Ken McClure is an award-winning research scientist with the Medical Research Council of Great Britain. His medical thrillers have been translated into fifteen different languages and are all international bestsellers. *Trauma* is Ken McClure's fifth novel, and follows the highly successful publication of *Pestilence*, *Requiem*, *Crisis* and *Chameleon*. He lives and works in Edinburgh, where he is currently at work on his sixth novel.

Also by Ken McClure

Trauma

Ken McClure

POCKET BOOKS

LONDON · SYDNEY · NEW YORK · TOKYO · SINGAPORE · TORONTO

First published in Great Britain by Simon & Schuster Ltd, 1995
First published by Pocket Books, 1996
An imprint of Simon & Schuster Ltd
A Viacom Company

Simon & Schuster Ltd
West Garden Place
Kendal Street
London
W2 2AQ

Simon & Schuster of Australia Pty Ltd
Sydney

A CIP catalogue record for this book is available from the British Library.

ISBN 0-671-85341-4

Printed and bound in Great Britain by HarperCollinsManufacturing,
Glasgow

We all labour against our own cure, for death is the cure of all diseases.

Sir Thomas Browne (Religio Medici)
1605–1682

PROLOGUE

John Main climbed to the top of the hill and turned to look out over the city to the Firth of Forth and the hills of Fife beyond. He was out of breath from the climb and his hands were muddy from the hard scramble over wet ground. It had started to rain again but it didn't matter. Nothing mattered. He wasn't sure what he was looking for up here, but it had something to do with perspective. The only other thing he knew was that he hadn't found it. In his heart he knew that he wouldn't find it here, but he had to go along with his instincts. He found a boulder and sat down. It was wet and covered with moss, but that didn't matter either.

Slowly the Forth and the hills disappeared from view as rain clouds drifted in from the west to obscure the horizon and foreshorten his view. Colours were lost as a universal greyness crept over the city. From here he could see the hospital that had played such a major role in his tragedy. Tragedy? Was that the right word? Was there a right word for what he was feeling? If there was, he couldn't think of it. Words described events that could be compartmentalised. He needed something to describe the complete destruction of his life, his family and all he held dear in the world. He couldn't see the A&E department of the hospital from his view point – it was on the other side of the building and it was too far away – but he knew it was there and it would be busy because it always was. Ambulances would be coming and going, trolleys would be taking breaks and fractures to X-Ray. Cubicle curtains would hide stitching and dressing from anxious relatives. Why? Why hadn't it all stopped after that awful night when the ambulance had brought the three of them in from the cold, wet motorway? Mary's beautiful body broken beyond repair, Simon deeply unconscious and he himself with . . . cuts and bruises. He had been the driver, and all he had sustained were cuts and bruises. He lifted his face to the sky at the almost unbearable thought. Was that some unseen deity's idea of a sick joke? He could still see the consultant's face when he had told him formally that Mary was dead. The man hadn't known it, but he was pronouncing a death sentence on John himself. He was condemning him to a living death, a living hell of loneliness and pointlessness stretching out before him like an endless desert. 'And Simon?' he had asked. 'He's very ill. It'll be a couple of weeks before we can say for sure.'

The weeks had passed and fate had played the final joke on him. It had invited him personally to take the final irrevocable step in the completion of his agony. The man in the white coat, a different one this time, had told him gravely that Simon had no discernible brain function. Machines were keeping his three-year-old body ventilated and nourished but Simon was, to all intents and purposes, dead. Could they turn the machines off?

'Yes.' The word echoed through Main's head like an

accusation. Such a small word: it was what Mary had said when he'd asked her to marry him. It was the word that had brought them both such joy when he asked her if she was pregnant. It was what the bank manager had said when they wanted to move to a bigger house, and what his sister had said when he asked her if she and her husband would look after Simon for a few days to let him take Mary off to Paris to celebrate their wedding anniversary in a few weeks' time. Now, the word had changed: he had just killed his son with it.

Two crows fluttered down to earth some thirty feet away and captured his attention. It soon became apparent that they had returned to the body of a dead rabbit. Main remembered them rising from the hill when he had arrived at the summit. They had been waiting to return to the feast and had now decided, in spite of his continuing presence, that it was safe. Main watched as they pecked at the body, spreading their wings to maintain balance as they grew in confidence and increased their efforts to eviscerate the corpse. Two more birds swooped down on the scene like collapsing umbrellas and a squabble broke out. How different it all was from the Disney scenes depicted on Simon's wallpaper at home. Anthropomorphic rubbish which they had all embraced happily in their ignorance of what was about to happen. That must be why everything was going on as normal down in the city, thought Main. They didn't know what reality was all about. His gaze drifted again to that part of the city where the hospital was situated. He knew that the staff there meant well and did their best. None of this was their fault. In fact, when it came right down to it, he couldn't understand why he hated everything and everyone.

1

Edinburgh, 14th February, 1993

McKirrop could feel the hot soup inside his belly like an island of warmth in the hollowness that lived there. He lingered over the last mouthful of bread for as long as he could before getting up slowly and stiffly to his feet. He buttoned up his coat laboriously and started towards the door. It was time to face the cold again. Rules were rules, and the rule was that you moved on again as soon as you had finished eating. The hall was too small for socialising and the queue got longer every week. Not that the place itself was overly warm or inviting but at least it afforded some respite from the icy east wind that was plaguing Edinburgh. McKirrop grunted a word of thanks to the Salvation army girl who stood by the door.

'Take care,' she said as he passed. 'See you on Wednesday.'

McKirrop looked at her and then quickly back at the ground in front of him. 'How come they all wear thick glasses?' he wondered.

The wind hit his left cheek as he stepped on to the wet pavement, so he turned to the right. Having nowhere to go afforded him that option. He heard someone call out his name, but ignored it until it was shouted again and he heard footsteps come up behind him. It was Flynn. McKirrop had seen him in the hall, some way back in the line, but had pretended not to.

'Where the hell have you been?' asked Flynn. 'Everybody's been asking about you. Bella's been pining for you.'

Flynn punctuated his remark with a burst of bronchitic laughter. He was a full head shorter than McKirrop with an unkempt mane of long greying hair which gave him a wild gypsy look. Both men were bearded and well past being taken for anything other than the down-and-outs they were.

'I've been away,' grunted McKirrop.

'You come into money or something?' demanded Flynn.

'Sure. I just choose to dine with the Sally Ann out of personal preference,' replied McKirrop sourly.

Flynn exploded into laughter again but his eyes were still suspicious. 'You always were a smartarse McKirrop.'

McKirrop didn't reply. He just looked at Flynn distantly as if thinking of something else.

'So you'll be back down the canal tonight.'

'Maybe.'

'You're up to something,' accused Flynn, narrowing his eyes.

McKirrop smiled vaguely and shook his head. 'Nothing like that,' he said.

'Well it's your loss if you don't,' said Flynn, pulling up his collar and shrugging his shoulders up round his ears. 'Figgy and Clark have got a bit of geld together. They're going to get in a few bottles and we're going to celebrate Bella's birthday.'

'Bella's birthday?'

'It's tomorrow. She's been telling us for days.'

'How old?'

'Christ, I don't know!' exclaimed Flynn. 'Who cares?'

McKirrop smiled again and Flynn read something into it. 'Except you maybe?' he probed.

'Why should I care?'

'Bella fancies you,' leered Flynn. 'She's always asking after you. Maybe it's mutual? A romance in our midst.'

'Jesus,' muttered McKirrop. 'I'd have to be desperate.'

'Well you know what they say,' whispered Flynn conspiratorially. 'Any port in a storm!'

'Christ! It would have to be a hurricane for Bella,' exclaimed McKirrop.

'So what do you say? Are you gonna come down or not?'

'Maybe,' replied McKirrop.

Flynn shrugged. 'Please yourself. I don't suppose you've got a swallow on you?'

McKirrop paused for a moment before bringing a half bottle of Bell's whisky out of his coat pocket. It was two thirds full.

'Jesus, good stuff!' exclaimed Flynn, grabbing at the bottle and removing the top with his palm, rather than his fingers. He took a long gulp before McKirrop grabbed it back from him. 'That's enough,' he growled.

'Drinking Scotch, are we?' muttered Flynn accusingly. 'No wonder you're not bothering with the likes of us any more. Not good enough for you, I'm thinking.'

'It's nothing like that,' said McKirrop. 'I did a bit of work for a woman up the Braids way; that's all.'

'I don't believe it,' leered Flynn. 'You're up to something.'

'I don't give a fuck what you believe,' retorted McKirrop with an abrupt change of mood, 'so piss off before I brain you!'

Flynn held up his hands in front of him in mock submission. 'I'm going, I'm going,' he said. 'Just don't come crawling back when whatever it is falls through.'

'Piss off!' repeated McKirrop with a swipe of his hand.

Flynn dodged the blow and moved away, looking back over his shoulder as he shuffled off. 'Tight bastard,' he mumbled before turning back and concentrating on where he was going.

It started to rain again as McKirrop made his way through the dark streets with his hands sunk deep in his coat pockets. It was a double-breasted military greatcoat, a gift from some charity, though he couldn't remember which. They were all the same. God how he hated their smiles, not that it mattered. What mattered was finding shelter for the night and getting a few drinks inside him. If his fall from grace had taught him anything, it was that it was 'now' that mattered. Not the past, not the future but 'now'. Every animal in nature seemed to know that except man. Human beings spent their lives wallowing in the past or planning for the future.

McKirrop glanced furtively behind him and saw that he was still alone. Flynn hadn't followed him. With a another glance in both directions he turned in through the iron gates of the cemetery and felt safe. He paused for a moment, feeling comfortably isolated before starting to make his way up to the far end. The cemetery was a large rambling place which had been allowed to become overgrown by owners who saw it as a real estate investment for the future. Many of the paths had succumbed to the ambitions of creeping shrubs and moss and were almost impassible but McKirrop knew his way around well enough. Using outstretched arms, he parted the undergrowth where necessary and ducked under low branches until he had arrived at his new 'home', as it had been for the past two weeks: a gravedigger's hut that was no longer in use.

Although parts of the cemetery were still used, contract workmen from outside were now brought in to dig and fill graves when required. Rationalisation of labour, if he remembered the term correctly. There was no longer a need to store tools and equipment on the premises. An ill wind for the Council Works Department had brought McKirrop a home.

It was quiet here and the hut was reasonably wind and water-tight. His new-found patron up in the Braids district had given him the opportunity to provide a few creature comforts. Cleaning out her garage, unused since her husband's death, had enabled him to acquire during the process a torch, some candles and a butane stove which came as a kit in a tin box complete with spares. She had paid him handsomely into the bargain, and there was a promise of regular odd jobs to come. There were also some nice tools in the garage that might need 're-locating' at some time, but for the moment he would continue to play his role as the honest artisan who had fallen on hard times and allow her to play Mother Theresa or the Good Samaritan or whatever it was that she saw herself as. *Symbiosis!* That was the word he had been trying to remember. He and the woman would continue in *symbiosis*. That was as far into the future as McKirrop

9

cared to look. He twisted the rusty padlock on the door and pulled it off. The tongue was broken, but it looked as if it was functional so it had deterrent value, and he was always careful to replace it when he went out in the morning. He stepped inside and pulled the door behind him, anxious to be inside out of the wind. The interior was cold and damp and smelt of earth and rough sacking but the air was still and that was a blessing in itself. He rummaged under the sacking in the corner and brought out the torch which he switched on while he erected the stove in the middle of the floor and brought it to life. The blue flame and the comforting hiss from the burner made him release a grunt of satisfaction. He glanced up at the single window to check that the sacking screen he had tacked over it was still in place. It was highly unlikely that anyone would come anywhere near here at night, or even in the daytime for that matter, but there was no point in taking any unnecessary chances.

The hut, small and square, heated up quite quickly. There was no ventilation, but that didn't matter. He liked the smell of the gas. It was suggestive of warmth, and if it helped him sleep so much the better. The Gas Board were hardly likely to come round and condemn it. McKirrop smiled at the thought and brought out his bottle to take a long swig from it. A drink by the fire in his own home. Another thought to make him smile. Home used to be a four-bedroomed villa not more than ten miles from this place with a Saab at the door and Laphroaig in the drinks cabinet. But that was a hundred years ago and didn't bear dwelling on. That was then and this was now, and this was what mattered. He had warmth, a roof over his head and a bottle in his hand. Everything was just fine. Those bastards down by the canal could get maudlin if they liked, with their bullshit about past glories, but he was doing just fine.

McKirrop was stirred into a groggy state of consciousness at about three in the morning; not that he knew the time, just that he had been asleep for some while. His arm caught the empty bottle as he struggled to prop himself up and he knocked it across the floor. There were noises coming from the cemetery which had wakened him. The thought that it might be the police cut through the haze inside his head and forced him into alertness. They might be having one of their bloody round-ups. De-lousing, a shower with carbolic soap and back out on the street again. Returned to the community. He sat still and listened like an animal in the night. He could hear clumsy movement in the nearby bushes and loud whispering. Periodically the noise level would rise and someone would urge silence.

McKirrop got to his knees and pulled back a corner of the sacking on the window a little. He couldn't see anything in the blackness but he heard a voice somewhere say, 'Get on with it then.' A few seconds later he caught a glimpse of a torch beam through the trees. It was about twenty-five metres away in the part of the cemetery that was still used.

Thankful that the intruders were apparently not the police and that they appeared to have no interest in him or his 'property', McKirrop relaxed and began to grow curious. He edged open the door a little in an attempt to hear more of what was going on.

He could hear the sound of shovels being used and it excited him. He had long held the view that the best place for a murderer to dispose of a body would be in

11

a cemetery, particularly one like this, one that nobody cared about. If they – whoever they were – were burying someone, it would be as well for him to know about it. There might be something in it for him; a possibility of blackmail, perhaps? A reward for information? But maybe it wasn't a body they were burying; maybe it was the proceeds from a robbery which he could dig up later and make off with. He could almost feel the sun on his back, hear the ice cubes clink in the glass. But first he had to find out.

McKirrop edged himself out of the door and crouched down close to the ground as he inched along towards where the sounds were coming from. There seemed to be four men involved; McKirrop could now see that two of them were digging while two others held torches. 'Get on with it!' snapped one of the torch-holders when one of the diggers stopped working. 'Maybe we shouldn't— ' began the one who had stopped digging, but he was interrupted by the man with the torch who shone the beam directly on his face. 'We all agreed, and we've come this far. Get on with it!'

Both diggers continued and McKirrop could see now that they weren't burying anything; they were digging something up or, more correctly, someone! They were digging directly in front of a recently erected tombstone!

'Bastards!' muttered McKirrop under his breath. Even to a man outside society in terms of almost everything else, the act of desecrating a grave seemed repulsive. True, the cemetery bore signs of various acts of vandalism, usually paint daubing and broken headstones, but he had never known any of them go this far before. He watched, spellbound, as the digging continued and the two torch-beams lit up a horrific tableau. Suddenly he heard the sound of one of the spades hitting wood and the silence ended.

'We're there,' announced one of the diggers.

'Pass it up,' said a torch-holder squatting down on his haunches.

The two diggers disappeared from view as they both bent down to grip the coffin and lift it up. McKirrop held his breath as he waited for them to bring it up out of the grave. They did so with surprisingly little trouble and McKirrop could see why. It was a small, white coffin. The coffin of a child.

McKirrop felt the bile rise in his throat. This was too much. He shook his head in impotent horror as he watched three of them get to work on the lid while the fourth held the torch-beam on it. With a final splintering sound the lid came off the coffin.

McKirrop watched the proceedings until he could bear it no longer. 'Bastards!' he yelled, getting to his feet. 'Dirty rotten bastards! Leave the kid alone!' He crashed through the undergrowth towards the light, arms flailing and yelling at the top of his voice which, in reality was little more than a broken yodel.

There was momentary panic among the four before the torch-beam was brought round to play on McKirrop and the holder called out to his fleeing companions, 'It's only an old wino!'

As McKirrop reached him, the man with the torch stepped aside smartly and hit him on the side of his face with the torch. McKirrop crashed to the ground beside the open coffin. He struggled to get to his feet while the four men re-grouped around him. A kick in the side made him fall to the ground again.

13

'Look at the old fool,' sneered one of the men above him. 'What a state.'

'Rotten bastards,' mumbled McKirrop but his head was aching and he couldn't think straight.

'Give the interfering old fool a kicking and let's get out of here,' said one of the men. 'Some nosey parker out there might have heard something.

Feet thudded into the prostrate body of McKirrop as he lay on the ground rolling ineffectually from side to side in futile attempts to avoid the blows. A particularly vicious blow in the stomach made him retch and he could taste whisky-flavoured bile in his mouth.

'Wait!' commanded one of the men and the kicking stopped. The man knelt down and brought his face close to McKirrop's ear. 'If anyone should ask you who you saw here tonight, you saw nobody. Understood?'

McKirrop grunted.

'You can't remember a thing, right?'

McKirrop grunted.

'Or else . . .'

More kicks rained in on McKirrop's helpless body and pain was replaced by unconsciousness.

McKirrop opened his eyes and screwed them up against the brightness of the light. He didn't have to ask anyone where he was. He could smell that he was in a hospital; that unmistakable smell of disinfectant and anaesthetic. There were screens round his bed but he could hear bustle beyond them. He ran his right hand over his chest and found that he was heavily bandaged. Moving his legs was painful and there seemed to be a large lump below his jaw on the left side. God! he could do with a drink.

He lay still, staring up at the ceiling and thinking

14

through what had happened at the cemetery. Would he be able to go back there, he wondered, or would the authorities have cleared out the hut and replaced the padlock with one that worked? What rotten luck. It had all been going so well. Now he would have to move back down to the canal with Bella and Flynn and the others. Flynn might make it difficult after their run-in the other day, but Bella would welcome him back. Either way, the sooner he got out of this place the better.

A nurse looked in on him and smiled as she saw that he was awake. 'How are you feeling?' she asked.

'Just fine,' replied McKirrop, his voice a croak from not having spoken for so long.

The nurse held back the screen for a young woman wearing a white coat to enter. Her cuffs were rolled back and she carried a stethoscope round her neck.

'You took quite a beating,' said the new arrival as the nurse left and closed the screens again. 'I'm Dr Lasseter.'

McKirrop looked at her and smiled weakly, partly because it was painful to move his mouth and partly because he was thinking how young she looked. Her eyes were bright and honest, her skin smooth and untouched by care. Her blouse was crisp and neat and her dark hair was swept back tidily and gathered at the back. What really struck McKirrop was that she actually looked as if she cared, and he found it disconcerting. It was the first time he had felt anything like vulnerability in ages. So long, he couldn't remember the last time. He didn't like the feeling; it reminded him of a different sort of life a long time ago, one he thought he had put behind him for good. He had thought himself to be immune from feelings like this. The Salvation Army girls were honest and meant well of course, but in a different way. It was somehow

15

impersonal with them, sort of same planet, different world. They didn't see you as a person in your own right, more as currency in some deal they had going. As for the middle-class do-gooders, they hardly saw you at all. You were just a number to be smiled at and patronised.

'I'll be all right,' he grunted.

'My boss will be here to see you in a few minutes,' said the doctor.

'Your boss?'

'I'm a junior doctor. Dr Stubbs will make sure I haven't missed anything.'

'No need. I'm fine,' said McKirrop, making an effort to prop himself up on one arm. 'If you'll just get me my clothes.'

'Not so fast,' said the doctor, pushing him gently down again and adding, 'There are some people who want to talk to you before you think of going anywhere.'

'What people?'

'The police for a start. You're front page news.'

McKirrop was alarmed. He suddenly felt himself becoming hemmed in by a society he saw as the enemy. 'What do you mean?' he demanded.

'I'll show you,' said the doctor, as if she had just had an idea. She left his bedside for a few moments before returning with a newspaper. She held it up for McKirrop to see. 'SATANIC HORROR IN CITY CEMETRY', said the headline.

McKirrop let his head fall back on the pillow, unhearing as the young doctor read out the story. He felt again the boots crashing into his body and heard the man's warning. 'You saw nobody. Understood?'

'That poor man must be going through hell,' said the doctor.

16

'What man?' asked McKirrop.

'The child's father.'

McKirrop screwed up his face. 'I don't understand.'

'Mr Main,' explained the doctor. 'A couple of months ago he and his family were involved in a car crash. His wife was killed outright but their three-year-old son was still alive when they brought him into hospital. He was put on a life-support system but he had suffered irreversible brain damage. Last month the man had the heartbreak of allowing the machine to be switched off.'

'Poor bastard,' muttered McKirrop.

'And now this,' she said. She laid the paper on the bed for McKirrop to read for himself. McKirrop felt his pulse quicken as he scanned through the tabloid text.

'Last night the scourge of Satanic ritual struck at the very heart of a city. The body of a recently buried small boy was disinterred and removed from its coffin leaving horrified church and police authorities with only nightmare speculations as to what might have happened to it. The boy's father, John Main (33) was last night too upset to comment. A man who had been sleeping rough in the cemetery and who is believed to have disturbed the intruders was admitted to hospital having been severely beaten after trying to stop the outrage. Police are waiting to interview him.'

The paper went on to report details of the car crash which had led to the death of Mary Main and, eventually, their son, Simon. Inside, the paper featured an interview with a church authority on devil worship in which he deplored the spread of the practice and warned that it was much more widespread than people realised. An editorial

17

headed 'Our Sick Society' went on to labour the point and blamed materialistic values for falling standards of behaviour.

'Do you think you'll be able to give the police any help?' asked the doctor gently when McKirrop had stopped reading.

He didn't reply for a few moments, and then he said, 'I didn't see anything.'

'But surely you must— '

'I told you! I didn't see anything,' he growled.

The house officer didn't take offence at McKirrop's sudden change of mood. She simply stood her ground and shrugged. She said, 'Well, if you didn't, you didn't. Now let's get you ready to receive your visitors.'

McKirrop again felt slightly vulnerable as he felt her hands fuss around him. 'I'm sorry I snapped at you.'

The words tasted like acid in his mouth. Apologies were like quadratic equations. It had been a long time since he had dealt with either.

'I get a lot worse,' said the doctor.

'What's your name?'

'Dr Lasseter, but more important, what's yours?'

McKirrop looked at her. 'Is that really necessary?' he asked.

''Fraid so,' said the doctor. 'If you won't tell us, you'll have to tell the police. We didn't find a wallet or credit cards on you— '

McKirrop saw the hint of a smile on her face and managed the semblance of a smile in reply.

'McKirrop, John McKirrop. No relatives mind you!' he insisted. 'Nobody.'

'As you wish.'

．　　　．　　　．

McKirrop was examined by the senior registrar of the Head Trauma Unit who didn't take too much trouble to hide his distaste for the job and made washing his hands afterwards seem somewhat more than a routine procedure.

'You've had simple concussion. You've got three cracked ribs and various bruises but otherwise you're okay.'

'Does that mean I can go?' asked McKirrop.

'The sooner the better as far as I'm concerned, but the police want to see you first.'

The doctor moved off, leaving McKirrop to glare after him. 'Toffee-nosed git,' he snarled as Sarah Lasseter retured.

'Dr Stubbs is a very good doctor,' she told him.

'Doesn't stop him being a toffee-nosed git does it?' retorted McKirrop, surprised at himself for entering into a dialogue.

'I suppose not,' agreed Sarah, taking McKirrop aback. 'Are you ready to see the police?'

McKirrop nodded. Sarah Lasseter took a few steps then turned round. 'You will try your best to help, won't you?'

He nodded again.

Two policemen arrived to interview McKirrop, an inspector who looked more like a bank manager to McKirrop's way of thinking – he was small and neat with a clipped moustache and a slight pot-belly – and a sergeant who obviously had a streaming cold. The area of skin beneath his nostrils was red raw. Both were hostile from the outset and obviously thought their best approach was to bully as much out of him as they could. When they failed to get anything using this tactic they became even more aggressive.

'So what the hell were you doing there in the first place anyway?' demanded the sergeant, removing the handkerchief from his face briefly.

'I told you! My room at Holyrood Palace was being decorated at the time so I chose to kip there.'

'Don't push your luck, McKirrop,' threatened the inspector.

McKirrop didn't feel threatened at all. He saw the police as his natural enemy. He had long since become immune to anything they could threaten him with. After all, when the worst they could do was lock him up in a warm, dry cell with three meals a day and a roof over his head, they didn't have a lot going for them. He was much more at ease with police bullying than he was with Sarah Lasseter's genuine concern.

'You must have seen something!' insisted the sergeant.

McKirrop shook his head. 'Didn't get a chance. They were on to me before I could open my mouth. I'm lucky to be alive.'

'You said "they". How many were there?'

'Hard to say. More than one.'

'Young? Old?'

'It was dark. Couldn't see.'

'Their voices?'

'They didn't say anything. Just beat the shit out of me.'

'Maybe you were part of it? Is that it? Were you the look-out man? How much did they pay you to keep your mouth shut?' demanded the inspector, bringing his face down close to McKirrop.

'Don't know what you're talking about.'

'Like fuck you don't. You're covering up for them, aren't you? What beats me is why. Those bastards dig up the body of a kid. A kid, for God's sake. And you say nothing! Doesn't it mean anything to you? Can't you imagine what agony that causes to the kid's father?'

'I told you. I didn't see anything.'

The two policeman looked at each other and shrugged. 'Take a look at life again soon,' sneered the inspector. 'I don't know why I've stuck this job so long, God help me. I need some fresh air.'

McKirrop remained impassive.

'We could always play our trump card, boss,' said the sergeant.

'All right then, go on.'

The younger man, holding the handkerchief to his face with one hand, took out a half-bottle of Vodka from his pocket with the other and stood it on the bedside locker so that McKirrop could look at it. McKirrop reached for it but the sergeant stopped him. 'First some information.'

McKirrop stared at the bottle. It was a cheap, supermarket brand with a Russian-sounding name, but he wanted it. He wanted it badly. He ran his tongue nervously along his top lip and imagined the fire in his throat from the spirit. His mind was in torment. He wanted the liquor but he was afraid of the men. He wouldn't get off with a kicking next time. On the other hand . . . perhaps it wouldn't matter if he . . . McKirrop laid his head on the pillow and said with a sigh, 'All right. I'll tell you.'

The sergeant brought out his notebook and parked himself at McKirrop's elbow. The inspector chose to stand at the end of the bed. McKirrop reached for the bottle but was prevented from doing so again. 'Talk first. Party afterwards.'

'There were four of them, but I couldn't see their faces because they had hoods on.'

'Hoods?'

'White sheets, like the Ku-Klux-Klan, with two slits for their eyes and one for their mouths. Except for their leader, that is.'

'What was he wearing?'

'He had on a sort of animal mask, like a sheep or a ram, with horns on it, and he was carrying some kind of stick.'

'What kind of stick?'

'Like bishops have.'

'A crook?'

'A crozier,' said McKirrop.

The policeman's mouth twitched as he looked for signs of mockery on McKirrop's face. McKirrop remained impassive. Only his eyes betrayed signs of dumb insolence.

'Get on with it.'

'Two of them dug up the kid while the others watched. They stood round the grave and chanted.'

'What did they chant?'

McKirrop shrugged and said, 'Don't know. I'm not a Catholic.'

'You mean it was Latin?'

'Could have been.'

'Ye gods,' sighed the sergeant.

'Then what?' demanded the inspector.

'They opened the coffin and took out the kid's body.'

'Go on.'

'They laid it out on the lid of the coffin and the leader said some words over it, then . . . he brought out this long knife and . . .'

'And what?'

'I couldn't stand it any more,' said McKirrop. 'I tried my

best to stop them but there were too many and they gave me a right doing.' He paused to finger his ribs tenderly before continuing. 'Their leader said that if I told a soul they would come back and cut my heart out.'

'You did the right thing, telling us,' said the inspector quietly. 'Did you get all that?' he asked his sergeant.

His colleague nodded, getting to his feet and snapping shut his notebook.

McKirrop reached out for the bottle but the sergeant beat him to it.

'We had a deal!' McKirrop protested.

'Everyone knows that it's against hospital regulations to consume alcohol on the premises.' He put the bottle back into his pocket.

'You rotten bastards. I told you everything! I've put my life at risk!'

The sergeant shrugged.

'Bunch of bastards,' mumbled McKirrop.

The sergeant looked questioningly at the inspector who nodded in reply. He removed the bottle from his pocket and poured some liquor out into the glass by McKirrop's bedside. McKirrop gulped it down greedily and the policemen turned to leave. As they reached the door the inspector turned back and said, 'About that hut, McKirrop – we've had the authorities put a new padlock on . . .'

Sarah Lasseter came in a few minutes later. She seemed pleased. 'I hear that you gave the police a great deal of help,' she said. 'I'm glad. The sooner they catch these people the better.'

McKirrop looked at her briefly before diverting his eyes. 'Can I go now?' he asked.

'If you insist. I don't think we can stop you.'

'Let's be honest. No one would *want* to stop me. If I was the Queen Mother they'd be tying me down to the bed with gold chains, but John McKirrop? Get that old bastard out of here. He makes the place look untidy. Right?'

'Something like that,' agreed Sarah Lasseter. She met McKirrop's gaze without flinching. It was he who broke off eye contact, feeling suddenly uneasy again. Sarah left and came back with his bundle of clothes and a piece of paper. 'You'll have to sign this,' she said.

'What is it?'

'It's a form to say that you are signing yourself out. It absolves us from blame if anything should happen to you because of your injuries.'

McKirrop signed the paper quickly and handed it back. '*Te absolvo, te absolvo,*' he said with a sigh.

'Thank you, Father,' Sarah smiled.

'You're a Catholic?'

'Yes, but did I overhear you telling the police that *you* weren't?'

McKirrop shrugged but did not say anything.

'I'll come back when you're dressed.'

McKirrop was ready for the road again. He had just fastened up the top button on his coat when Sarah Lasseter came back. She said, 'I know it's not very much, but I hope it'll buy you something to eat later on.'

She held out her hand. There was a five pound note in it. McKirrop looked at her – this was the last thing in the world he'd expected. 'That's very good of you,' he said, annoyed at the embarrassment he felt. He took the money and pushed it into his pocket.

'Good luck,' said Sarah, stepping back to allow him to pass.

McKirrop grunted and then paused uncertainly.

'Forget something?' asked Sarah.

McKirrop hesitated for a moment longer and then said 'About what you said . . .'

'Yes?'

'About the kid's father feeling bad . . .'

'What about it?'

'Nothing,' said McKirrop as an internal wrestling match came to an end. The values of an old life had almost triumphed over the present, but not quite. He turned and left.

2

McKirrop found an off-licence less than three hundred metres from the hospital. Sarah Lasseter's fiver bought him two bottles of Bulgarian wine on special offer and a can of strong lager. The transaction was carried out without either he or the shop assistant saying a word to each other. He was one of the clients the business liked to pretend it didn't have.

McKirrop turned into the first alleyway after leaving the shop and opened the lager. He gulped it down greedily and threw the can behind him without looking. He belched loudly and reached into the plastic carrier-bag at his feet to bring out one of the wine bottles. A quick rummage in his coat pocket and he came up with a small penknife which he used to deal with the cork. Practice had made perfect. He knew exactly the right angle to employ and the exact degree of insertion. Opening the bottle presented no more problem to McKirrop with his little knife than it would have done to the wine waiter at the Café Royal with his customised corkscrew.

With half a bottle of wine inside him, the edge had been taken off life and he felt ready for the road.

McKirrop saw Bella's group from the bridge. Bella was sitting on the wall laying down the law about something. She usually was.

'Well if it isn't our very own mega-star,' announced Flynn loudly when he saw McKirrop come down the steps leading to the towpath.

McKirrop ignored the comment and came over to sit down beside Bella on the low wall beside the water. He put the plastic carrier-bag containing the wine between his feet and asked, 'How have you been, Bella?'

'Careful, Bella,' urged Flynn. 'He'll probably whisk you away in his Porsche and take advantage of you.'

'Shut your face, Flynn!' snapped Bella. The comment froze the grins that were appearing on the other faces. Then, turning back to McKirrop, she answered, 'All right John boy. How about you?'

'Up and down.'

Bella was a large woman with hawk-like features and a florid complexion. She had some claim to be leader of the group by virtue of the fact that she had kept her strong personality despite her circumstances. For some unknown reason she seemed immune to the apathy which affected all the others. It was much easier to obey Bella than cross her. She liked McKirrop and didn't hide the fact. McKirrop found it amusing, and occasionally useful. Whenever he was around, her voice changed from its usual bark and took on a more gentle and refined tone. This always secretly intrigued McKirrop. Did she imagine he didn't hear her at other times? Her mannerisms changed too. She became almost coquettish, constantly putting her head to one side and flicking her hair back from her forehead, like a teenage girl talking to boys at the school gate.

For the benefit of the others, Bella said, 'We all heard about those bastards at the cemetery and what they did. I hope they catch them and cut their balls off. A bairn! I ask you. A bairn!'

There were murmurs of outrage and McKirrop nodded.

'You were very brave trying to stop them,' crooned Bella.

Flynn snorted.

'Never mind him!' snapped Bella, reverting to her bark. 'He's just jealous. If it had been him he would have slid all the way out the cemetery on a trail of his own shite!'

McKirrop and the four others in the group smiled as Flynn scowled and Bella stared him out.

'Did they hurt you bad?' Bella asked, her voice changing again to solicitous concern.

'They broke some ribs,' replied McKirrop, opening his shirt front to expose his bandages.

'Bastards,' murmured Bella. 'Has no one got a drink for this man?' she asked loudly.

'It's all right; I've got some here, Bella,' said McKirrop. He brought out the Bulgarian wine and handed it to her. 'Have a drink. Help yourself.'

Bella smiled and said, 'You deserve better after what you've been through.' She turned round and barked, 'Figgy! The gin!'

A small, emaciated figure, huddling inside a greasy anorak with matted nylon fur round its collar, came scurrying over. He must have been in his forties, but still had the features of a little boy despite the jaundiced complexion. His ears stuck out from his head and he was wearing a grin which exposed bad teeth. He reminded McKirrop of a chimpanzee, anxious to show the pack leader that he was perfectly content to be submissive. He handed a Gordon's gin bottle to McKirrop without changing the grin. 'Go on,' said Bella. 'It's not often one of us becomes a hero.'

McKirrop needed no second bidding. He took a large gulp of the gin and revelled in the fire in his throat. 'Christ, that's better!' he exclaimed.

'Take another,' said Bella, who had opened the wine and was helping herself. McKirrop took one more gulp and handed the bottle back to Figgy who scurried off with it back to his place.

'I've been thinking,' said Bella. 'You could sell your story to the newspapers. Lots of people are into devil worship these days. They'll probably pay you a fortune.'

'Do you think so?'

'I'm surprised they've not been after you already.'

'I signed myself out of hospital,' said McKirrop thoughtfully.

'Then that's why,' said Bella triumphantly. 'They're probably all looking for you right now.'

'You could be right,' agreed McKirrop, warming to the idea. 'We could all be on the brandy before the end of the week.'

'That's right, John boy,' said Bella. 'You won't forget your friends, will you?'

McKirrop saw the look in her eyes and knew that she was wondering about his absence in the last two weeks.

'I'll believe that when I see it,' muttered Flynn sourly.

'You shut up,' snapped Bella. Then, changing the subject, 'Christ, I'm starving. Who's got money?'

McKirrop brought out what little change he had from the fiver.

Bella looked over her shoulder and said, 'Come on you bastards. What have you got?'

A silent procession brought offerings to Bella. She counted the total and announced, 'Enough for a couple of fish suppers here. Figgy! You go down the chippy and get them. Clark, you go with him. Make sure he doesn't piss off with the geld.'

Figgy and Clark went off to get the food, leaving the others to pass round the Bulgarian wine. The man sitting beside Flynn refused his turn with a jerky shake of the head when Flynn handed it to him. The others looked at him questioningly.

'He's going to have one of his fits,' Bella warned.

At almost the same instant the man started to tremble all over. At first it was a moderate tremor, but it rapidly increased in magnitude until all his limbs were jerking and, balance lost, he fell from the wall to the towpath. 'Get something between his teeth!' exclaimed McKirrop, searching through his pockets for anything that might do. He couldn't find anything. Bella looked about her without any real sense of urgency. 'Leave him,' she said. 'He'll be fine. He always is.'

McKirrop tried to get a grip on the man to restrain him, but he was thrashing around so much that it was dangerous to get too near. As the fit started to subside he could see a trickle of blood flow down over the man's chin. 'He's bitten through his tongue,' he said. No one replied.

'There there, love,' said Bella as the man came round.

31

'You'll be all right in a minute. She spoke with so little concern that she might have read it from the back of a sauce bottle.

The man was helped up by two of the others and took his place on the wall again. He spat out blood intermittently.

'Where are those bastards with the grub?' complained Bella. 'They've had time to go to bloody Glasgow for it.'

'Here they are now,' said McKirrop as he saw a figure appear at the top of the steps.

'That's not Figgy,' Bella said as the figure started to descend slowly.

McKirrop could see that she was right. There wasn't much light, but the man coming down the steps was alone and he was too tall and erect to be either Figgy or Clark. The group fell silent as the stranger approached.

'I wonder if you could help me,' asked the cultured voice. 'I'm looking for John McKirrop.'

McKirrop was about to say something when Bella dug him in the ribs. 'Depends,' she said.

'On what?' asked the stranger evenly.

'On how much it's worth to you,' Bella replied.

The man reached into an inside pocket and brought out his wallet. He brought out a fiver and handed it to Bella saying, 'I really would be most grateful.'

Bella snatched at the note and pushed it down between her breasts. She turned to McKirrop. 'This is him here!' she announced with a triumphant cackle.

The stranger smiled weakly and looked at McKirrop. 'You're John McKirrop?' he asked.

McKirrop was suspicious. There was something about the stranger he didn't like, but he couldn't quite put his finger on it. Maybe it was simply the fact that the man was well-dressed and sober. He had all the trappings of success about him – not that he seemed overbearing, or even patronising at the moment. But then, he wanted something. He was smiling and spoke politely, but there was a look in his eyes that said he was playing a part.

'What if I am? Who wants to know?' McKirrop finally said.

'My name is Rothwell. I'm a journalist.'

Bella broke out in a huge beam. 'I told you, didn't I?' she said to McKirrop and then to the others. 'Didn't I just tell him?' There was a chorus of acquiescence.

'I wonder if I might have a private word with you?' Rothwell asked McKirrop.

'Don't see why not,' said McKirrop. 'We could go for a bit of a walk if you like.'

'You'll miss your tea,' protested Bella. 'Here's Figgy.'

McKirrop watched as Figgy and Clark arrived back with the hot food and handed the newspaper-wrapped parcel over to Bella to share out.

Rothwell watched for a moment before saying, 'I have a suggestion to make. You haven't really got enough there for all of you. Why don't you let me buy you some more, You chaps could go for it while I talk to John?'

'Sounds good to me,' said Bella. 'Maybe you could chuck in a few pickled onions?'

'Anything you want,' said Rothwell, taking out his wallet again. He handed over three fivers to Bella and turned his attention back to McKirrop. 'Shall we . . .?'

McKirrop and Rothwell walked slowly along the towpath together, neither saying anything until they were well away from the group. Eventually Rothwell said, 'I'll come straight to the point, Mr McKirrop. My readers want to know everything about what you saw in the cemetery last night.'

McKirrop paused before replying. He seemed to like Rothwell less and less by the minute. The man had an air about him: head held high, hands resting easily in the pockets of his expensive overcoat. It wasn't arrogance, just confidence he supposed, as if the man had never had a moment's self doubt in his life. The shine on his shoes was periodically emphasised by the odd reflection from the lights up on the road.

For some reason McKirrop kept thinking that Rothwell didn't look like the press at all but then, as he had to admit, he had never met a newspaper reporter before. His expectation had been influenced by how journalists were portrayed on television. He had, however, come into personal contact with many policemen in his time, and lawyers and solicitors. They were what Rothwell made him think of, a secure man who had the backing of the establishment, a professional man who normally had no trouble in having men like him moved on. 'Oh yes?' he replied. 'Why?'

'My readers are understandably alarmed at the prospect of grave robbers at work in the city. They want to know what's behind it. All sorts of rumours about devil worship and the like are doing the rounds. They'll be very interested in hearing exactly what you saw.'

'How interested?' asked McKirrop meaningfully.

'Shall we say two hundred pounds interested?'

'Let's say three,' replied McKirrop.

'Very well, three. Now tell me what you saw.'

'First the money.'

'First the story,' replied Rothwell pleasantly and evenly and without breaking the slow, even gait he was proceeding with.

They had come about half a mile along the towpath and were now walking along a particularly dark stretch where the canal curved under a bridge.

'There were four of them,' began Rothwell. 'They were wearing sheets over their heads so I didn't get a good look at them. And the leader, he was wearing a mask, a ram's-head mask and . . .' McKirrop told Rothwell what he had told the police. When he finished he was disappointed at Rothwell's lack of reaction. Rothwell just kept walking, slowly, evenly. He said, 'I got that much from my contacts in the police. I was hoping you could come up with something more.'

'I was scared out of my wits, I can tell you,' McKirrop added, hoping to elicit a more positive response.

'Must have been terrifying,' said Rothwell. 'Utterly terrifying.' He turned to look at McKirrop as he repeated the comment.

'It certainly was,' replied McKirrop with a grin adopted to counteract Rothwell's stare.

'Tell me about the child's body.'

'It was awful, awful,' said McKirrop, shaking his head. 'Poor little bastard. Makes you wonder what the world's coming to when they can do something like— '

'Quite,' interrupted Rothwell. 'Tell me what you saw.'

'The leader . . .'

'The man in the ram's-head mask?'

'That's right. He brought out this long knife and he cut open the kid's body.'

'How did he cut it?'

McKirrop shrugged and said, 'He sort of held the knife

35

in front of him with his arms outstretched like this.'
McKirrop demonstrated. 'Then he raised it up slowly and
plunged it straight down into the kid's body.'

'Then what?'

'He sort of moved it around. I couldn't see exactly from
where I was hiding but I think . . .'

'You think what?'

'I think he cut the kid's heart out.' McKirrop looked
to Rothwell for a reaction but Rothwell remained as
impassive as ever. In fact he showed so little emotion
that it was beginning to annoy McKirrop.

'What makes you think that?'

'He held something up above his head as if he was
offering it up to someone.'

'And then?'

'What do you mean and then?' snapped McKirrop. 'Isn't
that enough for Christ's sake?'

'They took the body away?' asked Rothwell, quietly
ignoring McKirrop's comment.

'That's right. They had this big bag and they put the
kid into it.'

Rothwell stared silently until McKirrop felt uncomfortable. McKirrop said, 'You're not writing anything down.
I thought reporters made notes?'

'I have a very retentive memory, Mr McKirrop,' said
Rothwell. 'How did our friends leave the cemetery?'

'They had a van.'

'A van,' repeated Rothwell.

'A black van, a black Transit van it was.'

Another silent stare.

'Do I get my money now?' asked McKirrop.

Rothwell brought out his wallet and counted out three
hundred pounds in twenty-pound notes.

'I don't suppose you have anything smaller?' McKirrop asked.

'No.'

'Oh well then,' grinned McKirrop. 'This will have to do.'

'And if anyone else asks what you saw at the cemetery . . .' began Rothwell.

'I know,' said McKirrop. 'Mum's the word.'

'On the contrary, you tell them exactly what you've told me. Understood?'

'You're the boss,' said McKirrop, shrugging his shoulders.

'I'm glad you understand that,' said Rothwell. 'I'd hate for you to forget.'

McKirrop felt the skin on the back of his neck tighten at the implied threat. He did not like Rothwell at all. 'I'd best be getting back,' he said.

'We'll go back together,' said Rothwell pleasantly.

The group had almost finished their fish and chips by the time McKirrop and Rothwell got back. Bella said to McKirrop, 'I've saved some for you. How about you Mr . . .?'

Rothwell held up his hand politely and declined. He turned to McKirrop and said, 'It's been nice doing business with you, Mr McKirrop.' The two shook hands and Rothwell turned to start up the steps to the road.

As he did so, McKirrop expertly flicked his toe at Rothwell's heels and Rothwell stumbled and fell. Bella and the others expressed their concern loudly and McKirrop went to help him to his feet. 'It's about time the bloody council did something about these bloody steps,' he said as he dusted down Rothwell. 'Are you all right Mr Rothwell? Nothing broken I hope.'

'I'm fine thank you,' said Rothwell, more worried about his loss of dignity than any physical damage. 'Good night.'

'Good night, Mr Rothwell.'

As soon as Rothwell was out of earshot, the group gathered round McKirrop. Bella's eyes shone like a child's on Christmas morning. 'Well?' she asked excitedly. 'How much did you get?'

'A hundred quid,' lied McKirrop.

'A hundred? A poxy hundred?' exclaimed Bella. 'Your story was worth thousands.'

'People like him can treat people like us like shit,' said McKirrop. 'And there's nothing we can do about it.'

There were nods of agreement all round and a moment's silent contemplation.

'At least I got a hundred,' said McKirrop, brightening up. 'What do you say we have a bit of a party? Get a few bottles of the good stuff, maybe some kebabs later?'

McKirrop was the hero of the hour. The others could not sing his praises high enough, with the exception of Flynn who just kept quiet.

'Who's going to go for the stuff?' asked Bella.

'How about you Flynn?' asked McKirrop before anyone else had a chance to say anything.

'Suits me,' said Flynn.

McKirrop handed over two twenty pound notes and Flynn set off, accompanied by two of the others. McKirrop watched them go and smiled. He knew he was back with the group. Bella came over to join him on the wall as he knew she would. She also took his arm and slid her hand into his pocket as he knew she would – ostensibly to massage his thigh but he knew what she would be looking for. That was why he had been sure to put three twenty pound notes in that pocket – the change he should have left from one hundred pounds. The rest of the money was stuffed down the back of his underpants.

'What's this?' exclaimed Bella, using her girlish voice as she brought out the notes, feigning surprise.

McKirrop took them from her lightly. 'My hard-earned cash,' he said. Bella smiled and McKirrop grinned. He handed one of the notes to Bella and said, 'Why don't you look after this one. After all, we're all part of the same family down here, aren't we?'

Bella took the note and slipped it teasingly down the front of her cleavage. 'Well,' she said. 'If you want it back, you know where to come.'

McKirrop grinned and got to his feet. 'I'm going to take a leak,' he announced and started to walk along the towpath. He had covered about fifty metres before he veered off into the shrubbery to his right. He cursed as he almost lost his footing in the drop and grabbed hold of some branches until he reached the bottom of the ditch. He had chosen this particular spot because there was some light here from a security lamp in the factory yard on the other side of the wall beyond the shrubbery. He wanted to see what he had managed to extract from Rothwell's pocket while he had been pretending to help him to his feet after tripping him.

It had been his intention to go for Rothwell's wallet – he had reckoned there was still a hundred or so left in it after he had paid out the three hundred – but that had proved too difficult. He had had to make do with whatever had been in Rothwell's right-hand overcoat pocket. It had felt like a card at the time and he had high hopes that it might be a Visa or

Access card. But as he examined it in the bushes he was disappointed. It was neither of these, nor was it a gold Amex card.

The little blue and white card was a University of Edinburgh library borrower's card and the only thing interesting about it, thought McKirrop, was that it had not been issued to a man named Rothwell. This was a staff card and it entitled one Doctor Ivan K. Sotillo to use the university's medical school library. McKirrop considered for a moment then slipped the card back into his pocket. This needed some thought.

Father Ryan Lafferty saw the man sitting in a pew near the back of the church. The man had avoided his eye when he had purposely looked in his direction so he had decided to leave it at that for the moment. He knelt and crossed himself as he broke the plain of the altar and then continued his journey through the narrow twisting corridor, smelling of dust and incense, to the adjoining church hall to see what the state of affairs was with regard to the jumble collection for Saturday's sale. Two ladies, one elderly and the other middle-aged, were engaged in sorting material into piles. The middle-aged lady held up a moth-eaten jacket with frayed cuffs and said, 'Some people, Father! They must think we're a rubbish tip down here at St Xavier's.' She tossed the offending article to one side.

'Maybe a bit thoughtless, Mrs Tanner,' said Lafferty. 'But I'm sure they meant well.'

Lafferty's charitable view about the coat was not typical. It had been forced on him in part by the guilt he was feeling at suspecting the motives of the man in the church. His first thought on seeing him had been that he might be after the contents of the offertory box or even the altar silver. For that reason he had been pleased to see that the stranger had been seated at the back, well away from the valuables. This unkind thought was now weighing heavily on his mind.

Lafferty was prone to self-criticism, and he was going through a particularly virulent spell at the moment. Recently, his time for reflection – usually around ten in the evening when he would sit alone with a glass of whisky by the fire – had been filled with fears that his church no longer represented the community at all. It was more like a club and, what was worse, a private club where the members were predominantly old and female. His discomfort at this thought was not so much due to the fact that it might be true but, rather, that he actually liked it this way. When he was searingly honest with himself, and he was in these late night sessions, he had no desire to change things, no wish to go out into the community: he felt no need to evangelise. He felt no need because he suspected that there was no point. The people in his parish didn't give a shit about Jesus Christ or his teachings and nothing he could say or do was going to change that. To imagine differently required a strong belief in the basic goodness of ordinary people. And that was where he was terribly afraid he was lacking. He was thirty-eight years old. He was a Roman Catholic priest and he was a cynic. He didn't want to be, but he was. The word made him afraid when he thought about it. Cynicism was like a cancer eating away at his faith. If only he could believe that it was a cancer – an illness – and not, as he feared most, a vision of reality.

'So what would you like done with it, Father?' asked the woman who had picked the jacket up from the floor and was treating it with exaggerated respect after Lafferty's rebuke.

'Throw it in the bucket, Mrs Tanner. I wouldn't wash my car with it,' murmured Lafferty absently. He was thinking about the man next door.

'Very good, Father,' said the woman with a shrug. So what was all that nonsense about 'meaning well', she wondered. She made a face at her elderly colleague.

'Will you ladies be all right on your own for a little while?' asked Lafferty. 'I have something to do in the church.'

'Of course, Father,' replied the older woman.

The man was still there. Lafferty stood in the shadows behind the altar for a few moments, partly obscured by a pillar, just watching. The man wasn't praying and he wasn't reading, but there was something about the way he moved in his seat from time to time that gave Lafferty the impression that he was trying to run away from something while sitting still.

Lafferty coughed to warn the man of his presence and came out from behind the pillar. He pretended to do something at the corner of the transept before walking up the side aisle to approach the stranger. 'I'm Father Lafferty,' he said. 'I don't think we've met before?'

The stranger smiled a little distantly and said, 'No, we haven't, Father.'

Lafferty was looking at a man in his early thirties, well dressed although in casual fashion, and with an educated tone of voice. He seemed deeply troubled. The lines round his eyes said that he hadn't slept for some time and his fingers were constantly in motion in a nervous wrestling match.

'Something is troubling you. Can I help?' asked Lafferty.

This was a simple enough question but, for Lafferty, it had a much greater significance. In truth, he wasn't at all sure that he could really help anyone at all any more, or if he ever had for that matter. He married couples whom he would never see again, buried the dead who had been born Catholic, and provided 'club leadership' in the automatic group activities of praying and singing hymns. All of these things, he reflected, could be done by a robot wearing the required vestments. He as a person didn't matter at all.

The man shook his head almost apologetically. 'I'm honestly not sure,' he said.

'Would you like to confess?' asked Lafferty.

'Actually . . . I'm not a Catholic, Father.'

'I see,' murmured Lafferty, although he didn't.

The stranger looked up and the priest saw the pain in his eyes. 'I really don't know what to do or where to go to make it better . . . I was passing and saw your church, and on the spur of the moment I thought perhaps . . . perhaps I could find what I was looking for here. Does that make any sense?'

Lafferty sat down in the pew in front of the stranger, his left knee up on the seat as he turned round to face him.

'I think you should tell me what's troubling you,' he said. 'You may not be a Catholic, but I'm a stranger and it often helps to talk to a stranger. I won't judge you and I won't discriminate against you because you're not a Catholic when it comes to confidentiality. I won't even ask your name if you don't want to tell me.'

'It's Main, Father, John Main.'

Lafferty held out his hand and Main grasped it briefly.

'We were driving through to see Mary's parents. Simon was their first grandchild and they doted on him. It was raining . . . It was raining very heavily. I remember the wipers were having difficulty coping with the water so I slowed down a bit. Mary had just made a joke about a boat being more use in this country when it happened . . .'

Lafferty could see that Main was reliving the event. He didn't say anything.

'I lost control of the car. I don't know why; perhaps a tyre blew or something. In retrospect it seemed to happen in slow motion. It suddenly slewed to one side and then skidded round in a circle when I tried to brake. We would have been all right if it hadn't been for the bridge across the carriageway. You know, one of those concrete flyover things. We just ploughed straight into it – or rather, the left side of our car, where Mary was sitting, ploughed straight into it. I was flung out on to the road but she was killed instantly.'

'I'm sorry,' said Lafferty. 'And your son?'

'Simon was badly injured, but he was still alive when the firemen freed him from the wreckage. The hospital put him on a life-support machine but when they had finished all the tests they told me that he had irreparable brain damage. They had to switch the machine off.'

Lafferty swallowed and felt inadequate.

'My son was buried five weeks ago. I never realised what true loneliness could feel like, but without Mary and Simon there seems to be no point to anything any more. I can't sleep, I can't work, I can't seem to think straight. And now this other thing!'

'Other thing?'

'My son's grave was dug up and his body was taken.'

'It was *your* son!' exclaimed Lafferty. 'I read about it in the papers. I'm sorry, I should have realised when you told me your name.'

'I can't cope with it, Father. They say it was the work of occultists, devil worshippers, and I can't come to terms with it. I'm not a stupid man, but I feel as if my son has been kidnapped. I know he's dead but it makes no difference, and not knowing what they've done to him is making it worse. I suppose I hoped that a priest might be able to give me some idea.'

Lafferty felt as if the roof had fallen in on him. He tried to keep the shock off his face as he struggled for words. 'My experience of dealing with the forces of darkness,' he began, 'has been mercifully limited. In fact,' he confessed, 'it's non-existent.'

Main nodded. He seemed to appreciate Lafferty's honesty.

Lafferty continued. 'This is not to deny their existence. Our universe is largely dependent on equal and opposite forces creating a balance. If we believe in the forces of light and goodness in the world then we have to acknowledge the opposites of darkness and evil.'

'I'm afraid, Father. I'm afraid for Simon's soul,' said Main.

'These people took your son's body, John, not his soul.'

Main looked Lafferty directly in the eye and said, 'I've tried telling myself that, but I'm not convinced. If that were so, why would they want his body in the first place?'

Lafferty felt his stomach tie in knots. 'I don't know,' he admitted. 'But I can try to find out. We have an ecclesiastical library in the city and there's a colleague I can speak to. What do you say we meet again in, say, two days' time, and I can tell you what I've found out?'

'I'd be very grateful,' said Main.

'Perhaps you could give me an address or a telephone number where I can reach you if I find out anything sooner?'

Main gave Lafferty both.

3

Sarah Lasseter had been on duty for thirty-five hours with only two hours' sleep. She had known what to expect when she started out on the course that would make her a qualified doctor, but that didn't make her feel any better about it. She was exhausted. What made it worse was that she really could not see any need for it. Like so many bad things, it had become 'traditional' that junior doctors should work themselves to a standstill. Because of that, there was no real impetus to change matters. If any attempt was made, it usually came from the junior doctors themselves, and in the end the more vociferous of their number would be patronised by the authorities as being young and 'bolshie'. The others tended to fade from the protest scene, fearing damage to their future careers.

Sarah's feelings on the matter remained unexpressed simply because she wasn't prepared to back them up with action. She felt that she had enough on her plate with the study and practice of medicine without getting involved in the politics of it. She also recognised that, as a woman, she was starting off at a disadvantage. Whatever anyone said to the contrary, medicine had a strong male bias. In the upper echelons, very few consultancies were filled by women. Sarah had quietly checked when she'd started at the hospital. The ratio was seven to one in favour of men. She hadn't mentioned this to anyone because she felt the feminist cause had been lost to the loonies. She accepted pragmatically that to be seen as an equal she'd have to be better. At the moment she was doing her one year obligatory residency work in hospital medicine, finding out her strengths and weaknesses, her likes and dislikes, with a view to future career direction. Her first six months had been spent in general surgery where she had performed well enough to be recommended for her current position in the prestigious Head Trauma Unit. When asked about future plans, Sarah would invariably say that, eventually, she planned to join her father in general practice. Just lately she had become aware of how much emphasis she had been putting on the word 'eventually'.

Sarah had been brought up in a small town in Norfolk, the only daughter of a country doctor and his wife, who was virtually a partner through her involvement in the day-to-day running of the practice. Sarah had inherited her father's intellect but, to her own regret, not her mother's inexhaustible patience and her capacity to see the good in everyone. Sarah regarded herself as much more of a realist. There had been a time in her teenage years when she had gone off the rails and had driven her parents almost to distraction. For a year and a half she had rebelled against the values her family held dear and had run wild. Her school work was ignored, her old friends were abandoned and she fell in with a crowd who were, to her way of thinking at the time, exciting. This unhappy time for all of them had ended almost as suddenly as it had begun and before Sarah had got into any serious trouble. The leather-jacketed boys who drank and smoked and 'borrowed cars' stopped being so exciting. Almost overnight they became boring and vacuous.

Ostensibly relationships with her father and mother were restored, but Sarah knew that the hurt she had caused ran deep, particularly with her father who had been ill-prepared for her antics. She had done her best to atone by catching up with her schoolwork and then gaining entry to Glasgow University's medical school.

Sarah knew how proud her father had been on her graduation day, but was aware that what he really wanted was that she should join him in general practice and one day take over care of the people who had come to mean so much to him. She had almost convinced herself that this was what she, too, wanted for herself, but knew that somewhere at the back of her mind guilt for the pain she had caused was still playing a part.

What concerned Sarah at the moment was not the fact that she was unbelievably tired and run off her feet, but that her immediate boss clearly did not like her. Dr Derek Stubbs, her senior registrar, was being less than helpful and she wasn't sure why. She suspected it had something to do with working-class snobbery. He liked people to know that he had clawed his way up from very humble beginnings and seemed to despise anyone who hadn't, although he had very clearly set out to distance himself from these very origins. Whatever the reason, Sarah found him difficult to talk to, and this was a problem, as there was a lot she had to learn. That meant asking questions, but asking Stubbs anything invariably brought a shrug of the shoulders and an equivocal response. His look always seemed to suggest that she should have known the answer to her question.

The consultant in charge of the Head Trauma Unit, Doctor Murdoch Tyndall, was the very model of good breeding and manners, a charming man in his fifties who looked as if he might have auditioned successfully for the part of an aristocrat in a Disney film. His appearance was complemented by a formidable reputation for his work with brain-damaged patients. But despite his professional success it was eclipsed by his brother's achievements. Cyril Tyndall was professor of viral epidemiology at the university medical school and a world authority on the design and development of vaccines.

Although the Tyndall brothers worked in different areas of medicine, Cyril Tyndall's success in the development of animal and human vaccines had had a direct effect on his brother's work. Gelman Holland, the pharmaceutical company which made a great deal of money from manufacturing Cyril's vaccines under licence, had not only endowed the medical school with substantial sums to provide the best facilities for Cyril to continue his work – a strictly commercial gesture – but had also made a further grant of two million pounds to the teaching hospital. This was seen by many as a high profile public relations exercise, but the company insisted that it was to emphasise their avowed commitment to front line medicine and research.

To everyone's surprise and delight, the Gelman Holland gift had been matched by an equivalent amount from the Department of Health in the unusual form of a direct grant. As agreed by both parties, the funds had been used to set up the Head Trauma Unit at the hospital. They had done this ostensibly to establish a national centre of excellence for the treatment of head injuries, but it was no secret that they also saw the propaganda value in illustrating how well public and private enterprise could work together for the common good in the field of health care. The government clearly saw this as the way ahead. Future funding would come less and less from the public purse and more and more from the involvement of commercial interests in health care.

The HTU – or more correctly, The Gelman Holland Head Trauma Unit, although no one ever called it that – had been open for fourteen months and had already earned an international reputation, particularly in the diagnosing of degrees of brain damage thanks to special monitoring equipment, the design of which was Murdoch Tyndall's special research interest. A consequence of Murdoch's research commitment was that much of the general running of the HTU was left to his senior registrar, Derek Stubbs. This was unfortunate from Sarah's point of view.

Sarah lived in the junior doctors' residency at the hospital, though she might have argued that she really lived in HTU; she spent so little time in her room. She was, however, due some time off now. She looked at her watch and saw that she only had another hour to do before she was relieved and would have a full twelve hours to herself. There was a patient she wanted to check on before she went off-duty. She went up to the ward and spoke to the staff nurse in charge.

The patient in question, a woman in her early fifties who had been the victim of a hit-and-run accident seven months before, was due to be discharged later in the day. Sarah felt that this was all right as long as her daughter was going to be around to look after her – as the patient herself had maintained she would be. The daughter, however, had been proving elusive. Sarah asked the nurse whether she had made contact yet, and whether in her opinion the woman could cope on her own.

'Her daughter hasn't phoned yet,' said the staff nurse, 'and I definitely think she won't be able to cope on her own.'

'I don't know what to do for the best,' said Sarah. 'She'll be heartbroken if she doesn't get to go home today. Maybe I should try calling her daughter's number again.'

At that moment Derek Stubbs came into the duty-room and, seeing the frown on Sarah's face, asked, 'Problems?'

Sarah told him what the trouble was and Stubbs said curtly, 'You're a doctor, not a social worker, Dr Lasseter. Let them get on with it!'

'Yes, Dr Stubbs,' said Sarah through her teeth.

'Leave it with me,' said the staff nurse kindly, and Sarah nodded her appreciation.

'Yes, Dr Stubbs. No, Dr Stubbs. Three bags bloody full, Dr Stubbs!' murmured Sarah as she walked into the lounge of the junior doctors' residency and threw down her bag. There were three others there, one woman and two men. They looked up.

'May we take it that you and Del boy have been having words again?' asked Harry Whitehead, a tall, gangling resident with rimless spectacles and a thinning quiff of fair hair. The vertical stripes on his shirt only served to emphasise his gauntness, but his voice was strong and deep.

'You may,' answered Sarah quietly. 'I can do nothing right as far as he's concerned.'

'Don't take it to heart, Sarah,' said the other man present, Paddy Duncan, senior house officer in general surgery.

'Sit down Sarah. Take it easy,' added Louise Vernon, who was doing a residency in obstetrics and gynaecology. 'It's only for six months, remember.'

'I'm beginning to count the minutes, and it shouldn't be like that! I can remember thinking I was the luckiest medic of my year when I got the job in HTU, but now . . .'

'Nothing ever turns out as it should. You have to learn to roll with the punches. Forget about him for the moment.'

'Easier said than done,' said Sarah.

'We're all going out for a Chinese meal. Come with us.'

Sarah felt cheered by the prospect. 'That sounds good; I'm sick to death of stale sandwiches and stewed tea.'

Lafferty was beginning to think that Main was not going to show up. He had expected him to come some time around mid-afternoon, but it was now nearly seven in the evening. He had even begun to consider what he should do next, and was deliberating over whether he should call Main at home or whether it might not be best in the long run to let the matter drop, when John Main came into the church and made the thought redundant. He was wiping snow from his shoulders.

'Cold out there?' asked Lafferty.

'Freezing,' replied Main. 'Mind you, it's not that much warmer in here.' He rubbed his arms to emphasize the point.

'I'm afraid we can't afford to have the heating on all

53

the time, but we can talk through here.' He made a gesture towards the head of the church with his arm. 'It'll be more comfortable.'

Main followed Lafferty through a small wooden door, painted blue and set in a stone arch to the left of the pillar behind the pulpit. It made Main think of Alice in Wonderland. Once through, they turned left again and entered a small room where Lafferty's vestments were hung on the back of the door. They were all on a single coat hook and it looked overloaded. Main was careful as he closed the door behind him lest they all fall in a heap.

There were two armchairs in the room, which looked worn and not very comfortable, placed on either side of an ancient gas fire, and mounted along the wall opposite the single window in the room were several laden book shelves. Below the window, arched and paned with leaded glass, stood a table stacked with hymn books that looked as if they had been withdrawn from service due to their tattered condition. A series of religious paintings were hung on plain walls that were a dull cream in colour, one of the chief colours favoured by institutions, thought Main, the other being green.

Lafferty invited Main to take off his coat and sit down while he himself knelt down in front of the gas fire and started to feed it matches cautiously as the gas hissed through. On the third attempt the fire popped into life making Lafferty withdraw his hand quickly. Even so, Main could smell singed hair. He noticed that one of the radiants was damaged; it emitted a flickering yellow flame while the others were blue.

'How are you feeling?' asked Lafferty.

'I'm OK. Did you find out anything?'

Lafferty frowned and said, 'In a negative sort of way.

54

I've spent many hours in the ecclesiastical library and I had a long talk with Father McCandrew down at St Agnes; he's made a bit of a study of the occult. The bottom line is that no one knows why these people would want your son's body.'

Main closed his eyes and rubbed his upper lip with his forefinger while he came to terms with the news. 'So I'm no further forward.'

'No,' agreed Lafferty. 'But on the other hand, it's as well to know that there's no known formal ceremony in Satanic ritual or in the annals of witchcraft that demands the body of a recently deceased child.'

'I suppose,' said Main philosophically.

'But you still have to know?' asked Lafferty, reading the signs.

Main nodded. 'I still have to know.'

'Have you been in touch with the police since it happened?'

Main smiled and said, 'That's why I was late. I was down at police headquarters trying to find out what they had come up with.'

'And?'

Main smiled bitterly and said, 'They've come up with nothing, or as they put it, their "enquiries are continuing".'

'They can't have much to go on. Unless they're actually aware of any Satanic activity going on in the community. Are they?'

'They say not.'

'In that case, they won't know where to start. These people, however evil they are, probably won't have criminal records and they probably don't consort with criminals so the police will be starved of information.'

'I'm sure the police will be grateful to you for putting their case so well,' commented Main sourly.

Lafferty let it pass. 'I've been wondering whether or not it might be a good idea to have a word with the man who was in the cemetery that night.'

'The wino's story has been in all the papers. Every lurid detail,' said Main. 'What else can there be to learn from him?'

Lafferty shrugged. 'Well, you never know. There just might be one little useful fact or observation that he overlooked in his efforts to give our noble press the kind of story they were after.'

Main thought for a moment. 'Maybe that's a good idea after all. I apologise for my earlier behaviour. I'm really very grateful to you for the trouble you've been going to.'

'No trouble,' Lafferty reassured him, 'and there's nothing to apologise for.'

'I'll start hunting down the man tomorrow.'

'No,' Lafferty said firmly. 'It's best if I do it.'

'Why?'

'You're too . . . intense. You might scare him off. It's best if I go. Who knows? He may even be a Catholic and, if he is, he wouldn't lie to a priest would he?'

Main smiled and thanked him. 'This must be taking up an awful lot of your time.'

Lafferty looked rueful. 'I could be thinking about the repair of the organ, the state of the roof, how many replacement hymn books we need or how little we have to spend on flowers at Easter, but all these things can wait. They can wait until your mind is put at rest about Simon. Christianity is about people, not bricks and mortar and budgets.'

56

Main left the church, saying he would come back in two days' time if he hadn't heard from the priest beforehand. As Lafferty watched him leave he thought about the upheaval his involvement with Main had caused in the smooth running of the 'club'. He had already had to go, biretta in hand, to the two ladies he had offended over the jumble sale and beg their forgiveness. He had yet to apologise to the Mothers' group for not turning up at their afternoon meeting, and to the senior Bible class for a similar offence.

He still had to have a word with young Mary O'Donnell, at her mother's behest, about recent behaviour with regard to the opposite sex. He looked at his watch and decided he had better do that this evening. He stretched his arms in the air and let out a huge yawn. Randy boys were bad enough, but randy girls . . . There was a whole lot of heartbreak still to come from that young madam, he feared.

John Main closed the door to the flat behind him and felt the quiet smother him like a cold, unwelcoming blanket. Noise and laughter and light and bustle had been replaced with silence and darkness. He rested his back on the door for a moment before urging himself not to dwell on this again. He switched on the lights – all of them – and then turned on the television. Next, he needed warmth, so he lit the gas fire to supplement the central heating until he had warmed up a little.

There were some messages on the answering machine, and he played them back as he took off his coat in the hall. The first was from his sister, Anna, suggesting again that he should get in touch with her as soon as possible and wouldn't he like to stay with her and her husband for a while? He hadn't been in touch with Anna since Simon's funeral. He hadn't been in touch with anyone since the bastards took Simon's body. He didn't want to talk to anyone about it. They couldn't help. They had already burdened him with as much sympathy as he could take over the course of two funerals. More of it wasn't going to help matters. He already knew how awful it was and how sorry they all were. It might sound ungrateful, but enough was enough.

Mary's mother was next on the machine with much the same message. He should get in touch. She was worried sick about him.

Main poured himself a large gin and noted that he would have to get another bottle tomorrow. Tonic was also getting a bit low. Maybe he should take a trip to the supermarket and get some food as well, instead of working his way through the tins and packets in the kitchen cupboards, rummaging through the freezer and bringing in take-away meals. Main smiled at the thought. Was this a step in his rehabilitation, he wondered? He resolved not to go to the supermarket where Mary had done the family shopping. That would be asking too much.

The third voice on the machine was that of Arthur Close, head of the English department at Merchiston School where he worked. Main was not to worry about anything. The others would be happy to cover his classes. He had their deepest sympathy and that of everyone else at the school, staff and pupils alike. He, Close, and the headmaster were in complete agreement that he should take off as much time as he felt he needed.

Main snorted at the bit about Close being in complete agreement with the headmaster. He said out loud, 'You're so far up the headmaster's arse, Arthur, it's a wonder you can see where you're going!'

Main immediately regretted what he had said. He thumped his fist into his forehead and berated himself loudly.

'Christ! What's wrong with you?' he demanded. 'They are ordinary, nice people, doing what they think is right. They're trying to *help* you, for Christ's sake!

Main slumped down in a chair with the gin and took a big gulp. 'Get a grip,' he said quietly. 'Get a grip.'

He gazed at the news on TV while the gin got to work on his fraying nerves, and then remembered that there had been some mail behind the front door when he came in. He brought it in from the hall and sat back down in the chair to open it. An estimated electricity bill for forty-seven pounds and eight pence, an exhortation from an insurance company to 'consider your family's future – what would happen to them if you were to die?' it wanted to know. Main threw it in the bin. The third envelope felt as if a card were inside and bore a second class stamp. Main opened it and saw the pastel coloured flowers on the front and the scrolled 'With Deepest Sympathy' across the top in gold. He flipped it open. 'Thinking of You, George and Martha Thornton', it said.

Main screwed up his face. Who the hell were George and Martha Thornton? Then he remembered. They were the couple he and Mary had met on holiday last summer. He was a grocer from Leicester and she was probably the most stupid woman he had ever met in his life. Main looked at the front of the card again and thought, thank God they don't make 'Sorry The Bastards Dug Up Your Son' cards. Eventually, he remembered that there was a packet of chicken curry in the freezer.

· · ·

McKirrop's celebrity status lasted three days. Three more reporters sought him out in that time, each hoping for a new angle on the Satanic ritual story, but McKirrop told them all exactly what he had told Rothwell. In all, he only made another hundred pounds. There was not a high premium on what an old wino had to say. There was a vague promise of some more money for the whole group if they agreed to be the subject of a social investigation for a 'Scotland on Sunday' colour supplement, but that would be at some time in the future, they said. The magazine was presently committed to covering the current vogue for Bonsai trees, the popularity of Western clubs in central Scotland – for which the clientele dressed up as cowboys – and an in-depth study of drug abuse in inner-city housing schemes. The reporter thought some time around August maybe.

McKirrop had shared £150 in all with the others. That left him £250 that he had hidden from them. Maybe it was time to move on. Maybe a move to London. It might be warmer down there. But first, he had resolved to try his luck with the library card he had taken from Rothwell's pocket. Maybe there was some perfectly innocent explanation as to why Rothwell had a doctor's staff library card in his pocket but, if there was, he wanted to hear it. After all, it was only going to be the cost of a phone call. And to a man of his means . . .

McKirrop brought the card out of his pocket and looked at it again. Maybe he wouldn't call Rothwell immediately. Sotillo wasn't a common name; there couldn't be many of them in the phone book. There might even be a reward for the card if he was to tell the good doctor that he had found it in the street. Every little helped.

There was no phone book in the booth. McKirrop had to ask directory enquiries for the number and then memorise it because he had nothing to write it down with, or on to. He repeated the number over and over while he sought out the digits with clumsy fingers. The number rang four times before it was answered by a woman.

'I want to speak to Dr Sotillo,' said McKirrop.

'Who shall I say is calling?'

'Just tell him he may hear something to his advantage,' said McKirrop. He could hear the woman laughing in the background while he waited. 'That's what he said, darling,' he heard her say. The receiver was picked up and a voice said, 'Hello, who is this? What do you want?'

McKirrop was taken aback. He remained speechless for a moment, then he put down the receiver without replying. The voice he had heard belonged to the man on the canal bank. Rothwell. There was absolutely no doubt in his mind.

This put matters into a new light altogether. Rothwell wasn't Rothwell at all. The man had lied. He had probably lied about being a reporter too, thought McKirrop. He had been right to be suspicious about that at the time. The question now was why? Why had Dr Ivan K. Sotillo pretended to be a reporter? What was his real interest in what had gone on in the cemetery that night? And most important, what was in it for John McKirrop?

As McKirrop returned to the canal, his mind worked overtime on what Sotillo might be up to. As he remembered, Sotillo had simply listened to his story, the same one he had told the police, and had seemed quite happy with that. In fact he had even been keen that he should tell any other reporters the same thing. So that was it! Sotillo had been making sure that the story he had told

61

the police was the story to be publicised. That suited Sotillo because . . . like him, he knew different!

That fact, decided McKirrop, was going to cost Dr Sotillo an awful lot of money. If he played his cards right, when this game was over he might well be able to afford a move to somewhere a good deal warmer than London. He remembered looking at a book in the local library last week while he was in there one morning keeping warm. *The Magic of Provence* it was called. The photographs had been beautiful. Provence, decided McKirrop, was the place for him.

Despite feeling that he held the whip hand, McKirrop was reluctant to take on Sotillo single-handed. He remembered the uneasy feeling that he had experienced when being alone with him on the canal towpath and how there had been a threatening air about the man. Sotillo might be a doctor, but he was no soft touch. There was more to him than met the eye, and just how much more McKirrop had an idea it might be better not to find out. He decided reluctantly that he would need help, some kind of back-up, even if it were only the presence of a witness.

McKirrop had to concede that his circle of friends and acquaintants had shrunk to practically zero over the past couple of years. If he was brutally honest he would have to admit that he did not have one true friend in the whole world. This had been true for some time, but it was the first time that he had been forced to confront the fact head on. He didn't like the feeling.

For one brief moment his acquired capacity for blocking out the past was seriously threatened. As if a veil had been lifted from his eyes, he was forced to remember a happy, successful individual with a wide circle of friends and colleagues who all liked him and saw him as the fun loving, carefree life and soul of any party. His name had been John McKirrop. The name was the same, but the only people he associated with these days were the people in Bella's group. If he were to recruit help it would have to come from there and that was not an encouraging prospect.

In his mind, McKirrop eliminated the members of the group one by one until he was left with Flynn and Bella herself. He didn't trust Flynn, but if matters should turn violent at any point he was the only one who would be of any use in that kind of situation. Could he be trusted if he paid him enough? His idea was to offer Flynn twenty pounds to accompany him to a meeting with Sotillo and to stand by to help in case of any threats or trouble, but McKirrop could imagine Flynn changing sides with no compunction at all if it suited him.

Bella was a woman and had therefore to be discounted from any participation in rough stuff. McKirrop smiled to himself at his gallant and mistaken notion – the truth was that Bella could probably beat the hell out of most of the group. He began to warm to the idea of using Bella. She was the nearest thing to a friend that he had, and she probably had deterrent value as a witness. Sotillo wouldn't try anything with a woman watching. McKirrop decided he would ask her tonight.

'Let me get this straight,' said Bella. 'You want me to go with you to meet this guy and if I do you'll give me twenty quid. Right?'

'Right,' said McKirrop, a little on edge that Bella had said it so loudly. He didn't want the others to know what was going on. That was why he had edged Bella away from the group a little.

'The guy owes me. I need you there as a witness to see that he hands it over.'

'Who is this guy? How come he owes you money?' asked Bella, whose credulity was being strained to the limit.

'The reporter,' replied McKirrop with a sudden thought. 'The reporter who came down here the first night I was back. Remember?'

'I remember,' said Bella. 'He was nice. He knew how to talk to a lady.'

'Well he hasn't paid me everything yet. I don't want him pretending to his bosses that he's handed over all the money when he hasn't.'

'But he gave you a hundred quid,' said Bella, displaying a better memory for figures than McKirrop would have liked.

'But he was to give me another fifty when the story came out,' improvised McKirrop. 'It must be out by now.'

'And you'll give me twenty?'

'Right,' said McKirrop. 'We're friends aren't we?'

Bella smiled, pleased at the notion. 'Friends,' she repeated. 'When do we see this guy?'

'I haven't set up the meeting yet,' said McKirrop. 'I'm going to phone him and ask for my money.'

'I'll come with you,' said Bella, getting up unsteadily.

McKirrop managed to dissuade her by handing over some money. 'Why don't you get us a bottle and we can enjoy it, because tomorrow there will be no drinking till after the meeting.'

Bella nodded sagely. 'Right,' she said. 'I always said that business and booze don't mix.'

. . .

McKirrop's palms were sweating as he put some change on the shelf beside the telephone in the booth. He dialled Sotillo's number, half hoping that there would be no answer.

'Hello?'

'I want to speak to the doctor, please.'

'Who is this?'

'Dr McKirrop.'

'One moment.'

McKirrop smiled at his little joke. He didn't have long to wait and could tell from the tentative way Sotillo answered the phone that he knew something was wrong.

'Dr McKirrop?'

'Just McKirrop. I'm no more a doctor than you're a journalist, Sotillo – or would you prefer Rothwell?'

'Who is this?'

'I think you know well enough.'

'What do you want?' asked Sotillo.

'Money. A lot of it.'

'Why on earth should I give you money? I've given you quite enough already.'

'Because if you don't I'll start talking and I have a feeling that you wouldn't be too keen about that. Am I right?'

'Start talking?' snorted Sotillo. 'Start talking about what? Who'd be interested in the ramblings of a drunken sot like you?'

'Maybe the police, maybe a real reporter. After all, it's a good story isn't it?'

'If you really think anyone will be interested in the babblings of an alcoholic misfit, go right ahead. You're welcome.' said Sotillo.

McKirrop had been prepared for this. He kept his cool and played his trump card. He said, 'Maybe they won't

65

believe me at first, Doctor, but your library card will help convince them. Then, when the rest of the gang describe you as the man who came down here pretending to be a journalist, the police just might get round to asking you for an explanation.'

There was a long pause and it pleased McKirrop. There was some background noise and he knew it would be Sotillo checking to see if his library card was really missing from his coat.

'What exactly do you want?' asked Sotillo. His voice had changed to a low whisper.

'I told you,' said McKirrop. 'Money, a lot of it.'

'What's a lot?'

'Five thousand pounds,' said McKirrop, shutting his eyes as he jumped in blindly with both feet.

Sotillo spluttered out the figure and said, 'That's ridiculous. You must be out of your mind. I just might run to five hundred, for the convenience of getting my card back you understand, but five thousand? You're crazy.'

'Please yourself,' said McKirrop matter-of-factly. He said it as if he was about to put the receiver down.

'Wait!' said Sotillo. 'Just let me think for a moment.'

McKirrop was excited. He knew he was on the verge of getting exactly what he wanted. It made him think he should have asked for more. Still, there would be other times . . .

'All right,' agreed Sotillo. 'But I need time to get that sort of money.'

'Tomorrow,' said McKirrop.

'That's not enough time,' protested Sotillo.

'Tomorrow, without fail.' That's what they always said in the films.

Sotillo sighed. 'All right,' he said. 'Come to the house at seven.'

'No,' said McKirrop. 'No house. Come to the canal, the bridge where we spoke last time. Seven o'clock.'

'Very well.'

McKirrop put down the phone and felt weak in the knees. He had done it! Five thousand pounds. Never in his wildest dreams had he thought he'd get the lot. He was on his way to Provence.

4

The O'Donnells lived on the eighth floor of a tower-block in Scotland Road. It was one of four blocks that stood in a square. The front two gazed out on to the bypass that ran round the east side of town. The rear two had an uninterrupted view of the railway marshalling yards. The height of the buildings ensured that there was a permanent echo down on the tarmac square they enclosed.

A group of teenage boys were playing football as Lafferty approached Melia Court. Their alternating laughter and curses drifted upwards on the night air. One of them noticed Lafferty's collar and started a sniggering chorus of 'All Things Bright and Beautiful' to the spluttering amusement of his friends.

'Good Evening Boys,' said Lafferty, facing them up.

Their heads went down and the football continued.

Lafferty held his breath all the way up in the lift lest the stench of urine should overwhelm him. The suggestion in spray paint on the corrugated metal wall of the 'vandal proof' car as to what should be done to the Holy Father barely registered with him. He had seen it so often before. The fact that Sharon loved Billy also failed to impress. The doors moved sluggishly back after an initial jerk, and he stepped out on to the landing. He walked over to the balcony to take in a deep breath and the view.

The air wasn't fresh; it smelled of fried onions and emulsion paint. There was a whiff of diesel and exhaust coming from the bypass and a faint drizzle settled on his forehead as he stood motionless at the intersection between two walkways. Laughter and curses and the sound of a plastic ball hitting against tarmac drifted up from below to compete with a nearby television set and an argument between a man and a woman on the floor below. Lafferty walked along to the O'Donnells' door and rang the bell.

A woman appeared in the doorway, drying her hands on a tea cloth. 'Father!' she exclaimed. 'I wasn't expecting you to call tonight.'

'Don't upset yourself, Jean. I just thought I might have a word with Mary if she was in,' said Lafferty. 'If she's not, or if it's inconvenient, there's no problem. We can fix up another time.'

'Oh, she's in, Father,' said Jean O'Donnell, looking back over her shoulder with an uneasy air about her. 'Come in. I'll get her out of her room.'

Lafferty followed the diminutive woman into the living room. Twin boys, aged about ten, were sitting on the couch watching television. 'Hello you two,' said Lafferty, sitting down opposite them. 'What are you watching?'

'The Bill,' replied one of them. His tone conveyed that they were not exactly pleased at being interrupted, nor were they at any great pain to conceal the fact.

'Put that television off, Neil,' commanded his mother. 'Father Lafferty has come to see us.'

Jean O'Donnell kept a fixed smile on her face as if hoping to counteract the surliness of her sons.

'Maybe they can watch next door?' suggested Lafferty. 'Do they have a set in their room?'

Jean O'Donnell looked vaguely unhappy at the suggestion, but the boys were off like a shot. 'It's not right,' she said. 'They shouldn't be watching television while you're here.'

Lafferty thought she seemed strangely vulnerable when she said it and could see what she was thinking. 'Times change, Jean,' he said.

Jean O'Donnell nodded briefly, as if she didn't want to acknowledge it, even when it was presented to her as fact. 'I'll fetch Mary,' she said and left the room.

Lafferty examined his surroundings, taking in the personal touches rather than the furnishings, which could be found with only minor differences in any of the other flats in the block. There was a shield on the mantelpiece with Joseph O'Donnell's newly-etched name. Crossed darts in the centre told how it had been won. A Maeve Binchey novel lay on the corner of the hearth with Jean O'Donnell's spectacles lying on the cover. Lafferty could see that it was a library copy from the plastic protector on the cover. How many other people in the block visited the library, he wondered – and concluded that the fingers of one hand might suffice for the answer. Apart from anything else, the nearest public library was a bus ride away. In fact the nearest anything to these flats was a bus ride away. It was a major factor in their unpopularity.

Lafferty could hear whispered arguing outside the door. It seemed to go on for an age before the door opened and a teenage girl was pushed into the room. 'She was just going out, Father,' smiled Jean. 'But she's got time for a word before she goes.'

Lafferty stood up and smiled. 'Nice to see you Mary, it's been a long time.'

The girl, dressed in leather jacket and tight jeans, looked up from beneath hair that cascaded over her eyes and said, 'Sorry, I've been a bit busy.' Her voice was laced with resentment. She shrugged off her mother's hand which was resting on her shoulder.

'Jean, why don't you leave us to have a little chat?' suggested Lafferty.

'I'll put the kettle on,' said Jean O'Donnell.

'Sit down Mary,' said Lafferty pleasantly. 'Are you off somewhere special?'

'Down the coast on the bikes,' replied the girl.

'The bikes? Motor bikes you mean?'

Mary nodded. She was a pretty girl, a little small for her fifteen years but well proportioned.

'Sounds exciting. But you don't have your own bike at your age surely?'

'I'm going on the back of Steve's.'

'Your boyfriend?'

Mary nodded and said, 'He's got a GPZ 500.'

'The Kawasaki's a nice bike,' said Lafferty.

'You know about bikes?' asked Mary, surprised.

'Just because I'm a priest it doesn't mean I'm boring.' replied Lafferty. 'I've always had a love of motor cycles. I keep abreast of what's on the road these days. There's a lot of nice machinery around.'

'Steve's bike is the nicest. He takes good care of it. He wants to make bikes his career. He's really good. Everybody says so.'

'How old is Steve, Mary?' asked Lafferty.

'About twenty-three. What does that matter?' said Mary defiantly.

'And you are fifteen.'

'I'm not a little girl! I know what I'm doing.'

'Maybe you do,' said Lafferty kindly. 'But your mother is worried sick about you and that's not right.'

'I keep telling her not to worry about me – but she won't listen! What else can I do?'

'Your mother worries about you because she loves you. Try to see things from her point of view.'

'She won't see them from mine!'

'Maybe you're both being a bit stubborn,' said Lafferty.

'I'm going out with Steve and nothing's going to change that!' insisted Mary.

Lafferty shrugged and asked, 'What's your father saying to all this?'

She lifted her hair from her forehead and revealed a black and blue mark above her right eye. 'This.'

'And you're still planning to go out this evening?'

'He's down the boozer playing darts. I'm going out with Steve,' said Mary defiantly.

'And your mother's left standing in the middle.'

Mary was stung into saying, 'She shouldn't be! I don't want her to be! I don't want to be like her! I don't want to spend my life in a dog kennel in the sky waiting for some drunken bum to come home every night. I want to live! I want to enjoy myself. Is that so wrong? Don't answer that. Your bloody church depends on people like her!'

Lafferty was wounded. 'What do you mean by that?' he asked.

'You know,' said Mary.

'Tell me.'

'Mugs. Gullible mugs. Always on the losing side, giving away everything they've got, doing what they're told. Yes Fathering, No Fathering, wasting away their dreary lives because they've been conned into believing things are going to get better in the hereafter. But they're not, are they? Because there is no bloody hereafter. It's all a bloody con!'

'Mary! Control yourself,' stormed Jean O'Donnell as she burst into the room. 'How dare you speak to Father Lafferty like that! I'm so sorry, Father. I don't know what's come over her. I honestly don't.'

Lafferty held up a hand and said, 'There's nothing to be sorry for, Jean. Mary has a right to her point of view and I am flattered that she confided in me. It's only healthy at her age to question everything, otherwise we'd never make any progress in this life.'

'You're too understanding, Father.'

Lafferty shook his head and said, 'Mary strikes me as an intelligent, mature girl who is well able to form her own opinions and decide for herself what is right and what is wrong. I think you should trust her.'

Jean O'Donnell looked at her daughter without saying anything but Lafferty was pleased to see a hint of softness appear in Mary O'Donnell's eyes.

'And you, young lady,' said Lafferty to Mary, 'should make sure that you are deserving of that trust.'

'Yes, Father,' said Mary O'Donnell. 'I'm late. I'll have to go.'

'Enjoy yourself,' said Lafferty. 'And if you'll take one word of advice?'

'Yes, Father?'

'Find a boyfriend with a CBR 600. It'll beat the hell out of a GPZ 500.'

. . .

When Mary had gone Jean O'Donnell served tea and put a plate of Digestive biscuits on the hearth between them.

'Help yourself, please,' she said.

Lafferty took a biscuit and said, 'You look worried Jean.'

'I'm thinking about Joe and what he'll do when he finds out she's been out with the bikers again.'

'He's not usually a violent man is he?' asked Lafferty.

Jean's face softened. She said, 'Far from it, but that young madam can push him over the limit. She did that the other night.'

'I saw the mark,' said Lafferty.

Jean O'Donnell was embarrassed. 'She deserved it,' she said quietly. 'After what she said to him. Called him a drunken sot to his face.'

Lafferty stayed silent, making Jean feel obliged to continue.

'Joe has never had the best of luck. He's been unemployed for longer than I care to remember, and maybe he does enjoy a drink or two, but basically he's a good man . . .'

'Do you think I should have a word with him?' asked Lafferty.

Jean considered for a moment then said, 'No, I don't think so. But I'll tell him you called and saw Mary.' Her eye caught Lafferty's and they both understood. Lafferty said a short prayer and then got up to go.

'Thank you for coming.'

'See you Sunday.'

Lafferty walked back along the walkway and paused for a moment at the same spot as before to watch the lights of the traffic on the bypass. He left the flats with a heavy heart. The O'Donnell girl had been upset but what she had said had hit home, and he had had to work hard at remaining composed about it at the time. The Church did depend a great deal on women like Jean O'Donnell. Decent, hard-working, good-natured and God-fearing women who saw their faith as a cornerstone of their lives. The real question was, did the Church depend on them, as he was willing to concede, or did it amount to exploitation as Mary O'Donnell had maintained? It was something he would rather not think about on top of everything else, but there would be no getting away from it, he feared. The best he could hope for was a respite while he set out to find the drunk who had witnessed the Main boy's exhumation.

McKirrop swung his arms across his chest as he paced up and down on the towpath on a repetitive ten metre patrol. Ostensibly he was doing this to keep warm – he kept remarking to Bella how cold it was – but nerves were playing a large part in his discomfort, not to mention the fact that they were both desperate for a drink.

'For God's sake, stand still!' snapped Bella.

McKirrop swung his arms all the harder and complained, 'Where the hell is he?'

'We've only been here five minutes!' retorted Bella.

'Seems like bloody hours.'

Bella watched the pacing figure in the gloom and began to grow suspicious. 'Why're you so edgy?' she demanded. 'What're you really up to?'

'I told you,' replied McKirrop. 'The bugger owes me money. Fifty quid.'

'So what's there to be so nervous about?'

'I'm just cold damn it! Now give it a rest will you?'

'Twenty quid for me, right?'

'Right. We agreed all that,' snapped McKirrop. 'What're you worried about? We're a team aren't we?'

'That's right, John boy,' said Bella quietly. 'But if you're holding out on me . . .'

'Nobody's holding out on you for Christ's sake! Where the hell is he?' McKirrop started pacing again but turned smartly when a voice from the bridge called, 'McKirrop?'

He looked up and saw the dark silhouette above the parapet. His throat tightened. 'Have you got my money?' he croaked.

'All in good time. Did you bring the card?'

'In my pocket.'

'Bring it up.'

'You come down.'

'What's all this about a card?' demanded Bella from the shadow of the wall beneath the parapet.

'He just dropped his library card, that's all,' said McKirrop dismissively, annoyed that Bella had opted for a speaking role.

'Who's down there with you, McKirrop?' asked the voice from above.

'Just my friend Bella, come to see fair play,' replied McKirrop. 'She's here to see that you give me my money.'

'I'm a witness,' crowed Bella. 'Give him the money you owe him.' McKirrop wished that Bella would just keep her mouth shut.

'I'm coming down,' said Sotillo.

McKirrop could feel his heart thumping in his chest. He was only a few seconds away from getting his hands on five thousand pounds. Five thousand pounds! He could hear the scrabble of Sotillo's feet on the steep earth path that led down to the towpath. The sound of a man bringing him five thousand pounds. McKirrop desperately wanted to urinate. He pressed his hands into his crotch from inside the pockets of his great-coat and shrugged his shoulders up around his ears. He took a step backwards to allow Sotillo to descend the last few metres in a sideways crab-like run.

'Where's the card?' asked Sotillo, straightening up.

McKirrop couldn't make out Sotillo's features in the darkness but was aware that Sotillo had the same problem as him. He figured that he had got the best of that bargain because, while Sotillo sounded unruffled and as urbane as usual, his own cheek muscles were twitching as if electrodes had been inserted in his face; his throat was as dry as the desert. 'Where's the money?' he croaked.

Sotillo's hand came out of his overcoat pocket. There was enough light to pick out the white envelope he held in it. 'Here.'

McKirrop snatched at it with his left hand and brought out the library card with his right.

'Here's your card.'

Sotillo took it and McKirrop ripped the envelope open to feel what was inside, rather than look at it. There was no mistaking the feel of bank notes. A thick bundle of bank notes.

'Did you get it?' asked Bella from the shadows.

McKirrop had almost forgotten about her. Confidence was flooding back through him like a cocaine rush. 'I got it,' he replied, his voice no longer a croak from a fear-tightened throat.

'Nice doing business with you,' he said to Sotillo. 'Maybe we'll do it again some time.'

'I was afraid you might think that,' said Sotillo. He

said it slowly and sonorously as if he had been expecting the worst and it had just happened.

'No,' he said. 'Our business, as you term it, will come to an end here and now.'

'As you say, squire,' said McKirrop lightly. But there was something about Sotillo's voice that threatened the reliability of his anal sphyncter. All his new found cockiness evaporated in an instant and he found himself wishing that he had not made any reference to future 'business'. 'Just a joke.'

'Let's get out of here,' said Bella, sensing that all was not well. 'You've got your money. Let's get a drink.'

Bella tugged at McKirrop's arm as she turned to start out along the towpath but suddenly the tugging stopped and McKirrop heard her exclaim, 'Who the hell are you? What's your game?' He spun round to see two large figures loom up out of the darkness. They were blocking the path behind them.

'What are you trying to pull, Sotillo?' demanded McKirrop with more courage than he felt.

'Give me back my money,' said Sotillo in tones that seemed to freeze the air.

There was an electric pause before Bella said, 'Give him it for Christ's sake. We don't need all this shit for fifty lousy quid.'

'Fifty pounds. Is that what he told you?' sneered Sotillo. 'I think perhaps your . . . colleague, hasn't been quite honest with you.'

Bella turned on McKirrop. 'You bastard! I knew you were up to something. A team, you said. We were a team! I'm going to get Flynn to kick your fucking head in! How much?' she yelled. 'How fucking much?' She flew at McKirrop.

The two figures moved in to separate Bella and McKirrop who were spitting venom at each other.

'When thieves fall out there's no telling what can happen,' said Sotillo to the two silent figures who were holding Bella and McKirrop. 'I think under the circumstances, gentlemen, they should perhaps do each other some serious and lasting damage.'

Lafferty had been down to the canal earlier to begin his search for the man he now knew to be John McKirrop. He hadn't remembered the name himself, but one of the two down-and-outs he found by the canal had given him the information and told him that McKirrop would probably be down later. The two of them had seemed pleased to help and seemed almost to compete in telling him everything they knew about McKirrop.

'A brave man,' said one. 'You know he tried to stop those bastards from digging the kid up at the cemetery?'

'So I understand.'

'Should be given some kind of medal, I reckon.'

The other drunk nodded sagely. 'Or at least some kind of compensation for the injuries he suffered.'

'Injuries?'

'They beat him up.'

'Beat him within an inch of his life,' added the other.

'I hadn't realised . . .' confessed Lafferty.

'Oh yes, but nobody gives a damn for the likes of us, Father. Begging your pardon, like.'

'God does,' replied Lafferty. 'Never forget that.'

'Yes, Father,' replied the drunk, obviously unconvinced.

'You will tell John that I'd appreciate a word with him later if he should show up?'

'Of course, Father.'

Lafferty could make out six figures as he descended from the bridge to the towpath. As he got closer he saw that the nearest man was either asleep or unconscious on the fringe of the group. He lay sprawled over the path with his head at a slightly raised angle where it rested on what looked like a railway sleeper. An empty bottle was still clutched in his hand. Lafferty stepped over him gingerly. 'Is he all right?' he asked the anonymous group in front of him.

'Who wants to know?' snarled a voice from the darkness.

'It's Father Lafferty from St Xavier's. I was down earlier looking for John McKirrop. Is he one of you?'

'McKirrop, McKirrop. Always McKirrop,' replied the voice. 'No he isn't.'

'Then can you tell me where I can find him?' asked Lafferty.

'Mr McKirrop is out courting at the moment,' came the sneering voice.

'Courting?'

'He is out walking with his lady, Father, the beautiful Lady Bella Grassick. And I do believe they're without chaperone.'

The group broke into cackles of laughter.

'I really would like to speak to him if I possibly could,' said Lafferty.

'They went that-a-way,' snapped the voice. 'About an hour ago.'

'Thank you Mr . . .?

'It doesn't matter,' said the voice.

'I think it does,' insisted Lafferty quietly.

'Flynn,' replied the voice.

'God bless you, Mr Flynn.'

'I'd rather He came up with a jacket and a pair of shoes,' replied Flynn sourly. The others supported Flynn with their laughter.

'There was a sale at St Xavier's last weekend,' said Lafferty. 'There were some things left over. Call round tomorrow afternoon to the church hall and we'll see what we can do.'

The silence behind him awarded some kind of moral victory to Lafferty as he set out along the towpath in the direction indicated by Flynn.

The towpath darkened with each step Lafferty took away from the canal basin and he began to feel cold. The temperature was now close to freezing. What had Flynn meant by 'courting'? Surely McKirrop and the woman, whatever her name was, couldn't be . . . or had the others back at the basin been making a fool of him? The collar round his neck sometimes had this effect. People confused celibacy with ignorance. Lafferty often regretted the downside of clerical garb. In many ways it seemed to act as a barrier between him and the people he sought to reach.

He recalled several instances in the past of priests removing their collars and going to live in deprived areas to find out what it felt like. In Lafferty's opinion, this had been a pointless exercise. Sitting in a cold flat on a housing estate all day did not tell you anything about the reason for being there. It did not tell you what it felt like to be unemployed and with no prospect of a job for the next twenty years. You couldn't simulate that. It had to happen to you before you could possibly know what it felt like.

The canal water to his left picked up a thin white

82

reflection and Lafferty looked up to see the moon slide out from behind a bank of steep cloud. He was grateful for any source of light; the path was now so dark. Something ahead scuttled across the path and rustled off into the undergrowth. He hoped it wasn't a rat; this was one of God's creatures that he had little time for. An owl called out from a distant thicket.

As he rounded the bend leading to the next bridge, Lafferty thought that he saw the silhouette of two or three people above the parapet. But he couldn't be sure, and besides, it didn't matter, they seemed to be heading away from the canal, not coming down to the towpath. Which was a relief – he did not welcome the prospect of joggers or, worse still, cyclists on mountain bikes coming hurtling towards him on the narrow path. The fact that he was wearing clerical black would not have helped matters in the darkness.

As he neared the bridge, Lafferty suddenly stopped in his tracks. There was a single street lamp up on the road leading to the bridge. A little of its light spilled down on to the towpath. Not much, but to eyes accustomed to the gloom it was enough to see what was there. He could see two figures lying on the bank by the water's edge. Could it be McKirrop and the woman?

'Are you all right?' he called out. And called again when the couple failed to respond. There was still no sound or movement. No cursing and scrambling around in the grass. Nothing.

'Hello there!' he tried once more.

Apart from the owl, who chose his moment well to emphasise the silence, there was no sound from the couple and they remained motionless.

Lafferty reminded himself that the two on the bank

were alcoholics. They could simply be blind drunk. He walked towards them and knelt down to shake one of them, the man, by his shoulder.

McKirrop's head flopped round to reveal a face lacerated on both cheeks and with a frightening wound on his forehead, where he had obviously been hit by something heavy. There was a large depression in his skull and blood had congealed in a black mess within it. The glass around his feet suggested to Lafferty that the weapon that had done the damage had been a bottle.

'God Almighty,' whispered Lafferty. He turned his attention to the woman. She was lying in McKirrop's shadow and he had to move McKirrop a little to get to her. It was only then that he realised that her head was not resting on the bank at all. It was hanging over the edge of the bank and was submerged in the water! Struggling to gain a foothold on the slippery grass, Lafferty managed first to pull the woman's head up out of the water, and then to pull her body up on to the bank. Her eyes were wide open, but they did not see the moon that had just emerged from the clouds again. One of her cheek bones had been smashed in and the eye above it had been dislodged from its socket. Her tongue lolled out of her mouth.

Lafferty whispered a prayer under his breath, but then recoiled as the woman's body made a gurgling sound. Water and weed slurped out of her mouth as if she had vomited weakly. She was quite dead, but some latent muscular spasm had been triggered. Some lost electrical brain impulse wandering around inside her body had conveyed its last message. As the body sank down into rest again Lafferty prayed over the woman and then turned back to McKirrop.

The word 'courting' came into his head again and it,

in turn, led to the phrase 'lover's tiff'. For some reason he could not put a rein on this surreal line of thought. A lover's tiff. Good God Almighty, how inappropriate a phrase to describe the scene at his feet. But it was not inconceivable that the papers might choose to report it as such. What had led to it? What had they fought over? The bottle? The lady's honour? There it was again, an intruding phrase from another world.

Lafferty said a prayer over McKirrop's body and then, as he opened his eyes, he saw McKirrop's hand move. He watched the dead man's fingers move like a white spider. A scar across the forefinger stood out in relief in the moonlight. Lafferty was mesmerised by the sight. He felt sure that this had to be another example of muscular spasm after death, but the fingers didn't stop. They went on searching, trying to make contact from the depths of some timeless abyss. Surely McKirrop could not have survived the horrific head injury he had sustained? Lafferty knelt down on the grass and felt at McKirrop's neck for a carotid pulse. There was none. And then there *was* something – very weak and very faint, but it was there. It caressed the tip of his third finger like a fluttering butterfly. McKirrop was still alive!

Lafferty scrambled up the steep muddy path to the bridge on all fours. The very urgency of his movements seemed to act against him and he kept losing his footing and slipping back. With a last, frantic effort, he pulled himself up on to the bridge path where he started to run towards the nearest houses, a small group of bungalows some two hundred metres away. He was breathing heavily and his trousers were covered in mud when he reached the nearest house and flung open the garden gate to charge up the path. He banged on the door with both fists until he saw the hall light come on and heard someone behind the door.

'Who is it?' called a timid woman's voice.

'I have to phone for an ambulance!' replied Lafferty. 'It's very urgent. Please open the door.'

'Go away!' said the voice behind the door. 'Go away or I'll call the police.'

'Look, I'm Father Lafferty from St Xavier's. There's a man badly injured down on the canal bank. He needs urgent hospital treatment.'

'I've told you once. Go away! Don't tell me any more lies! I'll call the police. I mean it!'

'Sweet Jesus!' exclaimed Lafferty. He dropped his hands to his sides in exasperation and moved his mouth soundlessly before giving up on the woman and crashing his way through the adjoining hedge to the house next door. Again he banged on the door. There was no reply and the house remained in darkness.

He had more luck at the third bungalow. The door was opened before Lafferty had even reached it by a man with a can of beer in his hand.

'What the hell is going on?' asked the man.

Lafferty told him.

After the ambulance and police had been called, the man asked Lafferty, 'Is there anything I can do?'

'Maybe some blankets and a torch?' suggested Lafferty.

'Of course.'

The man's wife was quick to come up with a pair of blankets from the airing cupboard in the hall, while he himself fetched a torch from the garage.

'Take this one; it's got a powerful beam. Want me to come back with you?'

'No,' said Lafferty. 'You stay here and tell the ambulance people where to come. I'll be down on the path on the east side of the bridge.'

'Will do,' said the man.

5

The police were the first to arrive on the scene, two officers from a Panda car that happened to be in the vicinity when the call went out. Lafferty felt relieved that his uneasy wait was coming to an end. For the past few minutes the only thing that moved had been the tiny pulse in McKirrop's neck that he kept searching for. He was still subconsciously unwilling to accept that anyone with such a horrific head injury could be alive.

'We'll take over now, Father,' said the elder of the two constables when they arrived on the bank; the other one looked like a boy. Lafferty straightened up and felt the stiffness in his back from having been in one position for so long. The policeman knelt down to examine the bodies with his torch and Lafferty heard him whisper, 'Sweet Jesus Christ.' He turned and said, 'Take a look at this Brian.' His colleague joined him in a squatting position and groaned before turning his head to the side to avoid looking any more.

'I thought you said one of them was still alive, Father?'

asked the first policeman as the wail of an ambulance announced its imminent arrival.

'The man is,' replied Lafferty. 'He doesn't look it, but he is. I found a pulse in his neck.'

Lafferty watched as the policeman took off his glove and put his hand to McKirrop's neck. 'There's nothing there now,' he said. Lafferty's motionless face reflected the moonlit ripples from the canal as he looked down at the scene, his eyes a mixture of sadness and bemusement. The policeman looked away again but remained on his knees, his fingers resting lightly on McKirrop's neck as if in deference to Lafferty's assertion that the man was still alive.

'God! I felt something!' he exclaimed. 'You were right. It's very weak, but it's there all right.'

Voices and the sound of running feet came from the bridge. The new arrivals were a paramedic team and more policemen from a second car. The two paramedics, dressed in green overalls and carrying cases packed with emergency equipment, arrived on the bank and got to work on McKirrop while Lafferty was invited by the newly arrived police inspector to tell him what he had discovered.

'Did you move the bodies at all, Father?'

'I had to move the man's body to reach the woman,' Lafferty confessed.

The policeman shrugged. 'Well, I don't suppose it's going to matter much anyway. Looks like a straightforward case of a couple of winos knocking hell out of each other. But we'll go through the motions. Where the hell are forensic?'

Lafferty felt himself drift into the background as yet more policemen arrived, this time from a white Bedford van. They wore overalls and wellington boots. More light was cast on the scene as a lighting generator arrived and was coaxed into life; it provided almost as much noise as it did light. The relevant area was marked out with plastic tape bearing the legend 'POLICE', and canvas screens were erected around the area the bodies lay in.

When he got the chance, Lafferty asked the inspector, 'I don't quite see who hit who, if you understand my meaning?'

'What do you mean, Father?' asked the policeman, giving the impression of being preoccupied with other thoughts.

'If you're working on the supposition that McKirrop drowned Bella . . .'

'You know these people, Father?' interrupted the policeman, hearing Lafferty use the names. He turned round to look at him directly for the first time.

'In a way,' replied Lafferty. 'I'd been looking for McKirrop to ask him a few things about Simon Main, the boy whose body was stolen from the cemetery. McKirrop was the man who was living rough in the cemetery at the time of the child's disinterment.'

'Was he now?' asked the policeman thoughtfully.

Lafferty pursued his original question. 'Say that McKirrop drowned Bella, he could hardly have done it after sustaining the head injury he's got, and if he did it before, how did he get the head injury?'

The inspector, looking down at the scene as the paramedics continued their work, replied, 'It looks to me as if the pair of them had some kind of argument; McKirrop hit the woman – that's what smashed her cheek in. She, in turn, hit him with the bottle – probably a reflex action – before she herself passed out, and fell with her head in the water.'

91

'I see,' said Lafferty in a voice that was filled with doubt. 'I hadn't thought of it that way.'

'We'll need a statement from you, Father.'

'Of course,' he replied.

After giving details to the police, Lafferty waited until the paramedics had lifted McKirrop on to a stretcher and were preparing to climb up to the bridge.

'I'd like to travel with him if that's all right? He may die before you get there.'

'Very well, Father,' said the leading paramedic.

As they started up the steep path to the bridge, Lafferty looked back to tell the inspector that he was going, but the man was engaged in instructing a photographer and members of the forensic team who were still busy by the canal. He looked back again from the bridge parapet at the illuminated scene below. There was a gap in the canvas screen. Bella's eyes were still staring at the heavens, oblivious to all that was going on around her. He thought of Hieronymus Bosch.

The ambulance gathered speed and its siren cleared the road ahead as they sped towards the infirmary. Lafferty held on to a grab-handle on the side of the vehicle and watched McKirrop's body respond to the unevenness of the road, despite the securing straps. A plastic airway protruded from his mouth and one of the paramedics constantly monitored his vital signs.

'How is he?' he asked the kneeling attendant.

The man shrugged and replied, 'Touch and go. You've already given him last rites?'

Lafferty confirmed that he had. As the journey continued, he wondered if what he was witnessing was innate human goodness. Could the experience be used to help bolster his flagging faith? Or at least to counteract the despair he felt on finding McKirrop and Bella, and seeing what they had done to each other. All the stops were now being pulled out to save the life of a man who had turned his back on society. Surely this was a sign of a compassionate, caring and loving community? Or did everything run on automatic pilot? Police, ambulance, medical services. Maybe it didn't matter too much in this case, Lafferty considered.

It was unlikely that McKirrop would recover from his injuries and, even if he did, society would not be finished with him for some time to come. Bella's death had yet to be accounted for.

The ambulance slowed and turned sharply to the right; they had arrived at the Infirmary. Almost before the vehicle had come to a halt, the rear doors were flung open and McKirrop's stretcher was slid out on to an Accident and Emergency trolley to be taken indoors. The paramedic who had sat with McKirrop throughout the journey reeled off facts and figures to the A&E team as they all disappeared inside, leaving Lafferty feeling anonymous and alone.

The driver of the ambulance closed up the doors of the vehicle and said to Lafferty, 'He's still hanging on then?'

Lafferty nodded.

'Sometimes it's bloody amazing how people can cling on to life,' said the man.

'Bloody,' agreed Lafferty as he started to walk towards the doors of A&E.

The receptionist affected a smile when she saw Lafferty's collar; she seemed oblivious to the state of the rest of his clothes. 'How can I help you, Father?' she asked.

'The man who has just been brought in. His name is John McKirrop. He has no fixed abode. I'd like to wait and hear how he is, if that's all right.'

'Perfectly all right, Father. If you'd like to take a seat through there, I'm sure one of the doctors will speak to you soon.'

Lafferty was joined within minutes by two of the policemen who had been down on the canal bank. When they had finished telling the receptionist their business, they came over to speak to him.

'I didn't realise we had a police escort,' said Lafferty.

'We drew the short straw,' said one of them. 'We've to wait to see if he comes round.'

Lafferty drew in breath. 'Could be some time.'

'That's what we're afraid of,' replied the policeman. 'We spend half our lives waiting around hospitals and court rooms. Did you know this man, Father?'

Lafferty shrugged and said, 'Not exactly, but I thought I'd wait to hear how he is. It's a terrible thing to have no one care about you.'

'Strikes me, if he'd just die it'd save us all a lot of trouble,' said the second policeman. 'If a couple of wasters decide to do each other in, it's fine by me – and anyone else with any common sense.'

'Kevin is a bit touchy about having his leave cancelled,' explained the first policeman with a sensitivity that obviously wasn't shared by his colleague.

'Really,' answered Lafferty drily.

'Well, what's the point?' Kevin grumbled on. 'All this time, trouble and expense over some drunken sod who, when he leaves here, will get smashed out of his mind and do the same thing all over again or worse next time. What's the point?'

94

Lafferty's philosophical roller-coaster started out on a downward slope again.

As time went on, the policemen drifted away from Lafferty as they all ran out of things to say to each other. The hospital had segregated waiting areas for patients and their relatives. The policemen had access to both, being part of the scenery in a large A&E department. But Lafferty felt obliged to remain with the relatives, not wishing to get in the way of the medical staff and knowing that there was very little he could do in a practical way. He tried reading one of the old magazines that were supplied on a table by the door, but the lighting was so poor in the room that he gave up as he felt a headache threaten.

There were several other people waiting in the room. A mother and daughter who huddled together for comfort and kept up a constant whisper of reassurance to each other, creating their own private island in a sea of adversity. There were two teenagers who drank cans of Cola from the drinks machine in the hallway. They didn't say much to each other, and constantly flicked through the pages of magazines without apparently reading anything. An elderly man in a raincoat sat with his hands in his pockets staring at the floor as if deep in thought. A group of four people, three men and a woman, who looked as if they came from the rougher side of town, kept muttering to each other about 'getting their story straight'. One man did most of the talking. He was in his forties and wore a light-blue shell suit with yellow diamonds on the sleeves and on the sides of the trousers. His black hair was slicked back like a fifties rock star and his teeth had several gaps in the front. On his feet, he had a pair of white trainers with fluorescent-green laces.

Lafferty did not recognise the make. It did not seem to be one of the top five he had heard were favoured by discerning schoolchildren.

The man got off his seat to kneel down in front of the other three and lecture them with the aid of a nicotine stained index finger. Lafferty heard him say in a stage whisper, 'If we all tell the same story there's nothing they can do. Nothing. We've just got to stick together. Right?' The two men nodded, but the woman looked frightened and doubtful. Lafferty reckoned that she was probably no older than thirty, but the lankness of her hair and the sallowness of her complexion made her look much older. He sometimes wondered why no research had been done on poverty-induced ageing. In his experience half the women living in the tower block flats suffered from it. So many beautiful brides were hollow cheeked hags by the time they were thirty. 'Right?' the man repeated for the woman's benefit. She nodded nervously but didn't argue.

The man looked up and caught Lafferty looking at him. He gave a slight smile and pretended to look past him before sitting back down again in his seat. Occasionally he would glance over his shoulder to see if he was still being watched. Lafferty did not attract any smiles or nods from the others – not that he sensed any hostility, just the feeling that his collar was out of place. Those present did not expect him to be waiting there like any other ordinary member of the public. He was part of the establishment. He should be 'doing' not 'waiting'.

A nurse appeared in the doorway and looked down at the clip-board she held in her hand. 'Mrs Simmonds?' she inquired.

The mother and daughter duo responded and the

nurse approached them with some news. When she had finished, Lafferty saw the mother break into tears, her shoulders silently heaving. He got up and walked towards them.

'Is there anything I can do?' he asked the daughter quietly.

'No, thank you,' replied the daughter sharply. She wrapped her arm further round her mother as if shielding her from Lafferty.

Lafferty retired gracefully and sat down again. But his head felt as though it was full of broken glass.

An Indian doctor came into the room, white coat flapping open and stethoscope protruding from his right-hand pocket. He looked around, saw Lafferty and came towards him. He exuded a faint aura of sweat. 'I understand you are waiting for news of McKirrop,' he said.

Lafferty noted the absence of any 'mister'. Society was putting 'McKirrop' back in his place already.

'Yes,' he replied. 'How is he?'

'Not so good, I'm afraid. It's pretty amazing that he survived at all, after that kind of head wound. He's stable for the moment and we will be transferring him to the Head Trauma Unit as soon as he can be moved. But as for when he might, if at all, regain consciousness, that's in the lap of the gods, I'm afraid.'

Lafferty wanted to ask, 'Yours or mine?' but didn't. 'Thank you for telling me,' he said. 'I'll phone in the morning if that's all right?'

'Of course.'

As he prepared to leave, Lafferty saw one of the policemen at the tea vending machine and stopped to speak to him. 'You're staying?' he asked.

'Yep,' answered the policeman with an air of resignation. 'Once they have him on one of those machines we could be here for the next six months, on the off chance that he'll come round.'

'That won't please your colleague too much,' said Lafferty, remembering their earlier conversation.

'Oh, Kevin's all right, Father. It's just that the job gets to you sometimes. Some of the things you see every day . . . you start to see things differently – well it just gets to you, you know?'

Lafferty nodded, 'I know.'

He glanced at his watch as he stepped outside and shrugged his shoulders against the cold. It was eleven thirty. He looked up at the sky to see that it had cleared completely. As a consequence, the temperature was now well below zero.

At three that morning, Sarah Lasseter's bleeper went off and she responded almost automatically. Her room was freezing as she pulled on a sweater and slacks – the hospital turned the heating in the residency off at eleven and it didn't come on again until six in the morning. Before getting into bed she had laid all her clothes out in order, so that she could dress quickly, and in complete darkness if need be. She reached under the bed for the pair of flat slip-on shoes she kept there and pushed her feet into them. She put on her white coat and clipped the bleeper to her top pocket before patting the other pockets to check that she had everything she needed. Satisfied, she sighed, 'Off we go again,' and slipped out of her room, closing the door quietly behind her to avoid waking anyone else on the corridor.

The coldness of the air outside almost took her breath

away as she crossed the courtyard from the residency to the main hospital; she had to watch her footing on the frosty cobbles as twice she nearly came to grief. It was a relief to enter through the swing doors and find herself cossetted with warmth, but she was still rubbing her hands together when she entered HTU and sought out the night staff nurse. 'You rang, master?' she joked in a deep voice when she saw the nurse approach.

'Sorry, Doctor, we have an admission from A&E.' The nurse handed over a clip-board with a single sheet of paper on it.

'John McKirrop?' exclaimed Sarah. 'The same John McKirrop?'

''Fraid so,' answered the nurse. 'He's really bad this time. Depressed fracture of the skull. The police think it was a bottle. He almost certainly has serious brain damage, but A&E say he's stable for the moment so they're keen to pass the buck.'

'Poor man,' said Sarah, reading the notes. 'Is he here yet?'

'He's on the way up,' answered the nurse.

Sarah heard the lift doors open and turned to see the night porter manoeuvre out a trolley. He had to swing his body wide to counteract the wanderlust of the front wheels as he pushed it in through the the primary unit doors. A nurse accompanied him.

'All yours,' said the nurse when the secondary doors had been opened to allow the trolley to enter. 'Where do you want him, Staff?'

'Alpha four,' replied the staff nurse, turning to lead the way to a bay in one of the three small 'wards' that comprised HTU. Each of the three patient service areas, alpha, beta and gamma, could accommodate four patients and each individual bay was equipped with life-support and monitoring equipment at the leading edge of technology. At this early hour the unit was only dimly lit by night-lights which gave off a peaceful, green glow. Sarah found that the lighting at night always made her think of an aquarium.

The three other beds in Alpha were all occupied, the patients having sustained head injuries which demanded that they have intensive care or brain monitoring or both. Each bed was surrounded on both sides by electronic equipment and chart recorders. Apart from the gentle hum of the heating and air-conditioning, clicking relays decided who would breathe and when. The A&E trolley was positioned parallel to the empty bed and McKirrop's body was lifted gently to its new home. The porter wheeled away the trolley followed by the nurse from downstairs, leaving Sarah and the staff nurse to deal with McKirrop.

'Let's get him plumbed in,' said Sarah, starting to connect the first of a range of tubes and electrodes to McKirrop's unconscious body. The staff nurse had turned on a small spotlight above the bed which provided a circular pool of white light on the patient without it encroaching on the dim green glow of the neighbouring bays. Sarah and the staff nurse worked silently until McKirrop was wired into the system and electronic information was now available for Sarah to note down on the patient admission sheet. When she had finished, Sarah looked down at him and said, 'Just how you're still alive, John McKirrop, is a mystery to me. You must want to live very much.'

'God knows why,' said the staff nurse.

Sarah smiled as they both watched McKirrop's chest rise

and fall in response to the ventilator equipment. 'Maybe he's an eccentric millionaire?'

'Or very much in love,' said the nurse.

'Or very angry.' Sarah looked at her watch and noted down the time on the sheet. 'Patient admitted to HTU and stable at three forty-six,' she said.

The staff nurse looked at the fob watch pinned to her apron. 'Check,' she answered.

'I think that's all we can do for the moment,' said Sarah, stepping back from the bed. 'How are the others?'

'No problems. Everyone's behaving tonight – so far.'

'Long may it continue,' said Sarah. 'I'm going back to bed.'

'I'll try not to disturb you,' smiled the Staff nurse.

Sarah had an undisturbed four hours' sleep before she was up again to begin the business of the day. It was Tyndall's ward-round today, so Stubbs would be particularly edgy and anxious to ensure that the unit was running smoothly. Sarah decided on a dark pencil skirt and a black roll-neck sweater. She tied her hair back in a bun. Finally, she chose to wear her large-framed spectacles, knowing full well the ensemble would make her look like a school marm – or Audrey Hepburn playing a nun, as Paddy Duncan had put it once before. Sarah deemed the measure necessary. Images were important, and she intended to be taken seriously.

Tyndall's ward-rounds always started at nine thirty precisely so Sarah was surprised when Stubbs was still absent at twenty-five past. She was beginning to think that she would have to brief Tyndall on her own when a breathless Stubbs appeared, cursing his car for having a flat battery. He smoothed his hair back with both hands and tugged his shirt cuffs down below his white coat before taking the patients' files from Sarah's hands without comment. Sarah watched the unit Sister and the day staff nurse exchange glances in response to Stubbs's rudeness.

Stubbs had not had time to read more than a paragraph before Murdoch Tyndall entered the duty-room dead on the half hour.

'Morning everyone,' said the smiling consultant whose eyes moved quickly round the room taking everything in. Stubbs let the asynchronous chorus of good mornings die down before he said, 'Good morning, sir. All ready for you.'

Tyndall rubbed his hands together and said, as he always did, 'Right, let's get started.'

Sarah smiled at Sister Roche, the unit sister, as Tyndall led the way followed by Stubbs at his elbow. The rest of them followed in single file in what Sarah always saw as a feudal procession. The Lord of the Manor being shown around his domain by his retainers. They stopped at each bay in turn and Stubbs read from the case notes which he hastily referred to for values and figures. Tyndall would nod and ask questions either of Stubbs or the nursing staff. Questions regarding nursing care were relayed through Sister Roche who would answer herself or refer the question as she saw fit.

When the group arrived at Alpha 4, the bay where McKirrop lay, Stubbs became flustered. He thumbed his way through the papers in his hand without finding what he was looking for. 'This is . . .' he began.

Sarah knew that Stubbs had no idea who the patient was. There had been no time to brief him beforehand. But as Stubbs had chosen to ignore her throughout the ward-round she decided to let him sweat as long as possible. She noticed Sister Roche look down at her feet to conceal a small smile and looked away in case it became infectious.

'I'm sorry sir . . . I don't seem to have any information about this . . .' stammered Stubbs. He looked at Sarah and said, 'Do you have any details on this patient, Dr Lasseter?'

'Yes sir,' smiled Sarah innocently. 'Mr McKirrop was admitted in the early hours of this morning after being involved in some kind of drunken fracas.'

She unclipped the new admission sheet that Stubbs had failed to notice on the end of the bed and handed it to him.

'No, you tell us, Doctor,' interrupted Tyndall.

'Very good sir,' said Sarah, taking the sheet back from Stubbs who looked daggers at her. 'Mr McKirrop was close to death when he was found on the canal bank last night. The A&E team managed to stabilise him and referred him to us because of his head injury. He has a depressed fracture of the skull with a concavity of over three centimetres at the mid point. I admitted him to HTU at a quarter to four this morning and assigned him to level one life-support systems.'

Tyndall took a pace forward and looked down at McKirrop. 'Level one life-support,' he repeated thoughtfully. 'No need for the patient to do anything at all for himself, eh? Do you think the day will come when we can do away with bodies altogether, Doctor?'

'We're a long way from that, sir,' replied Sarah. 'The machines are really very basic.'

'But they're getting better,' said Tyndall – a little frostily thought Sarah. She bit her lip as she suddenly remembered Tyndall's love of technology.

Tyndall frowned. He said, 'The patient seems familiar, Doctor, or am I mistaken?' He looked closer at the unconscious form of John McKirrop.

'No, you're not, sir,' replied Sarah. 'Mr McKirrop was our patient briefly last week because of concussion he received when he was beaten up. He was the man who disturbed the grave robbers in Newington Cemetery.'

'Ah yes, the man who lived in the cemetery.'

'The tramp,' added Stubbs.

'Not having the best of luck is our Mr McKirrop, is he?' commented Tyndall.

'Goes with the lifestyle,' said Stubbs.

Tyndall looked at him and said, 'There but for the grace of God, Doctor Stubbs.'

Stubbs smiled wanly. Tyndall turned to Sarah again and asked, 'What are the plans for Mr McKirrop today?'

Sarah looked quickly to Stubbs expecting him to interrupt, but he didn't, so she said, 'I think the full range of cerebral function tests, sir. It seems probable that he suffered extensive brain damage from the impact fracture.'

'Do we have X-rays?'

'Yes sir. A&E had them done last night. They're in the side room.'

'Let's have a look, shall we?'

The party adjourned to a small room with a series of light-boxes mounted along one wall. Sarah pinned up McKirrop's skull X-ray and stood back. Tyndall adjusted his spectacles on his nose and tutted under his breath.

'Quite a wallop. A wonder he survived at all.' He turned to Sarah. 'Can I have a look at his admission stats?'

Sarah handed him the sheet and Tyndall ran his eye down the figures. 'I'd go ahead with the tests,' he agreed, 'but I don't think we should formulate any long range plans for Mr McKirrop.'

'No sir,' answered Sarah.

Tyndall's attention returned to the sheet and he read out loud, 'John McKirrop. Age, early fifties, no fixed abode, no relations, next of kin . . . Father Ryan Lafferty?' He looked over his glasses at Sarah.

'I understand Father Lafferty arrived in the ambulance with Mr McKirrop, sir. He wanted to be kept informed about his condition, so A&E entered his name as next of kin. McKirrop has no one else.'

'What's Father Lafferty's interest in the patient?'

'I believe he wants to talk to Mr McKirrop about what happened in the cemetery with the Main boy.'

'Really?' asked Tyndall distantly.

'The police are also waiting to interview Mr McKirrop. I understand the other party involved in the fracas died,' said Sarah.

Tyndall gave a gesture of distaste and Stubbs did likewise. Tyndall's took the form of a little shake of the head, while Stubbs's lip curled in disdain.

'Well I suspect they'll all be disappointed, but you never know. Some of us have been in this business too long to be surprised by anything that the human body can do. I'd like to be kept informed of Mr McKirrop's condition, please.'

Sarah and Stubbs replied, 'Yes sir,' in unison.

When Tyndall left the unit the entire team seemed to breathe a sigh of relief. This brought smiles from everyone except Stubbs. His eyes flashed with anger, and Sarah did not need to guess at whom it was directed.

'A word if you please, Doctor,' he snapped as he walked out of the room. Sarah shrugged and accepted her cue to follow. She saw Sister Roche raise her eyes heavenwards and acknowledged the friendly gesture with a slight smile. Stubbs opened the door to the X-ray room and ushered Sarah inside before closing it again. 'What the hell do you mean by making a fool of me?' he demanded through gritted teeth.

'I don't know what you mean, Dr Stubbs,' replied Sarah coolly.

'You set me up over McKirrop. You know you did!'

'I assure you, Doctor. There was simply no time to brief you beforehand.'

'It was deliberate!' stormed Stubbs. 'You wanted me to look stupid in front of Dr Tyndall.'

'That's ridiculous! There simply wasn't time to tell you about Mr McKirrop's admission.'

'You did it to make an impression on Tyndall! Do you think I'm stupid or something?'

'What I think of you is neither here nor there and better left unsaid,' replied Sarah.

It was the first time she had done anything other than appease Stubbs, and it felt good. She noticed a hint of surprise appear on Stubbs's face followed by uncertainty, which made her feel even better.

'You'll be saying next that I flattened your car battery so that you'd be late!'

'I think you have said enough, Dr Lasseter,' said Stubbs, his voice rising to suggest a warning.

Sarah took a deep breath and said curtly, 'If you'll excuse me, Doctor, I have work to do.'

She turned on her heel and left Stubbs standing there.

Inside, Sarah's stomach was churning and she could feel the pulse beating in her neck, but she steeled herself to keep her head up and walk off with authority in her step. She went back to the duty-room and stood for a moment, looking out of the window, trying to regain her composure. Her hands were trembling.

'Everything all right?' asked Sister Roche.

'Yes thank you, Sister.'

6

Lafferty took a chance on finding John Main at home and went round to his flat. He had decided that a personal meeting would be better than a telephone call, and he didn't want to wait another day for Main to come back down to St Xavier's. At first he thought Main was out, but after the second ring of the bell he heard sounds from inside. The door opened and a groggy looking John Main stood there. He was wearing a sweat shirt with 'Merchiston School' emblazoned on the front, and a pair of denim jeans. His feet were bare and his hair unkempt. The heaviness of his eyelids said that he had been asleep.

'Father Lafferty? This is a surprise . . .'

'I was passing. I thought perhaps I'd pop in and tell you how I was getting on.'

Lafferty thought the white lie was justified in the cause of defusing the look of expectation that had quickly appeared in Main's eyes.

'Come in,' Main said, stepping back and opening the door wider. 'You'll have to excuse the mess, I'm afraid.'

'If only I had a pound for every time I've heard that,' Lafferty replied lightly. He walked into the living room and realised that Main had not been joking.

Main started to tidy things away or, rather, to concentrate the mess so that it was all in one place. Unwashed plates, cups, glasses and cutlery were collected and piled up on a coffee table, and Lafferty was invited to sit down. He did so, regretting that he had come without any good news to report. The empty gin bottle in the hearth and the glass standing beside it with a dried-up piece of lemon in the bottom explained why Main was looking so dishevelled.

'Can I get you something?' asked Main. 'Tea? Coffee?'

'Coffee would be nice but I don't want to put you to any trouble,' said Lafferty.

'No trouble, I could use some.'

The comment made Lafferty's eyes stray automatically back to the bottle in the hearth. Main noticed.

He said, 'I hope you're not about to give me a lecture on the evils of drink.'

'I wouldn't dream of it,' replied Lafferty. 'Drink can be an absolute blessing.'

The comment surprised Main: it had been made so matter-of-factly. He felt his liking for Lafferty, born at their first meeting, grow a little more, and he went to the kitchen to put the kettle on.

Lafferty looked around the room, noting the signs of an unhappy man living on his own. And then his gaze was caught by what he saw on the dining-table. A circle of white cards, each bearing a letter of the alphabet, and an upturned glass sitting in the middle. He got up slowly and walked over to the table. He was standing there when Main came back. 'Ouija?' he asked, turning to face Main.

Main seemed discomfited. He had obviously forgotten about it. 'Yes,' he said, trying to recover his composure. 'I thought I'd give it a try.'

'A try?' asked Lafferty gently.

Main's composure started to show cracks. He supported himself by putting both hands on the back of a chair and looked down at the table. He was having obvious difficulty in getting the words out. 'I wanted to . . . I needed to . . . I had to try getting in touch with Mary and Simon. I need to know what happened. I need to know that Simon is all right.'

Lafferty could read the pain in Main's eyes. It brought a lump to his own throat. 'You need more than one person for this business, I understand.'

Main nodded and said, 'I met this woman in a pub last night who told me that she had been in touch with her mother through a ouija board so I asked her if she would show me how it worked, and she did.'

'What happened?' asked Lafferty.

'Nothing.'

'Nothing?'

'Oh, there was some nonsense about Simon "being at peace" but I knew she was moving the glass.'

'I see. It can be a dangerous game, they tell me.'

'When you've nothing to lose the stakes don't matter,' said Main.

Lafferty noticed that there was an extra card lying in the centre of the table. He could read, *Simon Main*, *HTU*, *Beta 2*. There were some reference numbers and a Greek letter in the bottom left hand corner.

'It was the patient's name-card from the end of Simon's bed,' whispered Main. 'I took it the day they decided to switch off the machine. I thought it might help to have something connected with Simon on the table.'

Lafferty nodded, and then asked, 'You said something about coffee?'

'I'll get it.'

'Did you manage to get in touch with the wino?' asked Main a few minutes later as they sipped their coffee.

'That's really why I came,' admitted Lafferty. He told Main about the previous evening. When he had finished Main threw back his head and laughed bitterly. 'There's irony for you.'

'I don't understand,' said Lafferty.

'McKirrop, ending up in HTU with brain damage. That's where Simon was before he died.

'Oh, I see. I'm sorry.'

'Life's rich pattern. What are the chances of McKirrop pulling through?'

'Not good, I'm afraid. His injuries are pretty serious. They don't think he'll make it.'

Main shook his head resignedly and said, 'Well, it was a long shot anyway that he might be able to tell us anything more, wasn't it?'

Lafferty nodded. 'Yes, it was. But frankly, it was all we had.' The look of emptiness that appeared in Main's eyes made him wish that he hadn't added the last bit.

The two men drank their coffee in silence until Lafferty broke it by asking, 'Have you thought about a return to work? I think you might start to feel better if you had more to occupy your mind.'

Main smiled but there was little humour in it. He said, 'I know you mean well but I have to find out what those bastards did to my son. Going back to work isn't going to help with that.'

Lafferty nodded reluctantly and asked quietly, 'What are you going to do now? Do you know?'

'I'm going to try the newspapers,' replied Main.

'I don't understand,' said Lafferty, again.

'I'm going to try to persuade the newspapers to take up the story again so that our glorious police force will feel the pressure and start to get its bloody finger out.'

Lafferty opened his mouth to say something, but Main continued, 'And if you're about to say that they're doing their best, don't bother! It isn't good enough!'

'Fair enough,' said Lafferty.

He put down his empty cup and got up to leave, adding, 'If McKirrop should come round and I get a chance to speak to him I'll get back to you. In the meantime, I'll pay another visit to the library and see what I can come up with.'

Main relaxed a bit as he followed Lafferty to the door. He said, 'Don't think I'm not grateful. I am, I really am.' He held out his hand and Lafferty shook it.

'If you need me, you know where I am.'

When Lafferty got back to St Xavier's he found that his cleaner, Mrs Grogan, had made him lunch. This wasn't part of her duties, but she had a strong mothering instinct and often added to her cleaning and shopping role with the provision of an occasional cooked meal. Lafferty was grateful. He disliked cooking and his diet suffered accordingly. The downside to this kindness was that Mrs Grogan, being a woman of strong opinions, insisted on giving him her views on world affairs while he ate. Today she chose to expound her views on the common market. She was not in favour.

After lunch, Lafferty checked his diary. He had remembered the two home visits he had to make, but had forgotten about the meeting with the engaged couple, Anne Partland and her young man. It was pencilled in for three thirty. He liked Anne; she was a bright girl who had never caused her parents a moment's anxiety all through her teenage years and on through her course at teacher training college. One of the few, he thought. He had not met her fiancée but Anne and her parents wanted the marriage to take place in St Xavier's, so he had suggested a meeting. The boy was a Catholic so there would be no need for the usual 'mixed marriage' talk about the future upbringing of the children.

Sarah was relieved to find that, as the day wore on, Stubbs was obviously avoiding her. She was pleased she had stood her ground earlier, but her stomach still had butterflies over the incident. Although she had not said anything to the nursing staff, it was clear that they knew of her altercation with Stubbs and seemed to be going out of their way to be nice to her. It helped build her confidence to have them on her side.

She completed brain function tests on the six patients she had been assigned and plotted their progress, or lack of it, on their daily update charts. Four remained on a plateau; one had actually shown some loss of function; but the last, a patient named Trevor Brown in Beta 2, was showing a definite improvement in terms of electro-pulse readings. Brown had been in a coma for the past thirteen weeks, but Tyndall had predicted that he would recover. Many consultants were reluctant to make such predictions about coma patients, but the state of the art equipment that HTU was blessed with enabled them to detect the slightest of changes in brain function and to base their prognoses on them. In particular, the Sigma scan apparatus – which Murdoch Tyndall had played a major role in developing – was proving itself in the field trials it was undergoing.

Unlike the other monitoring probes which only needed the attachment of exterior electrodes, Sigma scan required that two electrodes be surgically implanted in the patient's skull. The procedure was not suitable for all patients, but in those who had had them implanted it had been possible to achieve an incredibly sensitive estimation of brain activity. Tyndall had worked out a table for the readings and, from that, a formula that could be applied to predict a patient's recovery potential.

Sarah applied Tyndall's formula to the figures for Brown and came up with the prediction that Brown would surface from the coma at some time during the next thirty-six hours.

As she was taking her work sheets back to the duty-room, she passed through Alpha and noticed that John McKirrop's admission sheet was still hanging on the end of his bed. She was puzzled. She thought that Stubbs would have wanted to carry out the tests on McKirrop himself – especially as Tyndall had asked to be kept informed. She looked for Stubbs and found him examining an electro-encephalogram with the aid of a magnifying lens and a ruler. She coughed to attract his attention.

'Yes, what is it?' asked Stubbs, without turning round.

'It's about Mr McKirrop's tests . . .'

'You do them. The tramp's all yours.'

'But Dr Tyndall specifically asked to be . . .'

Stubbs turned round and said coldly, 'He was being polite. But you're his blue-eyed girl of the moment, so you do them and inform him of your findings. As far as I'm concerned, McKirrop is a lost cause. A waste of my time. He's going to die. With a bit of luck we'll get permission to use his organs for transplant.'

Sarah bit her tongue, believing that Stubbs was deliberately trying to goad her into speaking out of turn. She ignored his callousness and simply said, 'Very well, Doctor.' It was important not to lose the ground she had gained with regard to Stubbs, and she had resolved to be cold and curt in her dealings with him. She returned to the duty-room and asked Sister Roche if she could have a nurse to help her with the tests on McKirrop.

'Of course,' said Roche. 'I'll give you Nurse Barnes. She's on the console at the moment. She could do with a change.

The 'console' was a computerised monitoring station that sat outside the entrance to Beta with Alpha on one side and Gamma on the other so that the duty nurse could see into all three from the swivel chair she sat on. In front of her, a bank of VDUs gave her a read-out of the vital signs of all twelve patients. A bank of red warning lights sat along the base of the unit ready to flash, along with an audible warning buzzer, should any patient falter in their tenuous grasp on life. Sister Roche herself relieved Nurse Barnes at the console.

Having established that McKirrop's blood pressure was acceptable and his pulse rate steady, Sarah set about adorning his head with a series of electrodes. First, she and the nurse had to make sure that as good an electrical contact as possible was achieved. This they did by depilating and cleaning the relevant areas of McKirrop's skull, and rubbing on high conductivity jelly before taping the electrodes into position. The injuries to the front of McKirrop's skull had ruled out the surgical implantation of Sigma probes.

'This always reminds me of these awful experiments we had to do in biology at school,' said Nurse Barnes. 'You know, the ones with the frogs.'

'Don't remind me,' said Sarah, screwing up her face. 'What a bunch of sadists we all were. How are we doing?'

'All ready I think,' replied the nurse.

Sarah made some last fine adjustments to the oscilloscope controls, getting the wave form as clear as possible on the screen. 'Will you check the recorder settings?' she asked the nurse.

Nurse Barnes moved away from the patient to stand by the roll-chart recorder. 'Shoot,' she said.

Sarah read out the settings on the oscilloscope. 'X-axis, 5.'

'Check.'

'Y-axis, 5.'

'Check.'

'Amp, 4'

The nurse moved a knob one click to the right before saying, 'Check.'

'Gain, 10.'

'Check.'

'Let's go for it.'

Nurse Barnes pressed the green START button on the recorder and the chart pen started to make its trace over a set time-course. The nib made a scratching sound as it rose and fell on the rolling chart, leaving a thin, red record of where it had been. A buzzer sounded and the pen fell to the base line. Sarah removed the completed chart and set up the next test. It took forty-five minutes in all to gather the information she needed for McKirrop's first condition appraisal. On completion, she thanked Nurse Barnes and took her file of graphs and read-outs to the doctors' room to begin a detailed analysis of them.

The 'doctors' room' sounded much grander than it actually was. In reality, it was one of the original ward side-rooms which had not been modernised at the time of the creation of HTU. It was close to the front door leading to the main corridor and lifts, and was sparsely furnished with a table, three chairs in varying states of decay, and a coffee percolator which Sarah switched on as soon as she went in.

There was a calendar sponsored by a local garage on the back of the door and various charts supplied by pharmaceutical companies pinned up on the walls here and there to break the monotony of vast areas of pale green paint. The only thing the room had going for it was that it was quiet, apart from the gurgle of water when it rained – there was a drain pipe situated immediately outside the window. At the moment it was fair. There was an unwritten rule in the unit that no one would disturb you there unless it was really necessary. For that reason the room had been dubbed 'The Ivory Tower'.

Sarah lost track of time as she analysed McKirrop's tests. The conclusion she was coming to was not what she expected, so she was forced to double-check everything. The fact that Tyndall had asked to be informed of the results had put an added burden on her. She mustn't make a fool of herself over this. She remembered the mug of coffee that was growing cold at her elbow and took a sip. 'Well, John McKirrop,' she said quietly. 'Unless I'm very much mistaken, you're not nearly as badly injured as everyone thought you were. The question is, why not?'

Sarah stared thoughtfully at the papers in front of her on the table for a few more moments before deciding to take another look at McKirrop. She met Sister Roche in the corridor, who was going off-duty.

'I didn't realise you were still here,' she said. 'Shouldn't you be off duty?'

'I won't be long,' smiled Sarah. 'Besides, I'm on call tonight.'

'Have a quiet one.'

'I wish.'

Sarah nodded to the night Staff Nurse who had taken up station at the console and walked through to Alpha 4. She took her pencil torch from her top pocket and opened McKirrop's eyelids, first right and then left, to shine the light in them. 'Well I'm blowed,' she murmured, putting the torch away again. She stood at the foot of the bed for a moment, watching McKirrop's face as if looking for clues, but the tubes and electrodes had deprived him of any sense of personality.

The tramp, as Stubbs had dubbed him, had obviously been a good looking man in his youth. He might still have been had he not been living rough for some time; the alcohol, wind and weather had taken their toll. He still had high cheek bones but his cheeks had hollowed below them and his eyes had sunk back into deep dark sockets. But the fact that the nursing staff had cleaned him up, and the wound in his forehead was hidden by pristine white bandaging, had restored to McKirrop some semblance of quiet dignity.

'I wonder,' she said as an idea occurred to her. She went to the X-ray room and searched for McKirrop's skull pictures. She found the one that had come up from A&E with the patient – the one she had shown Tyndall that morning – but she had a vague recollection of another envelope arriving from the X-ray department later.

After a brief search she found the X-rays still in their delivery envelope. Now she remembered. She had seen the porter bring them in, but had assumed that Stubbs was going to be doing McKirrop's tests so she had put them out of her mind. It looked as if Stubbs hadn't bothered to look at them.

Sarah pinned them up on the light box and adjusted her spectacles on her nose. One of the X-rays did not add anything to what she knew but the other confirmed exactly what she had begun to suspect. The slightly unusual angle of McKirrop's forehead had decreed that the frontal lobe of his brain was further back than normal in most patients. The injury that had appeared so horrific at first glance, although still very bad in terms of associated shock and trauma, would not have caused nearly as much brain damage as they had been assuming. This was why the tests she had run had given such optimistic readings.

With a bit of luck John McKirrop might actually survive his latest adventure and still be able to do the seven times table. In fact, there was a possibility that he might even recover consciousness before morning. This put Sarah in a quandary. Should she wait with the patient until he came round, and thereby witness the proof of her theory, or should should she call Tyndall right now with her diagnosis and prediction? She decided on the latter, despite realising how furious Stubbs was going to be. If he had opened the X-rays himself he would have seen what she had discovered, and he would have been counting the brownie points instead of her.

Sarah called Tyndall from the duty-room after laying out the relevant charts in front of her on Sister Roche's desk in anticipation of any question Tyndall might ask. She also had the X-ray beside her on a chair. She felt her mouth become a little dry as she waited for Tyndall to answer.

'Dr Tyndall please,' said Sarah when a woman answered. There was a short pause before Tyndall came on the line.

'It's Dr Lasseter here, sir,' said Sarah. 'You asked to be kept informed about Mr McKirrop's condition.'

'So I did,' said Tyndall pleasantly. 'He died I suppose?'

'No sir, far from it. I think he might pull through and quite possibly without any significant brain damage.'

'We are talking about the same patient, Doctor?' asked Tyndall. 'The down-and-out from the canal?'

'Yes sir.' Sarah went on to explain what she had found out from the brain function tests.

'Has Dr Stubbs had a chance to see your results?' asked Tyndall.

'No sir, he delegated the patient to me.'

'I see,' said Tyndall. Sarah could sense that Tyndall doubted the values she had obtained, but was too polite to say so straight out.

'I think I can explain sir,' she said. She told Tyndall how she had come to the conclusion that damage to McKirrop's brain had been minimised by the odd angle of his skull and how she had confirmed this by reference to newer X-rays.

Tyndall seemed much happier with this. 'Well done, Dr Lasseter,' he said. 'An alert mind is the physician's most valuable tool.'

'Thank you sir,' replied Sarah, feeling better than she

had done since she had started at HTU. The world was suddenly a much nicer place thanks to John McKirrop and his recessed frontal lobe.

'From the values you read out it sounds as if we can expect Mr McKirrop to regain consciousness in the not-too-distant future,' said Tyndall.

'Yes sir,' said Sarah.

'Thank you for letting me know.'

'My pleasure, sir.'

The conversation with Tyndall had imbued Sarah with new reserves of energy. She resolved to stay in HTU until McKirrop came round. It had been quite a day, all things considered. Standing up to Derek Stubbs had made it one to remember, but seeing John McKirrop regain consciousness would be the icing on the cake. She could not keep it to herself; she went to chat to the night staff nurse.

'With that head wound?' exclaimed the nurse when Sarah predicted that McKirrop would recover.

Sarah explained how it looked worse than it actually was.

'If you say so,' shrugged the nurse.

'Bet you fifty pence?'

'You're on. I'll call you if he stirs . . . Or maybe I won't. Fifty pence is fifty pence!'

Sarah went back to the doctors' room and carefully wrote up her notes on John McKirrop for inclusion in his case-notes file. Her handwriting was good, and she favoured a Schaeffer drawing pen filled with light blue China ink. Making sure that her notes were always clear and legible was almost a fetish with Sarah. It was born of an intense dislike of the way people made stereotypes of themselves. Many of her colleagues seemed obliged to write badly simply because they were doctors and it was expected of them. For the same reason, she could confidently predict what kind of cars they would drive, what clothes they would wear, what kind of houses they would aspire to and, in certain cases, what their answer would be to any given question. Her father had once explained kindly that his profession – and now hers – had to conform to certain standards because the public expected it of them. Sarah didn't accept that for a moment.

John Main lay awake and heard the fridge motor in the kitchen cut out, leaving the flat in absolute silence. He glanced at the clock at the side of his bed and saw the green digits register three in the morning, an hour he had seen a lot of in recent times. There was something about 'the wee sma' hours' that intensified fear and loneliness. Was it the quietness, or was it the darkness? Maybe the latter. Perhaps the absence of light allowed the forces of dark access to the fearful and vulnerable who lay unprotected by sleep. The loss of Mary and the fact that she was gone for ever was never more poignant than in these hours after midnight, when the dawn was still a long way off. Loneliness could be transcribed into actual physical pain.

But even this pain took second place to the agony of not knowing what had happened to Simon's body. It was something he did not properly understand, perhaps because it was a situation he could never have been prepared for; no one could. The nearest analogy he could think of concerned a woman he had once seen on television. The woman's daughter had been murdered, but the body never found. And the woman now spent all her time looking for it. He had not forgotten the look in her eyes. Now he knew how she felt.

The meeting with the newspaper people that day had not gone well; he had failed to persuade them to run the story again in any form other than a brief report, saying that the police had as yet failed to make an arrest. The journalist he had spoken to had been polite and kind, perhaps even to the point of humouring him, Main thought, but the affair was yesterday's story as far as the paper was concerned. His daily call to the police had only attracted the now routine reply about enquiries continuing. The priest, Lafferty, had done his best but had failed to come up with anything. So where did that leave him? What was he to do?

Main got out of bed and padded through to the kitchen to switch the kettle on. The coldness of the kitchen floor on his bare feet was a welcome distraction to what was going on inside his head. He lingered there in the darkness – he had not switched on the light – gazing out of the window at the silhouetted roof-tops, periodically testing the metal of the kettle with his fingertips until it became hot, when the pain of doing so provided even more distraction. The kettle boiled and clicked off; the spell was broken. Main took his coffee into the living room and turned on the television.

The film was in black and white. After a few minutes, he recognised it as being a Denis Wheatley story, though he couldn't remember the title, something to do with the devil, he thought. This was definitely not going to be a distraction; he clicked the channel changer. Although the screen changed to colour and noisy pop music, the black and white images from the film stayed in Main's head. He remembered reading Wheatley's books some years before and enjoying them at the time. There was something morbidly fascinating about the world of the occult, even to a disbeliever, as Main considered himself to be.

Perhaps that was what he should do next, take a personal interest in the occult, read up on it, find out about it? On the other hand, that's what Lafferty was doing. He had even consulted a colleague about witchcraft and devil worship. But there again, the man was a priest. His knowledge would be academic. He would probably be the last person to actually know about its practice in the community.

But what sort of people would he be looking for? There was no immediate answer to that one, and no obvious line of approach. The best he could hope for was to find someone who might know these things. The thought took him into the world of the spiritualist. If the police didn't know of any organised practice of the occult, and the Catholic church didn't either, maybe he should concentrate on the indirect approach and try to pick up some gossip or rumour on his own.

His experience with the woman and the ouija board hadn't given him much to be confident about, but as long as he realised that he might be treading on the stamping ground of the charlatan he might be able to pick up a useful lead in the spiritualist community. He would give it some more thought before doing anything.

Something made Main click the television channel back to the Wheatley film. The villain was about to get his come-uppance. A demon summoned up from the pit of hell was chasing him along a railway track and there would be no escape. He shivered and realised that he had not turned the fire on in the room. It was icy cold.

.   .   .

Ryan Lafferty was deeply troubled, so much so that he had got up at three in the morning and gone into the church to pray for guidance. An hour on his knees in the damp and cold had done little to help him physically, and he was very stiff, but he felt a little better mentally for having spoken his doubts and fears aloud. So far he had failed in his intention to help or bring comfort to John Main over the exhumation of his son's body, and his efforts at helping the O'Donnell family had been similarly ineffectual. What was more, he had been unable to get what Mary O'Donnell had said about the Church out of his head. Try as he might, he could not dismiss her angry outburst as being groundless – and this worried him.

Could it all be a test of faith, he wondered? Was God testing him? If he was, he was not coming through it very well. What had started out as a worry about his efficacy as a priest had now escalated into a full blown consideration of whether he should be a priest at all!

Lafferty had gone through crises before, of course, and thought that all priests must. At least the caring ones did, because self-examination was important to them. The alternative was smug self-righteousness. Looking back, his own first crisis had been during his third year at the training seminary, but it proved to be youthful panic and he had come through it with the aid of some kind words from the head of the college, who had seen it all before and knew just how to handle the situation. 'No one ever said being a priest was easy, Ryan. It isn't, it's bloody hard, it's meant to be.'

The second crisis had been more serious. He had fallen in love with Jane. Jane Lowry had been widowed after only three years of marriage when her husband, an RAF pilot, crashed into a remote hillside on a training exercise. She had sought solace from the Church and Lafferty had been the priest she had come to. She had newly moved out of her service home and had returned to the town where her parents lived. St Peter's, their local church, had been Lafferty's first charge.

Despite the fact that he and Jane were practically the same age and he was painfully inexperienced at the job, Lafferty had been able to guide her through the anger and despair she felt at her loss. Looking back on it now, it had been more like a brother looking after his sister than a priest-parishioner relationship, but it had worked for them and Jane had come to accept her loss and to keep her faith. Unfortunately for Lafferty the pity and compassion he felt for Jane turned into something deeper as time went on, and he had seriously questioned his vocation. He suspected that Jane felt the same way, but his love for her had remained undeclared and she, thankfully, had not made the first move. After a desperate struggle with himself, he had gone to his bishop and confessed all.

For the second time in his fledgling career, Mother Church had lent a sympathetic ear, this time in the form of Bishop Patrick Morrison, who had noted Lafferty's anguish and told him that he, too, had gone through a similar crisis at one time in his priesthood. 'You may be a priest but you're also a man. God knows that. God intended it that way.'

Morrison had persuaded Lafferty that his vocation would prevail, but it would be helped by a move to another town. As a consequence, he had come to St Xavier's. Morrison had been right. The love he felt for Jane mellowed to affection and he had been pleased some years later to hear from an old parishioner, who still sent him Christmas cards, that she had remarried and now had two children named Carol and Ryan. Just why the parishioner should have chosen to relay this information Lafferty had been unable to work out. Perhaps his face had betrayed more than he had imagined at the time.

Feeling that sleep would still be impossible, Lafferty returned to the church to pray. This time he prayed for Mary O'Donnell and also that John McKirrop might be allowed to recover, not least so that he might shed some light on the disappearance of Simon Main's body.

7

Sarah had fallen asleep in the doctors' room; she was sitting at the table with her head on her folded arms in front of her, where she had cleared away a little hollow among the papers. Just before half past three, she was wakened by the night staff nurse who gently shook her shoulder.

'Dr Lasseter?'

'Mmmm?' said Sarah sleepily.

'I think Mr McKirrop is coming round.'

The name brought Sarah to full awareness. She got up, rubbed her arms and said, 'Right, lead on.'

The nurse had already turned on the lamp above McKirrop's head so he was caught in a stage spotlight in the otherwise green auditorium. Sarah saw him move his head before she reached the Alpha 4 bay. He seemed to be in some distress, as if in the throes of some bad dream.

'Can you hear me, John?' Sarah asked, bending over him.

McKirrop stopped moving his head and Sarah felt

encouraged by the response. She nodded to the staff nurse. 'I think he can hear.'

'John, can you hear me?'

McKirrop grunted weakly and moved his head to the left.

'You're in hospital, John, the same one you were in last week after you were beat up in the cemetery. I'm Dr Lasseter. Remember me?' Sarah spoke each word slowly and clearly.

McKirrop said his first word, a slurred attempt at 'cemetery'.

'You've had another knock on the head. Can you remember anything about it?'

'Cemetery . . .' mumbled McKirrop. 'Yobs . . . beat me up.'

'That was last time, John,' said Sarah.

'Coffin . . . They dug up . . . boy's coffin . . .'

'That's right,' said Sarah kindly. 'You were very brave. You tried to stop them.' She was pleased that McKirrop did not appear to be suffering from any obvious brain damage. 'They took the boy's body, John, but you tried to stop them.'

McKirrop moved his head again as if frustrated at the struggle to get words out. '. . . opened the coffin . . . opened the coffin . . .'

His voice began to trail off as the effort of speaking tired him out.

'That's right John. That's excellent. You remember what happened. We'll have you right as rain in no time. Rest easy now. Get some sleep and we'll talk in the morning.' Sarah got up and stood beside the staff nurse, looking down at McKirrop as he sank back into sleep.

'That's fifty pence I owe you,' said the nurse.

'I'd better call Tyndall,' said Sarah.

'At this time?' exclaimed the nurse.

'He wanted to be informed when McKirrop came round.'

'I just hope for your sake that he included three thirty in the morning!' said the nurse.

The night staff nurse had planted the seeds of doubt in Sarah's mind. Tyndall *had* meant as soon as McKirrop came round, hadn't he? He hadn't meant first thing in the morning, had he? She tapped her fingers on the phone while she considered whether or not she should make the call. 'Oh, to hell with it,' she concluded and made it.

'Tyndall,' said the voice at the other end. He had a frog in his throat. Sarah knew that he had been asleep.

'Dr Tyndall? It's Sarah Lasseter here at HTU. John McKirrop recovered consciousness ten minutes ago.'

'Did he indeed?' replied Tyndall, clearing his throat. 'Is he lucid?'

Sarah gave a silent prayer of thanks. Tyndall did not appear to think the call unnecessary. 'Yes sir. A bit groggy, but I don't think there's any serious damage to worry about.'

'Does he remember anything about how he got his injuries?'

'No. I suspect he has trauma-associated amnesia about that, but he seems to remember the incident in the cemetery a couple of weeks ago, so there's no impairment to long-term memory.'

'Really? What's he been saying about that?'

'He remembers being beaten up and the boy's coffin being opened up.'

'What else?' asked Tyndall after a short pause.

'That's about it, sir. He's very tired and I didn't want to press him. He's sleeping at the moment.'

'Good,' said Tyndall. 'Let him rest. You are to be congratulated Doctor.'

'Thank you sir. What should I do about the police and the priest who wanted to be kept informed?'

'What about them?'

'The police wanted to speak to Mr McKirrop as soon as he came round.'

'Oh, I see. Well, I think we can leave calling them till the morning. It's not as if Mr McKirrop is going anywhere, is it?'

'No sir.'

'Good night, Doctor. Thank you for letting me know.'

Sarah replaced the receiver and felt pleased. She did a quick check of the patients and told the staff nurse that she was going back to the residency. She left the unit with a smile on her face – and fifty pence in her pocket. When she got into her room she was torn between making herself some coffee or getting directly into bed, knowing that she would only have about three hours' sleep at most. She opted for bed.

Sarah could feel the adrenaline surge of the last hour or so clearing from her veins, allowing tiredness to replace it. By the time she had laid out her clothes in order – just in case – she could feel her eyelids coming together. Her arm felt heavy as she reached out to turn off the bedside light. Within seconds she was asleep.

Sarah had an undisturbed three hours' sleep before her alarm woke her and she complained aloud as she always did. She reached out with her palm and made several attempts to connect with the 'off' button before the room was restored to silence again.

'Not already,' she grumbled. 'It can't possibly be . . .'

But it was, and she was up and getting washed after a few more minutes' grace. She was pleased to see Paddy Duncan at breakfast down in the dining-room; she hadn't seen him since the Chinese meal.

'Rough night?' Paddy asked.

'Not really,' replied Sarah. 'Well, yes and no,' she added after reconsidering.

'What does that mean?' asked Paddy.

Sarah told him about the McKirrop case.

'Well done,' said Paddy enthusiastically. 'And you say Stubbs gave him up for lost?'

Sarah nodded and said, 'I think he saw him as a sort of organ supermarket.'

'That's a particular hobby horse of his, I understand,' said Paddy. 'He reckons that people should have to opt out, rather than in, when it comes to transplant permission. It's a view that's gaining popularity.'

'It's something I've not really considered,' said Sarah.

'Maybe you should.'

'Why?'

'If you're working in a place like HTU it's a problem that's going to come up quite a lot.'

'Good point,' Sarah agreed.

'How are you getting on with dear Dr Stubbs anyway?' asked Paddy. 'Any better?'

'I don't think I could go that far,' replied Sarah. 'But I did let him know that I'm not his door-mat, and it seems to have improved matters.'

'Good for you,' said Paddy.

'How about you? Were you called out last night?'

'Twice,' replied Paddy. 'A patient we carried out a routine hernia operation on last Monday. He's developed a wound infection and it's been a bit slow to respond to treatment. I think it might be *Pseudomonas*, so I changed him to PYOPEN last night when his temperature was pushing a hundred and three. We should get the result of the lab test some time this morning. They were going to do a direct oxidase test on the wound exudate. I just hope to God I was right.'

'I'm sure you were,' said Sarah.

She looked at her watch and wiped her mouth with her napkin before saying, 'Another day of work and play beckons. See you.'

'See you, Sarah.'

Despite not having had much sleep, Sarah had a spring in her step as she climbed the stairs to HTU and walked in through the swing doors. Yesterday had been a good day and she hoped that the effects were going to last for some time. She remembered that her father had once said about medicine, 'every now and then you get a day that makes all the rotten ones worthwhile. Once you've tasted success, it's like a drug. You just go on wanting to have that feeling again. It's like being allowed to play God for a few hours.'

Almost at once, she could sense that something was wrong. Sister Roche crossed her field of view but failed to acknowledge her. Another of the nurses smiled as she passed, but didn't seem anxious to talk. Sarah went into the duty-room but found it empty. She came out again and walked through to Alpha 4 to take a look at John McKirrop. His bed was empty. The linen had been removed and the hi-tech equipment on both sides of the bay lay dark and silent.

Sarah stood there bewildered, unable to come to terms with the empty bed. Why on earth would anyone move him? She looked around and saw Sister Roche coming out of Beta suite. This time Roche acknowledged her and came over to join her.

'Where is Mr McKirrop, Sister?' Sarah asked, feeling embarrassed because the question sounded ridiculous. It showed on her face as vulnerability.

'Mr McKirrop died two hours ago,' replied Roche quietly.

'But that's impossible!' exclaimed Sarah. 'He came round at three thirty this morning. He was fine.'

'Dr Stubbs seemed to think that Mr McKirrop's death was not unexpected,' replied Roche.

'Dr Stubbs?' exclaimed Sarah.

'He was here when Mr McKirrop lost all brain function. He and Doctor Tyndall agreed that there was no chance of recovery, so the patient was allowed to pass away peacefully. That's why you weren't called out again, Doctor,' said Roche, anticipating Sarah's next question.

'Where does Dr Stubbs come into it?' asked Sarah, quite bemused by events.

'I understand Dr Tyndall called him in on the case,' replied Roche.

Sarah rubbed her forehead anxiously. 'Is Dr Stubbs here at the moment?' she asked.

'I think he's in the ivory tower,' replied Roche.

Sarah marched through to the doctors' room and entered without knocking. 'Just what is going on?' she demanded. Her only concession to ethics was the fact that she kept her voice down when she said it. It came out as an angry whisper.

'I beg your pardon,' said Stubbs angrily.

'What's all this about McKirrop having no brain function. I was *talking* to him at three thirty this morning!'

'Calm down, Doctor, calm down. You thought you were talking to him but it could only have been random disjointed function with the kind of damage that McKirrop had.'

'But he didn't have massive damage at all,' said Sarah.

'What nonsense!' retorted Stubbs. 'What did you think that was in the centre of his head? A birthmark?'

'I know it looked bad,' said Sarah. 'But McKirrop had an abnormal forehead. The unusual angle of his skull protected his frontal lobe which was recessed. It showed up on his X-rays.'

'I didn't see that,' said Stubbs.

'You didn't see the other X-rays. The X-ray department sent up two more films yesterday morning. You didn't bother to look at them.'

Stubbs paused for a moment to consider the implications of what Sarah had said. Deciding that he might be on shaky ground in an argument, he ignored the implied criticism and said, 'All this is academic anyway. He had an EEG like the Utah salt flats.'

'No he didn't. His brain function tests were very encouraging yesterday.'

'If you saw that, you must have had the settings wrong on the monitors,' said Stubbs.

'How dare you!'

'I dare because I'm a senior registrar and you are a wet-behind-the-ears resident,' said Stubbs, getting up angrily. 'You made a complete mess of things, Lasseter, and if you're thinking about a second chance I suggest an immediate change in attitude!'

.   .   .

Sarah ran all the way back to the residency, the way blurred by the tears that had welled up in her eyes. Not even she knew whether they were born of anger or of self pity.

'I can't believe it,' she muttered as she sat on her bed. 'I do not believe it. McKirrop was going to be fine. He was going to pull through. I know it.'

She had just blown her nose when her bleeper went off.

'Dr Tyndall would like to see you, Dr Lasseter,' said the nurse at the other end of the phone. 'Right now if you please.'

Sarah washed her face at the hand-basin in her room and held the towel to it for a good thirty seconds as she attempted to regain her composure. The last thing in the world she wanted to do was burst into tears in front of Tyndall. When she felt calmer, she took several deep breaths, dealt with some rogue strands of hair and set out for HTU. The spring in her step had gone.

'Dr Lasseter, do come in,' said Tyndall when Sarah knocked on the door and opened it slightly to look round. 'Please sit down.'

Sarah did as she was bid and smoothed her skirt. She had been unsure of what to expect in terms of Tyndall's mood. Even now, she was uncertain. Tyndall was urbane and smiling as usual.

'Dr Stubbs tells me you were rather upset about Mr McKirrop? Perfectly understandable. I like my doctors to remember their patients are people first and patients second. Any death is always a matter of profound regret.'

'I just don't understand it!' said Sarah animatedly. 'I

was so sure that he was going to be all right. His scans agreed, and when he came round this morning . . .'

'How often have you carried out a full range of scans?' asked Tyndall. He was still smiling, but Sarah knew that the first torpedo had been fired. 'On your own I mean,' he added. The torpedo was fully armed.

'Yesterday was the first time,' conceded Sarah. 'But I have seen a great many done and I feel sure there was no problem.'

'I understand Nurse Barnes assisted you?'

'Yes sir.'

'Sister Roche tells me that this was the first time for Nurse Barnes too.'

Sarah stayed silent. She hadn't known that.

'You didn't think to ask Dr Stubbs to check your findings?' asked Tyndall.

Sarah bit her lip. It went against the grain to drop even Stubbs in it. 'Dr Stubbs made me responsible for Mr McKirrop's tests, sir, and I felt happy with the way the scans went. There were no problems at any stage.'

'I see,' said Tyndall. 'You may, of course, be right. It's possible that Mr McKirrop's brain was able, for a very short period of time, to give indications of activity. But it's also possible that some kind of amplification error was made in the settings of the equipment.'

'I'm certain that they were all right,' said Sarah.

Tyndall shrugged his shoulders. 'Well, we can't turn back the clock, Doctor, but I must say that when I examined Mr McKirrop's head injury myself, I did feel that restoration to normal activity would be extremely unlikely.'

'But the X-rays sir! The angle of Mr McKirrop's skull at the front afforded his brain a good deal of protection. I explained that on the phone to you.'

'Ah yes, the X-rays. Do you have them to hand?'

Sarah excused herself for a moment and went to fetch McKirrop's films. She didn't think the light box would be necessary to make her point. She held up the films, one by one, against the light coming in from the window until she found the one she wanted, and then brought it back to the ivory tower for Tyndall to examine.

McKirrop held up the film in his left hand and traced the angle of the patient's skull with the pen he held in the other.

'The angle is quite unusual sir,' said Sarah.

'I see what you mean,' said Tyndall thoughtfully. 'But I suspect that the protection afforded was not enough. The PM will tell us for sure.'

'Yes, sir,' said Sarah, feeling deflated at Tyndall's dismissive attitude. 'He did regain consciousness,' she said, surprising even herself at her unwillingness to concede an inch.

'I accept that the patient spoke, but was it true consciousness, Doctor? Did you conduct a proper question and answer session?'

Sarah opened her mouth to affirm but suddenly realised that this would be untrue. McKirrop had not answered any questions directly. He had supplied words and phrases which she had interpreted as a two-way conversation. 'No sir, but he appeared to remember things about his recent past.'

'They could have been words snatched from the cosmos, Doctor.'

'I didn't get that impression, sir.'

Tyndall smiled but there was a suggestion of impatience about it. 'I'm sorry your chap died. Gaining experience in medicine can be a painful business.'

'Yes, sir,' said Sarah, realising that the time for any argument was over.

'I understand Dr Stubbs will be carrying out full brain scans on two of our patients this morning. Why don't you help out?'

Sarah took a deep breath and fought to control her temper. She felt like a naughty schoolgirl being given extra homework, but if she gave free rein to her tongue right now her time in HTU would be over. Maybe even her career in medicine.

'Yes, sir,' she said.

Sarah went through an awful day on auto-pilot. She assisted Stubbs with the scan patients, knowing that he was gloating over every second of her discomfort.

'It's very important that the gain control on the monitor matches the one on the recorder – it's something that can be so easily overlooked— '

'I'm sorry Dr Lasseter, was it something I did?' asked Nurse Barnes when she came on duty.

'No, Nurse,' replied Sarah. 'I'm quite sure neither of us did anything wrong but, if we did, it was my responsibility.'

'Maybe it was just one of these things?' said the nurse.

'Maybe,' replied Sarah. The comment had been meant kindly but Nurse Barnes was very wide of the mark if she really thought that. The last thing Sarah did before coming off-duty was to return fifty pence to the night staff nurse.

'What's this for?' asked the nurse.

'The official view is that McKirrop did not regain consciousness. You win the bet.'

'But I was there,' said the nurse. 'I saw it happen.'

'Random words and phrases from a destroyed brain,' said Sarah.

'Who said that?'

'Dr Tyndall.'

The nurse thought for a moment and then said, 'He may be my boss and he's certainly a very bright man and all that, but this time – he's talking rubbish.'

Sarah suddenly regained her confidence. Up until then she had been unaware of how it had been eroded away, and just how close she was coming to accepting the official view of things.

'Yes,' she said thoughtfully, 'He's my boss too, and you're right. He is.'

The nurse pushed the fifty pence piece back to Sarah, 'Off with you. You seem to live in this place.'

Sarah went down to watch the evening news on television. She was alone in the common-room, a large square room on the ground floor of the residency, furnished with a variety of unmatched furniture and which always reminded her of a dentist's waiting room. There were a couple of comfortable armchairs however, and she removed the pile of newspapers on the one nearest the TV to sit down. Being alone, she kicked off her shoes and put her stockinged feet up on the low table in front of her.

The national news was followed by the weather and then a bulletin of local news which she was about to turn off when the name 'McKirrop' stopped her. She sank back in the chair to watch. John McKirrop, the down-and-out who had witnessed the exhumation of little Simon Main's body and who had been injured in a brave attempt at tackling the culprits, had died in hospital that morning. He had been injured again in another violent incident in which a woman had died. This time McKirrop's injuries had proved fatal. The police were appealing for witnesses. There was some footage of the canal towpath and the police incident unit at the site. This was followed by a plan of the area and an approximate time of death for the woman. As yet, the police had failed to apprehend those reponsible for the outrage in the cemetery.

Sarah had been hoping for distraction from the television. Instead she found herself forced to think about McKirrop again. She had declined an offer to go out with several of the other residents for a drink at The Quill, the hospital's local pub, feeling that she wouldn't be good company after the day she'd had – she'd made an excuse about having some reading up to do. Maybe she should have gone to the pub after all, she thought. Apart from reminding her of the McKirrop case, the television story had forced her to consider the role of alcohol in their lives. The contrast between her colleagues laughing and joking over few drinks down at the pub and John McKirrop's alcohol-ruined life could hardly have been more stark.

Ostensibly it was a case of two different worlds, but only at first glance. In reality they were much closer than any of them would care to admit, especially in medicine. Pressure led to stress, stress to heavy drinking and heavy drinking, in turn, led to dependence, and then it was downhill all the way. Medicine was the profession with more suicides and more alcoholics than any other. That's what she'd been told at medical school.

Sarah got up and poured herself some coffee from the heated flask that sat on the sideboard. The residency had coffee available all day, but Sarah wasn't sure how often the domestic staff made a fresh pot. Certainly not within the last four hours, she concluded after sipping it. It tasted burnt. She put it aside after a few more sips and tried to concentrate on her book.

Her father had recommended that she read Renée Weber's *Dialogues with Scientists and Sages* as an exercise in perspective. But she found she couldn't concentrate. The McKirrop case was still uppermost in her mind. It wouldn't go away. Finally, after reading the same page three times without taking anything in, she put down the book and rubbed her eyes as she leaned back in the chair. She tried again to think things through logically but they were complicated by her inability to analyse her feelings properly. They were a mixture of disbelief, anger, sorrow and . . . unease. Yes, that was it, there was definitely an element of unease, the one feeling she had not been admitting to. Now that she had, she could start to define its cause.

She had recorded an encouraging brain scan on John McKirrop, one which suggested that he would recover consciousness, and some hours later he had – in her opinion. It was also the opinion of the staff nurse who had been with her. But instead of being on the road to recovery, as she would have predicted, McKirrop was dead and her superiors were telling her that the brain scan readings had been some kind of aberration, some quirk of fate or even a mistake on her part! A mistake due to her inexperience. What was more, they were telling her that McKirrop had not regained consciousness at all. Another mistake due to her inexperience.

Sarah had got the facts straight in her head, but they were not the cause of her unease – rather, they were the cause of her anger and frustration. Her feelings of disquiet were associated with questions that arose from the facts. If she was right and McKirrop had been on the road to recovery, then what was she suggesting? That someone else had made a mistake? Or that someone . . . someone had deliberately murdered John McKirrop? The notion was just too ridiculous, but the question remained. She needed a scientific way of dealing with it.

The post-mortem on McKirrop would, of course, define the extent of his injuries when they got round to doing it, but the pathologist would probably be Hugh Carfax, a friend of Derek Stubbs. Not that she was suggesting that Carfax might be influenced by Stubbs's notes and conclusions on the case, but people were people and human nature was human nature. McKirrop had been a nobody; he hadn't mattered in life so why should society care about his death or, more specifically, the exact cause of it?

Sarah felt embarrassed at the cynicism she was displaying. She felt the need to be more positive – but how? What could she do on her own? Suddenly she saw the crux of the matter. Tyndall had said that he doubted the unusual angle of McKirrop's forehead would have been enough to protect him from serious brain damage. Stubbs had, in effect, confirmed this view by recording a flat line on the patient's brain scan, indicating that McKirrop's skull had been pushed back into his brain causing massive damage. Why didn't she take a look?

She sat upright in the chair, and her pulse rate quickened at the thought. McKirrop's body would be lying down in the mortuary. She could go along and see for herself. The probing she would have to do would be disguised by the wound site. The pathologist need never know that she had interfered with the body. The thought made her pulse beat even faster. 'Interfere with the body' – that sounded serious. She supposed that it was.

For a medical practitioner to interfere with a cadaver before a legally required post-mortem sounded like a very serious offence indeed. 'Taking a look' could turn out to be professional suicide if she was found out, and someone chose to make it so. Despite the fact that she would not be altering or trying to cover anything up, the thought that Dr Derek Stubbs would be consulted in any repercussions if she were caught was not a comforting one. What should she do?

Sarah's need to know triumphed over the temptation to play safe and forget about the McKirrop case. She just had to know about that head wound. She checked her watch; it was just after nine fifty. The others wouldn't be back until around eleven. That gave her plenty of time if everything went smoothly. She returned briefly to her room to change into a sweater and jeans and slip on a suede jacket.

Sarah hit the first hurdle as she hurried along the bottom corridor to the stairs leading down to the basement where the mortuary and post-mortem suite were located, when she suddenly realised that the mortuary would be locked. She knew that she could get a key at the front office, but that would mean signing it out and then it would be known that she had visited the mortuary. But there was another key, she remembered. The hospital porters had a night key of their own for use when a patient died during the night and they had to remove the body from the wards. It was kept beside the 'dead cart', the nickname given to the covered trolley which was used to transport the dead from the wards when the occasion arose. The cart itself was kept in a little outhouse attached to the porters' lodge by the front gate.

She left the main corridor by a small side-door and made her way towards the porters' lodge. There was little in the way of lighting on the road between the main hospital and the lodge, so it was unlikely that she would be seen. But with each step that brought her closer to the trolley shed she felt more afraid. Her mouth became dry and something inside kept telling her to go back. Forget about it, it's not worth the risk! But her feet refused to listen. She was almost at the porters' lodge; light spilled out from the mess-room and she could see three men inside. One was reading a newspaper, the other two were arguing about something. She could hear their raised voices.

The trolley shed was comfortingly dark. She turned the handle slowly and felt the door release. The hinges squealed as she pushed it open, and she froze with her fingers on the handle, trying to think what she would say if the lodge door opened suddenly and the porters found her there. But the lodge door remained shut, the argument inside continued and Sarah let herself slowly into the trolley shed. She closed the door behind her, her teeth clenched as she tried to avoid making it squeal again. She was safe for the moment.

She knew that the mortuary key was kept on a hook on the wall with a skull and cross-bones above it. Some porter had seen fit to add this refinement in the past with red and black marker pens, and was largely the reason for her remembering the existence of the key. She had seen it when she and the other new residents had been shown around the hospital when they had first arrived – their 'orientation tour'. Right now it was too dark to make out

146

the skull and cross-bones; Sarah felt along the wall until her fingers touched the key and closed around it. At that moment she heard the phone ring in the lodge through the wall.

Sarah's heart skipped a beat as she thought of the worst possibility. There had been a death in one of the wards and the porters were being called out to remove the body. Any second now they would open the door and find her there. She stood behind the door, clutching the key in her hand with her eyes tightly shut, as if in prayer. The door of the lodge opened and the voices were suddenly loud.

'That's the third time that bloody staff nurse has called us out,' complained one.

'Maybe she needs the company,' said another.

'I know what she bloody needs.'

The door of the lodge was closed and the voices started to fade as the two porters moved off. Sarah let her breath out slowly and tried to steady her nerves. As soon as everything was quiet again she let herself out of the shed, steeling herself to do it as silently as she could, when all her instincts told her to make a run for it – there was still a porter next door in the lodge. With a final look round as she moved off, she started out for the mortuary.

The fluorescent lighting stuttered into life as Sarah clicked on the switch. Her heart was beating so strongly that she had to rest for a moment, leaning her shoulder against the wall. There's nothing to worry about, she told herself. You're almost there. She looked at the row of refrigerated body vaults in front of her. Her first task was to find McKirrop's body. There was a card index held in a metal holder on the front of each vault door indicating who lay inside and on which tier – there were three tiers to each. John McKirrop lay on the middle tier in vault 4.

Sarah undid the large metal clasp on the door and jumped back as the refrigeration plant sprang into life at the same moment. She chided herself for being so edgy and bent down to examine the label on the big toe of the corpse on the middle tray. It confirmed that the sheet-wrapped body was that of John McKirrop. Sarah dragged over the transporter trolley and adjusted it to the required height by winding the handle at the side. When it was in position, and the brake applied firmly, she slid out the tray with John McKirrop's body and locked it on to the transporter with the metal pin that hung down on a chain. She moved it back a few feet and shut the vault door. It closed with a clunk that seemed to echo throughout the whole suite.

Sarah wheeled McKirrop's body through to the post-mortem room and turned on the lights. The light switch also turned on a series of extractor fans which whirred into life. She reckoned that she would not need to get the cadaver on to a table; she could carry out the examination with it lying on the transporter. She doubted whether she could have manhandled McKirrop's body on to a table on her own. She did, however, wheel the transporter parallel to one of the three post-mortem tables so that she had access to water and electric power if required. She turned on the big, flat lamp above the table and angled it so that McKirrop was bathed in white, shadowless light. Next, she collected a series of instruments together on a metal tray and laid it on the table beside her. Then she undid the sheet wrapping McKirrop's head, grimacing a little at the cold clammy feel of it.

McKirrop's face had taken on the parchment pallor of

death and the wound in the centre of his head was so dark that it looked like a black hole. Sarah adjusted the lamp slightly so that the wound was illuminated perfectly. She picked up a metal probe from the tray beside her and investigated the depth. Her heart sank almost immediately. It was perfectly clear that the skull bone had indeed caused massive damage to the front of McKirrop's brain.

'But how?' Sarah murmured. Why had the X-ray of McKirrop's skull suggested that his frontal lobe had been protected? Why had it not shown actual penetration of the brain by the bone? After all, it had penetrated to a depth of – Sarah measured the extent of invasion – one and a half centimetres.

'Crazy,' she said, shaking her head. She ran the metal probe gently up and down the anterior surface of the bone and was suddenly struck by something odd.

'This wasn't the angle!' she murmured. She checked again and was now convinced that the angle of McKirrop's skull bone was different from the angle that had appeared on the X-ray.

Sarah's pulse rate, which had calmed down over the last ten minutes, suddenly started sprinting again. There was only one logical explanation. McKirrop's skull had been pushed back into his brain after the X-ray had been taken! Sarah dropped the probe she had been holding, and it bounced off the hard, tiled floor. For a few moments she stood absolutely still, then she started to think about priorities.

She needed proof! She needed solid evidence! The post-mortem carried out on this body would simply report that the patient had died from massive brain damage caused by his skull being broken by a large blunt object, the base of a wine bottle, and forced back into his brain. Exactly what everyone had suggested. She searched through the pathology cupboards until she found what she was looking for, a polaroid camera. Another brief search and she came up with film for it. She angled herself behind the trolley to photograph the wound, but stopped after taking two photographs. What was this going to show? she asked herself. A photograph of a gaping wound wasn't going to prove anything at all.

She thought for a moment, then came up with an idea. She ran through to the small office next door and rummaged through the desk drawer until she found a clear plastic protractor. She hurried back with it and positioned it to one side of the wound. She then inserted a metal probe so that it lay along the angle of the bone. She brought up the protractor close behind it, so that it showed the angle of the bone relative to the horizontal, and then took four photographs. The photographs, when compared to the X-ray of McKirrop's skull, should demonstrate a significant alteration in the angle of the bone.

8

Sarah began tidying up. She cleaned the wound site on McKirrop's head with a swab soaked in surgical spirit and did her best to obscure any signs of interference, not that there were many. The degree of invasion she had used was minimal, and there would be no reason for the pathologist to be on the lookout for anything out of the ordinary. She cleaned and returned the instruments to their rightful place and disposed of the used swabs and their wrappings in the discard bin for subsequent incineration. Finally, she wound the sheet back round the corpse's head and wheeled it back to the body vault.

To her frustration, Sarah could not remove the locking pin from the transporter in order to release the body-tray. She tried again but it was stuck fast and she broke out into a cold sweat. She could not get the body back into the vault! Her heart was thumping with the effort that she was expending, but with no success. She cried out in pain as her fingers slipped off the metal and she broke two of her fingernails. Tools! She needed tools!

She hurried back to the Post-Mortem suite and returned

with a chisel and mallet. They were really for use on human bone, but two blows with the mallet and the pin eased off. A third, and it sprang out to dangle on its chain in a mocking dance. The tray slid smoothly back on to its shelf.

With McKirrop's body safely stowed, Sarah checked twice that she had left nothing lying around before switching out the lights and listening at the door. She heard nothing, so she inched it open and took a quick look out in both directions before slipping out into the corridor. Locking the door behind her, she ran quickly along to the stairs leading up to the ground floor.

Sarah paused at the head of the stairs to calm herself. It was over; she had done it; she had found out exactly what she wanted to know. She started out along the main corridor, steeling herself to do so in a confident gait. The corridor was quite busy, mainly with nurses going to and from their meal break. No one was going to take much notice of her if she seemed purposeful.

Sarah reached the door leading outside and to the drive down to the main gate. She paused to consider for a moment. She had been being doing everything in reverse, almost without thinking, but now she fingered the mortuary key in her pocket and looked out through the glass doors into the darkness. Everything had gone well so far, but did she have enough nervous energy left to complete the exercise? Could she go through the business of returning the key? No, she decided after a few moments' thought, she couldn't. She had run out of adrenaline and it would be silly to push her luck any further. She simply couldn't face the stress involved. The key was about to go missing. No big deal. They could have another one made up. She turned away from the door and continued along the corridor. As she crossed the courtyard to the residency she dropped the key down a grating. The little splash it made marked the end of the operation.

Sarah closed the door of her room and felt weak at the knees. She sank down on to the bed and saw that her hands were shaking. Her mouth was dry and she felt that she might be sick. Thinking about what she had discovered made matters worse now that she had time to collect her thoughts. Fear was making a bid to take over from nervous exhaustion. In answering one question, she had opened up a Pandora's box of others. McKirrop had been murdered; he had been murdered by someone on the staff. It must have been someone on the staff, she reasoned. HTU patients were not allowed unaccompanied visitors, not that anyone had wanted to see McKirrop, anyway.

But who on the staff would want to kill a down-at-heel alcoholic – and why? What threat could he possibly have presented to anyone? Sarah could think of no good reason, but she did come up with a bad one: Derek Stubbs had killed John McKirrop because the results of her tests on the patient were embarrassing and were about to make him look foolish. McKirrop's sudden death had stopped that happening and had turned the tables on her. Her findings had been discredited and her professional competence brought into question.

But surely not even Stubbs could do something so awful?

Sarah found that she could not dismiss the idea altogether. She remembered Stubbs's distaste for McKirrop. He had regarded him as being a worthless object who was merely taking up space in HTU, his only value being as a potential organ donor. But had McKirrop mattered so little that his very life had been expendable? A pawn to be used in a career game move? Stubbs was a thoroughly unpleasant individual, but was he a murderer? Sarah baulked at believing it, but she was left with a list of questions seeking answers.

Could McKirrop's death have been some sort of bizarre accident? Perhaps the nursing staff had somehow made McKirrop's wound worse while they were changing the dressings? Sarah shook her head and admitted that this was a ridiculous idea. Its only merit was that it distracted her momentarily from thinking that someone on the staff of HTU had deliberately placed a blunt object into John McKirrop's head-wound and pushed his skull back into his brain.

After a restless night filled with bad dreams, mainly concerning McKirrop, Sarah was back on duty in HTU shortly after breakfast. Her first thought was to get her hands on the X-ray that showed the original injury to McKirrop's skull. This would be vital in proving her case. She went immediately to the X-ray viewing room and flipped through the large manila envelopes in the rack below the wall-mounted light boxes. She looked again, but there was no mistake. McKirrop's file had gone. She hadn't anticipated this, and frustration mingled with a hollow feeling in her stomach.

After one more search of the entire room she turned on her heel and went straight to the duty-room to find Sister Roche.

'Sister, Mr McKirrop's X-rays are not in the rack,' she announced.

Roche turned in her swivel-chair and looked over her

glasses at her. 'No, Doctor,' she said. 'Mr McKirrop is dead. His X-rays have been returned to Medical Records along with his case notes. That's what always happens.'

Sarah felt her cheeks colour. 'Of course,' she said. 'How stupid of me.'

'Was there something you particularly wanted to see?' asked Roche.

'Nothing really,' smiled Sarah, attempting to cover her embarrassment. 'A detail. I'll just nip along and see to it while I remember.' She turned with another attempt at a smile and left the room feeling as if her shoes were full of tin tacks.

'McKirrop, John McKirrop,' Sarah repeated for the benefit of a clerk who seemed hard of hearing. 'He died yesterday morning.'

The clerk turned away from the reception desk and put on spectacles that hung from a gold chain round her neck. She started to run her fingers along rows of cardboard folders, angling her head to see through the bottom portion of her bifocal lenses. 'And you say he was from . . . where?'

'HTU,' repeated Sarah.

'We have a John McCluskey . . . and a John McIntyre.'

'McKirrop,' said Sarah, through teeth that were beginning to clench.

'Ah yes, here we are. Couldn't see it for looking at it.' The woman chuckled. She pulled the file and handed it over to Sarah who opened the X-ray envelope. She pulled the films half way out of the envelope. There were two. 'There were three!' she murmured out loud. She removed the two X-rays that were there and held them up to the light. The one she wanted wasn't there. 'One of this man's X-rays is missing!' she said.

'I'm sorry. What's missing?' asked the clerk.

Sarah looked at her blankly. 'An X-ray,' she said, but her voice was distant. She was thinking that this was no accident.

'Typical,' said the woman. 'People are so careless these days. It'll be lying around somewhere in the ward.'

Sarah handed back the case file and left the Medical Records office. She felt dazed. Her proof that John McKirrop had been murdered had evaporated. Without that X-ray, she had nothing. If she made an accusation now she would be ostracised – if not thought to be mentally deranged. The whole notion would be deemed to be quite ridiculous. A tramp murdered by a member of staff? Absolutely ludicrous.

Sarah had an anxious hunt around HTU for the missing film, just in case it really had been left out of the file through error, but she found nothing. In her heart she had known that she wouldn't find it. She had been out-thought. That in itself was a chilling thought. It inferred that someone thought that she might go looking for the X-ray.

Derek Stubbs came into the doctors' room while Sarah was still searching. 'What have you lost?' he asked curtly.

Sarah felt gooseflesh break out on her neck. 'An X-ray,' she replied.

'You've lost an X-ray?' asked Stubbs sarcastically. It put Sarah's back up.

'Not me exactly,' she said. 'It appears to have gone missing somewhere between here and the Medical Records Office. I'm just trying to locate it.'

'Which X-ray are we talking about?' asked Stubbs.

Sarah looked him straight in the eye and said, 'One of John McKirrop's head X-rays.'

Stubbs held Sarah's gaze for what seemed to her like an eternity, before asking softly, 'What do you want that for?'

'I just wanted to see it again,' replied Sarah, watching him for any reaction she could construe as guilt.

'McKirrop is dead,' said Stubbs brusquely. 'Do you think we could concentrate on our living patients before any of them decide to join him?'

'Yes, Dr Stubbs,' Sarah answered through clenched teeth.

Before either had time to say anything else, an alarm went off on the console desk and the nurse monitoring it called out, 'Beta three! Cardiac arrest! Steven Miles!'

Stubbs and Sarah both ran through into Beta suite and personal animosity took second place to dealing with the emergency. Sister Roche and another nurse arrived close behind with the 'crash' trolley and Stubbs took charge. The cardiac monitor over the patient's bed had gone to flat-line instead of spikes, and a continuous monotone had replaced the comforting regular bleeps. The patient was a seventeen-year-old boy who had fallen from a third-storey window and fractured his skull. He had been in a coma for four weeks, but this was the first sign of complication. Stubbs alternated cardiac massage with injections of stimulants, and then Sarah took over while he prepared to shock the patient. One solitary green spike on the oscilloscope had been the only reward for their efforts after ninety seconds.

'I'm going to shock him,' announced Stubbs loudly.

The nurses cleared everything out of the way; Sarah

handed Stubbs the electrode paddles.

'Back!' said Stubbs, and everyone stood clear of the bed as the current was applied to the patient's chest. There was a loud thump and the patient's body responded to the voltage racing through him with an an involuntary jump. The monitor started to bleep again and the horizontal base line on the 'scope broke into spikes. But the sound was irregular, two bleeps followed by a pause then three quick bleeps followed by the monotone again. Stubbs applied the paddles again: two bleeps followed by the monotone. A third attempt was no more successful. Stubbs straightened up and put down the paddles.

'We've lost him,' he said, as the continuous monotone jangled everyone's nerves. He reached up and turned the monitor off.

Stubbs walked away leaving Sarah and the two nurses with the dead seventeen-year-old.

Roche turned to the younger nurse. 'He has Sigma probes. Call the lab will you?'

Sarah said, 'I'll do it Sister. I want to ask them for some more chart paper anyway.'

Patients with Sigma probes who died had to have them removed, and this was a delicate procedure. The probes were expensive, but could be re-used after cleaning and sterilising if undamaged. Technicians from the medical school did this. When a Sigma patient died, the HTU staff would call them and they'd come immediately to take the body. Sarah called the number written up on the wall beside the phone in the duty-room and was told that the team was on its way. They would also bring her more Sigma chart paper. Within ten minutes Steven Miles's body was removed from the unit.

· · ·

A shadow hung over HTU for the rest of the morning. It inevitably did when a young person died. It always seemed so unfair, as if an unjust mistake had been made and everyone felt aggrieved by it. But by three in the afternoon Beta three was no longer empty. A new patient had been admitted. He was a forty-four-year-old demolition worker who had been hit on the head by falling masonry. The empty bay was no longer a focus for grief and reflection: a new challenge had moved in to fill the vacuum.

The new patient had been stabilised by the A&E team before transfer to HTU. Sarah checked his pulse and blood pressure again to make sure that there had been no worsening of his condition during the move. Satisfied that he still seemed stable, she set about connecting the monitoring probes to his head. Stubbs arrived in the bay while she was positioning the last one. 'Everything all right?' he asked.

'He's still stable,' replied Sarah.

'How about blood tests? Did you take any?'

'Thirty mil. It's on its way to the biochem lab.'

'He's going to need surgery,' said Stubbs. 'Did you send some for cross-matching?

'Also on its way,' said Sarah. 'But surely he's too weak at the moment?'

'I agree. So what would you suggest in the meantime?'

'A full scan in the morning,' said Sarah. 'That should give us some information about the degree of damage sustained without putting him under any added stress.'

'Pencil it in then. You can do it.'

Sarah did not react to the suggestion. She simply said, 'Very well. Is he to have Sigma probes inserted?'

Stubbs shook his head and said, 'I don't think so. The

area of trauma is well defined and limited. But we'll decide after we see all the X-rays.'

'Very well.'

Sarah found it difficult to look Stubbs in the eye for fear that he might see suspicion there. Another part of her wanted to accuse him openly of complicity in John McKirrop's death, and she was glad when he left. Shortly afterwards, Nurse Barnes came hurrying towards her. 'Sister Roche asks if you would mind taking a telephone call?'

Sarah followed the nurse back to the duty-room where Sister Roche, with her hand over the mouth-piece of the phone, said, 'It's about Mr McKirrop.'

Sarah, feeling puzzled, accepted the receiver. 'Hello, this is Dr Lasseter. How can I help you?'

'Hello, Doctor. This is Father Lafferty. I was wondering how Mr McKirrop was?'

Sarah put her hand up to her forehead in anguish as she remembered the name from McKirrop's admission sheet, and the request that he be kept informed.

'Oh, I'm sorry,' she said. 'How awful, I should have telephoned you earlier. Mr McKirrop died yesterday morning. I informed the police but I clean forgot about you, Father. I'm most terribly sorry. You didn't see the television report?'

Lafferty could tell that Sarah's distress was genuine. He said as gently as he could, 'Actually, I don't have a television.'

'Oh, I'm sorry,' said Sarah. 'And it's no excuse anyway. I don't know what came over me. I really am most . . .'

Lafferty tried to assure Sarah that no great harm had been done before asking, 'I don't suppose that he regained consciousness at all then?'

'Well, yes he did,' stammered Sarah, feeling both embarrassed and ashamed at her oversight. 'That is to say, no he didn't . . .'

'I don't think I understand,' said Lafferty.

'I'm sorry,' answered Sarah, who had now gone into an apologetic spiral. 'It's sort of debatable really . . . The official view is that Mr McKirrop did not regain consciousness.'

'And the unofficial view?' asked Lafferty, bemused by it all.

'I think he did for a short while,' said Sarah weakly.

'Well, I'm sorry to hear of his death. I hope he has an easier time in heaven than he did on earth.'

'Quite so,' said Sarah.

'Thank you, Doctor.'

The phone went dead and Sarah replaced the receiver. She rubbed her forehead again, still angry at herself.

Lafferty let out a weary sigh and stared balefully at the telephone in front of him. He felt utterly dejected. McKirrop had died without his getting a chance to speak to him, and he was nowhere nearer finding out the reasons behind the stealing of Simon Main's body. He had read just about every book he could find on the subject of black magic and satanic ritual.

He was staring into space when Mrs Grogan came in and put down a cup of tea beside him. She had her outdoor clothes on.

Lafferty looked at his watch and said, 'You'll be off then, Mrs G?'

'Yes, Father. See you tomorrow.'

Lafferty watched Mrs Grogan close the garden gate and wave to him. He lifted his hand in reply before turning to the book lying behind him on the table: *Scottish Witchcraft* by Nicholas A. Macleod. Having failed to find anything of use in the general academic works on satanism, Lafferty had decided to investigate the possibility that the reason for Simon Main's exhumation might be related to some local or regional ritual or ceremony. There was precedent for this, in that many towns and villages around the country had fairs or customs of their own which dated back to pagan days.

John Main pulled on his leather jerkin and checked that he had his keys in his pocket before setting out for his second evening of pub crawling. John McKirrop's unforeseen death had given him a new idea, so he had decided to put his plan to ask around the spiritualist community on hold for the moment. The down-and-out's death had been reported on television, so the cemetery story would briefly be news again. People would talk about it in pubs. In these circumstances, anyone who knew anything might be encouraged to say something, if only to impress. Main had set himself the task of visiting every pub within a one mile radius of the cemetery in the hope of hearing some gossip.

The tenuous logic behind this was that outside this circle it would be more likely that another cemetery would have been chosen. This assumed, of course, that some – if not all – of those involved in the crime lived in the area. If this was so – and it was a big 'if' – someone else within this circle might know something: even a rumour would be a start. Last night had yielded nothing. That left tonight, and maybe tomorrow night, before public interest started to wane and the story was forgotten again.

· · ·

Main walked into the Cross Keys Bar and found it half empty. It was obviously a working man's pub. Three tables were occupied by domino players and two men in dungarees were playing darts in an alcove through the back. Not exactly the kind of place to find satanists, thought Main, but what did satanists look like? Christopher Lee? Peter Cushing? What did they wear? Black silk capes? If they did, there would be no problem finding them.

'What'll it be?' asked the barman as Main reached the bar counter, still looking around him.

'Half of lager,' answered Main. He would have preferred a large gin but the night was young, and there was a long way to go.

'Seventy-five,' said the barman, putting down the drink in front of him. Main handed him a pound coin and decided to push things along.

'I see McKirrop's dead then,' he said.

The barman looked blank. 'Who's McKirrop?' he asked.

'That old down-and-out who tried to stop the body-snatchers. It was on the telly.'

'Body-snatchers?' repeated the barman, who Main had decided was not rocket scientist material.

Another customer joined in. 'You know, Brian, those bastards who dug up the kid's body in the cemetery up the road.'

'Oh aye,' said the barman.

'Sick bastards,' said the other man.

'Aye,' said the barman.

No one else responded. Main finished his drink and left. He fared no better at the second bar, nor at the third. He ordered a gin and tonic at the fourth, partly to break the monotony of half-pints of lager, but mainly because he was feeling fed up. An unwelcome shaft of realism was starting to penetrate the clouds of his obsession. Maybe this was a stupid idea. If he were honest with himself, it was the act of a desperate man who had run out of ideas. It was time to see reason; time he pulled himself together, went back to work and started to pick up the pieces of his life. Main read all this in the bottom of his empty glass while he leaned on the bar counter. It was the first time his resolve had wavered, and he didn't like the feeling. It was very close to hopelessness.

'Same again?' asked the barman.

Main looked up and shrugged. 'Why not.'

Shortly after eleven, Main found himself in the lounge bar of a pub called the Mayfield Tavern. He'd lost count of the number of pubs he'd been in that evening, and with each failure he had become more and more depressed. His alcohol intake had reflected this and he was far from sober, although not overtly drunk. The alcohol, as alcohol always did, had merely exaggerated his mood. His lips were set tight and his eyes reflected the unbearable sadness he felt.

To the barmaid he was just another face at the bar, a man in the corner drinking quietly and keeping himself to himself. Just another sad man. The world was full of them.

The bar seemed to have a wide mix of customers, unusual these days, thought Main. Most pubs attracted allegiance from one sort of customer rather than another. Here, there were two tables occupied by students; they looked scruffy but their voices gave them away. They were obviously going on to a party and were trying to decide what they should take along in the way of drink.

'Not that rat poison you brought to Mandy's!' said

one boy to the long haired youth who was collecting the money. 'I was shitting through the eye of a needle for a week.'

'That was the thought of the exams – not the bloody wine,' said the collector.

'Don't mention exams!' exclaimed one of the girls who, despite her elfin appearance, was drinking pints of beer. 'I haven't done a thing.'

Main moved his attention to the various couples dotted around the room. Most were young, but there was a middle-aged duo whose complexions revealed that they drank a lot. The man had a small case at his feet and had kept his raincoat on. The case wasn't a brief-case, but a small version of the kind people in the fifties used to take on holiday with them to Blackpool; the sort that German spies used to carry in early British films or that Crippin might have carried his implements in. Main couldn't guess what the couple did. Shopkeepers maybe? An off-licence, perhaps.

There were two working-men standing at the bar, still in their overalls. They obviously hadn't been home. Both had hands that were stained with black grease. Main guessed at mechanics. He probably could have found out, had he wanted to, by listening to their conversation which had been animated for the last fifteen minutes, but half the verbiage seemed to consist of four-letter words. Main took in a sound bite.

'I fuckin' telt him fuckin' straight, I'm no doin' any more of these fuckin' jobs.'

'Fuckin' right,' replied the other.

There were three men in their early twenties sitting down at a table near the cigarette machine. They burst into laughter periodically, and Main guessed that some joke had been made at the expense of the students. He could sense the animosity between the two factions. There didn't have to be a specific reason, Main knew; students were like a red rag to a bull to certain groups of other young people. One of the girls got up from the student tables and went to the lavatory, passing the table at which the three men were sitting. One, the tallest, dressed in a leather jacket and denim jeans, leaned across and said something to her. Main didn't catch what it was, but the girl reddened and the man's companions burst into laughter. Main glanced back at the student tables where he saw a boy start to get up angrily. He was restrained by his friends.

'Let it go Neil, let it go,' he was advised. 'It isn't worth it.'

Sound advice, thought Main. The boy looked no match for the man in the leather jacket, no matter how sound his cause. The girl returned from the lavatory, pointedly avoiding eye contact with the three on the way as she passed. Nothing more was said and the students got up to leave soon afterwards.

As they passed out through the door a thickset young man in a denim jacket came into the pub. He had red hair, cut short with such a well defined shave line over his ears that he must have had it cut that day, thought Main. The man looked around him, spotted the three by the cigarette machine and came over to join them at their table.

Main was just about to lose interest in the quartet when he heard the newcomer say, 'I see that lying old bastard McKirrop's snuffed it.'

Main froze at the mention of the name. He had turned back to the bar but he could see what was happening behind him in the bar mirror.

'Who?' asked one of the others.

'The old wino in the bone-yard.'

Main's throat was tight with apprehension and anticipation. Just as he had been on the verge of giving up hope, someone had mentioned McKirrop's name. He remained completely immobile as he strained to hear every word that was being said.

'No kidding?' responded the man in the leather jacket.

'It was on the telly. Some geezer smashed his head in.'

'Serves him right.'

'He didn't mean any harm, really,' said another of the four, but he was pounced upon by the others.

'That old bastard could have gotten us into real deep shit, you stupid git,' said the newcomer.

'All right, all right!' protested the one who had dared run against the herd. 'I suppose you're right.'

'Of course I'm bloody right!'

'Well, he isn't going to get anyone into trouble now is he?' said another.

The four fell silent for a few moments before one asked, 'What else did they say?'

'Not much,' shrugged the red-haired man. 'Just that he was the geezer who put up such a brave fight in the boneyard.'

'Bunch of crap!' sneered the man in the leather jacket. 'Anything else?'

'Just that the police weren't getting anywhere.'

This brought laughter from the others.

Main could feel the blood pounding in his temples. At best, he had come out this evening hoping to pick up a rumour, a snippet of information, but he had hit the jackpot! These four were the actual men he was looking for. But satanists? These yobs? It didn't make sense. Unless, of course, they were just labourers and they had been paid by others to do the grave robbing. That seemed to make more sense. But what was 'sense' in all of this?

For whatever reason, Main recognised that somewhere along the line he had decided that satanism and witchcraft were middle-class 'pastimes', like tennis and skiing – the province of the white-collar worker. Maybe this was wrong. The truth was that he had no idea what sort of people were attracted to the occult. One thing was for certain, however: whatever these four were, satanists or paid lackeys, they knew something about the disappearance of Simon's body.

Main's eyes narrowed as he watched the men in the mirror. In his mind he saw them lift his son's body out of his grave to expose him to the night. The thought made him ball his fists and close his eyes tightly for a moment while he fought to muster self-control over the urge to create mayhem.

'Are you all right?' asked a female voice. There was no real concern in it. Main opened his eyes and said to the barmaid, 'Yes, thank you, fine. Just a bit of a headache.'

The girl looked at him suspiciously and Main sensed that she was wondering whether or not to summon the manager. He managed a smile in the hope of changing her mind.

'Migraine,' he said. 'It's the bane of my life.'

'Well, if you're sure you're all right . . .'

'I'm fine.'

The girl went about her business, but kept glancing

back at him every few moments. He saw her confide something to another customer who immediately looked in his direction. The customer said something that made the barmaid laugh. The sound made him think of a duck flying across the marshes.

One of the men had left the table to go to the Gents. This gave Main his plan of action. He would wait until the weakest of the four did the same. He judged the weakest to be the one who had shown some semblance of feeling about McKirrop's death. He would follow him and try to get whatever he could out of him. They were all drinking beer, so he shouldn't have to wait too long. Just as long as the silly barmaid did not try to bring some excitement into her dreary life by drawing too much attention to him. He noticed her looking at him again and summoned up another smile. It was hard.

Main's target was the third of the men to go to the gents. Main followed thirty seconds later. He had to stop himself from tackling the man immediately when he suddenly realised there was another man already in the toilet. He had overlooked this obvious possibility and alarm bells rang in his head. *Be more careful.*

Main pretended to look at himself in the mirror and ran his fingers through his hair until the unwanted man left. As soon as the door swung shut, Main turned round and walked up quietly behind the yob who was urinating at the wall. The man seemed to sense that something was amiss and stopped whistling. He had half turned his head when Main pushed his face up hard against the tiled wall and held it there.

'What the fu— '

The heel of Main's hand sunk into the yob's cheek,

making speech impossible. He had wet his trousers and his shoes before he managed to stop urinating.

Main felt an almost overwhelming desire to cause pain to the man he held. He wanted him to suffer. He wanted to smash his fist into this man's face with every ounce of strength he possessed and, just at that moment, it seemed formidable. With the greatest of difficulty he held back and hissed through his teeth, 'I am the father of the boy you dug up, you shit-faced little cunt! Start talking or, so help me, I'll turn you into a basket case. Where is my son?'

The yob's eyes filled with fear. Main relaxed the pressure of his grip so that he could speak.

'You've got it all wrong, Mister!'

Main re-applied the pressure. 'Wrong, my arse!' he snarled. 'I heard what you were saying back there about McKirrop. Start talking!'

'All right, all right! We were there that night, but you've got it wrong. You've got it all wrong.'

'Talk, you bastard!'

'I can't – You're hurting me!'

Main let the yob move upright and away from the wall. It was a mistake. As he straightened up, the man brought his right knee up into Main's groin and Main doubled up in pain on the floor. Just at that moment the door swung open and the fourth man from the table came in, the man in the leather jacket.

'What the fuck is going on?' he demanded of his companion who was holding the side of his face and standing over Main.

'This guy says he's the kid's father.'

'What kid? What are you talking about?'

'The kid's grave in the cemetery, for Christ's sake.'

'Jesus!'

The talk of Simon gave Main new strength. Despite his pain he launched himself at the yob who had kneed him and caught him in the midriff. The man fell backwards with a gasp on to the wet floor with Main on top of him. 'Where is he?' rasped Main through gritted teeth. 'Where is Simon?'

'You've got it all wrong pal,' said the man in the leather jacket, but Main persisted.

'Where is he?' he repeated, grabbing the yob on the floor by the throat.

'Get him off for Christ's sake!' squealed the man.

His companion kicked Main hard in the ribs, and as Main rolled over in pain he took another kick, this time to the side of his face. Pain exploded in his head, but he rose above it and struggled unsteadily to his feet to charge in again. 'Where . . . is . . . he?'

'The bastard's off his head,' complained the first yob; his voice had become high and almost girlish with fear.

Leather jacket caught Main with a vicious punch as he came in and again Main fell back. He saw his assailant grab a bottle of toilet cleaner which was perched on the window-sill and, through his pain, he thought that it wasn't going to make much of a weapon; it was plastic and soft. As he struggled to his feet the contents of the bottle were flung at him and caught him full in the face. In an instant, his eyes were filled with bleach.

Main let out a scream of pain and heard the door bang as the yobs ran out. His eyes were screwed tight shut, but there was no escape from the progressive burning of his eyeballs. He stumbled towards where he thought the wash basins were and groped wildly for the taps. Everything seemed hard, unforgiving and elusive. He found the top of one tap and water started to flow. Main splashed it maniacally up into his face, fearing that he was about to lose his sight for ever. He was only dimly aware of other people having come into the Gents.

9

The nightmare inside Main's head was taking him to the very limits of endurance, but he knew that he must not pass out. He had to keep flushing the chemical out of his eyes if he was to have any chance at all of keeping his sight. He had never known such pain. His eyes felt as if they were on fire and the pressure inside his head was slowly pushing them out of their sockets. The pungent smell of chlorine was catching his throat, making him splutter; his breathing was uneven through shock. His hands frantically sluiced water up into his face.

Very slowly, the pain began to subside and Main became aware of voices in the background. They had been there all along, but the fear of going blind, and his agonising pain, had blocked everything else out of Main's reckoning. At first it was just a hubub, but then he made out one voice that was louder.

'What the hell's going on?' it asked.

Main continued flushing his eyes. His breathing was returning to normal.

'I asked you a question!' demanded the voice.

'Bleach . . . in my eyes,' said Main haltingly.

'That was a stupid thing to do.'

Oh Christ! thought Main. He couldn't grace the comment with a reply.

'Just look at the mess in here!'

'If only I fucking could!' exploded Main as the sheer crassness of the comment reached him.

'How on earth did you come to get bleach in your eyes?' continued the questioner, backing off a little.

'Someone threw it at me,' answered Main through gritted teeth.

'Bloody hell, I'm not having this sort of thing in my pub. I run a respectable establishment. This sort of thing is not on!'

'Oh good,' said Main sourly. The pain had subsided sufficiently to let temper take hold, but he continued with the sluicing.

'I haven't once had to have the police here in all the time I've been licensee, and I'm not starting now. Pull yourself together and get out of here. I don't want your sort in my place.'

'Maybe we should call an ambulance, John?' suggested a voice from the background, but the suggestion was half-hearted, as if not to offend.

'I'm not having any ambulances either. You! Get out of here! Do you hear?'

Main felt the hand on his shoulder. He shrugged it off to continue cleaning his eyes.

'Did you hear what I said?'

Main raised his head from the sink at last, and paused for a moment to let the water drain from his face. He turned his head slowly and opened one eye cautiously.

His vision was blurred, but he could see – and that was all that mattered. The landlord's angry face swam into view. He was a fat man with heavy jowls and a large brown wart on the side of his turned-up nose, but Main thought him the most handsome sight he had ever seen. He straightened up and started dabbing at his eyes with his sleeve. He was a foot taller than the landlord, who took a pace backwards.

The man's voice took on a more conciliatory tone. 'I just want you out of here. I'm not going to call the police or ask you to pay for the damage; I just want you out of here. All right?'

Main looked at him sourly, but he felt good inside. He could see. He started to leave without another word. The small group of men near the door parted like the Red Sea, one of them brushing water off his jacket with which Main had sprayed him when he smoothed back his wet hair. As he left the bar he heard the barmaid's voice telling everyone how she had suspected there was something odd about 'that man'. He had been behaving strangely earlier.

'There's a lot of weirdos about,' ventured another voice before the door finally closed behind him and Main found himself out in the quiet street and the darkness which caressed him like a friend.

Main walked all the way home. There were a number of reasons, some connected with embarrassment about the way he must look after the fight in the pub, others with giving himself time to think on his own, but mainly because the cold night air felt good on his eyes. It was making them water, which interfered with his vision, but not unpleasantly so. There were haloes round all the street lights.

As he walked along he kept feeling his ribs, trying to decide whether or not any had been broken. He concluded not. He had already decided that the injury to his cheek was superficial, although it was quite badly swollen. He thought about the pub landlord and cursed under his breath, but all in all it had probably worked out for the best. Police involvement might have meant press interest – and having one of their English teachers involved in a pub-brawl might have proved less than popular with the governors of Merchiston School, extenuating circumstances or not.

Main made himself some coffee when he finally got home and sat down on the couch to drink it. He wanted to call the police and give them a description of the four men, but common sense prevailed. He decided that it would be best to wait until morning. The police were becoming used to his harassing them for action and he didn't want them dismissing what he had to say as the ravings of a dishevelled drunk in the early hours of the morning.

Main actually felt stone cold sober, despite his earlier drinking – which seemed like a year ago – but it would be better if he were to go to the police when he appeared calm and rational. At the moment the bathroom mirror said that he had fought a war single-handed and lost, quite apart from his eyes, which were appallingly bloodshot. He found some eye-lotion in the bathroom cabinet. It had been there since last summer. Mary and Simon had both suffered from hay fever. He paused for a moment with the bottle in his hand, but then opened it quickly to avoid maudlin reflection. He wet two swabs of cotton wool with the cool fluid and sat back down on the couch to apply one to each eye.

• • •

As he sat there in silence, the pain, discomfort and humiliation of the evening took second place to the knowledge that he had found the men who had disinterred his son. It was true they had got away, but only for the moment. The fact that he had found them at all proved his hypothesis. They must live locally. The police would find them and discover what had happened to Simon. His sense of hopelessness had gone.

Main started to go over everything he had heard the men say. There was a little thing that kept niggling away at him. They had kept insisting that he 'had got it all wrong'. What had he got all wrong? It wasn't just the words, it was the expression on their faces when they said it – and both had said it. They had looked aggrieved, even innocent, but they hadn't tried to deny that they were there that night. So what did it mean?

They had referred to McKirrop as a 'lying old bastard' and he assumed that they had been referring to McKirrop's tale of bravery in the cemetery, but now it worried him. Was there something else McKirrop could have been lying about? Surely McKirrop couldn't have been the one who had disinterred Simon?

Tiredness began to overwhelm Main, but before giving in he forced himself to write down everything that had been said and as detailed a description as he could remember of the four men. He found no trouble in remembering them. The faces of at least two of them would be with him until his dying day. He wished he could draw, but he couldn't; it would have to be a verbal description that he gave the police.

Ryan Lafferty turned over in his sleep for the umpteenth time and finally conceded that he was not going to get a good night's rest. He had not really been sleeping at all but had been caught in the uneasy no man's land between sleep and wakefulness, where troubles lie in wait like beasts in the forest. His earlier reading had compounded the problem. He had been going through a chapter in his witchcraft book about Aleister Crowley, perhaps the most infamous witch of the twentieth century. Crowley, once labelled the wickedest man in the world, had been included in the book on Scottish witchcraft by virtue of his connection with Boleskin House, on the shores of Loch Ness. It was written that, on one occasion, Crowley and his disciples had set out to raise Pan. He and another man had been locked away in a room to perform the satanic ceremony while the others had had to wait until morning before opening the door. When they did, they found Crowley a 'jibbering lunatic' and his colleague dead.

Lafferty opened his eyes and looked up at the patterns on the ceiling of his room. The shadow of the bare branches of the beech tree outside wove an intricate moving pattern as the wind stirred them. They looked like a spider's web about to ensnare him.

The telephone rang, startling him. He reached out his hand, trying to think which of his parishioners it could be. He could not think of any who were seriously ill.

Jean O'Donnell's voice brought him to full wakefulness with the urgency of her tone.

'Father? It's Mary!'

Lafferty propped himself up on one elbow. He said, 'What about her? What's happened?'

'Oh Father . . .' Jean O'Donnell's voice broke down in sobs.

'Take your time and tell me, what's happened?'

'An accident, Father. There's been an accident.'

'On the bike?'

'Yes. She's bad Father. She's really bad.'

'Where is she now?'

'In the Infirmary. The police have just told me.'

'What exactly did they say, Jean?'

Jean O'Donnell sobbed again before answering, 'That she's been involved in a serious road accident. She has bad head injuries. She's in something called the Head Tr . . .'

'The Head Trauma Unit?'

'That sounds like it.'

'That's the best place for her, Jean. They're experts on head injuries up there.'

'Oh Father . . .'

'I know, Jean. Are you going to the hospital now?'

'Joe's just getting dressed.'

'I'm on my way. I'll see you there.'

When Lafferty arrived at the hospital he found Jean O'Donnell and her husband already there. They were huddled together in the otherwise empty waiting room.

'No, don't get up,' urged Lafferty as he approached. He drew one of the plastic chairs out of the line and sat down facing the couple, leaning forward with his arms on his knees.

'Any news?' he asked.

'We're just waiting for the doctor to come down,' replied Jean.

Lafferty held out his hands and took a hand each from Joe and Jean in his own. He said a prayer and Jean said 'Amen' at the end, but Joe just stared at the floor as if in a world of his own. The sound of footsteps made Lafferty turn his head. A young woman in a white coat was coming towards them. He stood up.

The woman looked at Lafferty and then at the couple. She said, 'Mr and Mrs O'Donnell? I'm Dr Lasseter.'

Sarah turned to look at Lafferty and Jean O'Donnell said, 'This is Father Lafferty, Doctor, our parish priest.'

The name registered with Sarah and Lafferty smiled at the recognition in her eyes. He said, 'I think we've spoken on the telephone, Doctor.'

'How is she?' asked Jean.

'Not very well at all, I'm afraid,' replied Sarah. 'She's on a life-support machine at the moment. It's too early to say how severe her head injuries are, but I think it would be foolish to give you false hope. She's very badly hurt.'

Jean started to sob into her handkerchief and Joe wrapped his arm more tightly around her.

'Do you know exactly what happened, Doctor?' asked Lafferty gently.

Sarah said, 'I understand from my colleagues in A&E that she was the pillion passenger on a motor cycle. There was an accident involving another vehicle. Mary was catapulted off the machine.' Sarah's voice fell to a whisper. 'I believe she collided with a tree.'

Joe O'Donnell, who had stared resolutely at the floor throughout the conversation, suddenly looked up and said, 'I'll kill the bastard! I'll take his bloody life!'

Jean restrained him and Lafferty put a hand on his shoulder, too. Sarah said softly, 'If it's the young man who was riding the motor cycle you're talking about, I'm afraid he's dead. He was killed outright.'

Joe O'Donnell put his hands over his face and shook

his head as anger, grief and frustration threatened to overwhelm him.

'I'm sorry,' he sobbed through his fingers. 'I just . . .'

'Take it easy,' said Lafferty gently.

'Can we see her?' asked Jean.

'Of course,' replied Sarah. 'But she's on a life-support machine.'

'What does that mean exactly?' asked Jean.

'Quite simply it means that a machine is breathing for her. We place an airway tube into her throat, and she is ventilated artificially by a respirator. We also have tubes going down into her stomach and another tube going into a vein so that we can feed and medicate her. So be prepared.'

Sarah led the way upstairs to HTU. Joe and Jean followed, still with their arms around each other, and Lafferty brought up the rear.

In the early hours of the morning the stair-well seemed cold but Lafferty's momentary urge to shiver faded as they passed through swing doors into HTU and felt the warmth hit them. As if needing to break the silence, Jean said, 'It's very warm in here.'

'We have to keep it that way for the patients,' said Sarah. 'In a unit like this clothes and blankets get in the way.'

Lafferty saw what she meant. Mary O'Donnell was clad in a simple white hospital shift which left her throat and arms bare for ease of access. An unsightly plastic airway protruded from her mouth and her chest rose and fell in response to the ventilator that hissed and clicked beside her bed. Electrode wires snaked out from the bandaging on her head and she had suffered some superficial grazing to her face which had left an angry red weal. Her eyes were closed and there was no response from her when her mother, unable to restrain herself, knelt down by the bed and laid her face against her shoulder, sobbing her concern.

'Easy,' said Joe, placing a hand awkwardly on his wife's shoulder and helping her to her feet.

'Can we stay?' asked Jean when she had recovered.

'I really don't think there's much point,' responded Sarah gently. 'Nothing will happen tonight. We'll know more when we run tests on her tomorrow.'

'But if she should get worse and . . .'

'Mary will not die,' said Sarah. 'The machine is breathing for her.'

Jean looked puzzled. She asked, 'Are you saying that she can't die?'

'More or less,' said Sarah. 'As long as she's on the ventilator we can keep her blood oxygenated so, technically, Mary cannot die.'

Jean O'Donnell looked as if a great weight had been removed from her shoulders.

'It's wonderful what they can do,' said her husband.

'But,' cautioned Sarah, 'it may be that Mary's brain is so damaged she won't be able to recover.'

'You mean she could be a vegetable, don't you?' said Jean.

'It's possible,' said Sarah. 'We'll have to hope for the best.'

'And pray,' said Jean, looking down at her daughter.

'You will pray for her, Father, won't you?' she asked Lafferty without turning round.

'You know I will,' said Lafferty.

'Go home now,' said Sarah kindly. 'Try to sleep. We'll call you in the morning when we know more.'

Jean looked up at Joe who nodded. Joe wrapped his arm round her again and nodded his thanks to Sarah before setting off for the door. Lafferty was left standing there.

Sarah looked at him and said, 'I'm glad to get the opportunity to apologise to you in person, Father Lafferty. I really am most sorry that I didn't inform you of John McKirrop's death.'

'That's over and done with, Dr Lasseter. Don't give it another thought.'

'That's gracious of you Father. Can I offer you some coffee?'

'Most welcome,' accepted Lafferty, gratefully. He followed Sarah to the duty-room where she switched on an electric kettle.

'It'll be instant I'm afraid.'

'That's fine, but are you sure you don't want to get back to bed? I assume you were called out for Mary?'

Sarah nodded and said, 'That's okay. I could do with some coffee. You don't think I was too direct – too frank – with the O'Donnells, do you?' Sarah had turned to face Lafferty and he was surprised at the vulnerability in her eyes. His heart went out to her.

'Not at all. Can I take it from what you said that there's not much hope for Mary?'

Sarah shook her head. 'I don't honestly think so. The crash helmet she was wearing didn't fit properly and had actually been damaged in a previous accident. Her injuries are very bad. That's why I felt I had to try to prepare the O'Donnells for the worst.'

Lafferty nodded and said, 'You did it kindly.'

Sarah let out her breath. 'You don't know how relieved I am to hear you say that. You know, it's an awful thing, but when you see broken bodies and weeping relatives day in, day out, it's so hard to find . . .'

'New compassion?' asked Lafferty.

'Exactly,' nodded Sarah. 'I can feel it happening to me and I feel so guilty but I can't seem to stop the hardening process. There are times when I hate myself for it but I can't fight it.'

'No you can't,' said Lafferty. 'It's nothing to be ashamed of. It's your own body's way of telling you that it can't stand the strain of carrying everyone else's grief. It's too much for anyone. Don't worry. Underneath it all you haven't changed. You're still the same caring person you were before you came into medicine. The fact that you worry about it says so.'

Sarah looked at Lafferty for a moment before saying, 'Do you know, I probably shouldn't say this, but that's the first time I've ever heard anything comforting from a man of the cloth.'

Lafferty laughed and said, 'Then my day has not entirely been in vain.'

'More coffee?'

'That was fine,' said Lafferty who started to get up. 'I hope you don't mind my asking this, but what you said on the telephone about John McKirrop regaining or not regaining consciousness has been puzzling me.'

Lafferty noticed that Sarah visibly stiffened at McKirrop's name.

'If it's none of my business, just tell me and I'll shut up.'

Sarah desperately wanted to talk to someone about McKirrop's death, but she needed to think about it first. She confined what she had to say to the disagreement over whether McKirrop had been conscious or not.

'And you think he knew what he was saying?' asked Lafferty when she had finished.

'Yes,' affirmed Sarah. 'He didn't remember anything about the assault which brought him in here, but I'm sure he was quite lucid about what happened in the cemetery.'

'That's really what I wanted to talk to him about,' said Lafferty.

'Really?'

'I've been trying to help John Main find out what happened to his son's body,'

'I see,' said Sarah. 'Poor man, he's had quite enough to contend with without that happening.'

'You know him?'

'Not personally, but his son died here, in HTU,' said Sarah.

'Of course, I'd forgotten. Can you remember what McKirrop actually said when he came round?' he asked.

Sarah took a deep breath and said, 'It was really just a case of a few phrases but he clearly remembered the incident in the cemetery. He mentioned the coffin being opened and mumbled about yobs beating him up.'

'Yobs?' asked Lafferty with a puzzled frown. 'He used that word?'

'Yes, yobs.'

'Anything else?'

'No, I think that was it.'

'I'm grateful to you for talking to me about it,' said Lafferty.

'It's the least I could do.'

'Good night, Doctor,' said Lafferty. 'From what you said about Mary, I fear we may meet again before long.'

Sarah nodded slightly and said good night. Lafferty left.

•   •   •

There were grey streaks of dawn in the sky as Lafferty walked across the courtyard to his car. A milk float cruised past the main gate, its full load of bottles bouncing in unison in their crates as its small wheels made heavy work of the uneven surface. 'Yobs' was a funny word to use to describe satanists, he thought, as he struggled to put the ignition key in place in the darkness. Yobs conjured up images of tearaways, thugs – people who broke and destroyed things – but grave-robbing? That was something else. That wasn't their style at all. The engine of the old Ford Escort sprang into life accompanied by a squeal which suggested that the clutch release bearing needed attention. He really must get it fixed soon.

In theory, Sarah should have had the morning off, but it was Tyndall's ward round and it was expected that she should be there for that and the medical meeting afterwards. She arrived in the unit fifteen minutes early so that she could brief Stubbs on Mary O'Donnell. She found Stubbs with the patient when she arrived and noted that he had written her up for Sigma probes.

'Do you think it's worth it?' she inquired. 'She has massive brain damage.'

'Anyone under eighteen gets Sigma probes routinely,' replied Stubbs. 'It's written into the trial protocol. We have discretion with older patients, but the rules apply to our young friend here.'

'I see.'

'I thought you knew that,' said Stubbs.

'No one told me.'

Stubbs did not respond.

'Will you be carrying out the scans on Miss O'Donnell?' she asked.

'Unless Dr Tyndall says otherwise. Why?'

'It's just that I met her parents last night, and her parish priest. I'm interested in the outcome,' said Sarah. She felt uncomfortable saying it, as if she were inviting Stubbs to slap her down.

Sure enough, Stubbs said, 'Don't become personally involved with the patients. I think I've told you that before. It will drain you. You won't be able to function properly as a doctor. You'll be finished in this kind of medicine within a year. Think of them as cases, nothing more. Do your best for them, but keep it impersonal.'

'Perhaps there's a middle way, Dr Stubbs,' said Sarah in a tone that suggested Stubbs had missed it by a mile.

'I'm only saying this for your own good. You won't last a year.'

'I don't intend to make my career in this kind of medicine anyway,' said Sarah.

'Oh yes,' smiled Stubbs, 'I heard. You've set your heart on being a GP – just like Daddy.'

Sarah coloured with anger but she kept a rein on her tongue.

'That's different then. You can get involved all you want to with sore throats and boils on the bum. Demanding stuff.'

'There's a lot more to being a GP than that,' answered Sarah.

'I forgot about the ante-natal clinics,' murmured Stubbs.

Sarah responded with a look of disdain.

Stubbs seemed to take it in his stride. He looked at Sarah and said, 'Look around you! This is where it's at. Front line medicine! You've been given the chance to work at the very forefront of medical science and all you can think about is a career doling out HRT to the Women's Institute!'

'That is absolutely . . .!' Words failed Sarah as she tried to respond to Stubbs's sneer. What hurt her most of all was the awful feeling of disloyalty that had come over her because somewhere at the back of her mind a part of her agreed with everything Stubbs had just said.

'Good morning everyone,' said Murdoch Tyndall's voice, and Sarah and Stubbs froze mid-argument.

'Good morning, sir,' they replied in unison without breaking eye contact.

'Shall we begin?'

The consultant's round went smoothly enough, with Stubbs briefing Tyndall on the progress of each patient in turn and Sarah speaking when she was spoken to. Mary O'Donnell was the last patient to be considered as she was the latest admission. Tyndall read the notes and murmured, 'Doesn't look good, does it?'

'No sir.'

'Will you do the scans this morning?'

'Yes sir. About the Sigma probes? Will you implant them?'

'I'll do it before I go. Do we have a sterile set?'

Sister Roche said, 'Yes, sir.'

'Do we know about relatives?'

Stubbs turned to Sarah. She said, 'I saw both parents early this morning when we admitted her from A&E. The patient's parish priest was also here.'

'A little premature,' said Tyndall, beaming slightly to advertise his joke.

'I got the impression that Father Lafferty is a family friend,' said Sarah.

'Lafferty?'

'Yes sir.'

'Wasn't he the chap who had an interest in Mr McKirrop?'

'Yes sir.'

'If he keeps this up we'll have to make him chaplain to the unit!' said Tyndall.

Everyone smiled on cue.

'I hope you didn't build their hopes too high,' said Tyndall, becoming serious again.

'No sir, I think they realised the seriousness of the position.'

'Good,' said Tyndall gravely. 'We may have to see them after the scans are complete. We don't want this to drag on if there's no chance of recovery.' He turned to Sarah and asked, 'I don't suppose you can give us an indication as to what the priest's position might be on discontinuing the ventilator if it should come to that?'

'Not really sir,' replied Sarah. 'But he struck me as an eminently sensible man.'

'Good,' said Tyndall. 'The last thing we need is a self-righteous nutter causing all kinds of distress to everyone.'

'No, sir.'

'Well, that's it then. I'll do the probes if you prepare a tray, Sister.'

'Yes sir,' said Roche.

Tyndall went to scrub up for the minor surgical procedure involved in implanting the Sigma probes in Mary O'Donnell's skull. A few minutes later the phone rang in the duty-room, and a nurse announced that it was Mrs O'Donnell.

'You take it,' said Stubbs to Sarah. 'I'll prepare for the scans. You can tell her we should be done by twelve. We'll know more then. You know the routine.'

Sarah spoke to Jean O'Donnell and told her that Mary's condition was unchanged. She didn't remind her that it couldn't change with machines doing everything for her.

'Does that mean she's got a chance then?' asked Jean O'Donnell eagerly.

A lump came to Sarah's throat. She said, 'I'm afraid it doesn't in itself, Mrs O'Donnell. It means that her physical state is unchanged, but we don't know anything about the damage to her brain as yet. Dr Stubbs is just about to begin her scans. Can you call back about lunch time?'

'Yes, Doctor, and – thank you.'

'I'll speak to you later,' said Sarah.

Lafferty spent the morning in the church praying for the recovery of Mary O'Donnell, but also for strength to bring comfort to her grieving parents should it be necessary. After his conversation with Sarah Lasseter in the early hours of the morning he suspected that the latter would be more relevant. He wondered how Jean would take it. She had always had an unshakable faith. Please God it would survive the death of her daughter.

Joseph O'Donnell would be bitter and, when mixed with the guilt he was feeling, it might prove a heady cocktail to handle. Joe needed someone or something to blame. He and Mary had been at loggerheads for weeks over her boyfriend and the hours she kept. Joe clearly loved his daughter, but the fact that he would never be able to tell her this and that she had died with so much bad feeling between them would be hard for him to bear. He would feel resentful and betrayed.

Lafferty phoned to ask if there was any news. Joe O'Donnell answered.

'Still the same,' he said.

'No sign of improvement?'

'They're doing tests this morning.'

'I'll call back later, Joe.'

'Father?'

'Yes?'

'About the fight Mary and I had last week – the mark on her head – I didn't mean her no harm. I mean . . . I love her really.'

'I know that, Joe. Don't worry about it. I'll speak to you later.' Lafferty was sitting thinking about Joe when the phone rang. It was John Main and he sounded revitalised.

'I thought you'd like to know, I found them, Ryan. I found them last night.'

Lafferty had to think for a moment before he realised what Main meant. 'You mean, the people who took Simon?' he exclaimed.

'Yes. I found them, all four of them.'

'How in God's name did you do it?' asked Lafferty.

Main explained the thinking behind his pub crawl and what had happened when he had put the theory into practice. 'They were in the very last one I visited. I've just been down at police headquarters with their descriptions.'

'Descriptions?' asked Lafferty.

Main told him about the fight in the pub and how he'd nearly lost his sight.

Lafferty frowned and asked, 'Are your eyes all right?'

'Still a bit sore, but I can see. I'll survive.'

'So who are these people? Did the police have any idea?'

'I had a look through their mug shot books but I didn't recognise anyone. They seemed like plain, ordinary yobs to me,' said Main. 'But the police are confident they'll find them now they know where to look.'

There was that word again, thought Lafferty. 'Yobs'. 'How can you be sure these are the men?' he asked.

'They didn't deny it,' answered Main.

'You mean they admitted taking Simon's body?' exclaimed Lafferty.

'They didn't go that far. They tried to suggest I'd got it all wrong but they knew McKirrop, all right, and they admitted being there in the cemetery that night.'

'Thank God. I'm afraid I've been getting nowhere at the library. I hope the police pick these men up soon; this has all been a nightmare for you.'

'You can say that again,' agreed Main. 'But we're nearly there. It may be that these four were acting on behalf of someone else, but we'll cross that bridge when we come to it.'

'Indeed we will,' said Lafferty. 'Keep me informed.'

'I will.'

Lafferty replaced the receiver and put his hands to his cheeks. He massaged them gently while he thought about what Main had said. McKirrop had used the term 'yobs' in his semi-conscious ramblings and it had registered with him as being incongruous. Now Main had described the four men in the pub as 'yobs'. This meant that it hadn't been just a bad choice of word on McKirrop's part. The grave robbers really had been young tearaways. He returned to his earlier hypothesis that yobs didn't steal bodies. So what did it all mean?

Main's idea could be right. They could have been doing the dirty work for someone else, but it sounded as if they hadn't suggested that themselves when Main confronted them. According to Main, they had said he had 'got it all wrong'.

That was interesting, thought Lafferty. When an accused said something like that it was usually a precursor to a plea of innocence, but if the men admitted being there in the cemetery that night how could they possibly hope to plead innocence?

10

Sarah decided to stay for the tests on Mary O'Donnell although, in theory, she could have gone off-duty after Tyndall's departure. She was present when Stubbs completed the final scan. He sighed deeply and said, 'She's not even borderline; there's no activity at all.' He handed the results to her and she started sifting through the untidy bunch of papers, first separating the chart graphs from the print-out rolls. It did not take long to see that Stubbs was right; there was no doubt. To all intents and purposes, Mary O'Donnell was dead. Even the Sigma scan, the most sensitive test of all, was flat-lining. The young girl in the bed, whose chest moved up and down to the rhythm of an electric relay valve, was just an empty shell with no more living substance than a photograph.

'I'll call Dr Tyndall,' said Stubbs. 'Maybe you can get the parents to come in this afternoon? The sooner we get this over with the better.'

Stubbs went to the doctors' room to phone; he returned after a couple of minutes and said, 'Dr Tyndall can manage this afternoon, it now depends on the parents.'

'I'll call them,' said Sarah.

'Dr Tyndall will be here at two thirty. Ask them if they can come at two, will you? I'd like to have a word with them first.'

Sarah looked at Stubbs who met her stare without flinching. 'Very well,' she said.

'By the way, Dr Tyndall would like you to be present when he sees them. Part of your training.'

She walked towards the duty-room with a heavy heart. She knew that the O'Donnells would have spent all night hoping and praying that their daughter would pull through. Their nerves would be stretched to breaking point, and when the phone rang it would be snatched up with anxious hands. She tapped out the numbers with her index finger, slowly and deliberately, unwilling to initiate a train of events which would lead to such unhappiness. The phone was answered at the first ring.

'Yes?' said Jean O'Donnell's voice. It was filled with anxiety.

Sarah swallowed hard and said, 'Mrs O'Donnell, It's Dr Lasseter here at the Infirmary. I wonder if you and your husband could come in this afternoon to have a word with Dr Stubbs and Dr Tyndall?'

'What's happened? Is she worse?' asked Jean O'Donnell.

Sarah could hear Joe O'Donnell in the background asking what was going on.

'We've had the chance to run some tests, and it's now a question of discussing the results with you.'

'Discussing,' said Jean O'Donnell slowly.

'Dr Tyndall will explain everything this afternoon,' said Sarah gently.

'I see,' replied Jean distantly.

Sarah knew that Jean O'Donnell had understood the

implications of the meeting. She no longer sounded anxious. Her voice had lost its animation. Something had left her; Sarah knew it was hope.

'Would two o'clock be all right?'

'We'll be there.'

Sarah was glad that Tyndall always made a point of speaking to relatives himself when there was bad news to impart. He was good with the patients; he was equally good with the relatives. He had the great advantage of looking the part and at times like this it was important. He was the kind of man that relatives would want to see, a reassuringly establishment figure, well-dressed, silver-haired, charming, sympathetic, understanding. She suspected that Stubbs could be pretty awful, and worried about why he wanted to see the O'Donnells first. Surely he could not be considering pre-empting Tyndall in asking for permission for organ removal? Dealing with grieving relatives was an aspect of her work that she had so far managed to avoid, thanks to Tyndall's habit of seeing them himself. But it couldn't be avoided indefinitely. She suspected that Tyndall had asked her to be present at the meeting with the O'Donnells today for that very reason. Death was a constant visitor to a unit like HTU.

As two o'clock came with no sign of the O'Donnells, Sarah noticed that Stubbs was becoming anxious. He started looking at his watch at half minute intervals. At quarter past the hour he was clearly losing patience.

'Where the hell are they?' he demanded.

Sarah, not sure if she should reply or not, muttered something about them being delayed. She was secretly pleased that it was beginning to look as if the O'Donnells would not be seeing Stubbs after all. This proved to be the case when Tyndall arrived early at twenty past and the O'Donnells had still not arrived. Sarah heard Stubbs swear under his breath as he himself disappeared.

The O'Donnells arrived at twenty-five past with Joe apologising for having to change a wheel on the car.

'Bloody kids,' he muttered, but didn't elaborate.

Tyndall got up when Jean O'Donnell entered the room. She had done it tentatively, despite having been told to 'go right in'. She still thought it right to tap gently on the door with her knuckles and put her head round first. Tyndall smiled and shook her hand. Sarah noted that the smile was just right, not so broad as to indicate that everything was going well but not so wan as to suggest that it was just a social nicety. The smile was that given to a confidant, someone who understood and knew the score. Tyndall shook hands with Joe who followed behind and then with Ryan Lafferty who came in last, and who caused Tyndall to raise his eyebrows.

Lafferty explained, 'Mrs O'Donnell asked me if I would be present this afternoon, if that's all right with you, Doctor?'

'Of course,' replied Tyndall. 'Do sit down.'

Sarah exchanged smiles with the O'Donnells, and with Lafferty who asked her, 'Don't you ever sleep, Doctor?' Sarah replied with a smile.

Tyndall took off his glasses and laid them on the desk in front of him. He said gently, 'It's best if I come straight to the point. We have carried out a full range of tests on your daughter and, frankly, the news is not good.'

Tyndall paused and Jean and Joe drew closer together. Sarah noted that Jean was outwardly calm, but she saw that she was holding Joe's hand so tightly that her knuckles were showing white.

Tyndall continued, 'We have been unable to detect any indication of brain activity in Mary, using a wide range of tests and the most sensitive equipment available to medicine. None at all.'

Sarah noted that although the delivery of the words was sympathetic, the substance was quite brutally frank. Tyndall had taken no time at all to get to the point. Mary was brain dead; there was no hope for her.

'Couldn't she just be in a coma, like?' asked Joe after a short pause. His voice sounded rough and uneven compared to Tyndall's well modulated tones. It seemed to fracture the air in the little room.

'No. I'm afraid not,' said Tyndall. 'To all intents and purposes I'm afraid we have to conclude that Mary is brain dead.'

Jean looked as if time had stopped for her. Her expression froze, leaving her eyes as the mirrors of a deep sadness. Joe's face, on the other hand, took on a sudden flurry of animation, seemingly registering surprise, dismay and anguish all at the same time.

'What does that mean exactly?' he asked. 'Brain dead?'

'It means that your daughter cannot recover. She is beyond saving. I'm most terribly sorry.'

'But she's still on that machine isn't she?' said Joe. 'There's time yet, surely. I mean you read every day about people coming round after being unconscious for years even?'

Tyndall shook his head and said, 'I'm sorry, that's different. These people still have brain function, despite being unconscious. Mary has no such function. She is, in reality, dead. The machines are keeping her respiration and her circulation going, but these are simple mechanical processes. Mary will never be able to do them for herself again.'

'But . . .'

Joe started to protest, but his eyes were filling with tears and he kept shaking his head as if trying to free himself of the facts.

Jean raised his hand to her lips and kissed it. She was crying herself, but she said gently, 'Mary's gone love, we have to face it.'

Lafferty chose to stay in the background. He wanted to help, but the couple were comforting each other. He wasn't really needed.

After a few moments, Jean O'Donnell said to Tyndall, 'You will want to turn the machine off then?'

Tyndall nodded gently.

Sarah again thought the gesture absolutely right. Potentially this was the most emotionally agonising bridge to cross for the parents, but Tyndall had led them gently and sympathetically over it; he had almost made it appear a technical after-thought.

Jean and Joe held each other and nodded their assent. Lafferty remained as a spectator.

Tyndall put his hand to his head, as if uncomfortable, and said, 'There is just one other thing I have to ask you.'

Sarah took a deep breath and held it.

Jean and Joe O'Donnell looked at Tyndall attentively but did not speak. Tyndall continued as if the words were causing him pain.

'It is just possible that Mary could help some other patient.'

The O'Donnells looked puzzled.

'Help?' asked Jean.

Tyndall paused and then said, 'Her organs . . .'

Joe O'Donnell's face hardened, and his eyes took on an angry look. 'No way!' he stormed. 'No one touches my little girl. Is that clear?'

'Perfectly,' replied Tyndall gently. 'If you don't want it, then there is no question about it. Your wishes will be respected.'

Joe calmed down almost as quickly as he had flared up and Sarah thought that Tyndall might have another go at getting transplant permission, but he did not. He obviously considered it a lost cause.

'Could we see her just one more time?' asked Jean.

'Of course,' said Tyndall. He turned to Sarah, 'Would you?'

Sarah nodded her agreement and led the O'Donnells through to where their daughter lay. She felt a lump in her throat as the couple took what was to be a last long look at their daughter. Joe O'Donnell turned to Sarah at one point and asked in a hoarse whisper, 'She won't suffer will she?'

'No,' replied Sarah, fighting back her own tears. 'She's beyond all that.'

Sarah could sense a potentially awkward situation looming where neither of the O'Donnells would want to leave their daughter, knowing it would be for the last time. She herself was not sure how long she should give them before suggesting it herself. In the event, Tyndall solved the problem for her. He joined them and said gently to the O'Donnells, 'I'm afraid there are a few formalities we have to go through.'

He led the parents away, leaving Sarah on her own.

She was joined almost immediately by Ryan Lafferty who saw that she was about to lose the battle to contain her tears.

'The Lord giveth and the Lord taketh away,' he said.

'Sometimes I hate this job!' exclaimed Sarah.

Lafferty put his arm around her and the first tears started to roll down her cheeks.

'Look at me!' she sobbed. 'I'm supposed to be a doctor and I'm behaving like a silly schoolgirl!'

'Caring was never a crime, Doctor,' said Lafferty. 'The world could do with a lot more "silly school-girls".'

Sarah dried her eyes with her handkerchief and recovered her composure before nodding to Lafferty, saying, 'Thank you.'

It was time for Lafferty to take his own last look at Mary O'Donnell. The next time he 'saw' her would be at her funeral service.

'Would you like me to leave?' asked Sarah.

Lafferty nodded without turning round and Sarah melted away.

Lafferty felt the lump in his throat as he looked at the young face of Mary O'Donnell, so pale and peaceful. He read the ID card on the end of the bed. *Mary O'Donnell, d.o.b. 13.1.78.* Nineteen seventy-eight seemed like only yesterday. The passing of time seemed to accelerate exponentially as you got older, but fifteen was still very young.

Lafferty noticed the Greek letter in the bottom corner of the card and he remembered having seen it somewhere before. It had been on the card that John Main had placed in the centre of the Ouija board in his flat. At the time he couldn't remember what it was called.

Now, however, it came back to him. It was the Greek letter, Sigma.

Lafferty commended the soul of Mary O'Donnell to the keeping of the Lord while Joseph and Jean wept and Sarah bit her lip. Murdoch Tyndall switched off the respirator and Mary's chest fell for the last time to remain at rest. There was a moment when the silence seemed almost unbearable, but Tyndall quickly filled the gap and ushered the parents out of the room.

'Will you be at the funeral, Dr Lasseter?' asked Lafferty.

Sarah shook her head and replied, 'No, Father. It's against unit policy.' Then, realising how cold and impersonal that sounded, she added, 'There are just so many.'

Lafferty nodded and said quietly, 'Of course. How thoughtless of me.'

'No, not at all!' said Sarah, suddenly anxious to reassure Lafferty.

For some reason the last thing in the world she wanted to do was offend this man. Perhaps it was because he had been so kind to her when she had felt vulnerable, or perhaps it was because she detected a kind of vulnerability in him. She didn't know, but suddenly realised that she had to confide in someone and Lafferty was the man.

'I was wondering if I might have a word with you, Father.'

'Of course,' Lafferty said automatically before starting to wonder why. 'Just now?'

'No, I'd rather it was somewhere away from here,' said Sarah, looking over her shoulder.

'Perhaps you could come round to St Xavier's? I live in the house next door,' Lafferty suggested. 'Or . . .'

'That would be fine.'

'This evening?'

'Ideal. I have the evening off.'

'Shall we say, seven o'clock?'

A nurse came into the room and Sarah's voice changed. 'Yes, Father Lafferty, that would be perfectly all right,' she said in official tones.

She led the way out of the room.

Lafferty answered the door when Sarah arrived at two minutes past seven. He had changed out of clerical gear and was wearing navy-blue cord trousers and a matching polo shirt. Sarah was ushered into a comfortable, if old fashioned, room which had not seen a change of furniture in a very long time.

'Tea? Coffee? A drink?' inquired Lafferty when he had closed the door and the pleasantries were over.

Sarah, who was sitting awkwardly on the edge of a faded green sofa, dithered for a moment before replying, 'If a drink is really on offer I'd love one.'

'Whiskey, gin or sherry? That's your choice,' smiled Lafferty.

'Gin please.'

Lafferty opened up his drinks cabinet, grimacing at the squeal of the brass hinges, and extracted a bottle of Beefeater Gin.

'I used to buy Gordon's until they decided to reduce its strength and charge us the same for it.'

'I didn't know that,' said Sarah with a smile.

Lafferty rummaged through the bottles before saying, 'It will have to be bitter lemon, I'm afraid. I don't seem to have any tonic.'

'Fine,' said Sarah.

Lafferty poured himself a large Jamieson's whisky and sat down opposite her.

'Irish whiskey?' Sarah queried.

'A tribute to my roots,' smiled Lafferty. 'With a name like Lafferty and a job like mine, what did you expect?'

'You don't sound Irish.'

'My parents left Ireland when I was seven. I was brought up in Liverpool.'

'So you are one of these people with divided loyalties at rugby internationals?' smiled Sarah.

'No problem. I wear the green.'

Sarah nodded and took a sip of her drink.

'How can I help you, Doctor?' asked Lafferty, seeing the troubled look appear in her eyes.

'My name is Sarah.'

'Very well, Sarah.'

Sarah opened her mouth to start speaking but then she stopped and shook her head. 'Maybe I should have gone to the police, but they wouldn't believe me.'

'The police?' asked Lafferty.

Sarah nodded. 'I think a crime has been committed.'

'At the hospital?'

'Yes.'

'What sort of crime?'

'Murder.'

Lafferty's mouth fell open.

'Murder?' he exclaimed. 'But who?'

'One of the patients in HTU, John McKirrop. I'm convinced he was murdered.'

Lafferty took a few moments to get over the second shock – hearing the name, McKirrop. He composed himself before saying calmly, 'Have I got this right? You are telling me that John McKirrop was murdered while in hospital?'

'I think so,' said Sarah. 'In fact, I'm sure of it.'

'But why? How?'

'I don't know why, but I do know how,' said Sarah. She told Lafferty about her examination of the cadaver and the evidence she had found.

'You're absolutely certain about this?'

Sarah nodded. 'The trouble is, I can't prove it without the original skull X-ray. Without that, everything seems to be above board. Mr McKirrop was admitted to HTU with a depressed fracture of the skull and it caused massive brain damage. End of story. Only I and the killer know that the fracture got much worse after he was admitted to HTU.'

Lafferty shook his head, finding it difficult to take everything in. 'But why?' he asked. 'Who would want to kill a man like John McKirrop?'

'Needless to say, I've been thinking about that a lot,' said Sarah. 'The only thing I can come up with concerns a colleague, Dr Derek Stubbs. He's actually my immediate boss.'

Sarah told Lafferty about Stubbs being made to look foolish if McKirrop had recovered from his injuries. 'He dismissed the patient as being a hopeless case without even checking the X-rays.'

'I see,' said Lafferty thoughtfully. 'As an outsider, it all seems a bit extreme to say the least. Do you really think this man Stubbs capable of such an act?'

Sarah sighed and shook her head. 'Much as I dislike him, no I don't,' she answered. 'It's more a case of being unable to think of any other motive.'

'Then we'll have to look for one together.

'I've been trying,' said Sarah with a wry smile.

'Have you managed to come up with anything at all?'

'I suppose it's just possible that McKirrop knew something that other people didn't want him to talk about.'

'That makes sense,' agreed Lafferty. 'Any idea about what it could be?'

Sarah looked doubtful. She paused before saying, 'This may sound silly, but I think it could be something to do with the satanists and what happened in the cemetery with the Main boy.'

Lafferty's heart missed a beat. 'What makes you say that?' he asked, taking a sip of his drink.

'I saw John McKirrop the first time he was admitted to hospital, just after he had been beaten up by the men in the cemetery. There was something about him; it's hard to put my finger on it exactly, but I got the distinct impression he knew more than he ever said about the affair.'

'Why do you say that?'

'At first he wouldn't speak about what happened at all. He seemed scared. I had to urge him to tell the police what he knew for the sake of the boy's father. Apparently he did do that but I remember thinking at the time that he wanted to tell *me* something else. It was as if he . . .'

'Hadn't been telling the whole story?' added Lafferty.

'Exactly. How did you know I was going to say that?'

'I've been uneasy about what happened in the cemetery myself,' said Lafferty. 'I've read every book on the occult I can lay my hands on, I've talked to an expert on the black arts, and still nothing has emerged to suggest what kind of group would want the body or why. That's why I wanted to talk to McKirrop if he came round. I wanted to know if there had been something else he hadn't been telling us. Some extra clue.'

'I see,' said Sarah.

'There's something else that's bothering me. You told me that McKirrop had used the word "yobs" when referring to the men who had dug up the Main boy. John Main used the same word when he called me up this morning to tell me that he had found the men who did it. From what he said, they didn't sound like Black Mass material. It made me more certain than ever that McKirrop didn't tell the whole truth—'

'Did you say that Mr Main had found the men?' interrupted Sarah.

Lafferty nodded and told her briefly how Main had done it. 'The police are looking for them now.'

'Then we should know the whole story when they catch them,' said Sarah.

Lafferty nodded.

'But what could McKirrop possibly know that would be worth killing him to keep it quiet.'

Lafferty shook his head. 'I'm not sure,' he said. 'Perhaps there were other people in the cemetery that night? People who McKirrop never mentioned. Or perhaps there's something else that we haven't even thought about yet.'

'But there has to be a connection with HTU, if that's the reason McKirrop was murdered.'

'I suppose so.'

'I'm scared,' confessed Sarah.

Lafferty could see that she was. 'Have you voiced your suspicions about McKirrop's death to anyone in HTU?' he asked.

'No, you're the only person I've told.'

'Good, then no one knows that you suspect,' said Lafferty.

'Stubbs knows that I was searching for the missing X-ray,' said Sarah.

Lafferty frowned. 'But not why?'

'No.'

'Then I suggest that we do and say nothing until the police have come up with the four men. If they discover a strong enough motive for killing John McKirrop, perhaps you won't need the X-ray after all. Make sense?'

Sarah nodded and said, 'It does. I'm grateful to you for listening to me. I can't tell you what a relief it is to have shared this with someone.'

Lafferty smiled. 'I think you've just told a Roman Catholic priest that confession is good for you.'

When Sarah got back to the residency she found an air of excitement about the place.

'What's going on?' she asked Paddy Duncan when she met him in the corridor.

'You haven't heard the news?' he asked.

'What news?'

'Cyril Tyndall has come up with a vaccine against *Herpes* infections. It's reported as being a hundred per cent effective and Gelman Holland have been licensed by the government to manufacture it. It should be available for general use by the end of the year.'

'That's wonderful news, but what about trials and safety evaluations? Surely they can't just put it into production,' exclaimed Sarah.

'All done. The trials were conducted in secret with government approval.'

209

'But why in secret? And why would the government approve?'

'This is exactly the kind of research that the government wants to encourage,' smiled Duncan. 'Gelman Holland backs Cyril Tyndall with money and resources, Cyril comes up with the goods. The government smoothes the way ahead for them, keeps bureaucracy to a minimum, cuts red tape. Everyone benefits and the tax payer's contribution has been much less than usual for medical research. The propaganda value in something like this for the government is enormous.'

'But why the secrecy?' asked Sarah.

'Such sweet naivety,' teased Duncan. 'Do you realise how much money there is to be made with such a product? No scientist does anything these days without talking to his lawyer and the patents office. Some people are even trying to patent the human genome.'

'So this is not a traditional vaccine then?'

'No,' agreed Duncan. 'That's the really exciting thing. This isn't a traditional vaccine at all. Cyril Tyndall has taken a completely new approach to the problem and come up with a hi-tech solution to recurrent infections. He's used the techniques of genetic engineering to identify the DNA trigger mechanism in human cells which sets off dormant *Herpes* virus.'

'Brilliant!' said Sarah. 'He must have found a repressor binding site for the virus.'

'You sound as if you know about it.'

Sarah nodded and said, 'I got interested in the subject at medical school when we were studying phage lysogeny in bacteria. It struck me that the same thing might go on with the *Herpes* virus.'

'Tell me more,' said Duncan.

'Well, you know if you get an infection like a cold sore it appears to heal and clear up, but in fact it lies dormant within you until it's set off again by sunlight or stress or whatever?'

Duncan nodded and said, 'Once you've got it, you've always got it?'

'Exactly. Well, the theory was that the virus was kept dormant by a repressor substance until something happened to destroy or inactivate the repressor. When that happened, the virus was free to replicate and cause infection all over again. It sounds as if Professor Tyndall has identified the DNA trigger that does this, and come up with a way of keeping the virus permanently inactive. Do you know if it only applies to *Herpes simplex*?'

'No, that's the beauty of it,' said Duncan. 'It's said to be equally effective against the sexually transmitted form that's been sweeping the States, and against *Herpes zoster*. No more shingles. A complete cure.'

'There's even a school of thought that implicates *Herpes* virus in certain kinds of cancer,' said Sarah. 'This could put Cyril Tyndall in line for a major prize.'

'That's what everyone's been saying. And not only Cyril. Murdoch's name is on the paper as well. Quite a family affair.'

'Are you sure?' asked Sarah.

'Absolutely. It's in today's edition of *Nature*. There are four authors and Murdoch is one of them.'

'But Murdoch Tyndall isn't a virologist,' said Sarah, quite puzzled at the revelation.

'Maybe he made some kind of intellectual contribution,' suggested Duncan. 'Or maybe it's just a case of brotherly love. Cyril wanted his brother to share in a great moment in medicine.'

'The research councils take a dim view of honorary authorship' said Sarah.

'The research councils take a dim view of a lot of things that no one else pays any attention to,' Duncan replied.

Sarah smiled and said, 'I suppose you're right. Anyway, the main thing is that we'll have the vaccine.'

'And your boss will be in a good mood,' added Duncan.

'I hadn't thought of that little bonus.'

'I think the hospital is planning some little celebration in the meantime. Who knows, we dogsbodies may even be invited to it.'

'That would be nice. I've never met Cyril Tyndall.'

Duncan looked surprised. He said, 'I thought you would have, working for his brother and all.'

'Apparently he keeps himself very much to himself.'

'There might be something about the vaccine on the news – shall we take a look?'

Sarah agreed and they went along to the common-room where a dozen others had gathered excitedly for the same reason. The vaccine story was mentioned third in the headlines. There were loud cheers at the naming of the university and hospital, although there were no pictures either of the Tyndall brothers or the hospital. Instead, stock footage of the city was shown.

'I guess they didn't have time,' said Duncan.

The national news came to an end and was followed by local news. People began to drift away, but Sarah heard Duncan comment, 'God, what a mess,' as she was heading for the door. She turned round to see pictures of a burnt-out car, surrounded by firemen still playing their hoses on it. Four young men had lost their lives when the car they were travelling in had apparently burst into flames. No other vehicle had been involved and police were still trying to establish the cause of the fire.

John Main was about to go to bed when the phone rang. He hesitated before picking it up, fearing that it might be his sister or mother-in-law. He had not returned any of their calls for the past two weeks. He waited until the answering machine had put out its message and the bleep had signalled the caller to speak.

'Hello, Mr Main. This is Inspector Lenny at Lothians and Borders Police Headquarters. I'd like you to get in touch with us at your convenience, sir.'

Main snatched up the phone. 'This is John Main, Inspector. You have some news?'

'I think it might be better if I came round, sir, rather than talk over the telephone.'

'Very well, Inspector. As soon as you like.'

'I'll be there in about fifteen minutes.'

Main felt the excitement grow inside him. The police must have found the men. He was now very close to finding out what had happened to Simon. To fill in the time, he put his clothes back on and made some coffee, and he'd just finished a mugful when the doorbell rang. It was Lenny.

'Sorry to bother you at this late hour, sir, but you did seem anxious to get any news at all about your son,' said the policeman.

'Absolutely, Inspector. Have you found the men?'

The Inspector did not reply. Instead, he opened his briefcase and took out a manila folder. The briefcase looked new and Main could smell the leather. Lenny flipped the file open. He selected a photograph from among the papers and asked, 'Do you recognise this man, sir?'

Main took the photograph and looked at the smiling man standing on a beach with a glass in his hand. He was holding it up to the camera as if to wish the photographer good health.

'Yes, Inspector, I do. This is one of the men from the pub the other night. One of the men I told you about.'

Lenny took another photograph from the folder and exchanged it with Main for the one he had.

'And this man, sir?'

Main looked at the snapshot. It was a different size from the first one and seemed much older; it was dog-eared at the corners, and showed a tall man with his arm wrapped around a plumpish girl wearing a low-cut blouse. He was wearing a Hawaian shirt and she had a flower in her hair, although the background suggested that they were still in the UK, possibly at some seaside resort – Blackpool or Brighton perhaps.

'Yes, him too,' said Main. 'He's the ringleader.'

The policeman exchanged photographs again with Main. This time for one of a young man in army uniform. He was standing at attention and Main thought his cap a little too large. It seemed to dwarf his face. The background suggested a military establishment. Possibly a passing-out day photograph, he thought. The face was considerably younger, but Main recognised him as another of the men from the pub.

'He was one of them too, Inspector.'

'Perhaps you'd like to describe the fourth man to me, sir,' said Lenny, taking back the photograph.

Main thought for a moment. 'Let me see. Five ten, broad-shouldered, red hair cropped very short, shaved round the ears. I think he wore a single gold earring. He was wearing a denim jacket and jeans when I saw him.'

Lenny nodded and said, 'That's the man sir.'

'Then you've caught them?' asked Main.

'No sir,' said Lenny, 'I'm afraid not. I'm sorry to have to inform you that these four men all died in a car accident earlier today. We obtained the three photographs from their relatives. There was none available for the fourth man, but your description fits the one we have.'

Main felt as if his world had just collapsed. 'What kind of accident for God's sake?'

'The car they were in caught fire, sir. None of them got out. As far as we can tell no other vehicle was involved.'

Main shook his head as if doubting that fate could be so cruel. 'But they were my only chance of finding Simon's body,' he said in a despairing whisper.

He got up and walked to the window as if seeking distraction from the truth. After a few moments of staring silently out into the blackness he turned round to face Lenny.

'I don't understand, how could none of them get out? Cars don't just burst into flames like that. If there's an electrical fire, you smell burning, maybe see smoke. You stop the car and get out. You said yourself that there was no other car involved. They were young, fit men for God's sake, not paralysed cripples!'

'Our people are looking into that at the moment, sir,' said Lenny. 'It appears that the petrol tank in the car exploded for whatever reason. It was an old car; there may have been some kind of leak and an electrical fault. Forensic will sort it out.'

Main remained silent for a moment before asking, 'Will you be talking to the relatives about the men's involvement in the disappearance of my son's body?'

'Yes, sir. Once they've had a chance to come to terms with the deaths.'

'How did you know these four were the men, Inspector?' asked Main.

'I didn't, sir. One of my colleagues from Traffic left the men's photographs on the desk for distribution to the press. It just struck me when I looked at them that they fitted the descriptions you gave me the other night.'

'That was quick of you, Inspector. I'm grateful to you for telling me.'

'Not at all, sir. I'll be in touch if there's any more news.'

Main showed Lenny out and closed the door behind him slowly and deliberately. He stood for a moment with his forehead resting against it and his fists clenched. His eyes were tightly closed. He tapped his head lightly and rhythmically against the door as he whispered, 'Damn them to hell.'

11

Around two in the morning the wind, which had been strengthening steadily for the past three hours, achieved true gale-force status and drove rain horizontally into the windows of Lafferty's bedroom with unrelenting zeal. He had been lying awake for some time, so he couldn't accuse the weather of having woken him, but the sound of a storm at that hour did nothing to ease his troubled mind. He was about to get up and make some tea when the phone started ringing. It startled him and he stared at it for a few moments as if it were an unwelcome intruder. There was always something unnerving about a phone call in the wee small hours. It couldn't be a social call; it had to be bad news. The best he could hope for was a wrong number. He picked up the receiver hoping he wouldn't have to dress and go out into the rain.

'Have you heard? They're all dead.'

The voice was male and sounded slurred, as if its owner had been drinking. There was still a chance it was a wrong number.

'Who is this?' Lafferty asked.

There was a pause. 'It's me, John Main.'

Lafferty felt embarrassed at not having recognised him. 'I'm sorry, this line's very bad. Who's dead?'

'All of them, all four.'

It suddenly dawned on Lafferty who Main was talking about, and his throat tightened. He felt as if a steel band was slowly being applied around his chest. 'The men from the cemetery?' he croaked.

'Dead,' repeated Main as if he could not believe it himself.

'How?'

'A fire. The police think the petrol tank in their car exploded. They all died.'

'I see.'

'Well I bloody don't!' growled Main. 'How could it happen? Sometimes I just don't believe my bloody luck!'

'Maybe luck had nothing to do with it,' said Lafferty thinking aloud and then regretting it. Main was obviously very drunk and he didn't want to discuss anything with him in this state.

'I don' unnerstand; what d'ye mean?' slurred Main.

'Nothing,' said Lafferty flatly. 'I'll call you in the morning.'

He put the phone down to avoid any further discussion, hoping it would not ring again in a few moments. It didn't. Lafferty was left with only the sound of the wind and the rain as it continued its unrelenting assault on the panes. Just what the hell was going on, he wondered. A knot of unease settled into his stomach. If Sarah Lasseter was right, John McKirrop had been murdered because of something he had seen in the cemetery that night. She was also convinced that his killer had access to

HTU. Now four other men who had been there were also dead. An accident? He found that hard to believe. But, if it was so important to someone to conceal what had happened in the cemetery that night, why had it taken them so long?

Lafferty shivered as he came up with a possible reason. The killer or killers had been biding their time; they had been coolly waiting until the murder of all four could be achieved at the same time and even conceivably be made to look like an accident! Lafferty found the audacity of this quite breath-taking, but it also suggested something else. If the killers had been prepared to wait, they must have felt safe in the interim. They must have been confident that the men would not say anything of their own volition. But they must have been watching them all the same. And then, when Main had found them and reported the matter to the police, they acted . . .

It all made some hellish kind of sense to Lafferty. The only thing he couldn't see at the moment was any kind of connection between the four dead men and HTU.

A particularly vicious gust of wind hit the bedroom windows and rattled them in their frames. Lafferty shivered again and went through to the kitchen to switch on the kettle.

John Main woke up with a splitting headache to add to the feeling of depression he had gone to bed with. He remembered calling Lafferty, but not too much of what had been said. Had he arranged to meet him, he wondered. He had a vague recollection of something having been said about talking later. Maybe the best thing would be to call him when he felt a little better.

The first step towards rehabilitation would be coffee,

he decided, but almost changed his mind when he sat up to get out of bed. His headache soared to new heights, paralysing him into immobility for a moment. Should he attempt to get up or just sink back down on the bed again?

Against his better judgement, Main continued with his slow rehabilitation and made it to the bathroom before having to rest for a moment with his hands on the sides of the wash-basin. He looked at himself in the mirror and then closed his eyes. What a mess, he concluded. What would Mary have said about him looking like this? It wasn't hard to guess. He could almost hear her voice in his ear telling him to pull himself together. He sluiced cold water over his face. It reminded him of the incident with the men in the pub. He still found it hard to believe that they were all dead. Fate was seldom kind, but this was just too much to bear.

Thinking about the fickleness of fate triggered off a hint of a memory of something Lafferty had said on the phone last night. Something about it not being fate? He vaguely recalled the priest hanging up just afterwards. He couldn't blame the man. The thought of having phoned him while being stoned out of his skull made Main cringe inwardly as he filled the basin with hot water to shave.

Even his skin felt sore as he pulled the razor around the contours of his face. If the men's deaths hadn't been down to fate or bad luck, what was Lafferty suggesting? That it had not been an accident? That they had been murdered? Main paused with the razor an inch from his face. He found the idea both alarming and exciting. The theory was much more attractive than bad luck or a quirk of fate. Main finished shaving and turned on the shower. His head still hurt, but the air of hopelessness had left him. If the four *had* been murdered it wasn't the end of the affair at all. It was scarcely the beginning. It meant, of course, that there were other people involved in the removal of his son's body. The thing he had to work out now was how to get at them.

Main stepped into the shower and let the water cascade on to his upturned face while he thought it through. There was no obvious way he could reach these anonymous people but that had initially been the case with the four who had just died. He adjusted the shower regulator to make the water a bit hotter. Maybe he could start with a little publicity. That should unsettle them at least.

They, whoever they were, must be feeling pretty secure now that everyone who had been known to be in the cemetery that night was dead. Perhaps he might start people thinking and asking questions by letting the newspapers know that the four men who died in the car fire were the same four who dug up his son. The police already knew, of course, but having the glare of publicity upon them wouldn't do his case any harm at all. The suggestion of murder might provoke some positive action from them.

Main towelled himself down lightly so as not to exacerbate his headache. It was only when he bent over to dry his toes that the pain soared again. He steadied himself on the side of the bath for a moment before returning to the bedroom to get dressed.

Lafferty was in the side chapel when he heard the phone ringing across in the house. The little chapel was his favourite place at St Xavier's. It wasn't really a chapel at all in the strict sense of the word, in that it wasn't separate from the church – just a small alcove off the left-hand aisle

– but it was somewhere he felt comfortable. It had a small altar covered with a fading purple cloth edged in gold, six chairs with wooden backs and raffia seating and, above them, a single stained-glass window depicting scenes from the Crimea. The chapel had been added to the church at the behest and expense of a wealthy local family at a time when wealthy families in the community held much more sway in church affairs than they do now. The family had all but died out in the area and only one elderly lady in the congregation, Miss Catherine Bell, represented the original benefactors for whom it had been named. The Bell Chapel had not, as was so often supposed, something to do with the church bells.

The chapel had never proved popular with the congregation, either as a place for silent worship or simply for contemplation, but Lafferty used it a lot for both. For some reason he couldn't fathom, he felt closer to God here. It afforded him perfect solitude. It wasn't hard to see why the others didn't like it. It faced north so it was cold and dark; sunlight never backlit its window. Even if it had, the Crimean scene on the glass was one of despair rather than hope, depicting wounded soldiers with bandaged heads leaning heavily on crutches fashioned from tree branches, led in single file from the battlefield by a nurse with a large red cross on her apron.

Lafferty hurried the short distance across to the house to answer the phone, suspecting that it would be John Main. It was.

'I'm ringing to apologise,' said Main.

'No need,' Lafferty reassured him.

'I just felt so awful last night, I climbed into the bottle.'

'Really, no explanations are necessary.'

'Thanks. Something you said last night started me thinking,' said Main, abruptly charging the subject.

'What was that?'

'Something about luck or fate having nothing to do with the deaths. What did you mean by that?'

Lafferty paused for a moment, wondering just how far he should go in voicing his suspicions. 'I'm not sure myself,' he said eventually.

Main seemed to understand his difficulty. 'I know it's hard to suggest anything without proof, but the coincidence factor in this case is just too high to accept without question.'

'I agree,' said Lafferty, relieved that Main had taken the initiative.

'The question is what do we do about it?'

'Yes.'

'I've decided to give matters a little nudge,' said Main.

'By doing what?'

'By telling the papers about the connection. What do you think?'

'Good idea,' responded Lafferty after a moment's thought. 'That should get other people asking questions, not just us.'

'That's the idea.'

'You'll have to be careful,' Lafferty said hesitantly.

'What do you mean?'

'Just that . . . if the four deaths weren't accidental we are dealing with some pretty nasty and powerful people. You might be putting yourself in the firing line, so to speak.'

'I've thought of that,' agreed Main. 'I'll watch my back.'

Lafferty returned to the Bell Chapel and tried to put thoughts of Main out of his mind. He had to think about Mary O'Donnell's funeral, the reason he had gone there in the first place. He desperately wanted to get things right on the day. Unlike so many funerals these days, where he knew neither the deceased nor the family and had to improvise on what few sketchy details he could glean, he did know the O'Donnells and what they were going through. In particular, Jean was having a crisis in the faith that had meant so much to her over the years and Joe was agonising over the strained relationship he'd had with his daughter before she died. Lafferty had a duty to these people. He had to present Mary's death to them in a way that would allow them to recover from it without lasting doubt and bitterness, not only thanking the Lord for Mary O'Donnell's life but explaining satisfactorily why she had died. In effect he needed to convince the O'Donnells that the Lord had had a purpose in . . . sending Mary over the handlebars to smash her skull on a tree. Lafferty leaned forward in his seat to cradle his head in his hands. Above him, cold light came in from the Crimean window. How could he convince them, he asked himself, when he didn't believe it himself?

The moment of crisis passed. It was time to keep busy, he decided. There was a great deal to do and throwing himself into his work would stop him agonising, albeit temporarily. It was taking the easy way out, but what was the point in actively pursuing mental agony when it seemed to find him all too readily as it was?

Sarah smoothed the front of her dress and touched her hair lightly as she examined herself in the mirror. It had been ages since she had dressed up properly to go out, and she felt good. The irony was that she wasn't actually going anywhere, but the reception for the Tyndall brothers was a good enough excuse. Paddy Duncan was going to escort her and she was looking forward to the occasion. She felt like a human being again instead of what she had been for the past few months, an automaton waiting for the next call out.

Derek Stubbs had told Tyndall that he would remain on duty in HTU in order to let 'other staff' attend the party. Sarah felt sure that he had only been collecting brownie points with a display of selfless dedication for Tyndall's benefit – she even suspected that he must have weighed up the pros and cons of going or not going to the party and had decided that the opportunities for furthering his career would not outweigh the opportunity of impressing Tyndall. But it didn't matter. What mattered was that she was going and she felt like a woman again. She applied a thin film of pale lipstick to her lips and snapped the cap back on before making a final appraisal in the mirror. 'You'll do,' she muttered as she heard a knock upon her door. It was Paddy Duncan.

'Stunning!' exclaimed Paddy.

'Thank you,' replied Sarah before collecting her bag and opening it to make sure she had her key.

'All ready?'

'Ready,' smiled Sarah.

'I feel we should be going out to a swish restaurant with you looking like this,' said Paddy. 'Instead, it's going to be Bulgarian red and hospital chit chat.'

'I'm looking forward to meeting the great Cyril Murdoch,' said Sarah. 'It's not often you meet someone who has genuinely made a real advance in medicine – a major breakthrough.'

'Steady on, advances are being made all the time,' said Paddy.

'But not real advances,' countered Sarah. 'You get the "i" dotters and the "t" crossers who leak their "breakthrough" to the press and then declare coyly that everything's at "a very early stage", as soon as they've got the publicity they set out to achieve. That's usually the last you ever hear of them. But this is different. This is real! *Herpes* infections are an enormous problem, much more so than most people realise, and this is only the beginning. We've always been painfully short of weapons to use against viruses. Antibiotics are useless against them and many other possible "weapons" destroy our own cells as well as the virus. Viruses need the co-operation of the DNA in our own cells before they can multiply and cause infection and that's going to be their Achilles' heel. Molecular genetic techniques like those Cyril used are going to be the way to fight them on their own terms. Believe me Paddy, this is only the beginning.'

'I suppose you're right,' agreed Paddy, amused at Sarah's obvious enthusiasm. 'I just hope you're not reading too much into it all.'

Sarah was aware of heads turning when she and Paddy entered the reception-room above the hospital's main offices and it pleased her. She did her best to appear nonchalant and responded to Paddy's offer of a drink with, 'I think it's coming to us.'

'How posh,' whispered Paddy as he saw the waitress approach. 'They're really pushing the boat out.' He collected two glasses from her tray and said to Sarah in a stage whisper, 'But I bet it's still Bulgarian.'

Sarah took in her surroundings while she sipped her

drink and responded at appropriate intervals to Paddy's observations. She couldn't see Murdoch Tyndall and said so.

'Over there in the corner,' replied Paddy, 'He's half hidden by Hugh Carfax.'

Sarah found the pathologist easily enough by virtue of his red hair and did her best to look round him. She managed to glimpse the silver hair of Murdoch Tyndall and saw that he was standing beside a much shorter man. 'Is that his brother beside him?' she asked Paddy.

Paddy craned one way and then the other before replying. 'Could be. I've never met him myself.'

'Doesn't look much like Murdoch,' said Sarah. She saw that Murdoch was charming those around him, as he usually did in company. He flashed a smile at regular intervals like a lighthouse and she could see the others in the group move their shoulders as they laughed at what he was saying. The shorter man, however, seemed strangely detached. He wasn't smiling and he didn't appear to be interested in what was being said. No stomach for small talk, she concluded.

'Shall we try to get closer?' suggested Paddy.

Sarah nodded enthusiastically.

There was food on a table near Murdoch Tyndall's group, and they used this as an excuse for moving in that direction. Paddy picked up a plastic plate from the pile at the far end of the table and moved slowly along its length, collecting a formidable mountain of food. Sarah accompanied him but took very little for herself. There would be time to eat later. Some people moved away leaving a gap behind Tyndall's group. Sarah steered Paddy towards it, ignoring his protest that he hadn't finished heaping his plate.

'You can get more later!' scolded Sarah, 'I want to meet the great man.'

'You're a medical groupie!' hissed Paddy.

'I only want to talk to him,' replied Sarah with a smile. 'Find out what makes him tick, see what sets him apart from the rest of us.'

'Luck,' said Paddy. 'Being in the right place at the right time.'

Sarah shook her head and said, 'No, I think there's more to it than that.'

'The stamp of greatness?' smiled Paddy. 'Don't believe in it.'

He saw that Sarah's smile was being directed over his left shoulder and half turned to see who she was smiling at. Murdoch Tyndall had detached himself from his group and was coming towards them. Paddy moved aside slightly to allow Tyndall access to Sarah.

'Dr Lasseter, you look positively ravishing,' said Tyndall. His eyes showed that he meant it. 'I'm so glad you could come.' He half turned towards Paddy and said, 'And Dr . . .'

'Duncan, sir,' said Paddy.

'Ah yes, Dr Duncan. Glad you could make it.'

'It was good of Dr Stubbs to remain on duty this evening,' said Sarah.

'Quite so,' Tyndall agreed, 'but I've arranged some relief for him later so he won't miss all the fun.'

Sarah exchanged glances with Paddy. So that's it, she thought. Stubbs was getting the brownie points *and* the party. He would no doubt appear in a couple of hours' time, still wearing his white coat and playing the role of the selfless, dedicated medic who had just managed to tear himself away from the care of the sick for a few moments.

'Good,' said Sarah.

She changed the subject quickly in case Tyndall had noticed a slight smile appear on Paddy's face. 'I didn't realise you had an interest in immunology, sir?' she asked.

Tyndall smiled self-deprecatingly. 'It's my brother who's the star, Doctor, but we discuss everything, and I contribute the occasional idea.'

'I'm sure you are being far too modest, sir,' said Sarah.

'I don't think you've met my brother, Doctor?' asked Tyndall, turning to the group behind him.

Paddy shot Sarah an amused glance which she found irritating. 'Frightening!' he whispered, as Tyndall called to his brother to join them.

The man who joined them was the short man about whom Sarah had wondered earlier. He still didn't smile, but nodded curtly and shook hands with both Sarah and Paddy in turn as Murdoch Tyndall introduced them.

'Congratulations, Professor,' said Sarah. 'A brilliant piece of work.'

Tyndall smiled for the first time, a shy introverted smile which told Sarah that he was uneasy in the company of women. 'It's kind of you to say so, Doctor,' he said. 'Do you have an interest in this kind of research?'

'I got interested in molecular biology at medical school, Professor, but there were so many other things to learn at the time that I couldn't give it as much attention as I'd have liked,' explained Sarah. 'I understand that you identified the molecular trigger sequence of the virus?'

'We did,' replied Cyril Tyndall.

'May I ask how?'

'Basically, we identified the repressor substance which normally binds to the trigger sequence of the virus.'

'That's what normally keeps the virus in check?' queried Duncan, anxious to be part of the conversation.

'That's right,' confirmed Cyril Tyndall. 'Once we'd done that, we could design a protein which would bind to the sequence irreversibly instead of being subject to degradation by UV light, stress etc.'

'So the virus is still present in the body?' asked Sarah.

'Yes, but it's no longer subject to periodic triggering.'

'Absolutely fascinating,' exclaimed Sarah.

'I think we are being called,' Murdoch Tyndall murmured to his brother. They all looked in the direction Tyndall was looking in and saw that the chairman of the board of management and the hospital secretary were both beckoning to the Tyndalls. One was smiling and pointing at his watch.

'I'm afraid it looks like speech time,' said Murdoch Tyndall, making an apologetic gesture with his shoulders and spreading his hands. 'See you later.'

Sarah and Paddy watched the brothers make their way through the crowd to the front of the room, Murdoch enjoying the greetings and congratulations on the way, his brother obviously embarrassed by it all, keeping his head down as if intent on watching where he was putting his feet. The crowd broke into spontaneous applause as the pair mounted the small platform to be welcomed with handshakes from the chairman of the board and several other men, whom Sarah didn't recognise but assumed to be something to do with management.

The hospital secretary made a short speech congratulating the Tyndalls on their achievement and reflecting on how much kudos their work would bring the hospital. The board of management took particular pride in being the first – he felt sure – of many bodies to honour the

Tyndalls for their work. This reference to future prize prospects brought more applause and murmurs of 'Hear, hear'. In reply, Murdoch Tyndall made a charming, self-effacing speech, giving the lion's share of the credit to his brother and saying that their greatest pleasure came from the knowledge that they had made a contribution to the fight against disease. There was more applause and the speeches were over.

The crowd became small groups again and chatter took over as the Tyndalls started to circulate, Murdoch doing the talking and smiling and his brother following along behind.

'So what do you think of the great man?' asked Paddy.

'I think he's rather sweet,' replied Sarah. 'It's strange how two brothers can be so different.'

'Chalk and cheese,' agreed Paddy.

'But both brilliant.'

'There ain't no justice,' said Paddy. 'Two geniuses are a bit much for any one family.'

'Makes you believe in genetics,' smiled Sarah.

She was about to follow Paddy to the buffet table when she suddenly realised that Cyril Tyndall had detached himself from his brother's coat-tails and was coming towards her. She had a moment's indecision, feeling that it must be someone else he was making for, before saying to Paddy, 'You go on. I'll join you.'

Tyndall came up to Sarah and smiled without parting his lips. 'I don't think we finished our conversation, Dr Lasseter.'

Sarah felt a flush come to her cheeks. A possible Nobel prize-winner had come all the way over to speak to her, and she felt flattered beyond belief.

'This is really very good of you, Professor,' she stammered.

'It is always a pleasure to speak to people who are research-minded. Do you plan to move into research yourself, Doctor?'

For the first time in her career Sarah felt embarrassed about admitting to her plans of going into general practice. She didn't like the feeling and blamed Stubbs for it, sensing that she was betraying her father. She told Tyndall of her intentions.

'That's a pity,' said Professor Tyndall. 'My brother tells me that you are an exceptionally gifted doctor. It would be a shame to see such potential go untapped.'

'It's very kind of you to say so,' replied Sarah, feeling overwhelmed by the thought that the Tyndall brothers had been discussing her.

'Perhaps you would like to visit my lab one day soon and we could talk further?' suggested the Professor.

'That's very kind of you, sir. I'd like that.'

'Just give me a call then. Murdoch will give you my private extension number.'

'Thank you, sir,' said Sarah, feeling overawed by the whole conversation. Professor Tyndall excused himself and returned to his brother's side as Paddy approached with another food-laden plate. 'You're getting on well,' he said before taking his first mouthful.

'Professor Tyndall invited me to visit his lab,' Sarah told him, still slight dazed.

'I'm not surprised. That dress of yours is absolutely stunning.'

Sarah turned on him with an angry look in her eyes. 'Of all the sexist nonsense,' she stormed, trying to keep her voice down while making her point forcibly.

'Is it?' replied Paddy. 'He didn't ask me.'

'Professor Tyndall recognised that I was interested in the research. I am! That's why he invited me.'

'Of course,' Paddy agreed, tongue in cheek.

'I'm quite sure the professor wouldn't mind if you were to come along too, if you're interested,' Sarah insisted.

Paddy smiled. 'Wouldn't dream of it. Playing gooseberry is not my style.' He grinned mischeviously as he saw the anger flash again in Sarah's eyes.

Realising he was baiting her, she calmed down and said, 'Enough! I'm hungry.'

For once, John Main was lucky. No one had been murdered or raped in the city that day, banks and sub post-offices had remained inviolate and nothing substantial had burned down. The only national story was the latest wrangle over EEC farming subsidies – not a natural for the local evening paper. So, although the first edtion led with a council tenant 'slamming' the council over dampness in his flat, the second and final editions hit the streets with CEMETERY FOUR DIE IN HOLOCAUST.

Main bought a copy from the newsagent on the corner of his street and read it on the pavement. Below the headline was a photograph of the cemetery in which Simon had been buried. It was the same as that used in the original story, but the coverage was what mattered. The story began with a recap of his son's disinterment and how the police had failed to make an arrest. Main felt pleased with himself as he read on. This was exactly what he had set out to achieve. A second photograph showed the burnt-out wreck of the car in which the men had died. There had been no other vehicle involved, and the circumstances of the fire remained a mystery. The police had refused to comment at this stage but their inquiries were continuing. Questioned as to whether foul play was suspected, Chief Superintendent Hamish Anderson had declined to speculate.

The final paragraph of the story was what pleased Main most. It included an eye-witness report of the car fire. Main hadn't known about this: the paper must have sent out a reporter to ask around the houses near the scene of the fire. He had come up trumps. A Mrs Katherine Donaldson had been leaving her house to go shopping when she had seen a car outside her gate explode. 'It was terrible,' she had said. 'There was a loud bang that shook my windows and flames shot out from the car. There was glass everywhere. No one got out.'

Main felt a glow of satisfaction. There had been an explosion. He was more than ever convinced the holocaust had been no accident. The men had been murdered. He called Ryan Lafferty and asked him if he had seen the story.

'No. What do they say?' asked Lafferty.

Main told him and Lafferty whistled softly. 'That should shake the police up. You did well.'

'I was lucky.'

'So now we wait and see what happens.'

'The nice thing is,' said Main, 'I think the papers are obliged to follow this up. That will keep the pressure on the police.'

'Excellent,' replied Lafferty, and then asked, 'How are you feeling?'

'Better. A lot better.'

'Good.'

'I'm thinking of going back to work.'

'I'm delighted to hear it,' said Lafferty. 'It's about time.'

Main smiled at Lafferty's directness and said, 'You're right. I want to thank you.'

'There's nothing to thank me *for*.'

'Yes there is,' countered Main. 'I was on the verge of giving up hope and you stopped me. Things are beginning to happen now and it's down to you. I think we're going to get to the bottom of this.'

'I hope so,' said Lafferty. 'But what I said in the beginning still goes. I'm sure your son's soul has been in no danger.'

'I just wish I could believe that, Ryan.'

'I know. Get some sleep,' said Lafferty kindly.

12

Main decided against wearing a suit; he felt that it would be too formal and might suggest that he was being re-interviewed for his own job. He opted instead for a sports jacket and slacks, checked shirt and university tie. Casual, but acceptably establishment. He parked the car outside the school entrance and walked up the gravel drive past the playing fields where the third year were at rugby practice. Hargreave, the principal teacher of physical education, was cajoling them into cohesive action instead of individual bids for glory. 'Pass it, you clown!' yelled the track-suited man as a large fair-haired boy was caught in possession. 'That's what team mates are for!'

'Yes sir,' mumbled the boy as he got to his feet and looked down at them.

'Rugby is a team game, boy! *Life* is a team game!'

'Well, that's taken care of that,' thought Main as he turned away and continued up the drive. The bottom line to centuries of philosophy had just been supplied by Hargreave. Why didn't they ask him in the first place? he wondered facetiously.

After the five-minute obligatory wait – important people never saw you immediately, Main thought – the headmaster welcomed him with a handshake and the offer of sherry. Main declined politely, fearing it might be a test of his sobriety, a paranoid thought born of guilt about his less than sober habits of the past few weeks.

'How are you feeling, Main?'

'Much better, Headmaster, thank you.'

'A bad business all round,' remarked the headmaster sympathetically. 'So you feel well enough to come back to us now?'

'Yes sir, I'd like to, if that's all right with you?'

'Well, naturally we'd all be delighted to see you back,' began the headmaster. 'But are you sure you're well enough? You've been through an awful lot lately, more than any man should have to contend with and we all feel for you. Mr Close was saying as much yesterday.'

'Yesterday?' asked Main, suddenly suspicious of an uneasiness that had crept into the headmaster's manner.

'There was a meeting yesterday of the board of governors and, with the newspaper story and all – it couldn't have come at a worse time really – you were very much on everyone's mind.'

'I see,' said Main cautiously.

'All this witchcraft business, and now the suggestion of murder being bandied about, and everything coming on top of the loss of your poor wife, well . . . we all felt that it might be for the best if you were to take your time about coming back. Maybe go on extended leave until this whole unfortunate thing is cleared up.'

'You mean it's all a bit embarrassing for the board of governors?' said Main flatly.

'That's a bit unkind, Main.' The headmaster looked hurt.

'But accurate,' countered Main.

The headmaster leaned forward and spread his hands on the desk. 'The governors have to consider the parents, John, and they are the most fickle and delicate of creatures at the best of times. With the recession biting deeply, recruitment figures for the school are on a knife-edge. Next year will be touch and go. We have to avoid . . .' The headmaster searched the air for a word. '. . . association of the school with any kind of . . . unpleasantness.'

'I see,' said Main tersely.

'This business about exploding cars and burning bodies smacks of . . . criminality.'

'A side of life you would rather the pupils at this school knew nothing about,' said Main.

'I really expected better from you, Main,' responded the headmaster, looking hurt again. 'I thought you would see sense.'

'I do, Headmaster. I see it very clearly. So I'm suspended? Or would you prefer that I resign?'

'There's no question of that, Main. Let's just give it some time and, with any luck, this whole business will be behind us by the end of term.'

'And if it isn't?'

The headmaster spread his hands on the desk again and looked apologetic. 'Then you must do what you feel is right, John. What's right for the school, as well as anyone else. But let's not even consider that.'

'Very good sir,' said Main, taking this as his cue to leave. He got up and shook hands with the headmaster but avoided his eyes. As he opened the door the headmaster called out, 'And don't forget, John, we're all behind you!'

Main closed the door behind him and paused for a moment. 'Yes sir,' he murmured. 'Life is a team game.'

It was after nine in the evening when he returned home. His feet were sore and wet and he was hungry. After leaving the school he had driven out into the country and parked the car in a lay-by before setting off on a long walk. He had walked for over three hours in shoes that weren't up to the conditions, at first oblivious to the fact but then becoming all too aware of wet feet and aching ankles as the rough ground took its toll. It had also rained, so his clothes were wet through. For the first hour or so he had not really noticed the discomfort, he was so confused and angry. He really feared that he was beginning to crack up.

Just as he thought he was beginning to cope again, the visit to the school had pushed him deeper than ever into depression. He felt entirely alone in a world where everyone was playing a part and no one said what they meant. He was beginning to question just about every value he had previously believed in. What the hell was the school all about? Just what were they training the pupils to become? Thoughtless puppets existing in their own little world, isolated from reality by a sea of 'niceness', ignoring anything 'nasty' in the firm and sure conviction that it would go away if you disregarded it for long enough? Jesus!

Main tried to clear his mind as he climbed the stairs to his apartment. He searched in his pocket for the door key and had difficulty extracting his hand because of the wetness of the material. He cursed out loud, and then the words froze on his lips as he saw that the door was already open.

He looked at the lock for signs of splintered wood, but saw that it appeared to be undamaged. He considered that he might have left the door open earlier, but almost immediately dismissed the idea as a non-starter. He could remember closing and checking it as he always did. The flat had been burgled less than two years before and he could still remember the awful feeling of knowing that a stranger had been in his home, helping himself to anything he fancied, opening everything, touching things.

He remembered the look on Mary's face when she realised that the burglar had been going through her clothes. It had been physical assault by proxy. The fact that some cash and electrical equipment had been taken had been a minor consideration in comparison to the mental anguish the break-in had caused them. There was no question of him having left the door unlocked today. But it had happened again.

There was a light on inside the flat. Surely the burglar wasn't still here? He pushed the door open a little and was puzzled. There was something odd about the light. It was too dim to be one of the room lights and . . . it was flickering!

Oh my God! The place is on fire, thought Main as he pushed the door wide open, but something in his sub-conscious stopped him believing it. There was no sound of fire – no crackling or roaring – and there was no smell of smoke. The flat was cold and absolutely silent.

Still moving cautiously in case anyone was still inside, Main stepped quietly into the hallway and moved towards the source of the light. It was in the living-room. He listened at the door for a moment before pushing it slowly open. The light was coming from a candle. It was mounted on some kind of a stick in the middle of the floor and had five flames coming from it. It was shaped like a human hand. The flames guttered in the draught from the open front door, and filled the room with dancing shadows.

Main looked into the other rooms in the flat before returning to the living-room and turning on the light. Nothing appeared to have been disturbed, although he would have to check further. Nothing, as far as he could see, had been damaged and all the drawers were still in place. Last time every drawer in the place had been taken out and emptied on the floor. The television and hi-fi equipment sat where they always did and he could see that a five-pound note he had put under an ash-tray on the mantelpiece earlier was still there.

'So what the hell . . .' he murmured as he moved closer to inspect the candle, 'is all this about?' He leaned over and blew out the flames.

There was a strong smell of candle-wax from the still smoking object as he lifted it off its spike. It was much heavier than he expected; he nearly dropped it. He was filled with a sudden feeling of horror as he turned it to look at the underside. The candle wasn't just shaped like a human hand; it was a human hand!

Main felt himself go weak at the knees as he dropped it and took an involuntary step backwards. His hand flew to his mouth and he gagged back the impulse to throw up. The seconds passed and he steeled himself to take another look at the thing. There was no doubt about it. It was a human hand that had been severed at the wrist and covered in candle wax to make it the most macabre object Main thought he had had ever seen.

Main picked up the telephone to call the police and

then had second thoughts. He called Ryan Lafferty instead.

'Could you come over here, please? Something's happened. I need to talk to you.' Main had difficulty speaking. Shock had constricted his throat.

'Can you tell me anything about it?' asked Lafferty, a little surprised at the request.

'Not over the phone,' replied Main, still staring at the hand on the floor. 'But please come.'

'On my way,' replied Lafferty.

He was there within fifteen minutes, and found the door to the flat open. He knocked gently but there was no reply so he tried again, this time calling out Main's name.

'In here,' came the reply. It sounded weak and distant. Lafferty followed it through to the living room where he found Main sitting on the edge of an armchair staring at something on the floor. 'Are you all right?' he asked.

Main pointed at the floor and Lafferty saw what he was looking at. 'Oh my God,' he whispered softly. 'Is it . . .'

'It's real,' said Main. 'Look at the underside.'

Without touching it, Lafferty moved to where he could see the severed portion of the wrist, which had not been coated in candle-wax.

The raw flesh had taken on a dull brown appearance, but it was unmistakably real. 'I could do with a drink,' he said. 'How about you?'

Main, still staring at the hand, replied, 'I'm trying to give it up.'

Lafferty looked at him, trying to make sense of what he had said. It was obvious that Main was in a state of shock. He went to the drinks cabinet and brought back two large brandies. Main accepted the glass and drank without taking his eyes off the hand. 'Whose?' he croaked.

Lafferty sat down on the other chair and looked at it. 'The hand of a murderer . . .'

The comment seemed to bring Main out of his trance. 'What?' he asked, turning to look at Lafferty.

'By rights it should be the hand of a convicted murderer.'

'You know what this is all about?' asked an incredulous Main.

Lafferty nodded and replied, 'I think so. It's a Hand of Glory.'

Main repeated the phrase, obviously still bemused.

'It's a witchcraft symbol. The hand of glory opens any locked door. It gives the one who made it access to anything and everything it desires access to. There's no escape.'

Main considered what had been said before concluding, 'So they want access to me.'

'I think it's a warning,' said Lafferty. 'They're telling you to back off because they can get at you any time they want.'

'How do you know all this?'

'I came across it in the book on Scottish witchcraft I told you about. The last time one of these was used was in North Berwick, not more than twenty-five miles from here . . . four centuries ago.'

'North Berwick?' exclaimed Main. 'But it's—'

'I know,' interrupted Lafferty. 'It's a sleepy sea-side resort where the kids go to make sand castles in the summertime and businessmen play golf on a Sunday. But it hasn't always been that way. In days gone by it was a hotbed of witchcraft.'

'Ye gods.'

'In the late sixteenth century there was a Grand Sabbat called at North Berwick. There were three complete covens in the area at the time; that's thirty-nine witches. The Grand Master of the Sabbat was a man called John Fian, a schoolmaster by day in nearby Prestonpans. It was said that he could open up North Berwick Church at will using a Hand of Glory. They used it for their meetings. His followers used to raid the churchyard and dismember corpses for their charms.'

'Do you think that's what they did to Simon?'

Lafferty didn't know what to say. He could see the pain in Main's eyes, but he could think of nothing comforting to say apart from, 'All this was a very long time ago and even if it was, it wouldn't change the fact that your son's soul is safe. Those people couldn't touch it.'

Main shook his head. 'I still can't believe this is happening. I mean, God! This isn't the middle-ages and yet we're sitting here talking about witches. It's crazy! This was all centuries ago!'

'Jesus Christ lived nearly two thousand years ago, yet his followers persist. I'm afraid we have to consider that the followers of darkness persist likewise,' Lafferty replied.

'What should I do, Ryan?'

Lafferty saw that Main was looking hopelessly vulnerable but, at a loss, he shrugged his shoulders. 'Frankly, I don't know.'

Main broke into a smile which took Lafferty by surprise. 'Good old Ryan,' he said. 'No bullshit. I think that's what I like best about you.'

Lafferty smiled back. 'I've always thought of it as a curse. The truth can be such a hard taskmaster.'

'Well I appreciate it,' said Main. 'Neither of us knows what to do.'

'I can't quite see why they're trying to warn you off with powerful signs of witchcraft,' said Lafferty. 'It doesn't seem to make sense.'

'Maybe they're trying to impress me. They're showing me how powerful they are, earning my fear and respect? After all, my front door is undamaged, but they walked in.'

'But why?' asked Lafferty. 'The matter is really out of your hands. You've told the papers all you know and the police are handling the inquiry, so why warn you off?'

Main thought for a moment. 'Maybe they see me as the prime mover, the instigator of the investigation, the one who won't let go.'

'Maybe,' said Lafferty, but he didn't sound convinced. 'I can't think of any other reason.'

'Me neither,' said Lafferty. 'Do you want to come back with me to St Xavier's?'

Main smiled. 'Sanctuary?'

'Something like that,' agreed Lafferty.

'No, but thanks all the same. I'm going to stay and take my chances. And when you think about it, I don't have a lot left to lose. Do I?'

Lafferty smiled wryly. 'I suppose from your point of view you haven't.'

'What are we going to do about that?' asked Main, pointing to the hand. 'I don't see any point in calling in the police. Do you?'

'There's the question of whose hand it is,' said Lafferty.

'But the chances are, from what you've said, that it was taken from a corpse.'

'Almost certainly,' said Lafferty thoughtfully. 'Although

they would have been hard-pushed to come up with the hand of a convicted murderer. It was usual to cut the hands off a corpse while it was still hanging on the gibbet.'

'If we bring in the police and the papers get hold of this they're going to have a field day,' said Main.

Lafferty nodded. 'I wonder if that's what they intended?'

'But that doesn't go too well with trying to warn me off,' said Main.

'No,' agreed Lafferty. 'No it doesn't. Have you got a plastic bag?'

'I suppose so,' said Main. 'You're going to take it away?'

'I'll put it in the furnace at St Xavier's,' said Lafferty.

Main went to the kitchen and emptied a plastic Tesco bag which still had groceries in it. He gave the empty bag to Lafferty who picked up the hand gingerly and dropped it into the bag. It hit the bottom with a slap and Main screwed up his face.

'I know,' said Lafferty. 'You and me both.'

It was a little after one in the morning when Lafferty got back to St Xavier's. The house was cold; the heating had gone off at ten. He lit the gas fire in his room and paused in front of it for a few moments to warm his hands. He didn't look at the plastic bag sitting on the floor beside him, but he was terribly aware of its presence. He decided that the sooner he got it over with the better. He would take it outside to the old hut that stood between the church and the house; it housed the central heating boiler – although calling it that bestowed an air of modernity on it which was entirely unjustified. The heating system was ancient, so old in fact that no heating firm in the

247

city would take up the challenge of servicing it. The same applied when the system broke down. When repairs became absolutely essential they were carried out by an old ex-marine engineer in the congregation who did what he could.

Feeling as if the night were alive with hidden eyes watching him, Lafferty left the house and took the plastic bag to the hut. He opened the door and was assailed by the twin smells of oil and mustiness. Closing the hut-door behind him, he turned on the light – a bare forty-watt bulb that hung from an old flex draped over a roof support strut. He felt his pulse quicken as he grew closer to the moment when he would have to touch the thing. He was unsure of whether some form of 'service' would be in order, so he hastily improvised a few words of prayer asking that the owner of the hand be granted peace.

As he removed the hand from the bag, his reluctance to touch it made him fumble and it fell to the floor. The candle-wax covering split open and he saw that there was a scar on its side. What was more, it was a scar he recognised! The last time he had seen this hand, its fingers had been clutching at the moon on the banks of the canal. It was John McKirrop's! Lafferty fought his revulsion to consider the significance of his discovery and found some horrific logic in it. If McKirrop had survived his injuries, the odds were that he would have been charged with the murder of the woman, Bella. This object at his feet was as near to the hand of a murderer as the constructors of the Hand of Glory could get. Such dedication to detail frightened Lafferty. It also forged another link between this nightmare and HTU.

Lafferty steeled himself to pick up McKirrop's hand between his thumb and forefinger. He opened the small iron door at the front of the furnace and threw it in before closing the door quickly and resting for a moment to recover his composure. God! he needed a drink. He closed up the hut and returned to the house where he poured himself a large brandy and took it into the bedroom; the gas-fire had warmed it up a bit.

Lafferty sipped the brandy slowly while he thought over the events of the evening, one he feared that he would never forget. But why? The question nagged at him. Why go to such lengths to advertise the involvement of witchcraft in the Simon Main affair? If the police could find out nothing about the practice of black magic in the area, and no one else could either, it was obvious that these people managed to conduct their affairs in complete secrecy. Yet suddenly, here they were, doing something totally out of character. They must have realised that the newspapers would have a field day if Main had called the police, just as they had when McKirrop had given them his tale of ritual disinterment. Why would they want that?

The truth dawned on Lafferty with a suddenness that took his breath away. What had, only a moment before, been so Byzantinely complicated and puzzling was now quite simple and terrifyingly obvious. He rubbed his cheek nervously as he sought to come to terms with an entirely new hypothesis. Taking a sip of his brandy, he noticed that his hand had developed a slight tremor. He had to think everything through logically, but his mind was insisting on taking great leaps. The new theory might be simple but, in its own way, it was also very frightening.

There was a notebook lying on the table beside the old hymn books, which he'd been using earlier to make notes about what he should say at Mary O'Donnell's funeral in the morning. He brought it over to the fire and sat down with it on his knee to jot down notes. McKirrop had been in the cemetery that night and had seen all that had gone on; there was no doubt about that. The four men, the 'yobs' as both McKirrop and Main had called them, had been there too: they had admitted it. It seemed likely that they had all been murdered to keep them from telling what they really saw that night. McKirrop had been hiding something despite apparently telling all to the newspapers, and the yobs had insisted that Main had got it all wrong. So what had they really seen in the graveyard? Main had concluded that there must have been more people present that night; important, powerful people who wouldn't want their identity revealed. People who were prepared to kill to keep their association with the black arts secret. This was still possible, and might even explain the Hand of Glory as a grim warning, but Lafferty preferred another explanation. The Hand of Glory had been a stunt designed by someone with a knowledge of the history of local witchcraft. The gruesome object had been used to keep himself and Main – and the police, for that matter – on the trail of devil worshippers. But there had *not* been other people in the cemetery that night. There had been no Black Mass or satanic ritual. Simon Main's body was missing from its grave because . . . *it had never been there in the first place*!

Lafferty considered and assessed the implications of his new theory. It meant that the powerful people behind this whole awful affair probably had nothing to do with devil worship or black magic. And whoever had killed the yobs knew *why* Simon Main had never been buried at all.

Lafferty ran through everything again, making sure that

it all fitted. The Black Mass story had most likely been an invention of John McKirrop. He had made the whole thing up to attract attention to himself, or perhaps he had even been paid to do it. Come to think of it, that may have been the reason he had ended up in hospital for a second time. Maybe he had got greedy and asked for more.

The four yobs had been just that. They had been drunken louts who had dug up a grave for kicks – something they hadn't really denied according to Main – but the coffin had been empty! That was why they had said Main had got it wrong when he accused them of stealing his son's body. And why they had referred to McKirrop as a liar in the pub where Main had first found them. But they could hardly have come out with a story like that after McKirrop's tale. Who would have believed them?

The big question now was, what had happened to Simon Main's body? Some kind of mortuary mix-up perhaps? It was not entirely unknown for such things to happen. In fact, it probably happened a great deal more often than anyone cared to admit. If couples could occasionally leave a hospital with the wrong baby in the back of the car, then surely which body went into which coffin was even more open to occasional error.

Lafferty had to dismiss the notion almost as quickly as it arose. If five people had been murdered, it was nothing to do with any kind of mix-up or mistake, however embarrassing it might have been. It was something much more serious and organised than that. He checked the time and saw that it was a quarter to two. He had a funeral to conduct in just over eight hours.

A slight lightening of the sky warned Lafferty that morning had come. He hadn't been to bed at all and felt relieved that daylight had returned – problems always seemed worse during the hours of darkness. He got up from the chair where he had spent the last few hours wondering what he should do about his new idea and went over to the window to look out at what was a cold, grey world. His legs felt stiff and the stubble on his face rasped against his collar when he turned his head. It made him think about shaving and hot water but that remided him of the furnace that would heat the water and what was fuelling it. It wasn't a bad dream; it had really happened. He shivered and rubbed his arms before shuffling through to the bathroom in his stockinged feet – removing his shoes had been his sole concession to undressing.

Feeling better after a shave and a hot bath, he made himself toast and tea and sat down at the kitchen table to eat while examining his notes for the O'Donnell funeral, not that they were copious. He had failed to come up with a magic formula for providing comfort in the circumstances. He had no idea why God had allowed such a thing to happen. It was going to have to be a variation on the theme of the ways of the Lord being strange. Have faith and trust in him; there are some things that we are not meant to understand just yet.

His mind started to wander again. He was still unde-cided about telling John Main about his new theory. The man was on an emotional knife-edge; he would have to be awfully sure of his ground before saying anything. He did, however, decide to contact Sarah Lasseter and tell her of his suspicions. If he was right about Simon Main never having been buried in the first place, then the starting point for any investigation would have to be in HTU, where the boy had died. He suddenly realised that he had provided a motive for the death of John McKirrop at the hands of one of the staff in HTU, something that he and Sarah had failed to come up with at the time of their last conversation. It made him more certain than ever that he was on the right track.

But time was getting on. He started to look out his vestments for the funeral.

The O'Donnells had decided that their daughter's body should be cremated, but they had also expressed a wish that there should be a short service at St Xavier's before going down to the crematorium. Lafferty had readily agreed, hoping at the time that this was a sign that Jean's faith was winning through. His hopes had been dashed, however, when Jean had explained that she hated the chapel down at the crematorium. 'It's a toilet,' she'd said when Lafferty had questioned her.

It was a view he could sympathise with. The crematorium chapel did not have much going for it in the way of atmosphere. It was a bare, almost circular room with doors diametrically opposed to each other so that mourners entered by one door and left by another. This was so that the chain of the day was unbroken. As one funeral party left, another arrived and the mourners did not bump into each other. As for decor, there was none. It was as impersonal as a hotel room. Not even the flowers were a constant. When each funeral was over the flowers left too.

It had already started to rain as Mary O'Donnell's coffin was brought into St Xavier's and laid down gently on its catafalque, in front of which Lafferty stood. He watched the mourners file in. Their dress ranged from charcoal-grey suits to fluorescent-yellow bomber jackets. Some of the relatives had obviously not seen each other for some time and gave exaggerated smiles of recognition as their eyes met before mouthing silent greetings. A number of women were sobbing and Lafferty could see that it was going to be a distressing service. Sobbing, like laughter, could be infectious.

Jean O'Donnell was not weeping. She stood beside Joe, who looked red-eyed and vulnerable, but she remained quite composed. Lafferty sneaked a look at her and saw that her eyes were cold. She was being sustained by bitterness. At that moment he would have given a lot to have tears run down her cheeks.

'We are gathered here today to give thanks for the life of Mary O'Donnell . . .'

13

Lafferty managed on autopilot until the first hymn took the pressure off him for a couple of minutes. When it ended, the sobbing in the church had become widespread. Several of the men were now holding handkerchiefs to their faces. Only Jean O'Donnell remained cool and composed. Lafferty felt himself become mesmerised by her. As the last chord of the organ faded away he decided it was time to throw himself on her mercy.

'As your priest, it is my job to explain things to you when they might not be obvious in themselves,' he began. 'Today you look to me to explain why a young life, that of Mary O'Donnell, has been taken away in the manner it was and I have to say to you that I cannot.'

Some of the sobbing died down as surprise took over. A murmur ran round the chapel. Lafferty met Jean O'Donnell's eyes and thought he saw a slight reaction there.

'I have to confess to you that I have no idea why God took Mary's life. It's as much of a mystery to me as it is to you. I, like you, will have to hope that there was a reason, a good reason, something perhaps that we might not be able to understand, but a reason nonetheless. The only comforting thought I can offer you is that there are lots of things in the universe that we in this life cannot understand. It would be arrogant of us to pretend otherwise, although we constantly do; it seems to be in our nature. Scientists offer us 'explanations' that rarely stand the test of time. Astrologers make predictions couched in broad generalities, expert opinions are constantly foisted upon us, we accept them because we cannot bear not knowing. Having said that, I feel I have to offer you my apologies for not being able to do better. You expected more of me, I'm sure, and for that I am sincerely sorry. For what it is worth, you have my heart-felt apologies.'

Jean O'Donnell had been looking at the floor while Lafferty spoke. When he stopped she raised her head slowly and met his gaze. Her eyes softened and she gave him a slight smile. Lafferty felt relief flood through him like a warm glow. He smiled back and continued with the service.

Lafferty travelled in the first car behind the hearse along with the O'Donnells. He and Jean did not say much, but he knew that it was all right between them again. Joe had not proved to be the problem he feared he might, and had seemed well-comforted with his deliberate references to 'Mary's loving father'. He was sobbing slightly as he sat with his arm round Jean, but Lafferty thought that was a good sign. Tears were such a wonderful safety-valve. It was a pity that men could not use them more often.

As the hearse turned in through the gates of the crematorium, Lafferty turned to Jean and whispered, 'I'll make it as brief as I possibly can.'

Jean nodded and Lafferty got out first to hurry into the chapel to see that everything was ready. It was. There was a faint aura of perfume left by the mourners from the previous funeral party, but the chapel had been cleared and the pall-bearers had positioned Mary's coffin expertly over the hydraulic lift so that it would be clear to sink down through the floor at the right moment without impediment. For the moment, it was covered with a purple cloth trimmed with gold, worn in places through constant daily use. It was almost worn out where it draped over the corners of the coffin. Its only function was to cover the hole left in the floor when the coffin sank down for disposal in the ovens.

Lafferty said a last few words and raised his hand in blessing. There was a slight whine as an electric motor primed the hoist and the purple cloth started to sink to the floor. Lafferty watched it and paled as an awful thought came into his head. *Was Mary O'Donnell actually in the coffin?*

Mary had died in HTU . . . as had Simon Main. Lafferty found himself breathing deeply as if on the verge of a panic attack. This was ridiculous, he told himself. But it was no use, he couldn't get the idea out of his head. Quite suddenly, he snapped shut his Prayer Book and, without saying anything to anyone, he hurried out of the chapel and looked around for an attendant. He saw one talking to one of the drivers of the official cars and rushed over to ask him where the furnace room was.

The puzzled man stubbed out his cigarette with his foot and pointed him in the right direction, saying, 'There's a flight of steps just behind these bushes.' Lafferty gathered up his vestments and broke into a run.

The steps leading down to the furnace area were

dangerously worn and wet. Their location in perpetual shade meant that they were covered in green moss and Lafferty almost lost his footing as he hurried down them. The experience made him slow down and think ahead. How was he going to handle this, he asked himself. He paused for a moment, breathing heavily, with his hands resting on the old wooden door at the foot of the steps. The coffin must be in the furnace room by now. There was no time to think up some convincing excuse if he was to see for himself that all was well. He turned the handle of the door and it opened.

It was warm in the corridor as he hurried along to where he could hear voices. He could also hear the clang of metal, and in his mind he saw a furnace door being shut. Was he too late? Had the coffin already been consigned to the fire? He turned into the room to find two startled attendants.

'Has the O'Donnell coffin gone in yet?' he asked.

The two men didn't ask who Lafferty was. They noted his vestments and one answered, 'Not yet, Father, is there a problem?'

'Where is it, please?'

The man pointed to a small room on Lafferty's left. He looked in and saw it was where the hoist ended up. He could see the trap door in the ceiling leading up to the chapel. On the floor to one side was Mary O'Donnell's coffin.

'I want to open it,' said Lafferty.

The men looked at each other and looked bemused. 'I don't understand,' said one. 'What's going on?'

Lafferty's head was spinning. He couldn't tell the men that he wanted to check that there was a body inside because of the chain reaction he would set off if there wasn't! He couldn't expect the attendants to keep quiet about it and what the news might do to Joe and Jean O'Donnell was beyond imagination. 'I made a promise to this young girl,' he lied.

'A promise, Father?' asked one of the men uncertainly.

'I promised her that I would see that she had a crucifix in her hand when she was put in her coffin.'

Lafferty had his back to the men; he was staring at the coffin. He screwed his eyes shut at the weakness of his improvised excuse. He could hear the organ playing in the chapel above.

'I thought she was killed outright, Father,' said the man who did all the talking.

Lafferty screwed his eyes tighter shut. 'No,' he lied. 'She came round briefly at the hospital. I spoke to her.'

It was always the way, he thought. You tell one lie and, before you know it, you're in real trouble.

'I see,' said the man. 'Well, in that case . . .'

'Thank you,' said Lafferty taking a breath and turning round. 'It won't take long. Do you have a screwdriver?'

The attendant who had remained silent fetched one and handed it to Lafferty. He seemed as if he was ready to watch the proceedings, as did the other man.

'I wonder if I could do this privately, gentlemen, out of respect for the poor girl?' Lafferty asked.

The men mumbled their agreement and withdrew from the room. Lafferty closed the door slightly so that they couldn't see in easily from outside and started to undo the screws securing the lid. Even when all of them were removed the lid remained securely in place. Lafferty, whose pulse rate was now topping one hundred and thirty, cursed under his breath. He could see that the problem lay in the varnish, which was acting as a glue. It must have been soft when the lid had been screwed down. He inserted the flat blade of the screwdriver between the lid and the casket and rammed it in with the palm of his hand. He had to repeat this at intervals along the side until he felt the lid become free. He paused for a moment, whispering, 'Forgive me, Mary,' under his breath before pushing the lid aside.

There was no body inside.

Despite his suspicion that this might be the case, it still came as a shock. He stared at what lay inside: several plastic bags filled with some kind of fluid to provide weight. He picked one up and squatted with it in the palms of his hands while he wondered what to do next. One of the men coughing outside reminded him that he didn't have much time. He had to make a decision and he made it.

Lafferty replaced the plastic weight and positioned the lid back on the coffin. Replacing the screws quickly, he stood up to compose himself for a moment before stepping outside and saying to the attendants, 'All done, chaps. Thank you.'

'Right Father, we'll get on with it then.'

Lafferty watched as the two men brought Mary O'Donnell's coffin out of the side room and placed it on a roller-topped trolley in front of the oven door. He drew back a little when the door was opened and a blast of hot air swept past him. The coffin was manoeuvred into position and slid inside. The door was closed and the gas turned up.

'Thank you gentlemen,' said Lafferty. 'I'm obliged to you.'

Most of the mourners from the O'Donnell funeral

had already left when Lafferty returned to the parking area outside the chapel. The next funeral was already under way and he could hear the sound of the twenty-third psalm drifting out into the cold damp air yet again. Jean and Joe had not yet left. It was clear that Jean had been holding up matters to wait for him. The driver of the car was looking at his watch.

'Sorry about that, Jean,' said Lafferty as he joined the O'Donnells.

'Is something the matter, Father?' asked Jean.

Lafferty looked her in the eye and replied, 'No Jean, nothing at all. Just a technicality.' Lying was getting easier by the minute, he noted.

Jean O'Donnell looked extremely doubtful, but the moment passed and she said, 'You'll come back to the house?'

'Of course,' said Lafferty, ushering Jean into the car.

It was two in the afternoon when Lafferty got back to St Xavier's. Mrs Grogan asked him if he wanted some lunch.

Lafferty said that he wasn't hungry. He had gone back to the O'Donnell's flat and had had boiled ham sandwiches.

'You made your own bed this morning Father,' remarked Mrs Grogan.

'I didn't make it, Mrs Grogan,' he replied. 'I didn't go to bed last night.'

'I see, Father,' said Mrs Grogan. 'Are you feeling all right?'

'Why do you ask?'

'You've been looking a bit off-colour lately.'

Lafferty smiled and thanked Mrs Grogan for her concern and said, 'I'm all right. I've just had a lot on my mind.'

'I see, Father.'

He looked at her and thought, no you don't Mrs Grogan. You most definitely don't.

Lafferty shut himself away in his study and poured himself a drink. He felt like a rabbit caught in the headlights of some heavy oncoming vehicle. He desperately wanted to go to the police and hand everything over to them. God! that would be so good. He could be free of the whole nightmare in one fell swoop. But he couldn't. He had to think of what it would do to John Main and the O'Donnells. Neither Main nor the O'Donnell family could cope with the stress of his awful secret being made public. Besides, by allowing Mary O'Donnell's coffin to be burned he had destroyed the evidence that it was empty. He picked up the phone and called the hospital; he asked to speak to Sarah Lasseter at HTU. He was told that Sarah was not on duty.

'When will she be on duty?' he asked.

'Dr Lasseter is due on at six. May I say who's calling?'

'Father Lafferty.'

'Very good, Father, I'll tell her.'

More waiting, thought Lafferty as he drained his glass. He couldn't face being trapped indoors until six. He had to seek distraction in doing something – something that demanded physical effort; that would make him hurt and take his mind off the problem. It had been at least two years since he had last gone for a run. There had been a time when running for charity had been much in vogue and he had felt obliged to join a group of younger members of the local churches in running for 'the world'. In the event, he had enjoyed the training runs and even taking part in the final event – a half marathon. He had hoped to keep it up but, like so many other things, the notion had faded as other matters made demands on his time. He tried to think where the kit he had bought at the time might be. In the end, he asked Mrs Grogan.

'Track suit?' she exclaimed.

'A Navy blue one with a green flash down the trousers as I remember,' said Lafferty, slightly irked that the notion of him going for a run should provoke such astonishment.

Mrs Grogan shook her head slowly, then her face lit up as she remembered. 'Oh yes, I know,' she said. 'I'll get it.'

'Just tell me,' he said, but it was too late. Mrs Grogan had rushed off. He shook his head. Mrs Grogan was getting on his nerves today. He concluded that this was more a reflection of his own state of mind than any fault of hers. His nerves were strung to breaking point; that was why he was going on a run in the first place.

Mrs Grogan came back with the track suit and Lafferty thanked her. He knew where his training shoes were; they were in a cardboard box in the hall cupboard along with the table-tennis gear for the church hall. Within five minutes he was running out through the gates of St Xavier's and heading briskly towards the park. For the first mile or so Lafferty could do nothing but think about the aches and pains that were developing in his limbs, but as his bones settled down and accepted that he wasn't going to stop just yet, his mind turned again to the nightmare. Finding out that Mary O'Donnell's coffin had been empty had proved that his suspicions concerning Simon Main's fate had been right. He need have no qualms about alarming John Main unnecessarily now. The question was just when and where to tell him. Perhaps it would be a good idea to arrange a meeting between the three of them – Sarah Lasseter, Main and himself. They could perhaps decide on a joint course of action.

Lafferty came to a particularly steep section in his chosen route and stopped thinking until he had crested the top and his breathing had settled down again. There was only one thing against involving John Main, he thought, and that was the fact that he was personally involved. His heart might rule his head, and that might make him a liability. On the other hand, the man had a right to know what had happened to his son and the mere fact that satanic ritual and black magic were probably not involved after all must surely afford him some comfort. Main was an intelligent man. Perhaps he could be constrained into following a jointly agreed course of action.

Lafferty decided that this was the way ahead. He would call Main after he had spoken to Sarah Lasseter. He was now sweating freely and the original sharpness of the pain in his limbs was being replaced by a dull ache as fatigue began to set in. This was the pain he had sought. It was going to dull his senses to everything else for the next half hour.

Sarah Lasseter called at six thirty. 'I got your message,' she said.

'Can we meet?' asked Lafferty. 'We have to talk.'

'I'm on duty until the morning,' said Sarah.

'And then you'll have to catch up on some sleep,' said Lafferty thoughtfully. 'That would make it some time tomorrow evening . . .'

'I wish!' said Sarah. 'I'm back on duty at two in the afternoon tomorrow.'

'Oh dear,' said Lafferty. 'I didn't realise . . .'

'Most people don't, Father.'

'Are you the only doctor on duty tonight in HTU?'

'Yes, why?'

'Could I come up there?'

The suggestion took Sarah by surprise. 'I suppose so,' she said uncertainly.

'I don't want to cause you any problems,' said Lafferty quickly. 'Just say if you think it's not a good idea.'

'No,' said Sarah firmly, now that she had had time to think. 'I don't see that anyone could object. We can talk in the doctors' room and I'll be here if anyone needs me.'

'Good,' said Lafferty. 'What time would be best?'

'Let me see . . . Let's say, any time after eleven. The nursing staff will have changed by then and everything should be settled for the night. With any luck we won't be disturbed.'

'I'll come at half-past,' said Lafferty.

'See you then,' said Sarah.

'Oh, one more thing— '

'Yes?'

'I'd like to bring somebody with me.'

'Who?'

'John Main.'

'Simon Main's father?'

'Yes.'

'Can't you give me an idea what this is all about?' asked Sarah.

'Later,' said Lafferty.

'Very well,' she sighed.

•   •   •

Lafferty called John Main at home. He let the phone ring a good long time, but there was no reply. He berated himself for not considering the possibility that Main might be out and decided to try Main's number at half-hourly intervals until it was time to go to the hospital. Main answered at half-past nine.

'I tried to get you earlier,' said Lafferty.

'I went to a seance,' explained Main.

'I see,' said Lafferty, wondering about Main's state of mind and considering whether it was such a good idea after all to involve him at this stage.

'I thought I might meet someone to give me some idea how to get at these bastards,' said Main. 'But it was just a bunch of housewives playing themselves. They were about as close to satanism as Mother Theresa.'

Lafferty was relieved. Main hadn't gone to the seance in some kind of desperate attempt to contact his son, as with the ouija board incident, but in logical pursuit of his investigation. 'Can we meet?' he asked.

'Tonight?' asked Main, obviously surprised.

'It's important. I want you to come with me to the hospital. We're going to meet with one of the doctors there. I've got something to tell you both.'

'You know something about Simon?' asked Main.

'Yes,' replied Lafferty. 'I do.'

Main arrived at St Xavier's at eleven fifteen and Lafferty offered him a drink. He declined and asked what it was that Lafferty had discovered.

'I don't want to say just yet,' replied Lafferty. 'I want Dr Lasseter to hear what I have to say at the same time.'

'Can't you give me a clue?' asked Main, betraying his frustration.

'You won't have long to wait,' soothed Lafferty. 'I said we'd be there at half-past.'

Main looked at his watch. 'We'd best get started then. Your car or mine?'

'Mine,' said Lafferty.

The hospital was quiet at that time of night and Lafferty had no trouble parking inside the gates. He left the car in an empty bay of three spaces marked, CONSULTANTS ONLY, saying to Main, 'I'm sure there won't be too many consultants abroad at this time of night.'

Sarah Lasseter had been keeping an eye open for them; she saw them as soon as they appeared at the doors to HTU and let them in. She greeted Lafferty and was introduced to John Main. Sarah was keeping her voice low and the others took their cue from her to do likewise. 'In here,' she said, ushering them into the doctors' room.

Lafferty noticed the duty nurse crane her head from where she sat at the console at the head of the ward to see what was going on, but Sarah did not approach her to provide any explanation.

'Would anyone like coffee?' asked Sarah. Lafferty sensed that she was nervous. Both he and Main declined. Sarah poured herself some and sat down to face them at the table.

'This is all very mysterious,' she said.

Main said to her, 'If it's any comfort it's as much a mystery to me.' They both turned to Lafferty who was having difficulty in knowing where to begin.

'First,' he said. 'I must ask for your assurance that when you've heard what I have to say, it will go no further without all three of us agreeing?'

267

Sarah and Main exchanged glances before giving their assurances.

Lafferty took a deep breath and began. 'Yesterday I officiated at the funeral of a young girl called Mary O'Donnell. She died here in HTU, just like Simon. She was involved in a motor cycle accident.' Lafferty looked at the floor for a moment in silence before adding, 'Only I didn't.'

'I don't understand,' said Sarah.

'Nor me,' said Main. 'You didn't what?'

'I didn't really officiate at Mary's funeral because Mary herself did not attend. She wasn't in the coffin.'

Sarah's mouth fell open. Main looked equally shocked.

'She wasn't in her coffin any more than I believe your son, Simon, was in his,' continued Lafferty turning to Main.

'But this is . . .' Main could not find words.

'Beyond belief?' asked Lafferty. 'I thought so myself when the idea first occurred to me, but now I'm in no doubt. Simon's body, Mary's body, and God knows how many others, never actually made it to their funerals.'

'But what happened to them?' exclaimed Sarah.

Lafferty looked at her and said, 'That's what I was rather hoping you might be able to help with.'

'Me?' exclaimed Sarah.

'The answer must lie here in HTU. Both Simon and Mary died here,' said Lafferty.

'How do you know Mary wasn't in her coffin?' asked Sarah.

'I looked,' replied Lafferty.

'But how can you be sure about Simon?' asked Main who had been lost in his own thoughts.

'I can't be, absolutely,' agreed Lafferty, 'but everything points towards it when you think about it.'

He told Main how his suspicions had been aroused after the incident with the severed hand. 'It was just too over the top,' said Lafferty. 'Someone was too keen to have us believe in the satanist scenario. The down-and-out, McKirrop, must have given them the idea when he lied to the police and the press about that night. The only thing he saw in the cemetery was an empty coffin. That was why he was killed, to keep his mouth shut and perpetuate the devil worship theory. It's ironic really. It's my guess he made up the hooded men story to avoid identifying the yobs; they probably threatened him. As it turned out, this suited the real villains very well. There was no missing body for them to explain and the yobs could hardly speak the truth because no one would believe them, least of all after McKirrop's tale. McKirrop himself must have threatened to tell the truth, and that's what made him dangerous. They killed him, then when John got close to the tearaways and the police were called in that made them dangerous too.'

'It does make a lot of sense,' agreed Sarah.

'So what did happen to Simon's body?' asked Main.

'I don't know,' confessed Lafferty. 'That's what we have to find out and I think our best chance of doing that is if they, whoever they are, don't know we suspect anything.'

'Where do we begin?' asked Sarah.

'Tell us what happens when a patient dies in HTU,' said Lafferty.

Sarah shrugged her shoulders and said, 'The nursing staff prepare the body, the hospital porters are called and the body is removed to the mortuary. The relatives then instruct a firm of funeral directors and they take it from there.'

'What does that involve?' asked Main.

'The funeral directors either come and measure the body themselves or have some arrangement with the mortuary attendants to do this. They then come with the coffin, put the body in it and take it away.'

'So the funeral firm's men actually see the body?' asked Lafferty.

'Yes,' replied Sarah. 'Unless . . .'

'Yes?'

'Unless the patient has died from some highly contagious disease. In that case the body would be sealed in a special bag and then placed in a specially designed coffin which the director might supply, but he wouldn't necessarily be present when the body was enclosed.'

'That hardly applies in this case, does it?' said Main.

'No,' agreed Sarah.

Suddenly the door of the room was opened and Derek Stubbs came in. Sarah stiffened.

'I'm sorry,' said Stubbs in a tone that said that he wasn't. 'I didn't realise you were entertaining, Dr Lasseter. I thought you were on duty.'

'I am, Dr Stubbs,' replied Sarah. 'Was there something?'

'I came by to take a look at the Keegan boy. His tests this morning seemed to suggest he was going downhill. But if you're busy . . .'

Sarah got up and excused herself to Main and Lafferty. She followed Stubbs out of the room. The tension between them persisted while they stood on either side of the patient's bed and ran through the monitor read-outs together. As Stubbs finished noting down the last reading

270

into his Filofax he said, 'I thought you realised, Doctor, that being on duty meant giving your undivided attention to your patients.'

'When they need it, they have it,' replied Sarah, but she knew that Stubbs had the upper hand. He was not going to let her off lightly.

'I hardly think that socialising with your friends is compatible with giving "undivided attention" do you?'

'I am not "socialising with my friends", as you put it,' replied Sarah. 'Mr Main and Father Lafferty had something they wished to discuss with me.'

'Main?' said Stubbs.

'Simon Main's father,' said Sarah. 'You may remember, Simon was a patient here in HTU. He died.'

'I remember,' said Stubbs. 'What exactly do they want?' he asked, now more puzzled than annoyed.

'I'm not at liberty to say,' replied Sarah, intrigued by the change that had come over Stubbs.

'If it concerns HTU in any way, I should be told,' Stubbs said angrily. 'Do I have to remind you that you are a junior doctor in this unit?'

'I don't think so,' replied Sarah evenly. 'I think you have made that perfectly clear to me on every conceivable occasion.'

'I demand to be told what's going on.'

'And I must repeat that I am not at liberty to say.'

'You leave me no alternative but to inform Dr Tyndall of this,' Stubbs warned.

'As you wish, Doctor,' replied Sarah coldly.

Stubbs stormed out and Sarah let out her breath in a long sigh. The staff nurse at the console who had been out of earshot, though aware that all was not well, gave her a sympathetic shrug. Sarah returned to the doctors' room.

Lafferty got up from the table and said, 'This is all my fault. We should never have come here. Perhaps I could speak to Dr Tyndall and explain that you are not to blame?'

Sarah smiled her appreciation and said, 'Dr Stubbs and I simply do not get on. He wanted to know what you were doing here.'

'You didn't tell him?' said Lafferty.

'No, that was why he was so angry.'

'Maybe we should go?' said Main.

'No,' said Sarah firmly. 'He has already decided to report me to Dr Tyndall but that's of no consequence. We have to find out what happened to Simon and Mary. Now, where were we?'

Lafferty gave Sarah a look of admiration. 'We were discussing whether the funeral directors would know if a body was missing.'

'And there's something we have been avoiding discussing for my benefit,' said Main.

Lafferty and Sarah exchanged a silent look.

'We haven't discussed *why* the bodies went missing,' said Main. 'We haven't discussed who would want them.'

'No, we haven't,' agreed Lafferty quietly, a bit unsure of Main's intentions and considering the possibility of an imminent explosion.

'Dare I suggest that we all know why the medical profession might want to hang on to the bodies?' asked Main. When Lafferty and Sarah did not respond he added, 'Spare parts.'

There was a slight tremor in Main's hand, Lafferty noted, but he seemed to be well in control of himself. Lafferty said, 'I have to confess that the thought had occurred to me.'

'Me too,' agreed Sarah.

'I refused permission when I was asked at the time,' said Main.

'So did the O'Donnells,' added Sarah.

'But some bastard thought they would go ahead anyway,' said Main bitterly.

'Unfortunately, I think you may be right,' said Lafferty.

Main folded his hands on the table in front of him and made a gesture of frustration with his shoulders before saying, 'The ironic thing is, I don't really mind. At the time when I was asked, I was consumed with grief and couldn't bear the thought of anyone interfering with Simon's body. I refused point blank . . . it was almost a reflex action. But if I had been asked a little later, or in slightly different circumstances, I think I would have said yes. But I wasn't.'

Lafferty nodded his understanding and Sarah gave Main a smile of encouragement.

'The really ironic thing,' said Main, 'is that I actually had feelings of guilt after the funeral about having said no!'

Lafferty was glad that Main was speaking openly about his feelings. Main seemed much more comfortable with the new explanation of his son's fate than anything involving satanism or the occult. It was almost as if he felt relieved by it.

'So what we are dealing with is a scandal,' said Main.

'A scandal involving murder,' Lafferty corrected.

'So it's an organised scam . . . involving organs to order?' suggested Main.

'I suppose it could be,' agreed Sarah cautiously, 'but do you realise what sort of organisation that would involve?'

'Tell us,' said Lafferty.

'Our patients would have to be tissue-typed before their death to match up with the "orders". The organs would have to be removed very quickly after death, which would involve surgeons and theatre facilities standing by, and then there's transport. I just don't see how all this could be arranged secretly.'

Main said, 'Maybe I'm cynical but I tend to think that if the money is big enough most things can be arranged.'

'So who is doing it?' Lafferty asked Sarah suddenly.

'Stubbs,' she replied almost automatically.

'You're sure?' asked Lafferty.

'I know I'm biased because I dislike the man so much, but everything points to it,' said Sarah. 'He has a bee in his bonnet about getting transplant permission. He thinks Doctor Tyndall should press much harder for it and gets annoyed when he doesn't. I've heard him complain that Tyndall's been far too soft on several occasions.'

'I remember now,' said Main. 'Stubbs asked if he could have a word with me after Simon died, but Doctor Tyndall stopped him. I didn't know what it was about at the time but now what Tyndall said makes sense. He told Stubbs that the matter was closed. I had made "my decision".'

'This was after you had refused permission for organ removal?' asked Lafferty.

'Yes.'

'And then there's his involvement in John McKirrop's death,' said Sarah. 'I'm sure it was him.'

Lafferty told Main about the suspicious circumstances surrounding John McKirrop's death.

'Did Stubbs recognise us?' asked Main.

'I told him who you were,' replied Sarah.

'Then you must now be in danger,' said Main.

'I didn't tell him why you were here.'

'He'll work it out for himself,' said Lafferty.

'Maybe we could make something up?' suggested Main. 'An alternative reason for our being here.'

'At midnight? The father of a boy whose body went missing and the parish priest who has an interest in both John McKirrop and Mary O'Donnell? Would you believe an alternative explanation?' asked Lafferty.

'No,' conceded Main. 'I wouldn't.'

14

'So what do we do?' asked Main.

'I'll just have to be very careful,' Sarah replied.

'I don't think that will be good enough,' said Lafferty.

'Then what?' asked Sarah.

'You'll have to get out of here,' said Lafferty flatly. Main drew in his breath. Sarah looked shocked.

'But her career . . .' said Main.

'It's her life we have to consider,' said Lafferty. He looked at Sarah and said, 'Perhaps there's a way you could take some leave or arrange some kind of secondment until this business is over.'

Sarah put her hand to her head. 'I hadn't thought . . . I don't know . . . I don't want to run away. I'm in it too, you know.'

'But Ryan's right,' said Main. 'It's too dangerous for you to continue working here. You must see that.'

Sarah nodded reluctantly, then an idea seemed to strike her. 'I met Doctor Tyndall's brother at the reception the hospital gave for them over the new vaccine. It's just possible that I could spend some time in his research lab up at the university medical school. That way I would be away from Stubbs, but still be around to keep in touch with you two.'

'That sounds a good idea,' said Lafferty.

Main agreed. 'You'll speak to Doctor Tyndall about it tomorrow?' he asked.

Sarah promised she would.

'So how do we go about proving it?' asked Main. 'We can't go to the police without something concrete in the way of evidence. I suspect they will need more than Ryan's word that Mary O'Donnell's coffin was empty and an informed guess that Simon's was too.'

Lafferty agreed and said, 'Stubbs must have accomplices. I think we're all agreed on that. Maybe that's where we'll find the weak link. We need someone who'll talk. From what Sarah told us about the routine procedure after a death, someone must be being paid to turn a blind eye to certain irregularities. Do we know if the same firm of funeral directors was used in both Simon's and Mary O'Donnell's case?'

'I used Maitland Stroud in Morningside,' said Main.

Lafferty's shoulders sagged. He said, 'The O'Donnells used Granby's in Dalkeith Road.'

'They can't all be in on it,' said Main.

Lafferty looked at his watch and saw that it was after one. 'Let's sleep on it,' he suggested.

'Some of us,' smiled Sarah.

'Sorry,' said Lafferty. 'You'll call me tomorrow when you've spoken to Doctor Tyndall?'

Sarah said that she would. She accompanied Main and Lafferty to the door where they parted with whispered goodnights.

·   ·   ·

Main and Lafferty did not speak again until they were inside Lafferty's car. They both seemed to sense that the hospital was no longer a friendly place. It had become alien, threatening, a place to fear rather than trust.

'Do you think it's worthwhile asking the undertakers whether they actually saw Simon's body?' asked Main.

'No,' replied Lafferty firmly.

'Why not?'

'If they did we'll be no further forward and if they didn't, and didn't say anything about it, it means that they're involved so they won't tell us anyway. Either way, we would be advertising our suspicions. It would get back to Stubbs.'

Main accepted what Lafferty said without comment for a moment, preferring instead to watch the road as they twisted and turned through the dark and largely deserted streets. 'You're right,' he conceded. 'I'm just not thinking straight.'

Lafferty smiled as he flicked on the wipers to deal with the drizzly rain that had just started. 'You're doing just fine,' he said. 'None of this can be easy for you.'

'You know, I actually think I'm glad things have turned out this way,'

Lafferty stayed silent.

'It actually gives me a good feeling to think that part of Simon is alive inside someone else.'

'Good,' said Lafferty quietly.

'Even if it turns out that his body was used as part of some crooked medical scam involving millions, I'll still be glad. It won't matter who the patient is, whether he's the son of an Arab sheikh or a Texas oil millionaire. Just as long as the kid's alive thanks to Simon.

'I think that's the right view,' said Lafferty.

'I just wish I could have said yes at the time, instead of going through all this,' said Main. 'But Dr Tyndall asked me at precisely the wrong moment.'

Lafferty brought the car to a halt outside Main's apartment block.

'Would you like to come up for coffee or a drink?' Main asked.

Lafferty shook his head and said, 'Let's both get some sleep. We need it.'

As Lafferty drove back to St Xavier's his thoughts turned to Sarah Lasseter and the danger she was in. He comforted himself with the thought that Stubbs couldn't afford to harm her while he and Main were around. It would be too obvious. So what would Stubbs do? He would secure his position, Lafferty decided. He would take extra care to see that no one got careless. He would take no risks at all until Sarah Lasseter and her prying friends had disappeared from the scene. That might make the investigation doubly difficult but surely with something this big there had to be some way of getting inside it.

Lafferty decided to leave the car parked on the road rather than go to the trouble of getting out to open the gates leading to the parking area beside the house. He took the short cut through the old churchyard, his feet crunching on the stones of the path as he skirted the church to reach the house. As he rounded the last corner, he came to an abrupt halt and his blood ran cold at the sight that met him. There wasn't much light, but he could see that an animal was nailed to his front door. As he drew nearer he could see that it was a cat. Its stomach had been slit open and its entrails were hanging out. The smell made Lafferty put a hand to his face. He looked away for a moment and saw something else that made his heart stop. There was a body lying in the shadows beside the door.

He squatted down and turned the body so that he could see the face. It was Mrs Grogan! He felt for a pulse and found one; she was alive, she had just fainted. He gathered her up in his arms and carried her round to the side door. Once safely inside, he called the police and Alan Jarvis, whom he knew was Mrs Grogan's GP. He was also Lafferty's, though he seldom had need of him. Mrs Grogan came to before either had arrived and Lafferty had to calm her through her initial panic at the recollection of what she'd found on the door.

'I came round about ten o'clock,' she stammered. 'I'd forgotten to take my magazines home earlier so I thought I'd pick them up on my way home from my sister. But when I got to the door— '

Mrs Grogan buried her face in her handkerchief and Lafferty put an arm round her shoulders. Outside, cars were starting to draw up.

Lafferty glanced at the clock and saw that it coming up to two. This was shaping up to be another night without sleep, and it was beginning to tell on his patience. Mrs Grogan had been suitably soothed and sedated by her GP and the police had agreed to take her home. Other policemen, however, had remained to ask just about every stupid question they could think of, in Lafferty's view. He had expected the incident to be dealt with by a Panda crew but they had been joined by a full inspector and his sergeant from CID. It was Inspector Lenny, the officer who had attended on the canal bank.

'Because *you* are involved sir,' replied Lenny, when Lafferty asked why someone so senior had come.

'I don't understand,' said Lafferty, suddenly feeling apprehensive.

'It goes something like this, sir,' said the policeman, holding Lafferty's gaze as if it were some kind of test. 'You were the priest who was looking for McKirrop to ask him about witchcraft in the cemetery. You were the priest who found him dead. Now you are the priest who has a black cat nailed to his door. You seem to lead an exciting life, sir.'

Lafferty remained silent.

'And now you are going to tell me that you have no idea who did this or why. Am I right, sir?'

Lafferty nodded. 'Quite right,' he said. 'I've absolutely no idea.'

It was the police inspector's turn to keep quiet while he stared at Lafferty disconcertingly. Eventually he said, 'I'm no expert, sir, but I would think that a cat nailed to your door had something to do with black magic or satanic ritual, or am I wrong?'

'That would be my guess too,' agreed Lafferty.

There was another long pause before Lenny said, 'Frankly sir, we – the police that is – have been having a hard time over what happened to the Main boy. We've not been making any headway because no one will speak to us about black magic or devil worship.'

'I see,' said Lafferty. 'It can't be easy for you.'

'No sir. We're becoming paranoid about it. I'm even inclined to think that you just might know a good bit more than you are letting on.'

Lafferty shrugged and said, 'I assure you, Inspector. I know as little about the subjects you mentioned as you do.'

'Your cleaner had a bit of a shock tonight, sir,' said the policeman, changing tack.

'Quite so,' said Lafferty.

'My driver said she was still quite distraught on the way home. Mentioned something about you having books on witchcraft in the house, your bed not being slept in, things like that.' The policeman paused to watch the effect of what he was saying before continuing. 'I realise of course that she was upset and all this might be— '

'Ill informed tittle-tattle,' interrupted Lafferty. 'And that's exactly what it is.'

'If you say so, sir.'

'I do.'

Lenny exchanged glances with his sergeant and got to his feet. He said, 'Well, we'll be getting along, sir. If there is anything else you might like to tell us, please get in touch.'

'I will.'

The inspector smiled and said as a parting shot, 'After all, sir, we're all on the same side, aren't we?'

The policeman clearly thought he'd had the last word and had turned to leave when Lafferty said, 'Have you had the forensic report on the four men who died in the car fire, Inspector?'

The policeman stopped in his tracks and turned. He seemed surprised by the question.

'Yes sir, as a matter of fact we have. I understand there were no suspicious circumstances. A short circuit in the electric fuel pump seems to have been the culprit, caused by a leaking fuel can in the boot just above it. An act of God, you might say.'

'I'm not too sure that God will be happy to take the blame for that one, Inspector,' said Lafferty.

'What are you inferring, sir?'

'Nothing Inspector. Let's just say you are not the only one suffering from paranoia.'

Lafferty watched the police circus depart. His eyes followed the black plastic bag that contained the cat and its message of black magic. His lips broke into a wry smile. 'Not convinced,' he murmured. 'Not convinced at all.'

Sarah had little time for brooding. Several patients in HTU had a disturbed night and she was on call constantly. For the most part it was a case of altering the settings on the life-support systems, but for one patient, Martin Keegan, it was the end of the line. He was the patient that Stubbs had called in to see earlier when he had found her with Lafferty and John Main. Keegan had been involved in a road traffic accident. His car had swerved across the central reservation of the M8 motorway and hit an oncoming heavy goods vehicle. In addition to severe head injuries, he had suffered extensive damage to his left leg and foot where he had been trapped in the wreckage. Stubbs had been right about his condition; it had been worsening. At a little before seven in the morning, he lost all trace of brain function. Sarah repeated the Sigma probe tests at the most sensitive setting but still could find no trace of activity.

'No good?' asked the staff nurse.

Sarah shook her head. 'Afraid not,' she said.

'Dr Stubbs didn't think he was going to make it,' confided the nurse. 'He asked that he be informed if things got worse.'

'Really?' asked Sarah, surprised. 'I didn't get that message.'

The nurse was uncomfortable with this news. She said, 'There was a message left at the nurses' station.'

'I see,' said Sarah. 'Have you any idea why Dr Stubbs made this request?'

'I understand he wanted to speak to the relatives personally,' replied the nurse.

'But Dr Tyndall always speaks to the relatives,' Sarah said.

The nurse shrugged as if she was unwilling to get any deeper into this particular conversation.

'All right. Thank you, Staff,' said Sarah with a smile. 'You had better call him, but give me five minutes first will you?'

The nurse nodded her agreement and Sarah went back to the doctors' room. What the hell was Stubbs up to this time? Was this the new plan? Get in first with the relatives and brow-beat them into giving transplant permission before Tyndall spoke to them? That way he wouldn't have to steal the bodies. Sarah was furious; she picked up the phone and called Tyndall.

'Doctor Tyndall? It's Sarah Lasseter here. I'm sorry to bother you, but I thought you should know that Martin Keegan has lost all brain function. Dr Stubbs left word with the nursing staff that he should be informed if this happened. I understand that he intends to contact the family personally with a view to seeing them in the morning. I thought that you might like to be present too?'

'That's very considerate of you, Doctor,' replied Tyndall thoughtfully. 'I certainly would. Perhaps you would leave word to that effect for Dr Stubbs before you go off-duty. Just say that I should like to speak to the relatives as is my usual practice.'

'Yes sir,' said Sarah. She made a request for a meeting of her own with Tyndall and was told that four o'clock would be convenient. She put the phone down and felt pleased with the outcome of her call. 'Checkmate, Dr Stubbs,' she murmured under her breath.

Sarah was woken from a deep sleep just after midday by her door-bell ringing.

'All right! All right!' she complained as she struggled out of bed and fought her way into a dressing-gown. She opened the door to find Derek Stubbs standing there. He looked furious.

'What do you think you're playing at?' he demanded. He walked into the room so forcibly that Sarah had to step back sharply to avoid being trampled on. Stubbs closed the door behind him and Sarah felt afraid.

'What do you mean?' she stammered.

'You and Tyndall? What's going on?'

'I don't know what you mean. Get out of my room!'

'You told Tyndall about the Keegan boy, didn't you?'

'Yes, I did,' said Sarah.

'Why?' demanded Stubbs.

'So that he would see the parents.'

The honesty of Sarah's reply seemed to stop Stubbs in his tracks. 'For God's sake, why?' he asked.

'Because you have all the charm of an orang-utan with piles,' said Sarah, using up her last reserves of courage. 'I didn't want the Keegan boy's parents to be subjected to a charmless ghoul demanding their son's body.'

'Jesus Christ!' said Stubbs in a hoarse whisper. 'So you call in Saint Murdoch and he lets them off the hook without batting an eyelid. As you wish, Mr Keegan. Fiery Furnace it is then, Mr Keegan. Out with the Sigma probes and it's into the fire with perfectly good kidneys, lungs, eyes, you name it.'

'That's their right,' said Sarah.

'That's their right,' mimicked Stubbs in a sing-song voice. 'Don't you ever think?' he demanded. 'Don't you realise how much good these perfectly healthy organs could do?'

Or how much money you could make, thought Sarah.

'Do you know how many transplant permissions we've had in the last eighteen months in HTU?' asked Stubbs.

Sarah shook her head.

'None,' said Stubbs. 'Not one.'

Sarah remained mute.

'And all because our noble leader is more interested in promoting his own image as Mr Nice-guy.'

'That's unfair!' Sarah protested.

'Is it?' said Stubbs. 'Not one in eighteen months. That's an appalling record.'

'Not all doctors are fans of transplant technology,' replied Sarah, but it sounded weak.

Stubbs gave her a disparaging look. 'Come on,' he protested. 'We're not talking about twenty years ago when transplant patients lasted ten minutes on a good day. We both know what the modern success rate is. Why doesn't he try harder to get permission?'

Sarah did not reply. She was thinking how much easier it would be for Stubbs to run his scam with official permission.

Stubbs's expression suddenly changed and he drew in breath sharply as if he had just realised or remembered something. He turned on his heel and stormed out, leaving Sarah feeling exhausted, partly from tiredness, but mainly from fear.

She sat down on the bed as she felt her legs become weak and took pleasure for a moment in the fact that Stubbs had gone. He left in his wake a silence which was gradually invaded by the everyday sounds of normality. Traffic, a distant police siren, a meal trolley being wheeled across the yard outside. There was no question of going back to sleep. She would just lie back down on the bed and try to rest until it was time for her appointment with Tyndall.

Stubbs had been furious with her but he hadn't harmed her. She had feared for her life when he forced his way into her room but, to her surprise, he hadn't even mentioned the business of Ryan Lafferty and John Main being in HTU the night before. He hadn't tried to pump her on how much she knew. Instead, he had concentrated on Tyndall's failure to get transplant permission. Was he offering this as an excuse for what he was doing? The manner of his going had also been strange. What had made him suddenly turn on his heel and leave?

She tried to put Stubbs out of her mind as she thought about what she was going to say to Murdoch Tyndall. She hoped he wouldn't stand in her way, because she was excited by the prospect of meeting up with his brother, Cyril, again. If she was really honest with herself she would have to admit that the excuse of getting away from Stubbs had given her the chance to find out more about Cyril Tyndall's suggestion that she might conceivably have a career in research. Maybe it was fate, she reasoned. She had tried convincing herself that she still really wanted to go into general practice with her father, but there was no escaping the fact that Professor Tyndall had dangled quite a different prospect in front of her and it was undeniably exciting. For a moment she remembered Paddy Duncan's joking comment that she was a medical 'groupie'. It annoyed her.

Murdoch Tyndall put Sarah at her ease as soon as she

entered his office. 'Now then, Sarah,' he smiled. 'How can I help you?'

'It's a bit difficult,' began Sarah.

'Something's wrong, I can see that,' said Tyndall.

'I have to get away from HTU for a bit, only temporarily, but I do have to get away.'

Tyndall regarded Sarah in silence for a moment before spreading his hands on the desk in front of him and saying, 'Is that it? No explanation?'

'It's very difficult for me to speak frankly, sir, but Dr Stubbs and I do not see eye to eye and I'm feeling the strain.'

'A clash of personalities?' asked Tyndall.

'Something like that.'

'And what would you propose doing during this "temporary" absence?' asked Tyndall.

'With your permission, sir, I have a suggestion to make.'

'Go on.'

Sarah told Tyndall of her earlier conversation with his brother and asked if she might be permitted to spend some time in Cyril Tyndall's lab in the medical school.

'I see,' said Tyndall thoughtfully. 'But are you sure that laboratory medicine is something you want to do?'

'No sir, I'm not. But I would appreciate the opportunity to find out.'

'But if this is to be a temporary arrangement won't the problem still be here when you return?' asked Tyndall.

'I believe it will be resolved by that time.'

'Very cryptic,' smiled Tyndall. 'Is there something I don't know about?'

'Yes sir, but that is as much as I can say at the moment.'

Tyndall intertwined his fingers and said, 'Dr Lasseter, Dr Stubbs reported to me that you had been "entertaining guests" while on duty. Normally I would take a dim view of this, but on pressing him further he told me that your "guests" were, in fact, Father Lafferty and the Main boy's father.'

'Yes sir.'

'You obviously don't want to tell me more, so I won't press you, but can I ask if their visit had something to do with the "problem" with Dr Stubbs?'

'Yes sir, it did.'

Tyndall sat back in his seat and said, 'Very well, Doctor, I'll see what can be arranged. I'll call my brother before I leave.'

'Thank you, sir,' said Sarah, feeling relieved and getting up. 'I can't tell you how grateful I am.'

'I have to think of the patients,' said Tyndall. 'Discord between the staff is something we cannot allow.'

Sarah called Lafferty and told him how the meeting had gone.

'And do you think his brother will agree?' asked Lafferty.

'Unless he's changed his mind,' replied Sarah.

'Excellent,' said Lafferty.

Sarah told him of Stubbs's visit to her room earlier and of what had been said. Lafferty picked up on the fact that the incident had been prompted by the death of another patient in HTU.

'Tell me about the Keegan boy.'

Sarah gave him a brief resumé of the case.

'This may be our chance to catch Stubbs out,' said Lafferty. 'A young patient for whom transplant permission was refused. Presumably the boy's body should be in the hospital mortuary?'

'I think so,' said Sarah, but then she added as an afterthought, 'Actually I'm not at all sure. I've just realised I've been overlooking something.'

'What's that?' asked Lafferty.

'Some of our patients are fitted with a type of monitor we call Sigma probes. They are actually implanted in the skull. If a patient fitted with these probes should die, we have to have the probes removed by specialist technicians before anything else happens to the body.'

'Where do they do this?'

'I don't really know,' confessed Sarah. 'They come and remove the body from the unit. I'm not sure what happens after that. I suppose I assumed they took the body to the mortuary when they had finished with it and the undertakers would take over from there, but maybe not.'

'Maybe not,' agreed Lafferty.

'Do you think that— ' Sarah began excitedly.

'It's possible. Can you find out more about where the bodies go to have the probes removed?'

'I'll try,' said Sarah.

'But be careful!' warned Lafferty. 'In the meantime, I'll try to find out which undertaker is dealing with the Keegan boy's funeral.'

'You be careful too.'

'Let's both be careful,' said Lafferty gently.

The more he thought about it, the more Lafferty felt that they had discovered how the theft of the bodies was carried out. The 'specialist technicians' Sarah had mentioned would have to be in on the scam but that would be all as far as the hospital and the university were concerned. All HTU cared about was getting the Sigma probes back so, even if it meant Stubbs replacing them out of his own pocket, it would be a small price to pay in the stakes he must be playing for. It would mean, of course, that these same technicians were responsible for loading and sealing the coffins, otherwise the undertakers would know what was going on. He could check this if he could find out the name of the firm handling the Keegan funeral. He went out to get the local evening paper.

On the way back, Lafferty was stopped by one of his parishioners who seemed bent on telling him every detail of her medical history over the past five years. Lafferty made appropriate tutting and clucking noises at what he hoped were the right intervals but feared that his impatience might be showing. 'It's not an easy life you've had, Thelma,' he said to the small, fat woman standing before him, 'but you've a loving family and a God that cares about you. See you on Sunday?'

'Yes, Father,' replied the woman, taken unawares as Lafferty sneaked off.

Lafferty ran his finger down the *DEATHS* column and stopped at Keegan.

'Tragically, as the result of an accident, Martin John Keegan, beloved only son of James and Edwina Keegan. Funeral at Mortonhall Cemetery 11am on Thursday 18th. Flowers to Harkness and Glennie, Causewayside Lane.'

Lafferty checked Yellow Pages and saw that Harkness and Glennie advertised twenty-four-hour manning of their office. He would go there in person and ask about the Keegan boy's body. First he would phone Main and let him know what was going on.

'Well done,' said Main when Lafferty told him. 'It must be how they are doing it.'

'I think so,' agreed Lafferty. 'If we can just show that the Keegan boy's body has gone missing, we can call the police in and give them all our information.'

'How are we going to do that?' asked Main.

Lafferty told him of his intended visit to the undertakers.

'Do you want me to come?'

'Better if I go alone I think,' said Lafferty. 'Priests have an obvious connection with death. It'll arouse less suspicion if I go on my own.'

'As you wish. I'll be waiting to hear what happens.'

Sarah went on duty at six. She had left it as late as possible in order to minimise contact with Derek Stubbs. In the event, he was nowhere to be seen when she entered HTU and looked into the duty-room.

'Good evening, Staff,' she said to the nurse sitting there. 'What's cooking?'

'Dr Tyndall is having words with Dr Stubbs,' replied the nurse, as if she was imparting a secret. 'They've been going at it hammer and tongs for the past ten minutes.' The nurse held her finger to her lips and Sarah listened. She could hear raised voices coming from Tyndall's office. She shrugged her shoulders round her ears in order to empathise with the nurse. 'What's going on?' she asked.

'I don't know,' replied the nurse. 'Dr Stubbs suddenly appeared and walked into Dr Tyndall's office without so much as a by your leave.'

Sarah made a face. She was about to say something else when the arguing voices grew suddenly louder. Both she and the staff nurse pretended to be otherwise occupied as Tyndall's door opened and Stubbs emerged.

'You haven't heard the last of this!' Stubbs was saying, his face red with anger.

He saw Sarah standing there as he shut Tyndall's door, gave her a thunderous look that made the back of her neck tingle, and left.

'Something you said?' whispered the staff nurse who had noticed.

'Must have been,' said Sarah. Her throat was tight.

Twenty minutes later, as Sarah was checking the patient in Beta 4, Murdoch Tyndall came in and stood opposite her. He seemed unruffled by whatever had passed between him and Stubbs. Sarah thought it the mark of a gentleman.

'I spoke to my brother about your request and he suggests you pop up tomorrow in your off-duty if that's convenient?'

'Perfectly,' said Sarah.

Tyndall handed her a piece of paper with a telephone number on it. 'That's his personal extension. He asks that you call him before going up.'

'Thank you sir,' said Sarah. 'I'm most grateful.'

Tyndall smiled and turned on his heel. He made a point of saying goodnight to the nurses and left.

When she had a moment, Sarah called Lafferty, but he was out.

It was shortly after seven-thirty when Lafferty found the premises of Harkness and Glennie, a double shop-front with curtains in the window, half-way along a narrow lane and facing due north. The paintwork of the premises was a 'respectful' combination of grey and black. The door was locked, but Lafferty could see that there was a light on somewhere inside. There was a brass bell on the wall.

294

He pressed it and heard it ring. A shuffling of feet was followed by the undoing of locks and the door opened a fraction.

'Yes?' asked the unseen male voice through the crack.

'I'm Father Lafferty from St Xavier's. I wonder if I might have a word?'

Lafferty heard a chain being undone and the door opened to reveal a small man in pinstripe trousers and shirt-sleeves. 'You can't be too careful these days, Father,' he said as he indicated that Lafferty should enter.

'I suppose not,' said Lafferty as he waited for the man to secure the door again. What was anyone going to steal from here, he wondered.

'This way,' said the man. He led the way through to the back of the premises and into a small room which had a television on in the corner. A few chairs, a small table with a teapot and a half empty milk bottle standing on it and two or three newspapers lying around suggested that this was the staff-room. The man turned the television off and put his jacket on. 'Now Father, what can I do for you?' he asked.

'It's about the Keegan boy,' said Lafferty.

'A tragedy,' said the man, shaking his head. 'Eighteen years old.'

'Quite so,' agreed Lafferty. 'Is the lad in your Chapel of Rest?'

'No Father, he isn't.'

'He isn't?' queried Lafferty, hoping the man would say more.

'He's up at the medical school.'

'I see,' said Lafferty, waiting for more information.

'I understand he had to have some special medical equipment removed from him so we delivered the coffin,

295

and the chaps up there will let us know when we can collect it.'

'So you won't have anything to do with the boy's body?' asked Lafferty.

'We'll just collect it from the university in time for the funeral,' answered the man.

'I see.' The pieces now fitted perfectly. 'I'm sorry to have bothered you.'

15

Sarah managed to glean from the night staff nurse that Sigma probes were removed in a special laboratory up in Cyril Tyndall's department in the medical school. She called Lafferty just after midnight to give him this information. And he was able to tell her that he had largely found this out for himself, through his visit to the undertakers, and also that the technicians up there were responsible for seeing the corpse into its coffin.

'So that's it then,' said Sarah.

'I suppose so,' said Lafferty uncertainly.

'There's a problem?' asked Sarah.

'Why don't they?'

'Why don't they what?'

'Why don't they put the bodies back in their coffins when they've finished removing the organs? Why do they keep the bodies?'

'You're right,' said Sarah after a moment's thought. 'You'd think that would be the sensible thing to do. Otherwise they're left with them. what do they do with them?'

'Exactly.'

'Damn,' said Sarah quietly. 'Everything was fitting so well.'

'It's just occurred to me that Professor Tyndall's lab is where you intend to work up at the medical school,' said Lafferty.

'Yes.'

'It could be a case of out of the frying pan into the fire.'

'I'll be careful,' Sarah promised.

'I'm not sure this is a good idea after all. You could be in great danger.'

'Let me play it by ear,' said Sarah. 'Nothing has been agreed yet. Professor Tyndall wants me to phone him first.'

'Probably to arrange a preliminary meeting,' said Lafferty. 'If you're asked to go up there maybe you could use your visit to find out as much as you can about the set-up for Sigma probe management?'

'I'll certainly try,' said Sarah, adding, 'although it's quite hard to see how I could bring something like that into conversation.'

'As you said. Play it by ear,' said Lafferty.

'With a bit of luck, Stubbs's time is going to run out anyway,' said Sarah. She told him about the row she'd heard him have with Dr Tyndall.

'Did you manage to hear what it was about?' asked Lafferty.

'Fraid not.'

'Be extra careful,' urged Lafferty. 'He could be at his most dangerous if he thinks the net is closing in on him.'

'I will,' Sarah promised once more.

. . .

298

After an uneventful night in HTU, Sarah went off-duty and slept until her alarm woke her. She had set it for two o'clock so that she could telephone Professor Tyndall and, hopefully, arrange a meeting for later on that same afternoon.

'Professor? It's Sarah Lasseter. I think you've probably been expecting me to call?'

'Yes, my brother tells me you'd like to work with us for a while?'

Sarah thought that Tyndall sounded a little distant, as if she didn't have his full attention. 'If that's at all possible, sir?'

'This needs some thought, Doctor. Perhaps we should meet first and discuss which aspects of our research interest you most.'

'I was rather hoping I might be able to come up and see you this afternoon,' said Sarah.

'I think perhaps it might be better if we were to wait a few days. I'm up to my eyes at the moment. Give me a call in a couple of days.'

'Very good, sir,' said Sarah, feeling utterly dejected. Cyril Tyndall's interest in her career certainly seemed to have become lukewarm. She was forced into considering that Paddy Duncan might have been right at the reception when he suggested that his interest in her had more to do with her gender and the dress she had been wearing than any genuine regard for her professional skills. She decided that she would have to be philosophical about it, but it didn't stop her feeling more than a little foolish. Somewhere in the back of her mind she could hear her father say, 'Life is a learning process Sarah . . . and there are no school holidays.'

* * *

Sarah felt at a loose end. Instead of being on her way up to Cyril Tyndall's lab later that afternoon as she had planned, she would have to twiddle her thumbs for at least two days. She wondered how much time they had before the Keegan boy's funeral took place. Lafferty would know; she called him.

'The funeral is on Thursday,' said Lafferty. 'According to the undertaker I spoke to, they won't pick up the body until just before the funeral, so presumably it will lie in the medical school mortuary until then.'

'That gives us three days,' said Sarah.

'Not long, especially if you are not going to get a chance to go up there until Wednesday at the earliest.'

'And maybe even later than that,' said Sarah. 'It also depends on my off-duty. That's partly why I was hoping to see Professor Tyndall this afternoon. I'm off-duty until tomorrow morning.'

'I see,' said Lafferty. 'Look, John Main is coming round later. Why don't you come over and join us?'

'What time?'

'Come whenever you're ready.'

Sarah arrived at St Xavier's a little after seven to find Lafferty 'doing a bit of tidying up' as he put it. 'My cleaner will be off for a few days,' he said. 'She's had a bit of a shock.'

When Main arrived at half past, Lafferty told them both about the cause of her shock.

'How awful,' said Sarah.

'Another warning,' said Main.

'One for each of us,' said Lafferty. 'On the plus side it means that they still think it worthwhile trying to convince us that black magic is involved.'

300

'And on the minus?' asked Sarah.

'They know we are working together. That must have come from Stubbs seeing us together. It's just possible that Sarah might get a little 'present' from them too.

Sarah screwed up her face at the thought of it.

'In the meantime, we are running out of time,' said Lafferty.

'How so?' asked Main.

'The Keegan boy is due to be buried on Thursday and Sarah doesn't think she will get a chance to sniff around at the medical school by then.'

'Then maybe I could try?' suggested Main.

Lafferty and Sarah looked at each other in surprise. 'How?' Sarah asked.

'You tell me,' said Main. 'What sort of people visit the medical school?'

Sarah shrugged and said, 'Company reps, service engineers, undertakers, delivery men, all sorts.'

'Then there's lots to choose from,' said Main positively. 'We just have to decide what I'm going to be.'

'And which part of the building you want to be in,' said Sarah. 'It's a big place.'

'There is that,' agreed Main.

'But the bodies must all end up in the medical school mortuary, surely?' said Lafferty.

'I suppose they must,' agreed Sarah,

'That would fit with what the undertaker told me,' said Lafferty.

'Then I could be an undertaker's man,' Main said.

'Wouldn't you need a hearse?' asked Sarah.

'Not necessarily, I remember you said something a while ago about undertakers measuring bodies?' replied Main.

'That's right,' said Sarah, sounding more positive as she followed Main's line of thought. 'Most of them pay the mortuary attendants to measure the bodies for them so they can supply the right sized coffin, but a few firms prefer to do it themselves. You could turn up to measure a body.'

Main nodded.

'Are you sure you feel up to it?' asked Lafferty.

'I'm up to it,' replied Main.

'But who would you be measuring?' Sarah asked.

'I'll make up a name. The real point is to gain access to the mortuary. If I give a name and there's no body to match it then someone will have to check with somebody else and so on and so forth. Mix-ups and incompetence are a way of life in most public-service institutions. While they're looking for someone who's not there, I'll be taking a look at who is.'

'It might just work,' agreed Lafferty.

'There aren't that many undertakers in town,' said Sarah. 'It's likely that the mortuary attendants know them all. They'll spot you as an impostor right away.'

Main thought for a moment and then said, 'I could be from out of town. That's it! The hospital must have patients from all over the country. I could be acting for a firm in Aberdeen or Inverness – or anywhere.'

Sarah could think of no further objection. She looked at Lafferty who shrugged and said, 'Personally, I think it's worth a try.'

'Good,' said Main. 'Then it's settled.'

As she walked across the courtyard to the main hospital, Sarah saw Murdoch Tyndall's dark green Jaguar parked outside HTU. If Tyndall was in at this time in the morning, she decided, something was wrong. She wasn't surprised therefore when Sister Roche told her that he wanted to see her.

'Come in, Sarah, sit down.'

Sarah sat down in front of Tyndall's desk and saw that he wasn't his usual urbane self. 'I'm afraid Dr Stubbs has had to leave us for a while. Some family crisis, I understand. He may in fact be away for some time.'

'I'm sorry to hear that,' said Sarah with mixed feelings. She was feverishly trying to work things out in her own head. Had things become too hot for Stubbs to handle?

'This, of course, leaves us with a problem,' continued Tyndall.

'A problem, sir?' asked Sarah almost absent-mindedly.

'With Dr Stubbs gone, I am afraid I can no longer sanction your secondment to the medical school. We will need all the experienced people we have in HTU.'

'Of course,' replied Sarah.

'But as Dr Stubbs was the source of your discontent perhaps this won't come as too big a blow to you?'

'No, of course not, sir,' replied Sarah. She was still trying to work out the repercussions. Even if Stubbs had made a bolt for it, could they still nail him? They could, if they could show that Martin Keegan's body had been taken, she decided. It looked as if John Main was going to be their only chance of proving it.

'I'm arranging for a locum, of course,' said Tyndall. 'But for the meantime I would be grateful if you do your best to hold the fort. As soon as I get things organised today, I myself will take over Dr Stubbs's shifts.'

'Very good, sir.'

'Now that you're here, I'll take myself off to the

administration people and see if I can get some action out of them. I'll be wearing my bleeper. Call me if you need me.'

Sarah watched Tyndall disappear through the door and collected her thoughts for a few moments before walking through to the duty-room, where Sister Roche was sitting at her desk. 'Dr Tyndall has just told me about Dr Stubbs.'

'It's probably his son,' said Roche without looking up from her papers.

'His son?' asked Sarah, unaware that Stubbs was married.

Roche put down her pen and said, 'He was estranged from his wife. She lives in the south of England with their son. I understand the boy has a kidney problem. He's been waiting for a transplant for nearly two years.'

'I didn't know,' murmured Sarah. Her mind was a sea of confusion. This piece of information explained a lot.

Sarah started to read through the patients' charts. She glanced up at the clock on the wall and saw that it was just after nine-thirty. She wondered if John Main was on his way to the medical school.

Main checked his pockets to see that he had everything he needed. It was the third time he had done so in as many minutes. Satisfied again that his wallet and keys – and a measuring tape, his one prop – were where they should be, he left the flat and set off for the medical school.

At ten o'clock on a Tuesday morning the traffic was beginning to thin out a bit after the rush hour, but he still experienced a couple of hold-ups, both courtesy of the gas board who had dug up the road; in order to drink tea

and read newspapers inside Bedford vans, thought Main
uncharitably as the final hold-up extended to over four
minutes. He considered trying to park inside the hospital
gates on the grounds that he was there on official business,
but then decided against it. He had nothing on paper that
he could use to convince officialdom. He toured slowly
around the neighbouring streets until he found a space
being vacated by a delivery van. He noted that waiting
was 'limited to twenty minutes' in this area, but decided
to take his chances. If he managed to get what he had
come for, the fine would be a small price to pay. He
asked at the medical school gate-house for directions to
the mortuary and was given instructions by a uniformed
man who stepped outside in order to add pointing to his
words of direction. Main noticed that he said 'left' while
his hand pointed to the right, but he picked up the general
gist of it.

When he finally reached the door with MORTUARY
written above it, he could find no other instructions.
There didn't seem to be any kind of reception area or
office nearby. There was no one around, so he tried the
handle and the door opened. He stepped inside.

The mortuary was much larger than Main had anticipated,
but then he realised that he had overlooked the student-
training aspect of the place. Many of the bodies here
would be 'class material' bound for the dissecting tables
of first-year anatomy and physiology students, perhaps
not the noble end their owners had in mind when they
had donated their bodies for the furthering of medical
research, but necessary all the same.

'Can I help you?' asked a voice.

Main nearly jumped out of his skin. He hadn't heard

anyone come up behind him. He turned to find himself standing in front of a small, thin man wearing white overalls with a green plastic apron tied on over them. He was looking at Main through glasses that seemed so thick Main felt they must weigh a kilo. His skin was red, as if it had been exposed to the sun for too long, but this was Scotland in winter. There had to be a more pathological reason.

'I'm from Magraw and Littlejohn,' said Main. 'I've come to measure-up Andrew Lamont for his wooden overcoat.'

The eyes behind the glasses stared at him as if he was an insect under a magnifying glass. 'Who did you say you were from?'

'Magraw and Littlejohn, Aberdeen,' answered Main.

Another stare, but this time the man said, 'We've got no Lamont here that I know of.' He called out, 'Malcolm! Know anything about an Andrew Lamont?'

A second man appeared from an adjoining room. He was wearing the same clothes as the first and was holding a large sewing needle in his hand with what looked like a length of plastic thread trailing from it. He had obviously been disturbed in the middle of something. Main preferred not to think what.

'Have you checked the book?' asked the second man.

'No. Thought you might know,' answered the first. He left Main alone while he went off to check and the second man disappeared from sight again. Main started to look around. Most of the bodies would be in the refrigerated body vaults but he was looking for a coffin. There were four in the room, one on the floor in a far corner, and three were set out side-by-side on wooden trestles at the end of the row of body vaults. He moved quickly and silently across the room to the one on the floor, and saw there was no name-plate on the lid. He pushed his foot against the side and it moved. It was empty. Just as he was crossing to the other coffins the man with the glasses returned. Once again he did so silently and caught Main unawares. 'Big place,' Main said with what he hoped was a disarming smile.

The man with the glasses stared at him again, and then said, 'There's no one called Lamont in the book.'

'Oh shit,' exclaimed Main. 'There must be. You're not going to tell me I've come all this way and there's some bloody mix-up in the paperwork? Someone's probably forgotten to enter him in the book.'

The man with glasses pointed to the body vaults and said forcibly, 'If he was in there I'd know about it. Right?'

Main backed off. He raised his hands, palms outwards, and said, 'All right, all right, I believe you. But if he's not here, where the hell is he? Still lying up in the wards? I mean, shit, I can hardly tell my boss that the corpse isn't here and he'd better get the relations to cancel the funeral can I?'

The man with the glasses thought for a moment, and then said, 'Wait here.' He went off to confer with his colleague next door. Main decided that there wouldn't be enough time to examine the other three coffins. He was right; the man with the glasses returned quickly and said, 'I'll go up to the main office and check.'

'I'm obliged to you,' said Main as he watched the man go out through the door. As soon as it closed he hurried silently across to where the three coffins lay on their trestles and examined the first one. There was a brass plate on the lid. It said, Isabella Hartley, born 1910 died

1993. RIP. A paper label, also stuck on the lid, gave the name of the undertakers and the time of collection. Isabella Hartley was to be buried at two thirty that same afternoon.

Main was reading the name on the third coffin and drawing his third blank when the door opened and a man wearing a suit entered. His jacket was open to reveal a gold brocade waistcoat. He was carrying a case about twice the size of a conventional brief-case and had a rolled-up newspaper under his other arm. He saw Main and asked who he was in a tone of voice that suggested he had the right to ask these things. Main told him and explained that there seemed to have been a mix-up in the paperwork over the body he had been sent to measure.

The man frowned and asked, 'Who did you say you were here for?'

'Keegan,' replied Main, suddenly deciding to go for broke and improvise. 'Martin Keegan.'

'And you say he died in the hospital?'

'Yes.'

'Then why should he be here, and not in the hospital mortuary?'

'He had to have some monitoring apparatus removed from him. Sigma probes, I think they were called,' said Main, wondering who his questioner was. His dress and confident manner of speech suggested medical staff. A pathologist, perhaps.

'Ah, Sigma probes,' exclaimed the man. 'That explains it. He'll probably still be up in the Sigma lab. They haven't brought him down yet.'

'I see,' said Main. 'Perhaps I could go up there?'

'I don't see why not,' replied the well-dressed man. 'Do you know where it is?'

Main said not and was given directions. He had just repeated them back to the man when the attendant who had gone up to the office returned. Main knew he had to get in first. He said brightly, 'Problem solved. This gentleman has been kind enough to work out what has happened. I'm sorry to have put you to all this trouble.'

The attendant looked at the well-dressed man and said, 'Good morning, sir.'

'Good Morning, Claude,' replied the man. 'This chap's been looking for a Sigma patient. He's probably still upstairs.'

'Should have said,' said Claude dourly.

'I'm sorry,' said Main. 'Thoughtless of me. I'll be on my way then.' He left the mortuary, pausing for a moment outside to try to hear if anything more was being said. But the door was too thick. He just had to hope that the different patient names he had used weren't being compared.

Main realised that he could not use the body-measuring ruse to gain access to the Sigma lab. The Sigma technicians must supply that information to the undertakers; they could hardly have outsiders arriving to measure non-existent bodies. He'd have to find some other way of getting inside.

Main found the building he had been sent to. It was a modern, three-storey concrete block growing out of an older, blackened-stone one. There was a board about twenty metres from the glass-fronted entrance which announced it to be the Gelman Holland Research Institute. The text below explained that the building had been funded by Gelman Holland and that research there was carried out under the direction of Professor Cyril Tyndall. The building had been opened on the seventh of

June, 1991 by the Princess Royal. There was a photograph of the ribbon-cutting ceremony. None of this helped Main to think of an excuse for getting inside.

He found a place where he could watch comings and goings from the building without drawing attention to himself, and did not have long to wait. In the space of the following ten minutes three people entered the building. Two used an electronic key-card which they inserted in a slot by the front door. The third, who did not have such a key, pressed a bell and waited until the doors were opened by a man in uniform. After close scrutiny of a document he presented he was permitted to enter. No way there, thought Main.

Having given up on a frontal assault, Main walked round the outside of the building at a discreet distance, looking for alternatives. He thought he had found one when he saw a side-door open and a technician come out to put a large cardboard box in a rubbish skip. To make sure that he could get back inside, the man had propped open the door with a wooden wedge. Main was beginning to think of sneaking in when the man came out with the next load, but there was no next time. The door swung shut and the lock engaged with a loud clunk.

Main cursed under his breath and continued with his examination of the outside. There was one more door at the far side but it, too, was locked with no outside handles visible. After a further ten minutes he was considering giving up when he saw a van arrive outside the building. It had the name of a laboratory supplier on the side. The driver, obviously a stranger to the site, took a slow drive round the perimeter of the building before getting out to ring the bell at the front. He presented his delivery notes to the uniformed man who opened it.

After careful scrutiny, the driver was directed to the far side. Main saw this as his chance and circled round to be there before the van reversed back, its reverse-gear-bleeper warning of its approach. He watched as the driver waited for the door to be unlocked.

Once again his delivery notes were examined, this time by a man wearing a brown coat and sporting an Elvis Presley style haircut which seemed to be excessively greased, even from where Main was standing. The storeman, as Main took him to be, pointed to the inside of the building and made a gesture to his right. The driver nodded and opened up the back of the van while the storeman returned inside.

The driver disappeared inside the van for a moment before reappearing to pile up boxes along the rear of the vehicle. When he had ten arranged along the back edge, he jumped down and carried the first two inside. Main's pulse-rate rose. Could he risk it? Could he just nip over to the van and start carrying the next two inside? By the time he had finally decided that this was what he would do, too much time had elapsed and he steeled himself to wait for the driver's next trip. As soon the man had started off inside with the next two boxes, Main broke cover and ran over to the van on his toes. He picked up two of the boxes marked FRAGILE: *Laboratory Glassware* in red, and walked in through the open doors, noting that there was a fire release bar on the back of one of them; there would be no problem getting back out again. He was just in time to see the driver disappear round to the right at the end of the corridor.

Half-way along, and still unchallenged, Main found a flight of steps to his left. The fates were being kind; he put down the boxes about twenty metres past the foot of the steps and ran back to start climbing. With a bit of luck the driver would think that some helpful member of staff had given him a hand.

Main realised that he would now have to rely on the brief-case he was carrying to give him the apparent authority to be there. He was now in the first-floor corridor. Glass-panelled doors to the left and right enabled him to see that they were laboratories. White-coated workers sat on stools at benches, intent on what they were doing. One looked up as Main was looking in. Their eyes met, but the man showed no signs of alarm at Main being there. After all, why should he, Main reminded himself. This was a medical research lab, not a secret nuclear weapons facility. He was there to look for two rogue technicians in an otherwise highly respected institution. What he needed was some kind of a sign-board. He found what he was looking for at the landing of the stairs leading down to the main entrance. Unfortunately, none of the directions on it were helpful simply because there was no mention of the word Sigma and, not being a scientist, he didn't know what alternative heading the Sigma probe service might come under. Would it be 'Tissue Culture' or 'Stock Virus Laboratory' or 'Prep Room' or 'CSSD', he wondered. As he was puzzling over where to try next, he became aware of footsteps on the stairs. Someone was coming up from the ground floor. Main felt a momentary panic as he looked about him for some place to hide. There was nowhere. He considered bolting up the stairs to the next level, but then decided against it. He would stand and brass it out. He turned his back on the stairs and opened his brief-case, pretending to be searching for something as he heard the steps behind him get louder. Out of the corner of his eye he saw a white-coated figure pass him and move away along the corridor to the left. He was about to breathe a sigh of relief when the figure stopped and turned.

'Can I help you?' asked a male voice in tones that suggested that the real question was, who are you and why are you here?

Main gave a slight laugh which sounded terribly forced and said, 'I seem to have lost my bearings. I was looking for the Sigma probe lab.'

'The Sigma lab?' repeated the man who had come back along the corridor to stand directly in front of Main. Main noticed that his accent and tanned skin suggested that he might be Middle Eastern. 'What on earth do you want there?'

'My company manufactures the probes,' lied Main. 'I thought as I was in the neighbourhood I would call in and see if there were any problems.'

The man looked doubtful; he looked down at Main's brief-case and then back up at him. Eventually he said, 'The Sigma Lab is in the basement. How could you possibly lose your bearings and end up here? Who let you in?'

The game was slipping away from Main rapidly. His impulse was to push the man out of the way and make a run for it, but he doubted that he would be able to get out of the building in time. Besides, he had no wish to assault an innocent man doing his job, and neither did he want to end up in jail over this. He decided to go on with his implausible story. 'No one, actually. The door was open when I arrived so I just walked in. As there was no one about I started looking for directions and ended up here.' He gestured to the direction board.

Again the man looked doubtful. 'The door was open you say?'

'Yes,' replied Main.

'Come with me.'

The man started back down the stairs with Main following along behind. He thought how easy it would be to push him in the back and take to his heels, but again baulked at the consequences. At the foot of the stairs was the main entrance hall. A woman sat behind the reception desk and two uniformed security men were talking by the door.

'Jean, did you leave your desk unattended at any time in the last half-hour?

The woman looked at her questioner and then at Main. She replied, 'I don't think so, Dr Salman.'

The man summoned the two security men over and said, 'This man says that he just walked into the building. Is that possible?'

'No sir,' replied one of the men. The other just shook his head.

Salman turned to face Main again. 'Well?' he asked.

Main smiled and tried his last bluff. He turned to one of the security men and said, 'You were there all right. You were outside giving directions to a delivery driver. I just walked in behind your back. I didn't think I was doing anything wrong. Unfortunately there was no one at the desk I could ask for directions.'

Salman looked back to the woman sitting behind the desk. She shrugged uncomfortably and said, 'Maybe I went to the toilet. I can't remember exactly.'

Main felt relief flood through him, but it was short lived. The other security man said, 'But I would have seen him.'

Main had no answer to that but the man's colleague suddenly said, 'You went to put the kettle on while I spoke to the driver. Remember?'

'Oh yeah,' replied the man sheepishly. Main could hardly believe his luck.

Salman said to the three employees, 'We are trying to run a research facility where cleanliness and sterility are of the highest importance and yet apparently anyone can wander in here off the street!'

All three looked down at their feet.

'It won't happen again, sir,' said one of the security men.

'It had better not,' said Salman. 'Now, Mr—?'

'Main.' Main had little heart for continuing the charade.

'I'll call the Sigma people for you.' Salman leaned over the reception desk and picked up the phone. He punched in four numbers and waited.

'Mr Mace? It's Dr Salman. I have a man up here who says he's from the company that manufactures the Sigma probes. Would you come and have a word with him, please?'

Main watched as Salman replaced the phone. 'Thanks,' he said, feeling like a brave criminal of yore thanking his executioner. He did not have long to wait before two men appeared in reception. Both wore white tunics and trousers with the Gelman Holland logo above their left breast. Main took this to mean that these men were actually employees of the company, rather than the university. They wore name badges, Mace and Pallister.

'Your card?' asked Mace.

'I'm sorry, I've run out. I keep meaning to tell the office,' replied Main. He didn't bother to smile this time.

He was wondering if he was looking at the two men who had abducted his son's body.

'What company did you say you were from?' asked Mace, exchanging a doubting look with Pallister.

'Main Electronics,' said Main.

'How come we've never heard of you?' asked Pallister.

'The probes are made up by our research division. They don't carry our trademark yet. They're still under test, you might say.'

Mace looked at Pallister who shrugged and said, 'I thought Professor Tyndall's people made them up themselves.'

'So did I,' said Mace suspiciously. 'Wait there.'

Main had to wait once again while the reception phone was used.

'Dr Sotillo? It's Mace here, sir. Would you come up to reception for a moment sir?'

Main felt uneasy – even fearful – but his one crumb of comfort lay in the fact that they had not moved from the reception area and it was public. The opposition could not afford to do anything too awful to him here. A tall, distinguished looking man arrived and looked at Main as if he was something nasty on the pavement. He stood on the other side of the hall while Mace whispered an explanation to him. When he'd finished, Sotillo came over and said, 'The probes are made up here in the medical school. Who the hell are you?'

Main saw that Sotillo also had the Gelman Holland logo on his lab coat. He did not reply.

'He says his name is Main,' said Salman.

Main thought he saw a flicker of recognition in Sotillo's eyes. 'Does he indeed,' said Sotillo softly.

'Should I call the police?' asked the receptionist. 'There

316

have been a number of petty thefts recently. I know a woman up in pathology who— '

Sotillo gave a slight smile and interrupted her. He said to Main, 'Open your case.'

Main opened up his brief-case to reveal a copy of the daily paper and a measuring tape. Nothing else.

'Now your pockets.'

Main emptied his pockets. Sotillo looked through his wallet for identification and found it. He put everything back and handed the wallet to Main.

He said to everyone, 'He doesn't seem to have taken anything. I don't think we'll bother with the police. What's more important at the moment is, who let him in here in the first place?'

'I've already said something about that,' said Salman.

Sotillo looked at Main and said, 'Get out of here. You won't be so lucky again.'

Main needed no second invitation. The air had never smelt sweeter as he left through the front door without looking back. His first thought was to get to a telephone to call Lafferty. He had failed in his mission, but at least he had found out where the Sigma lab was and the names of three people concerned with it. As he came out of the medical school he made for the telephone kiosks he could see to his left.

Main was fumbling in his pocket for another coin to continue his conversation when the door of the kiosk was opened behind him and a gloved hand came down on the receiver rest, cutting him off. He felt a sharp pain in his right buttock as something was pushed into it, then everything started to become fuzzy. His legs became weak as the whole world seemed to start spinning in a whirl of colour.

When Main could think again he decided through the hazy fog of semi-consciousness that he must be dead. Everything was silent . . . he could see his son, Simon . . . but something was dreadfully wrong . . . this wasn't heaven . . . it was hell.

16

Lafferty looked at the receiver in his hand. The line had gone dead and he knew why. Main had been caught. He closed his eyes and offered up a prayer for his safety, but his conscious mind made him fear the worst. He replaced the receiver and saw it as an act of finality, the closing of a door, the severing of a link. He looked at the pad lying in front of him and read what he had written down during Main's call.

The Sigma lab was located in the basement of Cyril Tyndall's department, known as the Gelman Holland Research Institute. Martin Keegan's body was not in the medical school mortuary so it must still be there. Access to the Institute was by means of an electronic key-card which members of staff carried with them. There were two other entrances to the building but both were kept locked. The two technicians responsible for the Sigma probes were named Mace and Pallister, but a man called Dr Sotillo seemed to be in overall charge. The three of them seemed to work directly for Gelman Holland, yet Sotillo seemed to have some executive authority in the Institute; it had been he who had authorised Main's release.

Main had said he was phoning from a booth outside the medical school so he had obviously been followed. Why hadn't they just kept him in the Institute when they had him, Lafferty wondered, and then attempted to answer his own question. Because . . . either Sotillo wasn't involved in Stubbs's scam or . . . because he wanted other people in the Institute to think that he had let Main go. The odds seemed to be on Mace and Pallister being the ones who had followed Main and taken him prisoner. Whether Sotillo was involved or not was a moot point. It was conceivable that the two technicians had followed Main off their own bat. Lafferty pencilled in a question mark by Sotillo's name.

The big question facing Lafferty was what to do now. Should he call the police and tell them everything, or would the opposition have anticipated that and have hidden Main well out of the way by now? The police would turn up at the Institute simply to be told that Main had certainly been there, but had left. Lots of people saw him go. The truth was that Main could be held anywhere. What he really had to do was assess the danger that Main might be in. Was he right in assuming that they had taken him prisoner? Could something even worse have happened to him? Lafferty scribbled absent-mindedly in the bottom corner of his writing pad while he thought the whole thing through.

It seemed likely to him that the technicians would have figured out why Main had gone to the Institute. The chances were that he had probably been carrying his wallet with him, so even if he had given a false name, the opposition would have discovered who he really was. In fact, he recalled Main saying that he had been searched before Sotillo had let him go.

If they realised that Main was on to them, and had been looking for Martin Keegan's body, they would have to keep him out of the way until the evidence of the body-snatch had been disposed of. Main had said that the coffin wasn't in the mortuary, so the technicians had still to take it there for collection by the undertakers. Once the funeral was over there would be no evidence against them, but could they possibly afford to let Main go? Lafferty was afraid of the answer, but there was little he could do.

He decided that the main priority was to get to Martin Keegan's coffin before the funeral took place. It was now Tuesday afternoon. They had until Thursday morning. He called Sarah at HTU.

'Is it safe to talk?' he asked when Sarah answered.

'Yes,' replied Sarah. 'I'm here alone. Stubbs has gone off on compassionate leave. Professor Tyndall told me this morning.'

'Has he now?' said Lafferty softly, wondering where this fitted in with the rest. 'You don't think he's just made a run for it?'

'That was my first thought too,' said Sarah, 'but Sister Roche told me that he has a sick son. The boy lives with his mother and has been waiting for a kidney transplant for two years.'

'Good Lord,' said Lafferty, taken aback by the news.

'I know,' said Sarah. 'I just don't know what to think. This would explain Stubb's exasperation over the lack of transplant permission in the unit, but would it explain anything else?'

'I honestly don't know. I'm afraid they've got John,' he said.

'Oh my God.'

Lafferty noted that she was whispering, despite having said that it was safe to talk. 'Are you sure you can talk?' he asked.

'Yes, it's just that Dr Tyndall may come back at any moment.'

Lafferty told her about Main's call and how he was suddenly cut off.

'What do you think they've done to him?' asked Sarah in a hoarse whisper.

'I'm hoping they're just keeping him out of the way until the Keegan funeral is over. After that there'll be no evidence.'

'I hope to God you're right,' said Sarah. She sounded doubtful.

'But they shouldn't be allowed to get away with this, Sarah,' said Lafferty.

'But what can we do?'

'Are you still going to call Cyril Tyndall today?'

'No,' said Sarah. 'Stubbs running off like this has left us short-staffed. Dr Tyndall told me this morning that I couldn't be spared.'

'I hadn't considered that,' said Lafferty. 'You were our last chance of getting into that damned lab.'

'I'm sorry.'

'That just leaves the medical school mortuary on Thursday morning,' said Lafferty.

'Do you think that's possible?'

'It'll be difficult,' said Lafferty. 'The technicians will obviously leave taking the coffin down there until the very last minute, and even then they will be very much on their guard. We'd probably need an SAS squad to help us get near it.'

'So Stubbs and his friends are going to get away with it?' said Sarah.

'I hate to say it, but it looks very much like it.'

'Dr Tyndall will probably relieve me around four. Can I come over?'

'Please do,' said Lafferty.

Sarah arrived at St Xavier's at a quarter to five and got no answer to her first knock at Lafferty's door. After a second went unanswered she started to feel uneasy. Was it conceivable that they had got to Ryan as well as Main? She decided to look in the church.

The door closed behind her with a solid clunk that reverberated around the apparently empty church. It was dark inside, apart from the candles on the altar and on a long side-table to her left near the front. There were some dim electric lights switched on above the side aisles but they seemed to serve only to create shadows. Sarah moved slowly down the centre aisle towards the altar.

'Ryan?' she called when she thought she heard movement, but there was no answer. She looked at the confessional, off the right-hand aisle. It was dark and closed. Could Ryan be inside, she wondered. But her feet refused to approach it. Her imagination was moving into overdrive. 'Ryan?' she repeated, a little louder this time.

She heard a movement behind her and spun round to see Lafferty emerge from the shadows of the left aisle.

'Sarah? I'm so sorry. I seem to have lost all track of time. I was in the chapel.'

Sarah let out her breath and shook her head with relief. 'I thought . . .' she began. 'I thought you . . .'

'What?'

'Nothing.'

'Come on, let's go next door,' said Lafferty.

'Just a minute,' said Sarah. 'I want to light a candle for John. Is that all right?'

'Of course,' said Lafferty softly. He walked with her to the side-table and handed her a candle. Sarah lit it from one of the others already burning there and put it in its holder. She bowed her head for a moment and Lafferty put his hand on her shoulder. 'It'll soon be over,' he said gently. They went next door to the house.

'Have you eaten?' asked Sarah.

'No,' said Lafferty.

'Neither have I. What have you got in the house?'

'I'm not at all sure,' replied Lafferty cautiously.

'May I look?'

'Please.'

After a fruitless search through the kitchen cupboards Sarah said, 'All you seem to have in the house is half a packet of cornflakes, a loaf of stale bread and seven eggs.'

'Mrs Grogan's still off and I haven't had time to go shopping,' explained Lafferty.

Sarah smiled at his guilty expression and said, 'I am going out to get us some food.'

Lafferty opened his mouth to argue but Sarah put her finger to her lips. 'No arguments,' she said. 'Heat up a couple of plates.'

Sarah was back within ten minutes with a plastic bag full of Chinese take-away food. She extracted the two plates Lafferty had put under the grill and piled up the food on them. Using a tea cloth to protect her hands from the hot plates, she brought them through from the kitchen to the table. 'Eat!' she said. 'We'll talk afterwards.'

· · ·

'I hadn't realised I was so hungry,' said Lafferty with satisfaction when he'd finished eating. 'I really enjoyed that.'

'If you've been living on stale bread and eggs I'm not surprised,' said Sarah.

As they sipped coffee, Sarah said, 'From what you've told me it seems that what we really need is one of these electronic key-cards. If we had one, we could get into the building at night when no one was around and take a look at the Sigma lab for ourselves.'

'But we haven't got one,' said Lafferty. 'And what's more, we're not likely to get one either.'

'So what are we going to do?'

'I'll have to try getting to Martin Keegan's coffin in the mortuary before they take it away on Thursday,' said Lafferty.

Sarah's mouth fell open. 'But you said yourself they're going to be on their guard. You don't have a chance!' she protested.

Lafferty couldn't offer a sound argument. He simply said, 'I've got to try, Sarah.'

Sarah looked at him and saw that he was determined. She continued to watch him when he diverted his eyes and was suddenly very afraid for his safety. 'There might be another way,' she said quietly.

'What other way? said Lafferty.

'I could still try to arrange a meeting with Cyril Tyndall.'

'But you said yourself that you will not be allowed to leave HTU while they're short-staffed.' said Lafferty.

'That's true,' agreed Sarah hesitantly, 'but I might still be able to arrange a meeting.'

Lafferty looked blank. 'I don't understand,' he said. 'Why? How?'

Sarah looked a little embarrassed. She said, 'I was foolish enough to believe that Cyril was interested in me professionally when I met him at a reception in the hospital. That may not have been entirely true . . .'

Lafferty still looked blank. He said, 'I'm sorry, I don't follow you.'

Sarah smiled indulgently and said, 'Ryan, he was more interested in me as a woman.'

'Oh I see,' said Lafferty. 'Well, that's very understandable. You're very attractive.'

Sarah felt taken aback and was suddenly unsure of herself. She said, 'Thank you.'

Lafferty held Sarah's gaze for a moment that seemed suddenly to last too long for both of them. Sarah continued, 'If I could arrange some kind of meeting with Cyril, under false pretences, perhaps I might get a chance to "borrow" his electronic key.'

Lafferty's eyes opened wide. He said, 'That sounds like a very dangerous game to play, Sarah. You shouldn't lead a man on like that.'

'Cyril is a pussy cat,' said Sarah. 'He's hopeless with women, a shy, academic introvert.'

'I still don't like it,' said Lafferty.

'Let's face it, Ryan. It's our only chance.'

Lafferty scratched his head in anguish. He saw that Sarah was right but still didn't like what she planned to do.

Sarah smiled at his discomfort and said gently, 'It'll be all right. Really it will.'

Lafferty finally shrugged and nodded his agreement.

'Can I use your phone?'

'Of course.'

'I'd rather be alone,' said Sarah.

Lafferty got up and left the room.

Cyril Tyndall's secretary answered.

'May I speak to Professor Tyndall, please? It's Dr Lasseter.'

'I'm sorry, Doctor, I rather think he's just left . . . Oh no, hang on.'

Sarah could hear the woman calling out Tyndall's name in the background and then the receiver being picked up again. 'I've managed to catch him, Doctor.'

'Thank you,' said Sarah, looking at her watch. She hadn't realised it was getting late.

'Tyndall here.'

'Professor? It's Sarah Lasseter. I must apologise for not having called you earlier. Please forgive my rudeness.'

'Not at all, Doctor. My brother explained the position to me. I quite understand.'

'I really am most disappointed, Professor. I was so looking forward to renewing our acquaintance . . .' Sarah said in what she hoped was a sexy sounding voice. 'Your work is absolutely fascinating.' Sarah screwed her face up in embarrassment at what she was doing. She couldn't remember feeling so stupid. But it appeared to be working.

'Really?' said Tyndall slowly as if he was weighing up the possibilities. 'I should be delighted to tell you more, Doctor . . . perhaps we could meet sometime, even if you won't be coming here to work?'

Sarah blew a silent kiss into the air and said, 'I was rather hoping you might suggest that,' she cooed.

'When would be convenient?' Tyndall asked, sounding more than a little flustered.

'As soon as you like,' cooed Sarah, screwing up her face again. 'But you must be very busy . . .'

'My diary is rather full,' agreed Tyndall. 'Perhaps . . . It occurs to me that we might be able to meet, well, outside working hours?'

'What an excellent idea,' exclaimed Sarah, offering up silent thanks again. 'How about this evening?'

There was a pause before Tyndall cleared his throat and said, 'This evening? I don't see why not. Could you perhaps come to my house?'

'Sounds perfect,' said Sarah, trying to keep a note of triumph out of her voice.

'I'm afraid I live outside the city.'

'No problem,' said Sarah. 'I have a car.'

'Shall we say eight o'clock then?'

'Eight o'clock,' she repeated, and wrote down the address she was given.

Sarah opened the door and called Lafferty back into the room. 'It worked,' she exclaimed. 'I'm going to see him this evening at his house.'

Lafferty didn't know whether to be pleased or apprehensive, but he smiled at Sarah's obvious enthusiasm.

'If I succeed in getting the key, I'll come back here and we can go to the Institute tonight,' said Sarah.

'You mustn't take risks, Sarah. Apart from anything else, you have to think of your career. Not only are you leading the professor on, you are planning to commit theft with a view to breaking and entering.'

Sarah's elation suddenly died. She said, 'I wish you hadn't said that.'

'There's still time to change your mind,' said Lafferty.

'I'm going,' said Sarah firmly.

*   *   *

When it was time to go, Lafferty saw Sarah out to her car and wished her luck. He warned her once again not to take any unnecessary risks and she moved off with a last assurance and a wave of her hand. He stood for a moment by the kerb after her car had disappeared round the corner, wishing in his heart that she wasn't going.

Sarah made her way towards the city by-pass and picked up speed as she joined it from the slip road with a quick glance over her shoulder. With the car comfortably settled at sixty-five, and the traffic sparse at seven fifteen in the evening, she relaxed a little and turned on the radio. She changed station three times before finding some music she liked. She didn't know the name of the piece, but she did know it was Mozart.

As her Fiesta ate up the miles, she gave thanks for the by-pass which took her all the way round the outside of the city and brought her to the coast road, which she joined at the small village of Longniddry. Her speed dropped considerably on the winding road that now traced the shoreline eastwards, but a glance at her watch told her that she still had plenty of time to reach the coastal town – where Tyndall lived – by eight o'clock. Although it was dark, the night was clear and there was no sign of the rain promised by the local weather forecast at six. At five to eight she found Tyndall's road and started looking for his house.

The Elms was a large, detached Victorian villa which looked less than welcoming on a dark night. Apart from a dim porch-light, there was no sign of a light on in the rest of the house. This puzzled Sarah, but there was no mistake; this was the house. Its name was etched into the stone pillar that supported a gate which had obviously not been closed for many a long year. She locked her car and walked up the gravel path leading to the front door. There was a large, brass bell-push on the wall. She pushed it and heard it ring somewhere inside. After a few moments, she heard footsteps and felt her throat tighten with nerves. Cyril Tyndall opened the door.

'Dr Lasseter, how nice,' he said, extending his hand. Sarah shook it and found it moist. Tyndall was nervous too.

'I thought we might talk down here,' said Tyndall, leading the way from the main entrance-hall down a wide, carpeted flight of stairs to the basement rooms. This was why she couldn't see a light on from outside, thought Sarah. Tyndall opened a white-painted door and ushered her inside. She found herself in a long, low room, comfortably furnished as a sitting-room and welcomingly warm after the outside temperature.

'I live alone,' explained Tyndall. 'It makes more sense for me to live in the basement rooms. They're easier and more economical to heat.

'It's a big house,' said Sarah. Nervousness made her smile a little wider than usual.

'It was our family house,' said Tyndall. 'Murdoch and I were brought up here.'

'I see,' said Sarah.

'A drink, Dr Lasseter? Or may I call you Sarah?'

'Please do,' said Sarah, although it did little to put her at her ease. She really didn't like rooms that had no windows. 'Gin and tonic would be nice,' she said. She watched Tyndall pour her a very large measure and thought how amateurish his behaviour was for a respected professor and potential Nobel prize-winner.

She accepted the glass with a smile and took a small sip.

Tyndall poured himself a small malt whisky, added a little water and sat down on the chair beside her which he pulled a little closer. 'Now, Sarah, what would you like to know about my research?'

'Everything,' smiled Sarah. 'The development of the vaccine is such an enormous achievement. There are so many questions I'd like to ask; I just don't know where to begin.'

Tyndall gave a half smile as if he hadn't anticipated this response. Sarah noticed that he was sweating along his top lip. His eyes had taken on a flint-like quality which alarmed her a little. She had counted on Tyndall behaving like a shy, awkward academic. Maybe this wasn't going to be the case.

'How exactly did you identify the virus trigger?' she asked.

Tyndall looked a little reluctant to talk about work and Sarah wondered if she had overdone the sexy voice during the phone conversation. She was anxious to get things back on an even keel. Eventually Tyndall said, 'Using a new technique which we developed in the lab, we managed to isolate undisrupted viral DNA in its latent form. From that, we sequenced the upstream DNA and, from *that*, we identified a protein which bound reversibly to this sequence. When the protein was absent, the virus was free to replicate and cause an active infection. But when the protein reappeared and bound tightly to the sequence, the virus was inactivated. We went to work in the lab and designed a protein that would bind *irreversibly* to the trigger sequence.'

'Brilliant,' said Sarah. 'But how could you be sure that the binding was irreversible?'

Once again, Tyndall looked at Sarah strangely. 'Tissue culture,' he said. 'We challenged the virus in tissue culture.'

'I don't know too much about tissue culture, Professor. What little I know suggests that it's a technique of culturing human cells in glass bottles?'

'That's right,' said Tyndall.

'But is that really the same as testing the system in a human being?' asked Sarah.

'Not really,' said Tyndall as if the reply didn't matter. He was staring at Sarah in a way which made her regret having come. But she was here and she had a job to do, she told herself, as Tyndall moved even closer. She got to her feet and said, 'Phew, it's hot in here. Do you mind if I take my jacket off?'

Tyndall's features suddenly relaxed and he said, 'Of course not. Let's both get more comfortable.' He took off his own jacket and tossed it carelessly over the couch. Sarah noticed his wallet sticking out of the inside pocket.

'That's better,' said Sarah sitting back down again.

'You've hardly touched your drink,' Tyndall said, nodding in the direction of her glass.

'Actually, I'm rather thirsty,' said Sarah, putting a hand to her throat. 'I don't suppose you have anything soft. Orange juice? Coke?'

Tyndall let a slight look of irritation betray him before he said, 'I think I have some orange in the fridge.'

Sarah felt an adrenaline surge, fuelled by fear, as she watched Tyndall leave the room. This was her chance and she had to take it. With a supreme effort she overcame the nerves which threatened to paralyse her and picked up Tyndall's jacket to extract his wallet. Her fingers became thumbs as she searched through the contents, looking for the electronic key-card. She was almost sick with apprehension before she found what she was looking for. A black and blue plastic card marked ENTACARD. She slipped it into the side pocket of her skirt and stuffed the wallet back into Tyndall's jacket. Her pulse was still racing when Tyndall returned carrying a glass of orange juice. She accepted it with a smile and hoped that he hadn't noticed that her hand was shaking. Tyndall watched her like an owl eyeing up a mouse as she drank the juice.

'Better?' he asked.

'Much,' smiled Sarah. 'What I don't understand, Professor, is how you managed to do field trials on your vaccine. Surely if . . .' Sarah ground to a halt as Tyndall put his hand on her knee.

'Later,' he croaked.

Sarah gripped his hand and pulled it off her knee. 'I think you are presuming too much, Professor,' she said, hoping to rebuff him, but still keep everything on a civil basis. She was now very afraid. She had totally underestimated Tyndall, and she was now alone with him in the basement of a deserted house.

Tyndall's eyes flashed with anger. 'I don't think so,' he murmured, moving ever closer. 'We both know why you came here, so cut out the silly games. You want me, I want you, so let's stop teasing shall we?'

Sarah felt her knee being gripped so hard it hurt and she let out a little cry.

'What a nice sound,' murmured Tyndall, now almost on top of her. 'So feminine, so inviting . . .'

'Get off me!' cried Sarah. She could smell the whisky

333

on Tyndall's breath as his face bore down on hers. She struggled, but Tyndall was proving too strong for her. He had hold of both her wrists and was pulling her up off the chair. 'We'll be more comfortable here,' he gasped. He was breathing heavily when he pushed her down on to the couch and smothered her with his own body. She could feel the roughness of his beard on her cheek as he reached down with his right hand to start pulling up her skirt. She heard the material tear and her legs become free.

Sarah beat against Tyndall's back with her one free hand but it was useless. Her anger was now interspersed with sobbing and pleading.

'Get off me you animal!' she gasped, as she felt his right knee wedge itself between her legs, prising them apart.

Tyndall paused for a moment to lift his head and look down at Sarah. 'I've heard that some women like it rough,' he snarled. 'So be it.'

Sarah could not believe that she had been so wrong about the man. She simply could not believe that the beast on top of her was the shy, ineffectual little man she had met at the hospital reception whom she thought she could handle. The shyness must have been a mask for arrogance, the diffidence really a contempt for everyone around him. If only she had heeded Ryan's warning! She cried out as Tyndall bit her right breast through her top and forced his hand into her crotch in order to tear away her underwear.

Lafferty looked at his watch and saw that only half an hour had gone by. He couldn't relax; he had done little else but pace up and down since Sarah's departure. The worst of it was that he didn't know why he felt so uneasy. After all, Sarah was probably right: she was a grown woman and knew what she was doing. Once again, he failed to convince himself. He looked at his watch yet again. The thought that he didn't even know where she had gone suddenly occurred to him and made him feel even worse, if that was possible. He had been out of the room when Sarah had made the phone call so he had not heard her repeat an address. This fact niggled away at him for the next five minutes until he thought of something he could do. He remembered a boy scout trick from long ago. You could sometimes find out what had been written on a piece of paper by lightly shading the piece under it on the pad. Sarah had written the address down on his phone pad.

Lafferty rifled through two or three drawers before he found a pencil and then had to contend with the fact that it was broken. He couldn't find a sharpener so he used a kitchen knife. He returned to the phone pad and held the pencil almost horizontal to the paper as he scribbled back and forth very lightly and quickly across it. He put down the pencil and held the pad up to the desk lamp. He could read the address: The Elms, Seaforth Road, North Berwick.

Lafferty felt himself go cold at the mention of North Berwick. He froze with the paper in his hand. Tyndall lived in North Berwick? It had to be coincidence, he told himself. Lots of people must live by the sea in North Berwick and commute to the city. Why not Cyril Tyndall?

Despite this argument, Lafferty found he could not rest easy with the 'coincidence'. Tyndall, the director of Gelman Holland Institute, living in North Berwick with its past association with witchcraft and, in particular, the use of the *Hand of Glory*. There had to be a connection.

Lafferty could not bear the anguish he felt any longer. He grabbed his coat and ran out to the car. He was going to find Sarah.

The clutch release bearing on Lafferty's car gave an angry squeal as he took off a bit too quickly for its liking. 'Don't let me down now,' he murmured. 'Just one more night. That's all I ask.' The bearing decided on a compromise; it disintegrated as he changed down into third gear on entering North Berwick. Lafferty let the car coast to a halt and got out. He stopped the first person he met and asked them where Seaforth Road was. The man pointed in the general direction of the hill leading away from the main thoroughfare. 'About half a mile that way,' he said. Lafferty started running. He didn't even consider the possibility that he might be making a complete fool of himself until he had found Seaforth Road and had to rest for a moment in order to get his breath back. He didn't have to look for the house; he could see Sarah's car standing outside it.

As his breathing settled, Lafferty noticed how quiet it was. The houses in Seaforth Road were few and far between, large mansions standing in their own grounds, surrounded by high stone walls. The wind had dropped away to nothing as if the night was holding its breath. As Lafferty started towards The Elms he heard the sound of large rain drops hit the leaves of a dense laurel hedge to his right. He heard five or six before the first touched his cheek. Any minute now it was going to pour down. He fastened up the collar of his coat.

He paused at the entrance to the house and saw that it was in complete darkness. What did it mean? Had Sarah and Tyndall gone out somewhere? That seemed unlikely. Why would they do that? He walked up to the door and rang the bell. There was no answer, so he rang again and again. He couldn't think what else to do.

At last he heard a sound from inside and the hall light was switched on. 'What is it?' asked an angry voice as the door was opened.

'Professor Tyndall?' asked Lafferty, taking in the dishevelled state of the man in front of him.

'Yes, what is it?' snapped Tyndall.

'I am looking for Dr Sarah Lasseter,' said Lafferty calmly. 'I believe she's here?'

Tyndall's eyes took on a startled look. He patted his ruffled hair nervously. 'What makes you say that? Who are you?'

'Sarah's car is outside your gate. Where is she?'

Tyndall seemed unsure of what to say and it alarmed Lafferty. He started to lose his cool. 'Where is she?' he demanded.

'She's here,' admitted Tyndall. He stood back to allow Lafferty to enter the hall. 'Wait here a moment please. I'll tell her you're here.'

Lafferty watched Tyndall go downstairs. As he reached the foot of the steps he glanced back up at Lafferty before calling out pleasantly, 'Sarah, my dear, it's someone for you.' He disappeared from sight and Lafferty turned to look at the pictures and photographs which adorned one wall of the entrance-hall. One was a large print of North Berwick harbour. Lafferty leaned closer to examine the date when he heard a sound from downstairs. It was the sound of a lock being turned. Tyndall was unlocking a door. Sarah had been locked in!

Lafferty ran downstairs lightly on his toes and heard voices as he turned in the direction he had seen Tyndall go. They were coming from behind the white door. He put his ear to it and heard Tyndall rasp, 'You set me up! You led me on, you silly bitch. If it comes to it, I'll deny everything about tonight and you can say goodbye to your career, so think about it. Now pull yourself together!'

Lafferty opened the door to find Sarah wiping her tear-stained cheeks. Her skirt was torn. Tyndall turned round and opened his mouth to say something, but Lafferty hit him with a swinging right hand that carried all of his thirteen stones and a great deal of anger. Tyndall was lifted clean off his feet and tumbled over backwards to land in an untidy heap on the floor. Sarah flew into Lafferty's arms and the tears came. 'Oh Ryan,' she sobbed. 'I've been so stupid!'

Lafferty held her close to him while watching Tyndall over her shoulder. 'Are you all right, Sarah?' he asked gently. 'Did he . . .'

Sarah shook her head against his shoulder and said quietly, 'You arrived just in time.'

'Stupid bitch,' snarled Tyndall from the floor. He dabbed at his bleeding mouth with the back of his hand. 'There isn't a court in the land who would take her word against mine in the circumstances.' His face filled with fear as he saw the look in Lafferty's eyes as he gently disengaged himself from Sarah and started towards him. 'Keep away from me!' he squealed.

'No, Ryan!' called out Sarah, rushing forward to put a restraining hand on his arm. 'Don't! Please don't.'

Lafferty paused, looking down at Tyndall, his eyes filled with contempt. 'So this is what a potential Nobel Prize-winner looks like,' he murmured. 'The brightest and best of his generation!'

'Ryan, take me away from here,' said Sarah, her hand still on Lafferty's arm.

Lafferty turned and Sarah pulled him towards the door. They had almost reached the head of the stairs when they heard Tyndall's voice behind them. 'Wait!' he commanded.

Lafferty turned to see Tyndall standing at the foot of the stairs pointing a shotgun up at them.

'Oh for God's sake!' exclaimed Sarah. 'This is getting out of all proportion. Put the gun down, Professor.'

Tyndall started up the stairs towards them. The gun in his hands had brought back his confidence. 'Why did you really come here tonight?' he demanded of Sarah. 'What were you after? And why tell a priest you were coming here?'

'This is . . .' Words failed Sarah as she watched Tyndall level the shotgun at Lafferty's stomach. 'Stop this, Professor!'

There was a Chinese patterned vase standing on a small table next to Lafferty. Tyndall saw him glance at it and warned, 'Don't even think about it. That's a Ming.'

Lafferty had been thinking about it, although its size and weight had taken precedence over any consideration of origin or value. When Tyndall's eyes moved momentarily to the vase, Sarah saw her chance and flung her handbag at him. It opened in mid-flight and Tyndall was showered with keys, coins, lipstick and her hospital bleeper. It was the surprise factor more than the objects that caused him to over-balance and tumble backwards down the stairs. He let go of the gun and it clattered down the steps behind him to lie silently across his still legs.

'Oh my God,' said Sarah, putting her hands to her mouth. 'Is he all right?'

Lafferty was unsure about whether Tyndall was unconscious or just shamming. The gun was within easy reach for him. For a moment he was in two minds whether to go downstairs or not, but he overcame his reservations out of human concern and started to descend a step at a time. He reached the bottom and pulled the gun cautiously away from Tyndall by the barrels. Tyndall still didn't move. Lafferty put his hand to Tyndall's neck to feel for a pulse but couldn't find any. 'Sarah,' he said softly. 'I think you'd better take a look at him.' Sarah joined him at the foot of the stairs and knelt down beside Tyndall. After a moment she looked up at Lafferty and said, 'His neck's broken. He's dead.'

Lafferty closed Tyndall's eyes with his forefinger and thumb before picking up Sarah's belongings. Sarah herself seemed to be in a trance; she couldn't take her eyes off the body. Lafferty put a hand on her shoulder and squeezed gently.

'It's all my fault,' said Sarah quietly. 'If I hadn't been so stupid none of this would ever have happened.'

'Don't blame yourself, Sarah,' said Lafferty. 'Fate was holding the reins.'

Sarah shook her head and refused to listen, but Lafferty persisted. He made her look at him. 'This is not your doing,' he insisted. 'It just happened, that's all. His death was an accident.'

Sarah looked back at Tyndall's lifeless body. 'He was a gifted man,' she said. 'Whatever he tried to do to me.'

'Maybe,' said Lafferty coldly.

Sarah looked at him questioningly.

'Do you know how long he's been living here?' asked Lafferty.

'He told me that he and his brother were brought up here. This was the family house. Why?'

'Because this is North Berwick. An intelligent man who's lived here all his life must have known about the past connection with witchcraft and the Hand of Glory.'

'You think that Cyril was involved?' gasped an incredulous Sarah. 'But he was a brilliant scientist! Why on earth would he get involved in anything criminal?'

Lafferty shook his head and said, 'I don't know, but you didn't reckon on him being a rapist either.'

Sarah conceded the point in silence.

'Oh Ryan,' she whispered, her voice reflecting the hopelessness she felt. 'This is all just too . . .'

Lafferty drew Sarah to him and held her for a moment before leading her slowly up the stairs.

'What do we do now?'

'We should call the police,' replied Lafferty.

Sarah considered this for a moment before saying slowly, 'I managed to get the key to the institute . . .'

Lafferty looked at her as if he found it hard to believe what she was suggesting. 'You can't be serious – after all you've been through,' he said softly.

'I want us to see it through together,' said Sarah firmly. 'We've come this far.'

'If you're absolutely sure . . .' said Lafferty, his voice betraying the doubts he felt.

'I'm sure,' said Sarah, but she sounded as if her confidence was balanced on a knife-edge. 'If we call the police, these people might still get away with it. We owe it to John McKirrop, the O'Donnells, John Main and God knows how many others, to see that they don't.'

Lafferty saw the determination in Sarah's eyes and his heart went out to her. The feeling alarmed him but it was undeniable. 'Come on then,' he said. 'We'll have to use your car. Mine has given up the ghost.'

Lafferty drove the Fiesta back at Sarah's request. They didn't speak until they had cleared the outskirts of North Berwick, when Sarah asked Lafferty how he had come to be there in the first place.

'I was worried about you,' he replied. He told her about the trick with the phone-pad.

'Ryan?'

'Yes?'

'Would you take your collar off, please?'

Lafferty glanced sideways then complied without question. He tossed it over his shoulder on to the back seat. Sarah rested her head against his arm. 'That's better,' she murmured. 'And Ryan?'

'Yes?'

'Right now you are wondering what you should say. The answer is nothing. Just don't say anything.'

Lafferty remained silent.

Sarah remained with her head resting against his arm for the remainder of the journey. She wasn't asleep, but she kept her eyes closed until she heard the engine note slow as they approached a roundabout. She sat up straight and looked out of the window.

'How are you feeling?' Lafferty asked.

Sarah thought for a moment before replying, 'I don't think I've ever been so afraid in my life.'

As they drove through the outskirts of the city Sarah asked, 'Do you think we could stop off at the hospital? I'd like to change.' She fingered her torn skirt.

'Of course.'

Lafferty was glad it was still raining as he parked Sarah's Fiesta in the car-park outside the residency. It gave him a feeling of security. He supposed it was psychological, but a dark, wet night suggested that most people would be indoors. There would be less chance of being seen by casual passers-by.

Eventually, Sarah emerged from the building wearing jeans and her suede jacket. She ran down the steps and got into the car, brushing the rain from her hair with her hand. 'Sorry I was so long,' she said.

Lafferty ignored the apology and said, 'Sarah, you really don't have to do this. I can go alone to the Institute. Why don't you wait here and I'll get in touch with you later?'

Lafferty was puzzled when he saw a flash of anger cross Sarah's face. It was still reflected in her eyes when she said, 'Ryan, don't ever treat me like the little woman. Understood?'

'Understood,' replied Lafferty, a little taken aback.

Sarah wasn't finished yet. She said, 'This is as much my problem as it is yours and I'm the doctor in this team; I'm in a much better position than you to find my way round a medical research laboratory and understand what's going on. If anyone stays behind, it should be you. You may be a man but you are a priest and in my book that makes you . . .' Sarah paused as she felt her mouth begin to run ahead of her brain.

'As much use as a chocolate spanner?' ventured Lafferty.

Sarah saw the humour in Lafferty's eyes and her temper evaporated at once to be replaced by guilt. She let her body sag and she looked up to the heavens, saying, 'What am I doing? What am I saying to the man who drove through the night to save me from a fate worse than death, the man who laid out the villain with a punch that would have made John Wayne look limp-wristed. He does all this and I start playing the aggrieved feminist!' Sarah shook her head.

'It wasn't entirely unjustified,' said Lafferty. 'You actually made a very good point.'

'Why do you have to be so bloody reasonable?' exploded Sarah.

Lafferty looked puzzled and Sarah burst into laughter. 'What am I going to do with you?' she exclaimed.

When Lafferty still looked puzzled, Sarah said quietly, 'Let's both go to the Institute, shall we?' As the smiles faded, they both knew the time for laughter was over.

'Got a torch?' asked Lafferty.

'In the glove compartment,' Sarah replied. Lafferty started the car and they set off for the medical school.

A church clock struck one as Lafferty and Sarah made their way to the Institute. There was no security to speak of at the medical school, more a caretaker service to deal with late phone enquiries and keep a general eye on things. Despite the lateness of the hour, there were still a number of lights on in the main buildings. 'Emergency lab services,' explained Sarah.

When they reached the Institute Lafferty suggested that they wait in the shadows for a few minutes to make sure that there were no signs of activity inside the building. Being modern, a lot of glass had been used in its construction. Even a light on in a room at the back would have been visible from where they stood.

Sarah rubbed her arms as she became cold with the wait. Lafferty nodded and said, 'All right, let's go.' They flitted across to the door of the institute, and Sarah inserted the card in the electronic lock. There was a barely audible click and the door was released. Sarah ushered Lafferty inside, then closed the door again quietly. Both of them dropped to their knees to make sure they were not visible from outside; they waited a few moments until their nerves had calmed down.

Sarah pointed to the stairs at the back of the reception area and Lafferty nodded. But when they got to them they found that the stairs only went up. There were none leading down to the basement. Lafferty looked to his left and saw a door with a small glass panel in it. He went to have a look while Sarah checked the other side of the hall. Lafferty looked through the panel and saw steps leading down. 'Over here!' he whispered.

Sarah joined him and he opened the door to let her pass through first. With a quick glance over his shoulder to make sure that all was still quiet outside, Lafferty joined her and they descended to the basement corridor. There was a light on in the corridor – just a single bulkhead lamp, covered in a wire mesh, but it made Lafferty and Sarah look at each other apprehensively. They stood still for a few moments, listening, but there was no sound to indicate that they might not be alone.

'Maybe it's a safety thing,' whispered Lafferty. Sarah shrugged. They walked along the corridor, slowly examining the rooms on either side as they looked for the Sigma Lab. Sarah found it. The door had a white plastic sign on it with green lettering saying, SIGMA LABORATORY, AUTHORIZED STAFF ONLY. She tried the door but it was locked. Glancing at Lafferty she smiled wryly as if embarrassed that they had not reckoned on that possibility.

Lafferty placed his palms against the door to get an

idea of how solid it was. He moved his head from side to side to indicate that it did not seem all that secure to him and looked around for something he might use as a jemmy, but he found nothing.

'Well,' he sighed, taking a pace backwards. 'In for a penny . . .'

Lafferty threw his shoulder hard against the door and had the satisfaction of hearing splintering sounds. He did it twice more and the door swung back quietly on its hinges. 'Can we risk the light?' asked Sarah. 'There aren't any windows.'

'Better not,' replied Lafferty. 'These ventilation grilles may lead straight through to the outside.' He briefly highlighted two wire covered squares on the wall with the torch, then pointed it at the floor again.

The room was bigger than either of them had thought from the outside. It was actually a double room, with two doors leading out to the corridor. One half was obviously used for working on the bodies when they arrived. It had an operating table mounted on a central pedestal with a surgical lamp mounted above it. Instruments were arranged on metal trays on a side bench. There were two stainless steel sinks, one equipped with elbow taps so that they could be turned on and off without the operator having to use his hands.

'Could organs be removed here?' Lafferty asked Sarah.

'No,' replied Sarah firmly. 'The facilities are not nearly good enough. This set up is just what you would need for removal of the Sigma probes.'

'Nothing out of the ordinary?' asked Lafferty.

Sarah shook her head and they moved through a central partition into the other half of the room. On the left was

347

a small refrigerated body vault capable of accommodating two bodies. Lafferty swallowed as the torch beam picked out a coffin sitting opposite on the side bench. Sarah gripped his arm as they approached and looked at the lid. There was a brass plate fixed to it. On it was the inscription, MARTIN KEEGAN, RIP. The lid was loose and Lafferty pushed it aside. It was empty.

'The body's missing,' he said.

'Try the fridge,' said Sarah.

Lafferty pulled the clasp and released the fridge door. There was no light inside so Sarah held the torch while he examined the contents. There was one white-shrouded body inside; the label attached to the big toe of the left foot said, *Martin Keegan*. Lafferty stood up straight and felt thoroughly dejected. 'Well, that's that,' he said, berating himself. 'All wrong . . . we got it all wrong.'

'Not necessarily,' said Sarah softly. 'With Stubbs being away, they may have decided not to use Martin Keegan's body. It doesn't mean to say they didn't steal the others.'

'I suppose not,' agreed Lafferty. 'But this was our last chance to prove it.' He was about to shut the fridge door when Sarah suddenly said, 'Wait!'

'What is it?' asked Lafferty, alarmed at the note in her voice. He could see by reflected torch light that Sarah was staring at something in the fridge, but he couldn't understand what. Her hand was shaking slightly and the movement was amplified in the torch beam.

'His foot,' said Sarah.

'What about it?

'His left foot is undamaged. Martin Keegan's left foot was badly injured in his accident.

Lafferty gripped the end of the tray that the sheet-covered corpse was lying on and slid it out of the fridge.

The sheet was cold and damp as he unwound it from the head. He heard Sarah gasp as it came away. 'Oh my God,' she exclaimed, taking a step backwards. 'It's Derek Stubbs!'

Lafferty saw that she was right. He remembered Stubbs from the night he had caught the three of them together in HTU. 'The much maligned Dr Stubbs,' he said thoughtfully.

Sarah looked utterly bemused. 'I don't understand,' she confessed. 'What's going on?'

'I think we may have done Dr Stubbs a disservice,' said Lafferty. 'We let dislike colour our judgement.'

'You mean he *wasn't* involved in the body theft?' asked Sarah in astonishment. 'But he was always on about the lack of transplant organs and how Murdoch Tyndall didn't press the relatives hard enough for them!'

'We didn't know about his son,' said Lafferty. 'We should have listened more carefully to what Stubbs was complaining about. I think Murdoch Tyndall didn't press the relatives for permission . . . because he didn't *want* them to give permission!'

'What?' exclaimed Sarah.

'It makes sense now. John Main said that Tyndall asked him at precisely the wrong moment. You yourself suggested he did the same thing with the O'Donnells. He did that because he didn't *want* the relatives to give transplant permission.'

'But why not?'

'Because he and his brother wanted to use the bodies for something else,' said Lafferty.

Sarah's mouth fell open. 'But what?' she asked in a voice that shock had reduced to a whisper.

'I don't know, Sarah,' said Lafferty.

349

'But why kill Stubbs?' asked Sarah, desperate to seek out flaws in Lafferty's argument.

'I think when Stubbs came to see you about telling tales to Tyndall he suddenly realised that there was something fishy about the whole thing. He realised while he was speaking to you that Tyndall must actually have wanted the relatives to say no. He must have gone to Tyndall to have it out with him – the row you heard them having. When he didn't get any joy out of Tyndall he, like us, must have worked out that removal of the Sigma probes presented the best chance for "diverting" the bodies. He must have come here to the institute and this is the result.' They both looked down at Stubbs's corpse.

'Good God,' said Sarah.

A sudden whirring noise startled them. 'What is it?' asked Sarah, her voice betraying panic.

'A lift!' replied Lafferty, suddenly realising what the sound was. He caught a glimpse of light coming from a slight crack in one of the wall panels. Pulling Sarah out of the way, he indicated that she get under the bench. As soon as she was hidden, he joined her. A few seconds later they heard the lift come to a halt and the wall panel slide back.

Lafferty couldn't see who got out, only that it was a man, and he was wearing white surgical trousers and short, white rubber boots. The man crossed the lab and let out an oath when he reached the door to the corridor and saw the burst lock. 'Jesus H. Christ!' he exclaimed and then started running along the corridor.

'We're trapped!' said Sarah.

'Come on!' said Lafferty.

'But where?'

Lafferty indicated the lift and pulled Sarah towards it.

'If he's going to search the basement we can beat him to the front door!'

He slid open the door to the lift and they got in. The lift was long and narrow. Lafferty didn't have to be a genius to work out why. He pressed the 'up' button and nothing happened. He pressed it again and then four times rapidly in succession. Still nothing. He looked around for some kind of brake switch or emergency button that might have been holding the car, but there was none. There was only one other button. It had a down arrow on it. In desperation, he pressed it and the lift door slid shut. He looked at Sarah with amazement on his face as they both realised that they were going down. They had got on in the basement but they were definitely going down!

Sarah let her head slump forward on to Lafferty's chest and he shared her dejection.

Lafferty broke away from Sarah and bunched his fists in readiness. He had no idea what to expect when the lift doors opened, but he was going to go down fighting. The doors slid back to reveal nothing more sinister than a plain, green-painted wall. They stepped out into a narrow corridor leading to two swing doors. There was no point in going back up in the lift. It did not reach the upper floors. It simply connected the Sigma lab to this sub-basement. The long narrow car had been designed to carry coffins. The missing bodies did not go off to some fancy private clinic; they obviously came here.

Sarah looked first through the glass in the swing doors and let out her breath in a low whistle. Lafferty took a look and saw what seemed to him a unit very much like HTU. It was lit with low green lighting and each bed was surrounded with life-support machinery. The patients were enclosed by inflated plastic bubbles.

351

There did not seem to be any staff around, so Lafferty and Sarah went in through the doors and approached the nearest bubble. 'Oh my God,' said Sarah, putting her hand to her mouth. 'It's John's son! It's Simon Main!'

'But he's dead!' exclaimed Lafferty. 'What's he doing here?'

'They're all dead,' said Sarah, looking up the line. 'Brain dead. But their bodies are still being kept ventilated and nourished.'

They moved on to the next bubble and found Martin Keegan. Pumps and relays clicked and hissed perpetual life into him.

'I don't understand,' said Lafferty. 'What's the point of it all? If they are all brain dead, why keep them on the machines?'

'I'm not sure,' whispered Sarah. 'Maybe this will tell us something.' She had seen a plastic clip-board hanging on the wall between the two bays. She lifted it off its hook and read, 'MAIN, CHALLENGE DOSE 5, VARICELLA ZOSTER, 10.7 PFU per ml.'

'Mean anything?' asked Lafferty.

Sarah nodded thoughtfully and turned the page. 'KEEGAN, PROTECTION 1, PRIMARY COMPLETE, SECONDARY +2, CHALLENGE 1 DUE +14. H. SIMPLEX.'

'Well?' prompted Lafferty.

'They are using these people as human cell cultures,' said Sarah, not hiding her distaste. 'Their bodies are being used as laboratory animals.'

'What do you mean?'

'Viruses won't grow outside living cells,' said Sarah. 'To work with them in the lab you need some kind of cell culture system to keep them alive. This usuall takes the form of a tissue culture system – usually animal cells growing artificially in glass bottles with some kind of liquid nutrient. It's not as good as using human cells but the availability of human cells is, of course, limited – and they don't survive well in artificial culture anyway. They tend to die off after a few days.'

'But if you use a whole person . . .' said Lafferty, looking down at Martin Keegan.

'Precisely,' said Sarah. 'They're using whole bodies as living tissue cultures for viruses.'

'But what for?' asked Lafferty.

'The record cards suggest that Simon Main's body has been immunised with the *Herpes* vaccine and been challenged five times with the virus, the last time with *Varicella zoster*.'

'And Martin Keegan?'

'I think the code means that he has just been given his primary dose of vaccine. He still has to get a second injection in two days and then he will be challenged with *Herpes simplex* virus in fourteen days' time.'

'My God,' said Lafferty, his voice betraying the revulsion he felt. 'This is repulsive.'

'This must be how they developed and tested their vaccine so quickly,' said Sarah. 'They were using a human model from the beginning, so there was no need for small animal tests followed by time-consuming, expensive tests on primates.'

'But surely the Department of Health must have asked questions?' asked Lafferty. 'If they granted a licence for the vaccine they must have known how it was developed and tested?'

'You would think so,' said Sarah.

'There must have been paperwork, surely?'

Sarah said quietly, 'The government put up half the money for the Head Trauma Unit.'

'Good God,' whispered Lafferty as he saw what she was suggesting. 'They knew all along what was happening to these people.'

'Just another case of the end justifying the means.'

'It's incredible!'

'I remember my father telling me of the anguish that ran through the medical profession after the full extent of the Nazi medical experiments became known after the war. All that pain and suffering with people in the camps being subjected to nightmarish experiments. And all in the cause of advancing medical science. But the worst thing, he said, was not the fact that people who called themselves doctors had carried out such atrocities, it was the awful fact that they *had* advanced medical knowledge. In doing the unspeakable they achieved what normal researchers would have taken ten times as long to accomplish. It seemed somehow like a . . .'

'Triumph of evil,' said Lafferty.

'Yes,' agreed Sarah.

'Evil does triumph sometimes,' said Lafferty. 'The important thing is to continue recognising it as evil, and not to start crediting it as being anything else. And this,' he said looking around him, 'is evil.'

The sound of raised voices coming from the far end of the room interrupted them and brought home the hopelessness of their position. Lafferty looked around then pointed to the bed on which Martin Keegan lay. 'Get under!' he whispered.

Sarah slid under the bed and Lafferty followed with a great deal more awkwardness. He found his face pressed up against a glass tank that was receiving the waste product

354

from Keegan's body. The voices were getting louder and they could now hear what was being said.

Murdoch Tyndall's voice said angrily, 'This can't go on, Sotillo. We'll have to delay introduction of the vaccine.'

'Nonsense!' replied Sotillo. 'It's a chance in a million reaction. We can't let just one isolated case ruin the whole project. There's too much at stake.'

'But we don't know that it's just one case, Sotillo,' protested Tyndall. 'We don't have enough figures.'

The two men had stopped in front of Martin Keegan's bed. Lafferty could see by their feet that they were facing each other.

'Look!' said Sotillo. 'This is no time to get cold feet. There's always a risk with any kind of vaccination. We've just had a bit of bad luck, that's all.'

'And what happens if it isn't just a bit of bad luck?' argued Tyndall. 'I say we call a halt until we know for sure.'

'No!' said Sotillo. 'We go ahead as planned.'

Lafferty saw one pair of feet turn and head for the lift corridor. The other pair followed, Tyndall continuing to argue.

'What was all that about?' whispered Lafferty to Sarah.

'Sounds like something has gone wrong with the vaccine,' replied Sarah. 'Did you see where they came from?'

'Somewhere up the top end,' replied Lafferty, moving his head in the direction of the far end of the room.

'Maybe there's a way out up there?' suggested Sarah.

'Let's see.'

They slid out from under the bed and hurried up to the head of the room which was in deep shadow. They found a narrow passage to their left where they deduced Tyndall and Sotillo must have come from. Lafferty led the way cautiously along it, keeping his back against the wall and peering out slowly when they came to a right-angled turning. His heart sank when he saw the passage end in a door marked, ISOLATION SUITE. He straightened up and Sarah joined him at his side. 'No way out,' he said.

'Try the door,' said Sarah.

Lafferty nodded, recognising that they had nothing to lose by going on. There was no way out behind them save for the lift. The thought made him realise that Tyndall and Sotillo must have been told of the break-in by now. He pushed the door in front of him and it clicked open. The room was in darkness, but he could hear the now familiar sound of a life-support machine and could see the coloured LEDs blinking on the control panels. He felt along the wall to his right with an open palm and found the light switch.

The room contained one life-support bay, similar to the ones outside, but before Lafferty or Sarah could take a look at the patient lying there, they heard the sound of loud voices and Lafferty turned out the light again.

'They must know we're down here!' whispered Sarah urgently.

'Maybe not,' replied Lafferty. 'Maybe they're checking just in case. Get under the bed!'

Sarah got down on the floor in the darkness and crawled across to where she remembered the end of the bed was. Lafferty followed and urged her to hurry as the voice grew louder.

'I can't!' said Sarah. 'There are some boxes in the way. There's no room!

'Try going in from the side!' urged Lafferty.

Sarah slithered round to the side of the bed and managed to get underneath, but there was no room left for Lafferty.

'The boxes are too heavy. I can't move them!' said Sarah.

Lafferty clapped his hand to his forehead in anguish. The shouting voices outside were getting very near and there was nowhere else to hide except perhaps . . .

He tugged at the side of the plastic bubble enclosing the patient and it came free. He crawled in, feeling his way in the dark, warm, humid atmosphere inside the plastic, and lay down beside the patient. If the searchers, as he hoped they might, just switched on the light and took a quick look into the room they wouldn't see him.

Lafferty was very aware of the patient's chest rising and falling in response to the ventilator as he lay as still as a corpse. He tried to breathe as little as possible, partly through fear, but also because of the sweet, sickly smell that now filled his nostrils inside the plastic bubble.

'They can't possibly be down here,' he heard Tyndall say outside the door. 'It was probably yobs who broke in. They'd be looking for drugs. And even if it was one of these nosy parkers, they wouldn't have found anything up in the Sigma lab – and there's nothing to suggest that they found the lift.'

'We have to be sure,' replied Sotillo.

Lafferty heard the door open and the room was suddenly filled with light. For the first time he saw his companion on the bed and it was a vision from hell. He cold not stop himself gasping at the nightmarish face that was only a few centimetres from his own. For a moment he thought it was some kind of animal, but then he realised that the face was human. The skin was completely covered in suppurating pustules; they were the source of the sickly sweet smell. Even the eyes were affected with the sores and a sticky, yellow exudate oozed out from encrusted lids. The face jerked rhythmically as air was injected into the lungs by the ventilator.

Lafferty felt the urge to vomit become almost overpowering. He could taste it in his mouth as he kept his lips pursed and continued to fight the gagging in his throat. For some reason, he felt compelled to continue staring at the apparition in front of him, following the hideous contours of the face as guilt began to mingle with the revulsion he felt. This had been a human being, he told himself. He should be feeling compassion and pity, not fear and revulsion. He continued to stare at the horror until a new thought crept into the nightmare and exploded inside his head. This was not just a human being . . . there was something familiar about the outline of the forehead and cheek. His eyes widened as he realised the truth. The stinking, pustulated body lying beside him had belonged to Mary O'Donnell!

The realisation proved too much for Lafferty. He turned away violently to the left and threw up, fighting his way out of the plastic bubble as he did so. He ended up on the floor on his knees in front of Tyndall, Sotillo and two other men dressed in white. Sarah slid out from under the bed and put a hand on his shoulder.

'It's Mary,' he gasped, wiping his mouth with the back of his hand. 'It's Mary O'Donnell.'

Sarah got to her feet and looked at the body inside the bubble. She recoiled before saying quietly, 'Disseminated *Herpes*. The new vaccine did this to her, didn't it?' She looked Tyndall and Sotillo for an answer.

'A chance misfortune,' said Sotillo smoothly. 'It happens sometimes with vaccines. You're a doctor, you should know that.'

'But you don't know what the chances are with this particular kind of vaccine. Right?' asked Sarah.

Tyndall and Sotillo looked at each other as they realised that Sarah must have heard their earlier conversation.

'How could you possibly get involved in something like this?' Sarah demanded of Tyndall.

'It's not as if they were live patients we were using,' replied Tyndall. 'Can't you see the advantages to be gained by using such a culture system?'

'Culture system?' exploded Sarah. 'They were people, for God's sake, not culture systems!'

'Emotional claptrap!' snapped Sotillo. 'They were dead at the outset. Can't you rise above such pettiness? You're a doctor.'

'It's much to her credit that she can't,' said Lafferty, getting to his feet and standing beside Sarah. 'Maybe she recognises greed and avarice even when it's disguised as a quest for medical advance. People like you don't give a damn for anything other than their own glory and advancement. Money and prizes! That's what it's all about, isn't it?'

'I don't think we could expect anything else from an anachronism like yourself,' sneered Sotillo. 'You and your kind are two thousand years out of date!'

Lafferty made a move towards Sotillo but the two white-clad attendants blocked his way. 'Really, Father. Violence, and you a man of the cloth,' sneered Sotillo.

'I'm looking at the face of evil, Sotillo,' replied Lafferty. 'I don't think my church would have the slightest problem with me smashing it through the back of your head.'

Sotillo seemed discomfited with the look on Lafferty's face. He said to one of the attendants. 'Prepare two bays out there.'

Lafferty smiled ruefully and said, 'And now there are to be two more murders in the cause of medical science. Right?'

Sotillo didn't reply and Tyndall looked at his feet in silence.

'Well, Doctor?' said Sarah. '*Are* you going to murder us?'

Tyndall seemed embarrassed and lost for words.

'It shouldn't be too difficult. After all, it's not as if it's the first time, is it?'

'What do you mean?' demanded Tyndall.

'John McKirrop,' said Sarah. 'And Main, and Stubbs. You killed them all, didn't you? You came back to the hospital that night after I phoned you and pushed McKirrop's skull back into his brain. And later on, when Stubbs knew too much and Main found the lab, you disposed of them too.'

'McKirrop was a no-account tramp,' said Tyndall. 'He'd probably have drunk himself to death within a year anyway. As for Main and Stubbs, we couldn't allow them to get away either. Don't you understand? This work is far too important to let anything get in the way. The *Herpes* vaccine is only the beginning. We're on the threshold of being able to fight viruses at molecular level! We're talking about an end to disease!'

Sarah and Lafferty did not reply.

'We're wasting time,' said Sotillo. 'Lock them in here until the bays are ready for them.'

18

As Sotillo and Tyndall turned away, Lafferty threw himself across the room in a last-ditch attempt to fight his way out. He knew that the odds against him were hopeless, but he felt he owed it to Sarah and himself to try. Sotillo and Tyndall were surprised at the sudden rush but Mace, the attendant who had remained while Pallister went to organise the bays, was obviously prepared for it. As Lafferty lunged forward he simply stepped aside like a matador dealing with a clumsy bull and hammered his fist into the side of Lafferty's head. Lafferty went down and lay still on the floor.

'No more silliness, please,' said Sotillo, looking down at Lafferty's prostrate form.

Lafferty came round to find Sarah pushing heavy boxes against the door. He sat up slowly and asked what she was doing.

Sarah jerked her head round and said, 'Good. You've come round. Are you all right?'

'I think so,' said Lafferty, confused by the activity.

'Can you help me?' asked Sarah.

Lafferty got to his feet unsteadily and rubbed the side of his head. 'What on earth are you doing?' he asked haltingly.

'I'm barricading the door,' replied Sarah. 'I've decided I'm not going to go meekly like a lamb to the slaughter. I want to hold on to life as long as possible. I think we should put up a fight. What do you say?'

Sarah didn't wait for an answer, and Lafferty watched her manoeuvre one of the life-support machines into position with a determination he found compelling. There seemed to be no point in emphasising the hopelessness of their position. He turned to look at the space above Mary's bed where the machine had been. 'You disconnected it?' he asked.

'Mary doesn't need it. She's dead,' replied Sarah. 'We do. Come on. Lend a hand. Bring the other power-pack over.'

Lafferty did as he was bid. He was still puzzled, but it felt a whole lot better to be doing something rather than just sitting around. He shook off the last of his drowsiness and got to work. He pulled out the remaining heavy boxes from below the bed, carefully avoiding the glass waste-tank, and found that they were full of spares for the life-support machines: diaphragms, filters and pump-bodies. He dragged them one at a time across the floor and started adding them to the barrier. When he had stacked the last of them in position, Sarah took a step back to look at the barricade. She screwed up her face. 'There's not going to be enough weight,' she said anxiously.

Lafferty joined her and had to agree. After a moment's thought, he said, 'Wedges!' He pulled some of the plastic tubing from the tube ports on the machines and started pushing it into the crack along the bottom of the door.

'Good thinking,' said Sarah, but her voice still betrayed doubts.

'What about the bed itself?' asked Lafferty when he'd finished.

Sarah looked round and nodded. 'I'll move Mary.' She tore away the plastic bubble from over the bed and used it to wrap Mary O'Donnell's body.

'I still don't understand what happened to her,' said Lafferty as he watched.

'The new vaccine didn't work on Mary,' said Sarah. 'It had the complete opposite effect to that intended. It left her without any protection at all. So, when they came to challenge her with an injection of live virus it simply rampaged through her body.

'But that might happen to other people too,' said Lafferty.

'Precisely,' agreed Sarah. 'That's what Sotillo and Tyndall were arguing about. Sotillo wanted to dismiss Mary's case as a chance in a million occurrence. Tyndall had cold feet; he wanted to withdraw the vaccine.'

'I see,' said Lafferty as he stepped in to lift Mary's body gently from the bed and lay it on the floor. As he did so, a deep sigh came from her throat and Lafferty almost dropped her.

'It wasn't real,' said Sarah, quickly putting her hand on his shoulder to reassure him. 'Just trapped air in her lungs.'

Lafferty nodded nervously and joined Sarah in pulling the bed across the floor. They propped it up against the door as they heard sounds outside it.

The door moved in a little as someone tried to open

it, but the wedges held without allowing too much strain to fall on their barricade.

Another attempt was made to open it before Sotillo realised what had happened and banged on the door.

'What is the point of this, you stupid people?' he demanded. 'You can't escape!'

Neither Lafferty nor Sarah replied. Both of them were concentrating on keeping their weight against the bed-frame.

Sarah inclined her head to look at her watch. Lafferty didn't ask why, although he did wonder. He couldn't imagine anything less important in their current circumstances than what time it was. A tremendous crash at the door put the thought out of his head as Pallister and Mace took a running charge at it together. The door jerked open a few inches before the wedges and the weight of the barricade stopped it.

As Lafferty applied his full weight in an attempt to close it again, he saw either Pallister's or Mace's hand come through the gap and try to get some purchase on the edge of the door. He had a box of pump spares lying at his feet and, picking up one of the heavier components, a round, chromium-plated pump-body, he smashed it across the invading fingers. A yelp of pain was followed by a quick withdrawal of the hand. Lafferty and Sarah managed to close the door again, but the wedges had been displaced. Lafferty dropped down on his knees quickly to push them back into place. He was squeezing the last one into the crack when a vicious kick to the door caused it to move back an inch or two and caught his forefinger in the gap along the bottom. The skin was torn back from the base of his nail and it was his turn to cry out in pain. He got to his feet with his indured

finger in his mouth and kicked the last wedge into place
with his shoe.

'Are you all right?' asked Sarah anxiously.

'I'm OK,' replied Lafferty, briefly taking his finger out
of his mouth to spit out blood.

'Get some tools!' shouted Sotillo outside the door.

There was a lull in the proceedings while either Mace or
Pallister or both went off to find tools; then Sotillo spoke.
'Why don't you stop this foolishness? You know there's no
escape. Why don't you just accept your fate and make it
easy on yourselves? There will be no pain or suffering,
I promise. A simple injection of a neurotoxic chemical
and it will all be over. You won't feel anything.'

Sarah whispered to Lafferty, 'Personally, I don't fancy
a simple injection of a neurotoxic chemical. Do you?'

Lafferty admired Sarah's bravery and wished he could
match it. In the circumstances, all he could manage was
a weak smile.

'But if you persist in this time-wasting nonsense,' continued Sotillo, his voice becoming harsher, 'I might not
be inclined to be so charitable. We could be talking about
new dimensions in pain before I'm finished with you!'

Lafferty saw that this time Sarah had visibly paled.
Somehow it seemed to give him courage. 'Chin up!' he
said. 'We'll give them a run for their money.'

Sarah smiled and said, 'You're a very special person,
Ryan. In the circumstances I think I'm allowed to
say that.'

Lafferty gave a slight nod.

'Maybe we should both be honest with each other?'
suggested Sarah tentatively.

Lafferty, leaning against the barrier, held her gaze for a

moment before saying, 'Maybe it would be wrong to leave certain things unsaid, Sarah. I think you know that I've come to feel a lot for you. More than I should, perhaps, but I can't deny it and I'm not ashamed of it.'

'Good,' said Sarah quietly. 'I'm glad. It's also mutual.' Lafferty could hear that Mace and Pallister were back outside the room. He and Sarah turned their attention back to the door and braced themselves. A metal object began rhythmically battering against the outer skin. Lafferty didn't think it was an axe – it didn't sound heavy enough – but he could hear the sound of splintering wood.

He watched as the inner surface of the door begin to blister under the onslaught. A hole appeared and started to get bigger as the long metal spike Pallister was wielding ripped into the wood. Lafferty reached out to the wall and turned off the room light so that the opposition would not be able to see in through the hole. He, on the other hand, could see them as the hole got bigger. The jagged opening was the size of a tennis ball but it was getting bigger by the second.

When it reached the size of a football, Lafferty picked up another of the heavy, metal pump-bodies and waited his chance. He knew that pretty soon one of men outside must try to get an idea of what the barrier looked like. In the event, it was Pallister. He stopped working with the spike for a moment and his face suddenly filled the gap as he tried to see into the room. Lafferty let fly with the pump-body and it caught Pallister squarely between the eyes. There was a sickening crack and the man went down without a sound. Lafferty knew there was a very real chance that he would never get up again. He had put all his weight behind the throw.

Sotillo was furious. He shouted at Mace, telling him

to continue with the spike before angrily confirming that Lafferty and Sarah would know what suffering was all about before he was through with them.

Lafferty had to fight off a sudden wave of hopelessness that swept over him. What they were doing was pointless. They couldn't hold out much longer, and all they had achieved was the probable death of one man and the incitement of Sotillo to a sadistic rage. But there was no going back. They had to fight on to the bitter end. He armed himself with more pump spares and continued to hurl them through the hole in the door, but Mace was keeping well out of the firing line, using the spike from the side rather than head on. Lafferty was running out of ammunition. He looked about his feet but couldn't really see anything useful in the darkness, and they couldn't afford to turn the light on. One thing that did catch his attention was one of the power packs they had pushed against the door earlier. The light coming in through the hole in the door illuminated the words DANGER: HIGH VOLTAGE along its front. It gave him an idea.

'Sarah!' Lafferty whispered. 'Take over!' He pushed the box of spares over to Sarah with his foot and added, 'Make them count.'

As Sarah let fly with her first missile, Lafferty found the connecting leads from the power pack and started to strip the ends off them with his teeth. When he was satisfied with the length of the bare wire he had created, he plugged the other ends, those fitted with jack plugs, into the power pack. He attached one of the bare ends to the metal bed frame, then started to feel around the base of the wall for a plug socket. He found one but it was a good two metres from the door. Would the cable stretch? He started pulling the power pack towards the socket but found that the main cable was jammed below the base of the bed frame. It was half a metre short. Lafferty raised his eyes towards the ceiling and muttered through gritted teeth, 'Give me a break!' He tugged and pulled until sweat broke out on his face but the cable was jammed tight. 'It's no good!' he gasped. 'I can't budge it.'

'Only two left,' said Sarah anxiously, as she hurled another missile through the hole to clatter harmlessly off a wall outside. 'Oh God, Ryan! There's not going to be enough time!'

Lafferty looked up at her but couldn't make out her face in the darkness. 'Time for what?' he asked.

Sarah paused before replying, 'I didn't tell you, but when I went in to the residency earlier to change my clothes I telephoned Paddy Duncan. I told him where we were going and why. There's a chance he'll phone the police when he realises I haven't returned. The longer we hold out, the more chance there is that help will come.'

'Why didn't you say this earlier?' asked Lafferty.

'After what I said to you about being treated as the little woman I didn't want to admit to being so scared that I told someone what we were going to do.'

Lafferty shook his head in the darkness but the knowledge that they still had a slight chance of survival gave him new energy. He squatted down at the base of the bed frame and prepared for a final try at moving it. He gripped the base of the frame with both hands and pressed his cheek to it as he started to heave. The veins on his forehead stood out with his effort, but he kept his eyes closed and concentrated on the image of a car with a blue light speeding towards them.

The frame moved slightly and he knew that the cable

was free. There was no time to rest. He immediately pulled the power pack into range of the socket and positioned the plug below it.

'Move back, Sarah!' he hissed.

Sarah moved away from the door and Lafferty carefully placed the remaining bare wire on the floor in the centre of the doorway. It would not stay in place. It seemed that no matter what he did, the wire still preferred to curl up into the air. As a last desperate resort, he tore off his shoe and placed it on top of the wire to stop it moving. Satisfied that everything was now in place, he turned up the voltage dial to maximum and pushed the plug into the socket. He held his breath as he threw the switch. A single red light illuminated to indicate that the wires were now live.

Lafferty crawled across the floor on his hands and knees to join Sarah before positioning himself behind the glass waste tank that had been plumbed in to Mary O'Donnell's bay. He tore off the plastic cover and Sarah saw what he intended to do. She placed herself at one end of the tank to help, and they waited in silence.

'They've run out of ammunition!' Sotillo shouted at Mace. 'Get on with it!'

Sarah and Lafferty saw Mace appear in front of the hole in the door and quickly enlarge the hole so he could now see the form of the obstructions behind it.

Lafferty took Sarah's hand in the darkness and whispered, 'We can do it!' He felt a slight squeeze of her fingers in reply.

As Mace started to lever the door open, Lafferty braced himself for the final gamble. Mace switched on the light in the room and the look of apprehension faded from his face as he saw Sarah and Lafferty crouching down against the far wall as if in fearful acceptance of their fate. The door opened and Sotillo stepped into the opening. He paused to smile down at them.

Lafferty kept his eyes on the hands of the men in the doorway. Mace had gripped the bed frame; he was about to try to make the opening a little wider. Sotillo stepped forward to help him and Lafferty made his move. 'Now!' he shouted, and he and Sarah heaved the glass waste tank over on to its side so that a tide of foul-smelling liquid swirled over the floor to engulf the feet of the men standing there. In doing so it completed the electrical circuit between the bed frame and the bare wire lying on the floor. Sotillo and Mace were electrocuted, adding a new, awful burning smell to the already foul atmosphere.

Only Murdoch Tyndall was left alive, and his face was a mask of fear. As Lafferty got up and started towards him, Tyndall picked up the metal spike that Mace had been using and flung it at him. Lafferty was too exhausted to move out of the way quickly enough and the shaft of the spike caught him on the forehead. Tyndall took to his heels as Lafferty fell to the floor. Sarah cried out in anguish and dropped to her knees to cradle Lafferty's head in her arms. The wound didn't seem too bad, but Lafferty was unconscious.

Sarah realised that she and Lafferty were alone. She could hear the lift taking Tyndall up to the Sigma lab and relaxed a little. 'We did it,' she whispered as she looked down at Lafferty. She felt totally exhausted and let her head slump forward on to her chest. She closed her eyes for a moment, crooning softly to Lafferty that it was all over.

Suddenly, Sarah became aware of a fierce crackling

sound. Her eyes jerked open. The short-circuited power pack had burst into flames and the fire was spreading rapidly.

Panic replaced exhaustion for Sarah and she struggled to her feet to start dragging Lafferty's unconscious body towards the door. The fire had already spread to a coil of plastic tubing and noxious fumes were beginning to fill the air.

Sarah found great difficulty in moving Lafferty at all; he was so heavy. But she managed to clear a path through the debris round the door and drag him out of the room. She tried closing the door to contain the fire, but it had jammed against the bed-frame and the flames were starting to lick round it. She returned to Lafferty to start dragging his unconscious body down between the patient bays to the lift corridor.

Frustration and anger vied inside her as her strength began to fail with the effort required. Progress was now painfully slow and the fire had spread out of the room into the main ward. It was catching up on them. If only she had been able to close the door. It might have given her an extra few minutes. As it was, the flames had now reached the first patient bay. The plastic bubble was alight.

Sarah had to lean back fully on her heels to drag Lafferty along by the arms a foot at a time. The fumes were making her cough, interrupting her rhythm and heightening her fear. It seemed likely that the short-circuit Lafferty had caused had tripped out the ventilation system. As the smell of burning flesh reached her, she was filled with panic and given a final surge of adrenaline. She managed to make it to the swing doors, dragging Lafferty's lifeless body, and almost fell through them backwards. A final tug and Lafferty was through them too. She just had to get him to the lift and they would be safe. The fire was now half-way down the unit but there would be plenty of time to summon the lift and, if need be, the swing doors would afford them some protection from the fire. The air, however, was becoming increasingly foul.

Sarah checked Lafferty's pulse and found it strong. 'Wake up!' she urged. 'We're nearly there!' There was no response, so she pulled him slowly along to the lift and pressed the button. Sarah's heart almost stopped as she saw that the little light above the button had failed to come on. She stared, unwilling to believe it. She pressed it repeatedly, but still nothing happened. It was not just a bulb failure. There was no sound from the lift machinery.

The truth dawned on Sarah like a knife in the ribs. Tyndall had turned off the power to the lift. There was no way out. What little strength Sarah had left in her legs drained from her and she slumped slowly to the floor beside Lafferty. Tears rolled down her cheeks for the first time. It had all been for nothing. They were both going to die. Lafferty groaned as if he was about to come round and Sarah shushed him. 'Ssh,' she whispered through her tears. 'Sleep on Ryan, sleep on.'

It was becoming increasingly difficult to breathe. The fire was using up all the available oxygen and the air was filled with toxic fumes. Her only comfort was the thought that they would both be unconscious or even dead before the flames reached them. Sarah closed her eyes and rested her head on the wall behind her. Lafferty's head was in her lap.

She was on the point of losing consciousness herself when she heard the lift machinery start up. She opened her eyes and blinked, not sure if she was imagining it.

Lafferty groaned loudly and she said sharply, 'Ssh!' It wasn't her imagination. The lift was coming down! She struggled to her knees and had half-turned round when the lift doors opened and Paddy Duncan stepped out. Two policemen were with him. 'Sarah! What the hell?'

'Oh Paddy, thank God you've come. I'd given up hope. I thought we were going to die,' gasped Sarah. She tried to stand up but collapsed into Paddy Duncan's outstretched arms.

One of the policemen got Lafferty into the lift while Paddy helped Sarah inside. The other policeman went to look through the swing doors at the fire. He held a handkerchief to his mouth. 'What about the patients?' he yelled back to the others.

'They're dead,' said Sarah weakly. 'They're all dead. Leave them be. Let's get out of here.'

Fresh air had never tasted sweeter as Sarah and Lafferty lay on the ground outside waiting for the ambulance to arrive. The Fire Brigade were doing their best to contain the blaze, but it was a hopeless task. The very fact that the secret lift was the only access route to the sub-basement meant that they could not tackle the seat of the blaze. The ground floor was now alight and it was more a question of stopping the fire spreading to other buildings than attempting to save the Institute.

'How are you feeling?' asked Sarah.

'You saved my life,' said Lafferty, taking her hand.

'It was the least I could do,' replied Sarah, 'after all you'd done for me . . . Maybe we're good for each other?'

Lafferty turned to look at her in the light coming from the fire. 'Maybe we are,' he agreed, squeezing her hand.

He turned away to look at the fire and started to think about what they would tell the authorities. Would anyone believe them?

Sotillo and his henchmen were dead. Cyril Tyndall was dead and all the evidence against Murdoch Tyndall was going up in flames in front of his eyes. Apart from that, there was the disturbing question of how easy it had been for Gelman Holland to obtain a government licence for the new vaccine. Sarah had pointed out that the government had put up half the money for the Head Trauma Unit. Gelman Holland had put up the rest. Could the partnership have had a deeper significance? Was it conceivable that the government actually knew that brain-dead patients were being used as human guinea pigs for faster vaccine development?

Suddenly he caught sight of Murdoch Tyndall out of the corner of his eye. Tyndall was at the far end of the building, talking to a group of policemen. They weren't restraining him in any way. In fact, they seemed quite deferential, looking occasionally at the flames together as if sympathising with his loss. As Sarah and Lafferty watched, a distinguished looking man wearing a dark coat was allowed through the police barrier to join the group. Lafferty didn't recognise him but Sarah did.

'I've seen him on television,' she said. 'He's a junior minister in the Scottish Office.

Lafferty nodded but didn't say anything. He was wondering if the presence of the newcomer answered his earlier questions. He could see that Tyndall had recovered all his old self-confidence as he engaged the government man in conversation. 'Tyndall doesn't know we're alive,' he said.

'The bastard,' spat Sarah.

'It may turn out to be our word against his,' said Lafferty, voicing his fears about lack of evidence.

'He is *not* going to get away with it,' said Sarah resolutely. 'Even if it means sifting through the ashes of that building and checking dental records for the next year to establish the identity of the patients.'

Lafferty did not reply immediately. He was thinking about the obstacles that would be put in their way and the almost certain lack of cooperation they could expect from the authorities. He became aware that Sarah was waiting for him to say something. 'Are you with me?' she asked.

Lafferty looked at Sarah and smiled. 'I'm with you,' he said.